4/14

# DASH OF PERIL

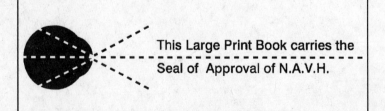

This Large Print Book carries the Seal of Approval of N.A.V.H.

# DASH OF PERIL

## LORI FOSTER

**THORNDIKE PRESS**
*A part of Gale, Cengage Learning*

GALE
CENGAGE Learning·

Farmington Hills, Mich • San Francisco • New York • Waterville, Maine
Meriden, Conn • Mason, Ohio • Chicago

**GALE**
CENGAGE Learning·

LIBRARY OF CONGRESS CATALOGING-IN-PUBLICATION DATA

Foster, Lori, 1958–
    Dash of peril / by Lori Foster. — Large Print edition.
        pages cm. — (Thorndike Press Large Print Romance)
    ISBN-13: 978-1-4104-6867-3 (hardcover)
    ISBN-10: 1-4104-6867-4 (hardcover)
    1. Large type books. I. Title.
PS3556.O767D37 2014
813'.54—dc23                                              2014001575

Published in 2014 by arrangement with Harlequin Books S.A.

Dear Reader,

For those of you with good memories, you're going to read this book and then recall that I was rehabbing a broken elbow while writing it. So I need you to know I was already well into the book before I broke my elbow. Honest. My editor can vouch for me on that!

Pretty please don't think, even for a second, that anything Margo goes through is in any way related to my own experiences. :::Grin:::

I very much hope you enjoy Dashiel "Dash" Riske and Lieutenant Margaret "Margo" Peterson. I love hearing from readers, so feel free to drop me a line. Oh, and before you ask, *yes,* Cannon is getting his own book, *No Limits.* His story will actually be the first book in a new series. To check on release dates, my website should always be your go-to resource, www.lorifoster.com.

Happy reading!

Lori Foster

To Shana Schwer, best friend extraordinaire. Not only because you find me an answer for every police question I have, and love the UFC as much as I do, and are such a terrific pet lover. But because you're you, a pretty terrific person all the way around.

And extra thanks to Nancy Glembotzky, the true owner to Oliver the cat, the ragdoll puppy-cat I used to show Margo's softer side. I love when my readers are also animal lovers like me! Thank you, Nancy, for sharing Oliver with me.

# CHAPTER ONE

Frozen pellets of sleet carried by the icy March winds stung Lieutenant Margaret Peterson's face. The late snowstorm wasn't uncommon.

Welcome to Warfield, Ohio.

With one gloved hand Margo held her coat closed at her throat. The other hand, ungloved, remained in her pocket as she hurried to her new car parked in the lot across from the bar. At 1:00 a.m. the streets were dark with minimal traffic. A lone streetlamp lent an angelic glow to the beautiful pearl color of her Lexus.

Closing out a bar wasn't new for her; usually at times like these, in the quiet of the night after hours of being sized up by hungry men, she felt like Margo, not Margaret, a woman instead of a lieutenant. Despite her reasons for being at the bar this time, playing the game left her feeling sexier, softer, more vulnerable — the opposite of her kick-ass cop persona.

But right now, she was both soft woman and commanding lieutenant, balancing the image she needed to convey with the ability she'd honed.

For months she'd been unofficially undercover, hoping to glean information on the bastards who ensnared women, forcing them into seedy porn movies that included bondage, domination and some sick, sexually inspired discipline.

If the women had been willing, well then, she'd leave them to it. Who was she to judge? She wasn't a hypocrite; she believed in consenting adults doing as they pleased.

But abducted women? Abused women?

The first young lady who'd come to them had been disoriented, confused and so incredibly scared. The bastards had grabbed her, blindfolded her and taken her to a vacant building, where they'd forced her to star in an underground porno. Maybe they'd let her go because they knew they'd be cleared out by the time anyone would find their location.

And maybe, just maybe, they had planned to only do one video. But like most sick fucks, once they got a taste of their perversion, they wanted more.

Margaret detested all bullies, took great

pleasure in bringing down criminals, but she had a very special, deep-rooted red-hot hatred for men who sexually mistreated women. It was the worst type of degradation, the most demoralizing thing that could happen to a female.

Her heart beat harder, faster, just thinking of it. Fury rivaled the cold, heating her from the inside out with molten hatred.

Eventually, one way or another, she would crack this case and annihilate the ones responsible — or die trying.

Hanging in local bars — the very locations where the women were often targeted — had seemed an ideal setup. For too many months, right through the holidays, she had spent several nights a week on the prowl . . . without a single nibble.

Others had given up. The captain believed the bastards had either shut down or moved their enterprise elsewhere. In her bones, Margo sensed they were still around. And then, just last week, a woman showed up at the station. Bruised, traumatized, hysterical, she had barely escaped.

That made four instances now, two of them fatal. Margaret was determined to get to the bottom of it, so on top of the reignited but routine investigation, she kept her eyes and ears open while trolling the "less respectable" bars.

Nothing new in that, really.

Being a female lieutenant with tough-as-nails notoriety complicated dating. And with her particular tastes . . .

"You shouldn't be out here alone."

Before she could register that deep voice as someone she recognized, Margo had her coat open, her loaded Glock in her hand.

The weapon didn't faze him.

Tall and handsome and far too carefree, he stared into her eyes. Even in the dim light through the never-ending sleet, she saw his crooked smile and she felt his anticipation.

Well, hell. Spending hours in a classless bar amid nasty drunks had less impact on her tension than Dashiel Riske's half smile.

She didn't lower the gun, but she did keep her finger off the trigger. "Stupid move, Dash."

"Approaching you in the dark?" He stepped closer and, moving her gun hand aside, put his fists in the lapels of her coat and pulled it closed against the blustering wind. The position had his hands near her breasts — and caused her heartbeat to stall. "Would you shoot me?"

"No." She was trained enough to discern a threat before firing. "But I might slug you."

Taking liberties, he slid his hands up and under her collar to draw her closer. "Is that forthcoming?" He angled his face down to hers. "Should I duck for cover?"

"No." If he weren't so warm, she'd have pushed him away. Maybe.

Dash was such a player, never taking anything seriously — most especially not women. Where other men hesitated, he forged on with sensual confidence born from success.

For a while there he'd hung at the bars with her, specifically Rowdy's bar, Getting Rowdy, the closest to where the women had been grabbed. He'd adequately allowed her to use him as a prop in her scam. With Dash, she could pretend to be an easy drunk and easier prey.

Even though she'd sometimes sat on his lap, kissed his neck or ear — even felt him up — other women had come on to him. She didn't like to think he'd done without during their ruse.

But she hated even more to think of him hooking up.

When she'd started to feel jealous, she knew she had to cut him free.

At first he'd objected, but then the holidays had come and the department had given up on finding the sick fucks responsible. . . .

"What are you doing here, Margo?"

After a glance around, she tucked the Glock .40 back into the specially designed inside pocket of her coat, where she also kept another fully loaded magazine. "What are *you* doing here?"

"I vote we sit in your car out of this ice storm and then I'll tell you."

It beat freezing to death, so Margo turned and, with a touch of her hand to the driver's-side handle, released the autolock. Sliding into the leather seat, she pushed the keyless ignition button. Dash walked around the hood and folded his big body into the passenger seat. The small, sleek car fit her perfectly. But Dash's muscular frame looked a little squashed, making her almost smile.

"You can move the seat back," she told him.

"Thanks." He adjusted it, which allowed him to stretch out his jean-covered legs a few inches.

The interior felt like a meat locker from having been in the dark, bitter cold. She turned up the heater, set the climate control for both heated seats and relocked the doors.

"New ride?"

"A gift to myself." But she didn't want to

talk to Dash about that. She'd spent too many months blocking him from all personal thoughts.

He studied her in silence. "How long were you at the bar?"

Far too long considering it had turned out to be a waste of time. "Why?"

"Just wondering if you might have had a little too much to drink."

"Of course I didn't." He'd done this routine with her enough times to know she never let herself get tipsy. She had the slightest buzz — but was as rock-steady as ever. "A few beers, that's all."

"Beer, huh? Longnecks?"

"Of course." She varied her routine from one bar to the other, just in case her drinking habits factored in to the minds of the psychopaths preying on their victims. She showed up at each bar pretending to be already drunk and then added to that perception by her loose behavior.

"I suppose you're as good at holding your liquor as you are at everything else?"

Was that a condescending tone she heard? "I know my limit." Anything she did, she did well. It was sort of family law — if you weren't going to excel, don't bother.

Tapping her fingers on the steering wheel, she said, "Well? Let's hear it. Were you fol-

15

lowing me or will you claim this is happenstance?"

"I didn't follow you, but I was looking for you."

"Scouring bars?" And why now? Months had passed without him seeking her out, when she'd been almost positive that he would.

Not that she was bitter about it or anything. She'd ended things for a reason — a reason that still existed.

Dash gave an infuriating shrug. "Before you gave up, this is the night we would have met at Rowdy's."

"So?"

"Call me sentimental, but I miss it." After the slightest pause, he added, "I miss you."

"Really?" She refused to be sucked back in by his charm. The holidays had been almost intolerable — in part because she'd spent too much time thinking about him. Spring was upon them, and with it came a renewed sense of purpose, a purpose that didn't include Dashiel Riske.

"Don't you?"

"What?"

In that warm, teasing voice of his, he said, "Miss me." He shifted, sending electrical awareness into the air. "Just a little maybe?"

Fond memories made her fight a smile.

"We did have some fun." Rowdy's bar had quickly become her favorite hangout. Getting Rowdy was a clean but comfortable place that served simple meals, good drinks and fun entertainment, like pool and darts, and a dance floor.

Best of all, badass Rowdy Yates stayed around to run the place himself. That was incentive enough to turn the staunchest teetotaler into a booze hound.

Though Rowdy and his bartender, Avery, had married over Christmas, he was still a sinfully gorgeous hunk surrounded by an aura of danger and sensual menace, more than worth a fantasy or two.

"Admit it," Dash murmured, watching her with probing intent. "Admit that you missed me."

She reluctantly gave her attention back to Dash — and wanted to groan. A lonely streetlamp gave faint illumination to his features, but she knew every nuance of his gorgeous face. No, he didn't have Rowdy's bad-boy rep, but his razor-sharp sensuality and construction-worker physique churned up a different type of fantasy.

Too bad she knew they'd never suit.

"Maybe," she agreed. "Just a little."

"I'm wounded — especially considering I wasn't your first pick."

No, he wasn't. She'd initially wanted Rowdy to play her counterpart in the role of bar trollop, but Avery Mullins, now Yates, had already staked a rock-solid claim. Not a big deal because she knew she never would have gotten involved with Rowdy anyway, not beyond a one-night stand.

"As I recall, you offered."

"More like insisted."

She inclined her head in agreement. As second choice, she'd accepted Dash's help with her cover, help she needed to give her a reason to hang around the bar without getting hit on by every lonely sap alive. She wanted to look the part of helpless, vulnerable, female boozer, but she didn't want to appear too pathetic.

The first woman who'd escaped had initially been at the bar with a boyfriend. They'd parted ways at the door, and she'd gotten snatched right off the street.

So Margo set herself up as easy prey by following the same scenario — with Dash.

"I'd love to know what you're thinking." Dash looked her over in a way that felt far too physical.

*That I missed you so much, too.* Blocking that response, she asked, "What are we doing here, Dash? It's getting late and I've had a full day."

His gaze narrowed, proving she'd hit a nerve. "If you wanted to start back at the bar scene, you should have given me a call."

"I'm a big girl. I can handle it alone."

His gaze moved over her face. "Do Logan and Reese know what you're doing?"

Oh, now that just pissed her off. She settled into the corner of the seat, getting comfortable for this long-overdue confrontation. She would have preferred somewhere less . . . confined, maybe a location where his presence didn't fill every inch of her space, where she didn't breathe in his scent, where his tall, ripped body wasn't so temptingly close.

But all she had was the here and now, so she'd make her point and then send him on his way. "You're confusing yourself, Dash. My detectives answer to me, not the other way around."

He disregarded her commanding tone and clear umbrage to say, "So they don't know?"

"I don't answer to anyone, especially not you."

As if finally realizing her mood, he raised his brows. "You know it's dangerous."

"I can handle danger." Hadn't she spent too many nights being dangerously attracted to him?

"What if your ploy works and someone

grabs you?"

"That's the plan." And yes, it was dangerous. Deep down, she knew it wasn't right. But deep down, she had so damn many issues. . . .

"You need backup." Before she could say anything, Dash whispered, "Let me be your backup."

"You and I have different objectives."

"I want to sleep with you," he admitted without reserve. "You want to catch some creeps — so sure, our main objectives are miles apart."

Plainspoken Dash. Margo shook her head, denying what he wanted and how his brazen words affected her.

"But," Dash said with emphasis, "the two aren't mutually exclusive. I'd like to see the creeps caught, same as you."

*He'd like to see them caught.* No sign of outrage or disgust at what happened, at what the men did — or what the women suffered.

Margo blew out a breath. If she involved Rowdy Yates, he would go after the bastards with single-minded intent.

Dash's brother, Detective Logan Riske, one of the most honest, honorable, driven men she knew, always attacked injustice. He was seriousness personified.

Funny how the two brothers were so dissimilar in personality.

Logan saw her as a sexless superior, not a woman.

But Dash had been making his interest known almost from the moment they'd met. Unlike Logan, he played at life and enjoyed every moment.

In many ways, Margo was just like the rest of her family. Being a cop was in her blood.

But other things . . . other genetic ties . . .

"I'm pretty sure," Dash went on, interrupting her disturbing thoughts, "that you want to sleep with me, too."

A denial would be pointless. Dash knew women. Instead, she gave him the truth. "It won't happen."

"Because?"

"For one thing, I'm the lieutenant at a station previously plagued by corruption. I spent a lot of time and made a lot of enemies clearing out the trash." More than one bad cop had lost his job. Other, less conscientious cops resented her for turning out their friends.

Logan and Reese were two of only a handful of good cops who had backed her 100 percent.

With anything work-related, she trusted them both. Away from the station . . . she preferred they stay out of her business.

Sleeping with the brother of a lead detective would definitely blur the lines.

"It's important that I keep my personal life completely separate from work." Few would understand her personal life, and too many others would use it against her.

"You think I'd gossip with Logan?"

"Probably Reese, too." Logan and Detective Reese had been buddies forever; Logan and Dash were as close as two brothers could be. They all hung out together.

That made the circle far too close for her peace of mind.

"Seriously?" Dash angled his broad shoulders into the corner of the car to better face her. "You think guys sit around and share conquests?"

"Conquests?" Margo smirked. "Is that what you call it?"

"I might if I was the pathetic type to brag about how and when and with whom I had sex." Getting comfortable, he unzipped his coat, showing a black thermal crew-neck shirt beneath. "But here's a news flash for you — I don't screw and tell. At least, not since I was seventeen. And trust me, even if I was the type — and again, I'm not — do you really think Logan or Reese wants to hear about us doing the nasty?"

Curiosity finally got her attention off his throat and up to his dark brown eyes. She tipped her head. "Would it be nasty?"

Dash watched her for several seconds before replying. "Entirely up to you." His voice went deep and dark. "It can go any way you want — as long as it goes."

She imagined sex with Dash would be . . . fine. Satisfying, sure. The man exuded testosterone and confidence. But it'd be the same old run-of-the-mill bang-for-fun encounter. He'd be polite, a gentleman. Considerate. It'd take the edge off, but there'd be no real depth. No risk.

No danger.

Unfortunately, that just didn't do it for her.

Not that she'd ever tell Dash what *did* do it for her. That, by necessity, she reserved for fleeting adventures with strangers. Men she could control.

Men she would never see twice.

She did not share with guys closely related to her detectives.

"You know," Dash said, "Logan prefers to think you're made of stone. Reese, too. Must be a cop thing, right? To them, you're a peer, not a supersexy woman."

She and Logan had always shared mutual respect. Reese . . . that had taken a while but they were on good terms now. Both Logan and Reese were incredible detectives and she was lucky to have them.

But they weren't peers. "I'm their superior."

Dash grinned. "Maybe that attitude of yours helped to form their perspectives."

Even now he couldn't be serious. "Maybe." Other than how it pertained to being a cop, she knew little enough about how men thought. What she did know she didn't particularly like.

"I'm not the only one who sees it."

She cocked a brow. "Excuse me?"

"You being sexy." He watched her far too closely, maybe judging her response. "Rowdy sees it, too."

A little thrill of excitement uncurled inside her, but she hid it. "Rowdy married his bartender."

"Doesn't make a man blind now, does it?"

No, but maybe it should. She detested men who cheated almost as much as the guys who were physically abusive.

"You know, honey, Rowdy has a distinct dislike of cops. You and he never would have happened."

Dear God, had he read her thoughts? Did he know she'd once set her sights on Rowdy?

Did anyone else know?

She tried to put on her poker face, but he'd caught her off guard. Instead, she just spelled out the truth to him. "Rowdy has a certain appeal, but even if he'd been interested, I never would have gone down that road."

"Ah," Dash said, a little mocking. "Still too close to home, huh? I mean, his sister is married to Logan and you're all uptight about that possible gossip —"

Margo lost her temper. "Is there a point to this chat? Because if so, I wish you'd get to it."

"All right." Taking liberties, Dash adjusted the climate controls, turning down the heat now that the car had warmed. "I want your answer."

"About?" She glanced at the illuminated clock. If she didn't get home soon she may as well plan on staying up. Her shift would start in less than five hours.

Before she realized his intent, Dash moved toward her, leaning over the console and stealing the breath in her lungs.

She frowned — and his mouth brushed hers.

In a rough whisper, he said, "This."

Margo couldn't deny that it felt good to be near a man, *this man,* soaking up his heat, hearing the husky timbre of his voice, feeling the restrained power innate in all good men.

He put scant space between their mouths and waited.

When she didn't pull away, Dash leaned in again, nudging her lips apart with his own. She relaxed at the damp touch of his tongue, first tracing her lips and then dipping inside.

God, he tasted good, like a man should. Her heart pumped faster. More so than the average guy, Dash was muscular from work in his construction company. Tall, handsome, friendly . . . *and sexy.*

What would it hurt if she gave in? If she took the brief pleasure he offered? It wouldn't last, and in some ways it'd only make her want more, things she couldn't have.

Unreasonable things.

Twisted things.

Margo flattened her hands on his chest and levered him away. "That's enough."

His forehead rested against hers. "Our definitions of enough are further apart than our motivations."

"I . . . can't."

Remaining close, frowning just a little, Dash studied her face, her eyes . . . her soul.

"Tell me why."

She couldn't. "I'm sorry." Did she have to sound so breathless? "You should go now." Before she changed her mind and complicated her life horribly. It wouldn't be fair to him . . . and it wouldn't be fair to her.

Dash didn't press her, but his tension increased. One hand still on the side of her face, he brushed his thumb over her temple. "You've been as clear as you can be, you know? Not interested. I hear you say it and I believe you. I see you like this, and I'm convinced."

She couldn't get enough oxygen to relieve the restriction in her chest. "But?"

"But I'm getting mixed signals all the same."

So damned astute. Maybe he had a few things in common with Logan after all. God knew his brother rarely missed even the most subtle clue. "I'm sorry."

"That's it?" He dropped back to his seat, his eyes glittering in the darkness. "That's the explanation?"

She shook her head. "I don't explain myself. It was only an apology." Without meaning to, she licked over her bottom lip — and saw the heat in his dark eyes increase. "I don't owe you anything, Dash." And no way would she tell him she did want him —

just not enough to overcome the problems. Sex with Dash would be like bungee jumping when she wanted to skydive.

"No," he said softly, "I don't suppose you do." His expression flat, all his natural humor squashed, Dash buttoned up his coat again, opened the door and stepped out. A blast of wintery air slapped her heated face — but it couldn't compete with the sudden frigidness of his mood. "Drive safely, Margo."

He was one of the few people other than family who called her that. To the rest of the world she was Margaret, a rigid, by-the-books, untouchable lieutenant.

He didn't slam the door, just calmly closed it — and walked away, his shoulders hunched against the relentless sleet.

Standing beneath the overhang of the bar with snow and sleet trying to blind his view, the chill of the winter storm reaching down deep to his bones, Saul Boyle watched the man exit her car. Must've been a short convo. His brother, Curtis, would be pleased.

"She's all alone now," he said into the cell.

"The roads are shit," Curtis mused, and then added, "I'd feel better about this if Toby was with you."

28

That made Saul bunch up in jealous anger. "He won't be available until tomorrow, and then we might miss our chance."

"There would be other chances."

He clenched his teeth. "I don't need Toby. I told you. I got someone to help me."

"Yes, that pathetic dopehead who needs the cash for his next fix."

Why did Curtis have to ridicule every decision he made? "He'll be solid, Curtis. I swear."

The lengthy pause had Saul sweating before finally, his tone gentle, Curtis said, "I'm trusting you with a lot, Saul."

"I know." It made him giddy, the idea of proving himself to Curtis. He was as good as anyone. He was *better* than Toby. "I got this."

"Make sure, Saul. I need the police off my ass, not digging deeper into my business."

"She's the one leading the dig, so once she's gone, the others will back off." Saul started walking toward the van, where his disposable hired hand waited. "After tonight, she'll be a distant memory."

"Perfect. Let me know when it's done." And with that Curtis hung up.

Anticipation building, Saul grinned as he trod through the accumulating snow. Curtis loved the slow torment inherent in their playtime, but Saul lived for the brutality of a surprise attack — as long as it wasn't directed at him. Curtis could be unpredictable . . . but no. His brother was fair. Vicious when necessary, but he knew what he was doing.

Curtis was the brains. It was his money and power that made it all possible. Saul enjoyed being the muscle.

Together, they made an unstoppable team.

With hurt coiling around her, Margo watched Dash go until he disappeared into the darkness. For reasons she couldn't understand, defeat burned her eyes.

Damn him, why did he need to confuse things?

She turned on her headlights, fastened her seat belt and put the car in gear. With no other cars on the road, she pulled out of the lot and onto the icy street, going slow to accommodate the worsening weather.

The defroster and her wipers couldn't quite counteract the ever-forming ice on her windshield. Twice she felt her tires slipping and slowed even more. Before the night was over the station would be bombarded with calls. The wrecks would pile up. Hopefully none of them would be too severe.

Lost in deep thought, she'd traveled a little over a mile when suddenly from her left, bright headlights emerged from the obsidian night. Blinded, she threw up a hand to shield her eyes . . . and several realities crashed through her mind.

She was about to be T-boned; given the speed of the approaching car it had to be deliberate. The impact was going to hurt her, maybe even kill her.

Damn it, now she'd never know what it was like to sleep with Dash Riske.

The last thought had barely formed when metal hit metal with a great grinding crash. The force of the impact jarred every bone in her body. Her forehead connected with the steering wheel . . . and as a great blackness slowly swallowed her up she didn't see or hear anything else.

# CHAPTER TWO

The van barreling toward Margo's driver's-side door snapped away Dash's brooding annoyance.

She was about to get ambushed.

Fear and rage slammed into him, but neither of those emotions would help the situation, so he went on autopilot. Slowing his truck to keep from sliding on the slick roads, he locked his hands on the wheel and said a quick, silent prayer that she wouldn't be hurt.

Thanks to the shitty weather, he'd made the decision to follow her home to ensure she got there safely. He hadn't planned on her ever knowing about it, but subterfuge no longer mattered.

His guts twisted when the bulky van rammed headlong into her petite Lexus. Heart hammering, he half-assed parked his truck at the side of the road and, keeping one eye on the van, launched out the door.

Knowing he had to reach her, he moved fast, sliding every other step of the way.

Her car careened sideways, spun once and collided with a telephone pole. The air bags released and glass shattered. From overhead wires, clumps of accumulated snow and ice dropped hard.

Even before the sound of the crash faded away on the dark night, Dash reached her. Seeing her demolished door buckled in, the glass everywhere, sent fear jamming into his throat.

"Jesus." The obscene sound of grinding gears and a revving engine told Dash the driver of the van was okay — and desperate to disengage from the snowbank.

Dash reached for Margo's door handle.

He jerked at it twice, pulling with all his strength until finally with a sharp screech of bent metal, it wrenched open. Margo lay slumped over the steering wheel and deflated air bags, her small body lifeless.

Carefully, Dash put his fingertips to her throat . . . and blew out a breath when he felt her steady pulse. *Thank God.*

How much time did he have before the van freed itself from the snowbank?

And once it did, what would happen?

"Margo? Come on, honey, talk to me." In case she had neck or spinal injuries, he didn't want to move her. He pulled out his cell phone and almost by rote dialed his brother instead of 911.

Logan answered with "What's up?"

"Margo was just in a wreck. Bad. We're at . . ." He looked around and found the street signs. "Corner of Second and Main. She's unconscious."

Calm and commanding, Logan asked, "Any other cars involved?"

Dash could hear Logan moving and knew he was already on his way. "An old cargo van." Except for the glare of headlights off Margo's car and the van, inky darkness blanketed the empty streets. Tension prickled along his spine — he could almost smell the sense of danger.

"Are you hurt?"

"I'm fine, but . . ." Dash could barely believe it, but he knew what he'd seen. "She was rammed, Logan."

"You mean deliberately?"

Sure looked that way to him. With the roads like an ice rink it was possible the idiot behind the wheel just didn't know how to drive.

But Dash wasn't willing to take chances. "That's my bet."

A new urgency entered Logan's tone. "If she's out, don't move her unless you have to. But if you get any vibes at all, grab her up and take cover. You got me?"

Fuck. He looked again at the van still trying to rock out of the packed snow. "Yeah."

"Take her gun if you have to."

Funny that Logan didn't even ask if Margo was armed. He knew she went nowhere without a weapon. "Got it."

Suddenly Margo sat back with a heart-wrenching moan. Blood trickled from her temple down her ear and jaw. Her short, dark hair glittered with chunks of glass from the shattered windshield.

Gasping, she opened her eyes, flinched and gave a weak, muffled curse.

Dash crouched down beside her outside the car door. "She's awake."

"Tell her backup and an ambulance are on the way. And Dash? Watch your ass."

" 'Course." Dash disconnected the phone and dropped it into his pocket. "Sit still, honey. Logan is sending help."

"Dash?"

"Yeah, it's me." Was she concussed? He smoothed back her hair and winced at the gash he found near her hairline. He didn't want to alarm her, but if at all possible, he'd prefer to get her in his truck so they had a way out if it became necessary. "You hit your head. Anything else hurt?"

"Everything." As if personal injuries didn't matter at all, she whispered, "The other car?"

"A cargo van." He glanced that way but behind the windshield all he saw was darkness. "They're stuck for now."

Instead of being reassured, she drew her gun and tried to turn toward him — probably to leave the car. The seat belt caught her and she sucked in a painful breath.

"Let me help." She hadn't yet moved her left arm, so he used extra care as he reached in around her, gently opened the latch on the seat belt and freed her.

Looking past him, Margo swallowed hard, blinked twice and rasped, "Move."

Her voice was so weak he barely heard her — but he didn't try to disarm her. Looking back, he asked, "Any idea who that is?"

"Yeah." Stark pain narrowed her eyes. "Trouble."

The wheels of the van finally found purchase. It shot forward a few feet, slewed to the side and, oddly enough, did a U-turn to face them again.

"Ah, hell." His first instinct had been right. "We have to go. *Now.*"

Margo clenched her teeth and slid one leg from her car.

*Not fast enough.* The van barreled toward

them again, so Dash did the expedient thing and hefted Margo up against his chest. On a short cry, her body shuddered before going deliberately still.

So brave. So damned stoic.

The van sped forward and he knew he'd never make it to his truck in time. Instead he headed for the sidewalk and ducked toward the questionable safety between two brick buildings. Fuck. No outlet.

Margo groaned raggedly, shifted to take aim and a loud blast sounded far too damn close to his ear.

He nearly dropped her.

Seconds later he heard return fire and hunkered down with her, trying to shield her with his body until he could get them both behind a heavy metal trash bin.

She locked her jaw as he set her on the dirty, icy ground behind the hulking steel bin. A thick layer of ice covered every surface. Her breath frosted in front of her.

"Are you okay?"

Small, wounded, dazed, she still pulled it together and gave him a stiff nod.

He could tell she had extreme pain. From her head — or somewhere else? What could he do about it anyway? More blood ran down her jaw, her neck. An overhead utility light showed the whiteness of her face.

They both heard the van's engine idling right outside the alley. Not liking their odds, Dash put his shoulder to the giant grimy bin and scooted it catty-corner to provide a few more inches of cover. He eyed the windows in the two buildings sandwiching them. One had bars and was too high to reach anyway. The other would leave them exposed. No way would they get through it without getting shot.

"Dash?"

Absently, not wanting her to worry, he said, "Help will be here soon." Reassurance and the physical protection of his body was the best he could give. In the refuse, he located a long thick pipe and lifted it. It'd make an adequate weapon if it came to that. He glanced back at Margo. "Don't suppose you have a second gun with you?"

"No. Extra magazine and handcuffs . . . but those were in my purse."

"Still in the car?"

"Yes."

"Any other weapons in there?"

"AR-15 in the trunk."

Dash chewed his upper lip, considering his odds of making it to the car and back. . . .

"No." Margo shifted, winced. "Don't even think it."

Given her condition, he wanted her gun — but no way would he take it from her. The way she held it he knew it gave her comfort. His brother was the same. Logan had often said he felt naked without his sidearm.

A sudden barrage of gunshot blasted the metal bin and ricocheted off the brick building. Cursing, Dash dropped over Margo, doing his best to cover her with his chest and arms, protecting her head from the flying debris of brick and mortar. They were so close they shared breath.

When the bullets stopped flying, he sat back and looked her over, smoothed his hands over her face, her hair. No new injuries, thank God.

Moving away from his touch, she swallowed audibly. "I have vertigo."

From her head wound. A strange combustible mix of rage and worry left him taut. Margo had ability and experience, so he'd happily take direction from her. "What can I do to help?"

With the wrist of her gun hand, she swiped blood from her face. Even that movement made her clench with agony. She bit her bottom lip, sucked in two slow shallow breaths. "I need to return fire but my coordination is blown."

He brushed her hair back to eye her injury again. "Logan is on his way."

"Until he gets here, we're sitting ducks and they're determined."

Meaning if they didn't fire back, the goons would press forward. "Why don't I return fire?"

Face stiff, she held her breath, peeked around the bin and ducked back again. Slumping against him, she stated, "They want me dead."

Like hell. Dash kept his voice calm with supreme effort. "That's not happening."

As if he hadn't spoken she carried on an internal debate, gripping the Glock in her right hand while trembling uncontrollably. "I can't steady my arm."

"I can shoot," Dash said again. He stripped off his coat and tucked it around her legs.

She wavered in indecision. "Are you any good?"

"Logan taught me." And that said a lot. "I'm good enough to fend them off until he gets here."

Out on the street, the low drone of voices carried on the turbulent night. The bastards thought they had them. They were making plans.

"It's now or never, babe."

Margo gave one small nod. "You'll have to take it from me."

Dash didn't at first understand, but when she just sat there, bloodied and battered, her hand locked tight on the weapon, he realized what she meant. "Easy now." He gently pried the heavy black weapon from her stiff, cold fingers.

"Don't you dare hit an innocent bystander."

Given the dark of the night, the lousy weather and the obvious firefight, there shouldn't be any innocents hanging around. "It wouldn't be my first plan." Keeping the gun at the ready, he eased forward a little bit at a time . . . and spotted one man taking aim from the driver's-side window of the van.

It took only that split second for him to mentally record the man's face, his features.

Shots came their way, the noise unsettling. Dash felt Margo flinch, and rage calmed his frantic heartbeat.

He let out a slow breath, braced as he eased forward and squeezed off three rapid rounds before taking cover again.

Watching him with something like blurry admiration, Margo asked, "Hit anything?"

"The van." Maybe. He was a decent shot, unless compared to Logan and Reese . . .

and probably Margo.

Using only her right arm, with her left held at a strange angle, she scooted farther back to the brick wall to give him more space. "Keep shooting." Dash saw her every shallow breath, and he felt her unwavering strength.

Damn, she needed medical care. But first things first.

Creeping forward again, he put two more shots into the van. This time he knew for certain that he'd hit a tire and the grille. Curses filled the air.

"Next one is through your window, ass-holes!"

Unbelievably, Margo snickered.

Maybe realizing that their position out in the open — especially since their victims were willing to fight back — wasn't the best place to be, the attackers gave up. The van accelerated, and even with one tire demolished, it managed to flee the scene.

Peeking out, Dash watched until they disappeared from sight. "Stay put."

She made a small sound that he chose to take as affirmation.

Standing, he crept along the brick wall to the open street and glanced out again. Nothing but empty buildings and shining ice. The wind howled, reminding him that he was without a coat. He ignored the bitter cold because that was all he could do.

The taillights of the van disappeared into the night, and still Dash watched until the *flop-flop-flop* of the destroyed tire faded away to nothingness.

When he returned to Margo, he found her slouched against the wall, her eyes sinking shut. Her utter stillness scared him.

"Hey."

She didn't bother to look at him. Maybe she couldn't. "Gone?"

Relief nearly took out his knees. "For now." He hoped like hell they wouldn't circle around and come back again, but he'd stay alert just in case.

It felt like an hour had passed, but it was probably less than five minutes. Surely backup would arrive soon.

He placed the Glock on the ground between them, lifted his thermal shirt and ripped away a section of his white undershirt.

"What are you doing?"

"It's okay. I'll only be a second." He ducked out of the alley, cautiously approached the main street and found it still empty. All around him, ice sparkled beneath stars and moonlight. Like muted wind chimes, the continuing fall of sleet made a faint tinkling sound. The air was so cold, so crisp, that it hurt his lungs to breathe.

It would be a beautiful sight if goons weren't trying to kill them.

As far as the van had gone, it'd take the shooters at least a few minutes to sneak back on foot, but he doubted they would. They had to know the police had been called.

Stepping through the deep snow, grateful that he'd worn his boots, Dash gathered packed snow and ice into the ripped cloth and tied it shut. After one last look around, he returned to Margo with his makeshift ice pack.

He went to his knees beside her, impressed by her fortitude, worried about her lethargy and exploding with protective instincts. "Keep your eyes closed." With tender care, he brushed the chunks of gravel-like glass out of her short dark hair and off the shoulders of her black wool coat before pressing the ice to her head.

Pain drew her brows together, but she said not a word.

He held the pack in place and looked her over. "Are you hurt anywhere other than your head?"

With exaggerated effort she opened her eyes to look up at him. "Afraid so."

His heartbeat jumped. Dreading her answer, he asked, "Where?"

A slow, deep breath expanded her chest. Her colorless lips parted for faster breaths until she almost panted. "It's unfortunate, but my left elbow is dislocated."

What the fuck? Dash looked at how she held her left arm slightly out from her body in such an awkward way. His brows flattened. Her right hand — the hand that had gripped her gun so tightly — was bare, but she wore a leather glove on her left. "You're sure?"

Her red eyes mocked him. "Quite sure."

Anger ignited. "Why didn't you say something?"

She again closed her eyes, almost like she couldn't help herself. "What could you have done about it?"

No idea, but she still should have told him. "When I took you from your car —" God, he'd thrown her half over his shoulder then literally jogged with her in that position.

"It hurt like hell, but being shot would have been worse." Pale with pain, Margo added, "You did great, Dash. Better than I'd expected."

What had she thought? That he'd fall apart? Maybe hide behind her — the big, bad lieutenant?

More anger simmered to the surface, and that really pissed him off. He never got angry. He was the easygoing one, damn it, the one who enjoyed life and all its vagaries. He didn't get riled, and why should he? He'd been blessed in too many ways to count.

He had parents who adored him and a brother that would make anyone proud.

Most would call him wealthy, but because the money didn't mean that much to him, he preferred the term *financially secure.*

Inherited genes gave him height and strength, a fit body that he'd honed in his construction company — a body that appealed to women.

That brought him back around to his disgruntlement toward Margo . . . the one woman who rebuffed him at every opportunity. Now he knew she considered him a wimp.

In the face of more pressing problems, he decided to work that out with her later. He could hear her teeth chattering — when she didn't have them clenched in pain — so he settled back against the wall beside her and carefully drew her to his side to both support her and share heat.

She sighed and sank closer, wedging into

his shoulder. "Mmm, you are so warm."

Her voice sounded drowsy, and that, too, bothered him. "I'm sorry, but you can't go to sleep yet." She surely had a concussion to go with her other injuries. God, he couldn't believe this. He wrapped himself around her as much as he could. "The ambulance should be here soon."

Even as he said it, they heard the distant whine of approaching sirens. He probably had only a minute more alone with her. Shaking out his coat, he tucked it around both their legs, trapping his warmth in with hers. "You'll be able to rest soon."

"I don't need to be babied."

"I know," he soothed. He looked beneath the ice pack at her bruised but beautiful face. "I think the bleeding has stopped."

Her lashes lifted, treating him to the sight of her dazed blue eyes. "You're a mess, Dash. You have blood everywhere." Her gaze moved over his neck, his chest. "From me?"

"Yeah."

"I'm sorry."

Why did she keep pushing him? "Don't worry about it." Ruined clothes were the least of his concerns.

Her slim brows pinched down. "You followed me."

47

"Instinct," he said without apology. "I know you're a cop, and I know you can take care of yourself. But I'm a man and I couldn't help seeing you as a woman alone leaving a bar late at night."

"Sexist."

"Guilty." He tried a small smile to counter the possible insult. "Under the circumstances I hope you don't mind too much."

"If you weren't here . . ." she whispered, then stopped, swallowed, stared at him some more before starting over. "If you weren't here, I would be dead."

"No." He wouldn't even consider that possibility. He kissed her head, tucked her face against his throat.

"I can handle almost any situation."

"I know." Even now, her stubborn pride showed through.

"But I won't lie to myself. I'm still a little disoriented. My head feels like it's splitting in two and even though it's not my gun arm injured, I'm not sure I could have shot straight enough to hit anyone."

"So? My shots were off, too, but they still didn't like their odds." He was incredibly proud of her, and he needed her to know it. "They wanted you completely disabled after the wreck."

"I was."

"No." He tipped up her face. Her eye was swelling, her forehead bruised, and blood ran down her cheek. And still he wanted to kiss her. Why not? He brushed his mouth so very gently over hers, then whispered against her lips, "Instead, your first instinct was to grab for your gun."

"It's ingrained," she said just as quietly.

"Because you're a cop through and through. According to Logan, one of the best he's ever known."

"He said that?"

"You don't realize how he and Reese admire you? Why do you think they don't see you as a woman? The cop in you is too dominant."

"I guess that's a good thing."

For Logan and Reese, sure. But Dash wasn't one of her subordinates. Eventually — if she'd give in just a little — he'd get her under the sheets and law enforcement would be the last thing on her mind. "If those miserable fucks had walked up to you, you would have shot them, Margo. I know that."

She continued to look at him until her eyelids grew heavy again. She gave in, closing her eyes and snuggling close again. "It's not easy for me to admit, but I'm so glad I'm not alone."

"Yeah, me, too." He had no problem admitting it.

She swallowed, let a few seconds of silence pass. "What I hate is that now you're stuck in this mess."

"I know." He understood the ramifications. His truck sat out there where the goons could have easily read his plates. If they wanted to uncover his identity, they would.

But he was here with Margo, holding her, protecting her, and he wouldn't have it any other way.

Because he couldn't stop kissing her, he put another soft peck to the top of her head. He had a million questions, but they'd all have to wait. Now that he'd thought of license plates, he said, *"E-K-B 8-9-3-2."*

"What is that?" she asked.

"Plates for the van. I'm just making sure I don't forget."

She stirred. "You noticed them?"

"They rammed you. Hell, yeah, I noticed." The sound of the sirens swelled louder, closer, and finally dimmed as the squad cars arrived. The reflection of red-and-blue lights bounced off ice everywhere.

Logan bellowed his name.

"Here!" He kept Margo close to his side, aware of her limp against him again, her eyes remaining closed. "We're in the alley."

Logan was the first in, his gun drawn until he spotted them. His gaze scanned the alley for any threats, then shifted to search over Dash's body before locking on his face.

Logan held himself perfectly still. "You're hit?"

"No, I'm fine. It's Margo's blood from her head. Her elbow is dislocated and she probably has a concussion, too."

Some of the stiffness eased from Logan's rigid shoulders and he began giving orders. Even now, in the thick of it, Dash had to smile at how easily his brother took control of any situation.

Pride was there, but fear for Margo overshadowed it.

Reese, dressed in jeans and a pullover sweatshirt, walked in ahead of the paramedics. His messy hair and casual clothes were proof that he'd left his bed to join Logan. Whistling when he saw them huddled together there on the ground, Reese hunkered down in front of Dash. He nodded at the Glock. "The lieutenant's gun?"

"Yeah."

Reese retrieved it from him.

"She said she has more weapons in her trunk."

"I'll take care of it." Resolute and calm, he said, "You need to come with me."

Dash turned his head to look at Margo. "She's hurt."

Reese's gaze shifted to his lieutenant. Without an ounce of sympathy, he said, "Peterson, you hanging in there?"

"Yes."

At her faint voice, Reese cocked one brow but said nothing about it. He eyed the blood everywhere, noted how Dash held the compress to her temple, as well as how he cradled her close. "The EMTs are getting a stretcher."

Rousing herself, Margo got her eyes open and tried to struggle up to her feet. Dash could tell she did her best to hide her pain from Reese — a pain she'd allowed Dash to see. He hurried to help her, taking extra care not to jostle her injured arm.

Suspiciously satisfied, Reese half grinned. "Gonna walk out on your own steam, huh?"

Dash scowled at Reese. "Don't be an ass."

He shrugged. "It's what Logan or I would do."

But Margo wasn't a man, she wasn't large and muscled or —

She pressed away from Dash's hold. "I'm sure as hell not going to be carried."

Reese gave Dash an I-told-you-so look.

The EMTs crowded in, and she said, "Give Reese the plate numbers," as she limped toward them — leaving Dash behind without a word.

Dash watched two medics offer her assistance, saw her give a few whispered commands, and he felt so incredibly helpless that it enraged him. "She is the most stubborn woman."

"Proud more than stubborn," Reese said with a slap on Dash's shoulder that staggered him forward a step. "Stop fretting. They'll take good care of her." He scooped up Dash's coat, shook it out and offered it to him. "I need to know what happened, right now before you forget any of the little details."

Shoving his arms into the sleeves, Dash stated, "I'm going to the hospital with her."

"I'll drive your truck," Reese said, "and we'll all go to the hospital."

Blood oozing between his fingers, Saul held his aching head. But the pain from where he'd hit the dash was nothing compared to the dread he suffered as he waited to see how Curtis reacted to the fuckup. *He'd let her get away.* Rage built, but Saul kept his expression impassive.

Curtis wouldn't need more reason to

unleash his caustic temper.

At just that moment Curtis strode in, his body bunched in anger, his face florid with it.

Saul grimaced, but it was Toby who took the meaty blow on the chin. It half knocked him off his seat, and sent blood trickling into his goatee.

Slowly, Toby righted himself. His eyes squinted in fury, but he kept silent. With the back of his hand he wiped away the blood.

*"You should have fucking been there."*

Without reacting to the blow, Toby pushed to his feet and kept his attention glued to Curtis.

Curtis rounded on Toby again. "You know Saul can't handle this shit!"

Knowing better than to object to the insult, Saul inched back — out of harm's way.

Toby worked his jaw. "You'd sent me elsewhere."

"You took too fucking long. If you'd gotten back sooner . . ." His anger slipped away, filled with nothing more than rank disgust. "Find me a woman," Curtis ordered, and Saul knew he was talking to Toby, that he wouldn't trust him again for a very long time.

Enigmatic, Toby asked, "Personal use, or for a project?"

Saul always admired Toby's poise under extreme circumstances; it wasn't the first time Curtis vented on Toby to keep from assaulting his own brother.

If Curtis wanted the woman for himself, then the requirements would be far different than any woman they'd use in their playtime. Saul waited to hear the answer, hoping it'd be for a project so he could take part.

In that, he never disappointed Curtis.

His brother clenched and unclenched his fists. "A project." He shot a mean look at Saul — but he refrained from striking him. "Looks like I'll have to take care of that bitch cop myself."

"Setting a trap, then." Toby nodded. "Got it."

Saul sat forward. "What's the plan?"

"I'm going to do what you fucking couldn't. That's the plan." Curtis turned to walk away. "Let me know when you have the woman."

Toby caught Saul's arm and hauled him up. "I'll take care of it right away."

The second they were away from Curtis, Toby turned and sank a fist into Saul's gut.

Saul doubled over, wheezing, unable to

catch his breath as the pain radiated out, making him light-headed.

Toby pulled him upright. "Your brother might spare you, but I'm not going to. Remember that."

As Saul watched him walk away, he thought about getting even — but he dismissed the idea. In fact, he laughed.

His brother was ready for another project, and Saul could hardly wait.

# CHAPTER THREE

Dash related everything to Logan, then told it again to Reese, then to the uniformed cops. Everyone wanted to know everything — repeatedly. He paced, hungry, tired, and as Reese had accused, fretting.

Because he didn't sit, Logan got up to prowl the hallway with him. "So you met Margo at a bar?"

"Yeah." For the fifth time. "I was looking for her and found her and . . ." He waved a hand. Logan knew the rest, for crying out loud.

"I thought you were done with that."

On a humorless laugh, he said, "No." He'd tried, damn it. He'd spent the holidays visiting his folks with Logan and Pepper. Of course their parents adored Pepper. She was unique, beautiful, blunt and a perfect match for Logan. Unfortunately, his mom had seen Logan all happily married . . . and wanted the same for Dash.

"So you're still interested in her?"

Logan didn't sound happy about it. Thanks to his mother's attempts at hooking him up, he'd taken to hiding out in his cabin on the lake. The solitude hadn't been as peaceful as usual. He'd given up, and instead gone through a string of one-night stands.

But that ended up a waste of time because none of the women measured up to Margo. So he'd started shopping anew for a retreat cabin. One without memories of Logan and Pepper.

"She'll need some help for the next few days."

Logan frowned. "Who?"

Pushing past him, Dash headed back to the waiting room. "Margo."

"Peterson can take care of herself and she won't appreciate you trying to coddle her." Logan kept pace beside him.

"Wrong." Dash shoved his hands in his pockets to keep his fists from showing. "She wouldn't appreciate *you* coddling her."

"But you're different?"

"Damn right." He had to believe that. "Now stop needling me."

"I wasn't," Logan said in that ultracalm tone that for some reason had Dash on a ragged edge tonight. "What can I do to help? Want me to go grab you a few things? Your shirt is a mess."

With Margo's blood. Jesus. What the hell was taking so long? "A shirt, socks, maybe a razor — I'd appreciate it."

"No problem. My house is closer to the hospital than yours. I should be able to get back before you and Peterson leave here."

Dash was taller, so he couldn't share Logan's jeans, but he said, "Throw in a pair of sweatpants or something, will you? I'll do some laundry in the morning."

"If Peterson lets you hang around that long."

When Dash glared at him, Logan bit back a smile and raised his hands in surrender.

"I'm sure she'll welcome you with open arms."

Standing in the doorway to the waiting room, Reese asked, "Who? Peterson? Is that a joke?"

Dash shouldered past him, almost making Reese spill the coffee he'd just refilled. Normally he could take their jokes about Margo having ice for blood and balls to rival any guy.

But not tonight.

A minute later, Reese came in and sat across from him. "Logan headed off to get some stuff. Said he'd be right back."

Had they found something more wrong with her? Was that the holdup? Was she even now headed in to surgery? Would someone let them know if that was the case?

Reese's phone rang and for the next few minutes, Dash had to listen to his muted conversation with his wife. Until recently, Dash hadn't envied his brother or Reese for their marital status.

But now . . . He got up to pace again but got only as far as the door when Reese spoke.

"Alice said if there's anything she can do to help, let her know."

Dash nodded. "Thanks." He propped himself against the wall. "How's the kid?"

"Doing good." Reese sat back in his seat and sprawled out his long legs, then started rubbing his left thigh where an old bullet wound still pained him during times of fatigue. "Finally over the flu, poor little guy."

So that's why Reese looked so beat. "Few sleepless nights?"

"Alice is a wonderful mother hen. And Marcus . . . Well, it still breaks my heart to look at him."

Meaning both Alice and Reese had stayed attentive to Marcus's needs.

Dash said only, "Yeah," because there were no other words adequate enough to cover it all. At only nine, Marcus had seen a world of hurt. His dad was now behind bars, where he belonged, and his junkie mother had died from an overdose.

But if anyone could make Marcus whole again, it was Reese and Alice.

Silence filled the waiting room for a few minutes, and then they both heard the *squeak-squeak-squeak* of rubber-soled shoes approaching. Dash met the guy halfway — but that didn't stop the doctor. Still walking, he asked, "You're with Margaret Peterson?"

"Yes." Dash trailed him back into the waiting room, where Reese had sat forward in anticipation.

"I'm Dr. Westberry." He held out a hand, so Dash took it.

"Dash Riske. I'm a . . . friend."

The doctor looked at him over his glasses, sized him up, then turned to Reese.

"Detective Bareden. Peterson is my lieutenant."

"I see. There's no family present?"

Dash shook his head. "No."

"Okay, then." The doctor opened a clipboard to peruse notes. "The good news is that she'll be fine. No nerve or bone damage. No surgery needed. But we had to

61

reduce — that is, put back in place — her elbow."

"I've heard that hurts like hell," Reese said.

"Very painful, yes." The doctor scowled. "She refused a sedative, but we gave her something for the pain both before and after. She's still going to be in very real discomfort for a few days at the least."

"Why did it take so long?" Dash asked. "Her head was bleeding, too, and she might have other injuries —"

Looking back at that damn clipboard, the doctor said, "On top of the tests to check for injury to the arteries and nerves in the arm, and the possibility of broken bones, we also evaluated her head injury."

"And?" Reese asked.

"We didn't find any other damage. We stitched her head, and a nurse cleaned up some of the blood." He looked at each of them. "She has a concussion. It would be best if someone could stay with her tonight."

Dash took a step forward. "Me."

One brow lifted, Reese looked at him.

Gaining steam, Dash said, "I'll be staying with her. Just tell me what I need to do."

"Yes, well, if she agrees for you to be there, you'll need to monitor things. Every two hours while she's awake, every three hours while sleeping, do a neuro-check — ask for her name, the date, make sure she knows where she is. Make sure her pupils are equal."

Dash listened as the doctor gave more details, ready to do whatever needed to be done.

"I gave her a prescription to control the pain, so if you can, make sure she uses it. It'll help her to rest."

Dash had no idea how she was supposed to rest if he had to wake her every few hours, but he'd do it all the same.

Tiredly, the doctor sank down to a seat and finally closed the clipboard. "She's in a splint to keep her elbow bent and to prevent her from moving it. The sling is to help her support her arm, but she can remove that when it's more comfortable for her. However, she has to wear the splint, she cannot move her elbow and she should keep it elevated as much as possible. Ice every couple of hours during the day for swelling."

"Got it."

Somewhat skeptically, the doctor said, "It's important that she not be too active for the next few days. We don't want to risk a new injury." Then half under his breath, he added, "Not sure how you'll manage that one, but I wish you luck with it."

Reese grinned. "Did she give you hell?"

"Let's just say she has a very strong will."

Dash didn't see any humor in the situation. "Anything else?"

"She's been given instructions to follow up with an orthopedist in three days. Overall we prefer to keep immobilization limited otherwise we see too much stiffness in the joint. She'll be told then when she can remove the splint entirely and start light exercises to regain range of motion."

"Is she going to be out of commission for long?"

"Most achieve full activity in four to six weeks."

Reese whistled. "She's not going to like that."

Dash knew it was true — and dreaded the frustration she'd feel.

The doctor pushed back to his feet, his clipboard tucked to his side. "Overall, she should be fine."

Dash again shook his hand. "When can I see her?"

"The nurse will let you know. Shouldn't be too much longer now."

After the doctor left, Reese scrutinized him. "You need some rest, too, you know."

"Says the guy who's been up with a sick

kid." Now that Dash knew Margo would be okay, the exhaustion sank in. He dropped into the chair beside Reese.

It didn't make any sense for him to be this invested. Okay, sure, he hated to see anyone hurt, especially a woman. He would always do what he could to help someone in her situation.

But he felt so much more than mere concern for another person. Only family had ever engendered this much caring.

But Margo wasn't family. She wasn't even a casual date.

If she got her way, they'd be acquaintances and nothing else.

Dash didn't plan to let her have her way.

Reese snorted. "I was going to suggest you let your brother take her home so you can catch a few hours sleep before you start playing Florence Nightingale —"

"No."

"— but given your expression, I think I'll save my breath."

"Good plan." Margo would kick Logan out, and then she'd never let Dash in. Dash had to take advantage of her current vulnerability because once she had a chance to catch her breath, she wouldn't admit to needing help. "Don't worry about it, Reese. I've got it covered." He pulled out his cell

65

phone and called his foreman. Owning a company meant he could take days off when needed.

And though Margo might not realize, it also meant he was used to calling the shots. She might run roughshod over most men, and intimidate others, and she probably mistook his good humor for weakness — but very soon, Lieutenant Margaret Peterson would get to know him better.

And she'd learn that appearances seldom told the whole story.

Getting her clothes off was the hardest part, especially that damn leather glove. Her fingers had swollen so badly that they had to cut it away. After that, the meds they gave her kicked in and although they didn't obliterate the pain, they did make it more manageable.

Now if only they could medicate her frustration and worry.

By following her, Dash had become a target, same as her. Never, ever, did she want to involve him like this. He wasn't a cop, wasn't equipped for the danger about to come their way.

But every time that worry wormed into her mind, she recalled Dash's quick thinking and capability in fending off two armed men. She remembered how he'd cared for her without being condescending. She recalled his concern, and how he'd deferred to her.

Such a nice surprise. And sort of . . . a turn-on. Thinking of Dash was easier than concentrating on her aches and pains.

Through the long process of X-rays, exams, setting her elbow and the numerous tests on her noggin, he'd stayed with her at the hospital.

Why would he do that? She wasn't an infant in need of help. She could have taken a taxi home. It especially unsettled her when she found out Logan had brought Dash a change of clothes and toiletries because Dash planned to go home with her.

And now her two top detectives knew it.

It was so humiliating, and so . . . comforting, that she almost couldn't bear it. She had not come from a family of coddlers. Pep talks, commonsense commands and a good push in the right direction were given at times of need.

Nothing else was needed or expected.

Her family knew she'd been injured, but none of them were willing to run out in the predawn hours to check on her. During a very brief phone call, her dad had asked, "You'll be okay?"

Without a single hint of pain in her voice, she'd replied, "Yes, sir, of course."

She could hear the approval in his voice when he said, "Good. We'll talk later."

That's how mature adults treated minor injuries. Not that Dash seemed to understand the protocol. She was a lieutenant, for crying out loud — the youngest woman ever promoted to that rank in their city. She was not a frail, helpless civilian.

She didn't need anyone fussing over her.

But he'd stayed anyway, and by the time they got out of the hospital, her head stitched and her arm snug in a splint and sling, the sun was already on the rise.

Slumping against the passenger door, her left arm cushioned by his coat, Margo kept her eyes closed. That was easier than seeing his concern.

"We're almost there," Dash said softly.

Red splashes of dawn glistened off every ice-covered surface of road, trees and buildings in blinding display. It amplified the ache in her head. Each small bump in the road made her elbow throb. She had more bruises than she could count. Over her entire body, a never-ending pulse of discomfort tried to claim all her concentration.

But a few minutes later, with Dash pulling into her driveway, Margo had other things on her mind, more important things.

Thanks to her, Dash was now in danger. Would he be safer away from her — or with her? More importantly, would his presence hinder her from doing what needed to be done?

What she damn well intended to do.

"Easy," Dash told her as he parked. He circled around the hood of the truck and opened the passenger door. The ground looked a fair distance away and she dreaded the effort it would take to get back on her feet.

She half turned, and Dash carefully slid one arm under her thighs, the other behind her back so he could lift her out. He handled her weight without a single sign of strain, cradling her against his broad, warm chest.

A lesser woman would have stayed put and let him carry her in.

She had not been raised to be a lesser woman.

"Thank you." She truly appreciated the assistance since his truck rode so high off the ground. The very prospect of hopping out made her ache all over. "I can walk from here." *I hope.*

At close range, his deep brown eyes took her measure. "You'll insist?"

"Yes."

"Shame, since I like holding you." He treated her to a molten look, and then slowly bent so that her feet touched the ground. He continued to hold on to her until she'd steadied herself. Tucking her coat back around her, he asked, "Okay?"

It hurt to breathe, but she nodded.

"So stubborn." He reached in to the floor and snagged up her purse, the stuff Logan had brought him and the bag of her bloodied clothes. The clothes she would pitch, but thank God he'd had the foresight to retrieve her purse from her car.

*Her brand-new ruined car.*

That alone warranted a groan, but she bit it back and tried not to drag her feet along the lit walkway to her front door. Because of the splint and sling, her coat was only draped over her left shoulder and the bitter wind easily tore it away again. The borrowed scrubs were no barrier at all and the chill cut right through to her bones. Tiredly, she readjusted her coat again.

Dash transferred his load to one hand and with the other wrapped her up close. "Come on. The last thing you need is a cold on top of everything else."

Given her hectic work schedule, she got home at all different hours. The outdoor lights were automated, set to come on at dusk and go off again at dawn. She had plenty of mature trees that blocked the rising sun in the front, but they'd be flickering off very soon.

"Nice place."

Ha. Dash hadn't looked around; ever since the doctor had allowed him behind the curtain at the hospital, she'd felt his constant attention focused on her.

No one had ever scrutinized her as he did; it went beyond the intimate way a man watched a woman he wanted. What it meant, she didn't know for sure because she'd never encountered it before.

She knew Dash was worried because he only smiled when he knew she was watching. But the emotion in his eyes held more than worry — and it unnerved her, making her uncomfortable in a very foreign way.

They reached the front door and, knowing it'd be futile, she turned to face him. Maybe it was the pain meds or the confusion from the concussion — or even plain-old indecision. But she hadn't been able to work up a credible way to refuse him. Not that he'd really asked for permission. Because the doctor announced she shouldn't be alone given her concussion, Dash had volunteered himself to babysit. Now that she'd had some time to get her thoughts together, she decided he'd be safer well away from her.

And she'd be safer . . . without his presence making her feel things she shouldn't.

Staring him in the eyes, hoping she sounded convincing, she said, "Thank you for the ride." She lifted her chilled fingers for a handshake — and Dash grinned.

Folding her fingers in his and drawing her hand to his chest, he asked, "Is that your way of trying to get rid of me?"

Yes. "You don't need to stay."

He shifted so that his body blocked the wind, stepped close enough that his broad shoulders shielded her from daylight. "Would you rather have Logan or Reese?"

She shuddered at the thought. "No." If it was truly necessary, she *did* have family. Albeit, not anyone she'd want around when she wasn't 100 percent. But she had an alarm she could set, and —

"Are you seeing anyone?"

"No." What a stupid idea. When did she have time for a committed relationship?

"Then I'm it, right? The doc said you couldn't be alone, so if you make me leave, I'll have to call my brother, and he will probably call —"

"All right!" She winced, pain slicing into her brain. Damn him, he knew she didn't want her detectives seeing her in a debili- tated state. "Do not call Logan."

"I won't," Dash soothed. He lifted her purse and spoke in a rough whisper. "Your keys are in here?"

She was too cold, utterly fatigued and achy to debate this on the front porch. And contrary to common sense, she was also a little relieved that she wouldn't be alone tonight. Eyes squeezed shut, she nodded. "Side zippered pocket."

"Hang in there, honey. I'll have you inside in a moment." He set down the bag of clothes, located the keys and unlocked the door.

Immediately, Oliver stepped out, rubbing his downy white head against her shins.

Dash went still. "You have a cat?"

He could see that she did. "No, he must've broken in. Quick, call the cops."

"Smart-ass." With a little more incredulity, he said, "You have a really *old* cat."

At the sound of Dash's voice, Oliver halted, then hunched his back and hissed.

"He's my puppy-cat." It hurt like hell, but Margo bent down to him. "It's okay, Ollie." She stroked his head, tickled under his chin. "Come on, sweetie. Let's go in."

It wasn't easy to walk with the cat wind- ing nervously in and out around her ankles.

She stumbled her way to the sofa and gingerly sank onto the cushions so that Ollie could join her. He jarred her injured elbow when he leapt up beside her. She gritted her teeth and let him butt his head on her free hand, then rub the length of his body against her uninjured arm.

Dash closed the door and now, with him inside her home, the reality of her situation really hit. She looked at him, saw him watching her curiously, and wanted to curl up and sleep for days.

Instead she said, "Ollie is blind."

Dash stayed silent, but his expressive eyes gave him away. He thought her softhearted.

Sweet.

He thought she was gentle, like most women.

She should disabuse him of those notions ASAP, but she didn't have the energy. Not right now.

Almost like a reminder of what they'd just endured and how proficient he'd been under pressure, Dash still wore the shirt with her dried blood all over it. Disheveled brown hair and beard shadow added a rugged edge to his good looks. Even holding a purse didn't detract from his machismo.

She swallowed. "When I got him, Ollie already had a long list of medical issues, but he was so affectionate, such a big loving mush, that I couldn't turn him away." Maybe she was softhearted after all, at least when it came to her cat. "We suit each other."

"Because you're a big loving mush, too?"

Yes. "That's not what I meant." But what had she meant? She shook her head.

Dash let it go. "He lost an eye?"

"Yes." Ollie tilted toward her, demanding she pet him harder, wanting her to use both hands. Poor guy. No way for her to explain that he'd only be getting one-handed pets for a few days. "He can't really see out of the other. He survived a tornado but was so damaged that his original owners couldn't care for him anymore. They already had to rebuild and . . ."

"And," Dash said, his brows pinching down, "he was a member of their family."

That's how she'd always looked at it, too, but she didn't want to harshly judge others who'd been through so much. "He's mine now." And she would never abandon him.

Dash came farther into the room. "Will it spook him if I get too close?"

"Yes, but don't take it personally. He still has nightmares from the horrors he went through." Ollie pawed her thigh in time to his loud rumbling purr.

"Nightmares?"

"He'll start crying at night like something is wrong. But the vet says he's fine. Usually he just needs to wake up enough to realize he's safe." *With me.* Her arm throbbed more insistently. She needed to bathe, change her clothes and get some rest.

But what to do with Dash?

Her modestly-sized home shrank with him in it. Where would she put him? He would overflow the couch, and she didn't have a guest bedroom . . .

"How do you get him to settle down again?"

She wanted to sleep, not talk, but complaints had never been accepted in her family, so she sucked it up and put on a good front. "During the bad nights, I'll hold him a while and finally he'll go back to his bed."

"He doesn't sleep with you?"

She drew her hand along Ollie's back all the way to the end of his tail — just the way he liked it. "His choice. I've never forbidden it."

By small degrees Dash seated himself on the sofa. The cushions dipped with his weight. Denim stretched over his strong thighs. He brought with him the scent of man and the brisk outdoors. *How could she possibly be aroused right now?*

"You called him your puppy-cat?"

At the moment, even his deep voice seemed a turn-on. What the hell was wrong with her?

Ollie turned his head toward Dash, sniffed the air and backed up into her side, reminding her to reply.

"Being blind hasn't stopped him. He'll listen to me and follow me everywhere I go, just like a happy puppy."

"Cute nickname." Carefully, Dash held out his large hand. His fingers were long, his palms calloused. A working man's hands. "Your voice and presence must reassure him."

"Yes." Those hands had touched her gently in the alley, brushing back her hair, skimming over her bruises — taking her gun from her. Sexy, competent, compassionate.

What would it be like to feel those hot palms firmly moving over her naked body?

"Margo?"

She struggled to get her gaze up to his face. "Ollie doesn't take well to strangers." But Ollie didn't strike out with his claws. He sniffed Dash's palm for the longest time, and when Dash slowly turned his hand over, Ollie butted his head into him for a pet.

Her traitorous cat liked him!

And there was Dash's beautiful smile.

That particular tilt of his mouth affected her like a touch in secret places.

She shuddered, and Dash lifted a brow. "You okay?"

"Yes." Maybe. She cleared her throat to remove the huskiness. "I can't believe he's letting you pet him."

"I love animals and they know it. Helps with winning them over."

Margo could only stare as Ollie sidled closer to Dash and began his loud, rumbling purr — the purr he saved for special moments of affection.

"Yeah, you're a good boy, aren't you, Ollie?" As he'd watched her do, Dash brushed his hand over Ollie's head to his back, all the way to the tip of his tail, while Ollie arched in bliss. "You like that, don't you, my man?"

Her parents disdained her cat, or disdained her for loving him, yet Dash seemed pleased to have the cat's approval.

It had to be the meds, but damn it, her eyes grew wet. "You haven't yet been exposed to his bad habits."

"Yeah? Like what?"

"He sometimes misses the cat box."

That turned Dash's smile into a soft chuckle.

*A chuckle.* Oh, God, how she liked the

sound of that. She squirmed in her seat.

Dash gently rubbed Ollie's ear . . . leaving her mesmerized. "Given he's blind, I'd say if he's hitting it fifty percent of the time, he's doing pretty good."

Not understanding her reaction to him, Margo said in distraction, "I put a large rubber mat under the box. When he misses, it doesn't hurt anything."

"He looks like he's going to nod off." Dash treated the cat to another long stroke. "Soft fur."

"He's a rag doll." To divert her concentration from Dash's gentle touch, Margo looked away at the clock on the wall. Nearing 7:00 a.m. "He was probably frightened when I didn't come home, so he hasn't slept as much as usual. Before he goes to sleep, I need to feed him."

"Why don't I take care of that for you?"

How easy would it be to let him take over? Too easy. "I can do it." Now that her arm was encased in the splint, she could walk without jarring it. But even the smallest movement amplified the ache in her head.

Dash moved around in front of her, caught her under her arms and easily brought her to her feet — without causing her any more pain.

So tall and leanly muscled. Other than the

ruined shirt and beard shadow, no one would know that Dash had been up all night with her. The comparison to her present pathetic state made her want to throw up. Or maybe that was the concussion, too.

She could not be this pitiful.

Not with him. Not ever. "You don't need to stay."

He followed her sluggish path to the kitchen. "We already sang this tune, remember?"

"You can't treat me like an invalid."

"Trust me, Margo, that's not how I see you." When she stopped and stared at him, he held up his hands. "Sorry, but I can't help it. Even wounded, you're impressive."

Her back teeth clenched. "That's a joke, right?"

He lowered his hands — and his eyes. Taking her in from breasts to thighs, he said roughly, "No." He looked up at her face. "It can be frustrating as hell, but overall I like it that you're not the average woman."

She absolutely could not have this conversation right now. "Fine. Suit yourself." She pointed to a cabinet. "The cat food is in there. Open him up a can, but put it on a big plate by his water fountain."

Dash looked at the gurgling water bowl. "That makes enough noise for a . . ."

Realization dawned. "A blind cat to find."

She turned away from his admiration. "I need a shower."

"No."

Disbelieving, she stared at him.

"You aren't supposed to get the splint wet."

*Here we go again.* "But I can't sleep with blood in my hair."

He stepped up behind her. "It's not as bad now that the nurse cleaned you up, but . . ." He touched his fingertips to her short hair, skimmed those rasping fingertips down her throat to her shoulder. "How about I run a bath for you?"

"I can't wash my hair in the bath."

"You'll ruin the splint in the shower, and you're not supposed to get the stitches wet."

"I'll take the splint off."

"No." He quickly amended that with, "Be reasonable. You could end up back at the hospital. Three days, the doc said. Wear it three days and then maybe they'll move you into a brace."

It annoyed her that he was right. "Oliver is impatiently waiting to be fed."

She felt Dash's hesitation, then he said, "Sorry, boy."

Already missing the heat of his body, Margo turned to watch as he took a can out

81

of the cabinet and peeled off the lid.

He glanced her way. "If you take a bath, I could wash your hair."

"In your dreams."

Ollie smelled the food and began an impatient meow, winding in and around her legs.

"I have dreamed about it. At least the part where you're naked and wet."

Her breath strangled in her chest. She was already on the ragged edge. She didn't need Dash adding to her confusion.

As if he hadn't just said something so outrageous, Dash opened three cabinets before finding the plates. He dumped out the food and put it down for the cat. "C'mon, Ollie. Here you go, kitty."

Margo stood there, the last of her resources quickly fading. "If you think for even one second that I'd —"

"Margo." Dash watched Ollie dig in, then straightened again to face her. "I take it you haven't looked in a mirror lately, have you? You're sort of impersonating the walking dead."

She knew that. The gash on her head had only required five stitches to keep it from scarring. It had swollen like a goose egg, then settled to a mere bump that caused purple, blue and green bruising over half her forehead. Her makeup was only partially washed off and the dried blood had her short hair sticking out in odd little clumpy curls.

A yawn took her by surprise, and even that — stretching her mouth wide — hurt like the devil. The yawn ended in a broken groan and she muttered, "Feel a little like the walking dead, too."

Sympathy softened his voice. "I can only imagine. But you know, blood and bruises and lusty groans of pain have a way of discouraging a guy from making a play."

"I thought you said I was impressive."

"You're still standing, right? Most people would be curled up and crying."

Trying for a sneer, she asked, "You?"

"I'm getting there." His warm smile curled her toes. "It's past time for your pain meds." He dug the bottle out of his pocket and shook out a pill. "Water?"

She hesitated for far too long before nodding. "Thanks." With any luck the pain medicine would numb her enough to let her sleep after she got clean.

He filled a glass and carried it to her. After she'd swallowed the pill, he tipped up her chin. "If it makes you feel any better, I promise you don't have anything I haven't already seen."

She was so worn out, she had a feeling she'd pass out the second she got settled somewhere. Which probably meant a shower really wasn't a great idea. "Fine. Run the bath if you want, then stay out of my way until I'm done."

"Spoilsport." He started down her hall, peeking into each room, studying her spare bedroom, then her home office, until he finally found the right one. "A shallow bath. And I'll be right outside the door waiting . . . just in case you change your mind."

# CHAPTER FOUR

Dash leaned against the wall outside the bathroom, listening to the occasional ripple of water. In his mind, he could almost see her, so strong and brave and independent.

But equally small and soft and so badly hurt.

He pressed the heels of his hands to his gritty eyes, trying to fight off the exhaustion. Now that he had her back in her own home, safe and sound, the adrenaline dump left him weary. "You okay in there?"

"I won't melt in warm water, if that's what you mean."

"You're not getting the splint wet, are you?"

"No, I'm not."

Hearing the strain in her voice, he wanted to curse. She'd taken clean clothes in with her, but he had no idea how she would manage to get dressed. The doctor claimed her arm would cause considerable pain for at least a few days.

Struggling in and out of the tub, washing her hair, soaping up her body . . .

Damn, but the visuals were killing him.

"Margo? You sure you don't need any help? You have to be hurting."

"I'm okay."

Damn it. Why wouldn't she trust him a little? Okay, sure, letting him bathe her would cross a few boundaries, especially considering the lack of intimacy they'd shared.

But they were both adults. True, damn it. "We're both adults," he said aloud.

"Go away."

Was there a funny note to her voice? Something more than discomfort?

He pushed away from the wall, paced a few feet and came back. He felt ridiculous, fretting outside her door, waiting for her to admit that she needed him. "I understand why you think you have to be so tough."

Nothing.

"Logan and Reese treat you like you're Superman, or the Hulk or something equally macho." Most of the time he doubted Logan and Reese ever noticed her as a female.

"I prefer it that way."

He had a feeling she would prefer everyone see her as a hard-ass. When it came to him, she was doomed to disappointment.

He waited another five minutes, then said, "You need to come out now, Margo." Much as he relished the thought of assisting her, if she fell asleep in the tub she could end up hurting herself more.

"I am."

He clenched at the sound of water sluicing over her body. "Be careful that you don't slip on the wet floor."

Seconds passed in tense silence. "Hey, Dash?"

She sounded a little drunk, and that alarmed him. "Yeah?" He reached for the doorknob.

Voice slurring, she said, "If you could use only one word to describe me, what would it be?"

He dropped his hand again. Had the medicine affected her that quickly? Probably. He'd always thought drugs were a no-no with a concussion, but apparently things had changed. That, or the pain of her dislocated elbow trumped the concussion.

Resting back against the wall, he fought a smile. "One word, huh?"

"Just one."

He chewed his upper lip, giving it quick thought, then decided she could handle the truth. "Fuckable."

Silence.

He waited. Margo wasn't herself right now, not with everything she'd been through. Her injuries and the powerful pain medicine . . . if she were any other woman he'd be treating her with kid gloves. But this was Lieutenant Peterson, the ballbuster, and he knew her well enough to know she'd detest sympathy.

When the door opened, he slowly straightened in anticipation.

She hadn't really dried her hair and little rivulets of water ran down her silky neck and disappeared into the collar of a large, soft robe that fit over her splint and was only loosely tied around her petite frame. Without makeup, the stitches and bruising were even more obscene.

His heart gave a soft thump — and he knew he was a goner.

Even fatigued, she tilted up her chin. "So . . . not impressive, as you said earlier?"

He could see the fogginess in her gaze; it took away some of her edge, making her softer, more accepting. It nearly leveled him. "The meds have you loopy."

"Maybe. I can hold my liquor, but . . ." She stumbled, and Dash caught her right arm, up high near her breasts, carefully steadying her again. "The Peterson family doesn't indulge weakness."

His brows pulled down. "Meaning what, exactly?"

"We're not pill takers."

"Even prescribed medicine?"

"Meds are for wimps." She leaned into him. "A strong person toughs it out."

Who the hell had come up with such an asinine rule? "An *intelligent* person follows doctor's orders."

She didn't acknowledge the truth of that. "Shhh. Don't tell anyone I took pain meds, okay?"

"I'll make you a deal." He cupped her face, drawn by the warmth and silkiness of her bruised skin. "I'll keep your secret as long as you continue to take them when you need to."

"We'll see." She smiled sleepily — and with sexual intent. "Now, about that one word . . ."

Knowing what she wanted, what she needed, Dash drew his gaze from her naked mouth to her shadowy blue eyes. "I'm sticking with *fuckable.*" His thumbs moved over the delicate hollows of her cheekbones. "But *impressive* would be right behind it."

Their gazes held for the longest time.

She leaned toward him. "Washing my hair

89

one-handed wasn't easy, especially with those stupid stitches in the way."

"You should have let me help." Another trickle of water trailed down her neck. "I can at least dry it for you."

Staring up at him, practically begging to be kissed, she finally nodded.

Before he forgot his good intentions or she regained her usual starch, Dash stepped around her into the bathroom. He bent to drain the tub — something else she couldn't manage — and picked up a spare towel.

He saw the discarded scrubs half-sticking out of a clothes hamper — and her clean clothes sitting on the side of the sink with the sling on top. It struck Dash that other than the splint she was naked beneath the robe.

He jerked around to look at her again. Though small, she had noticeable curves, the back view as curvy as the front.

As if she felt his hot stare, she said, "I have bruises."

His chest tightened. "Want to show me where?"

With a helpless shake of her head, she whispered, "Everywhere."

He moved up behind her, his hands at her tiny waist. He would have loved to kiss each and every mark, but not with her like this.

"I'm going to help you now."

"How?" A shiver ran up her spine — and no wonder.

Wet hair and exhaustion and only the robe for covering.

Dash grabbed her clothes, then guided her forward. "Come on. Let's go to your room."

Her small bare feet left damp marks in the plush carpet as she moved ahead of him. "Where's Ollie?"

"Curled in his bed in your living room, sound asleep." Just as she'd said, the cat ate, cleaned himself, then snuggled down to sleep. "What about you? Are you hungry?"

"Not enough to stay awake."

Without his prodding, she went past the home office, the spare bedroom and into her own room to gingerly sit on the foot of the bed.

Dash gave a quick glance around — and didn't find a single surprise. Everything was as orderly as he'd expected it to be, her comforter a neutral cream color without the adornment of throw pillows, her nightstand and dresser clutter-free. He didn't see a single speck of dust or a shoe out of place.

With Logan being a cop, he recognized the quick-access safe in the corner of the room. Since Reese had taken her weapon in the alley, he wondered if she had other guns

91

locked in that safe. It was big enough to hold a rifle or two . . . and more.

"I'm cold."

Dash took in her bare calves and feet, her narrow wrists, her slender throat. So fragile, but still so strong. "Does anything hurt besides your head and arm?"

"Pretty much everything. But it's not bad."

Or were complaints of any kind as taboo as medicine? Had she come from a family of stoic martyrs?

"Your legs? Shoulders?"

Damp lashes shadowed her big blue eyes. "Mostly my arm and head."

If she weren't drugged, Dash doubted she would admit that much to him. "Okay. I'm going to dry your hair first." Otherwise it'd just get her clothes wet. "Then we'll get you dressed and you can sleep."

"It's short, so it doesn't take long."

Feeling equal parts tender and horny, Dash set her clothes on the bed beside her. "I like your hair, Margo. A lot." He ran his fingers over her head. Her hair, in a Halle Berry sort of style, was curlier wet, but when dry it looked silky soft and feminine — a great contrast to her shark persona.

"Thank you. I like your hair, too. It's always a little messy, and a lot sexy."

Flirting? "Is that so?"

"You know how you look." Her gaze moved down to his waistband. "You know how women react to you."

Other women, sure. But Margo never made things easy. Despite her claims to the opposite, he already knew she was attracted to him. He felt her interest every time she looked at him. But she fought it.

She fought *him*.

Usually. Now . . . not so much.

But damn it, given her drugged state, he couldn't really do anything about it. Or could he?

Pretending it meant nothing at all, Dash pulled both the soiled thermal shirt and the ripped undershirt off over his head and dropped them to the floor. The waistband of his jeans had loosened from extended wear and they hung low on his hips.

Margo's lips parted. Breathing more deeply, she stared at the worn denim of his fly. Her pale throat worked as she swallowed. "What are you doing?"

"Don't want you to get messy again now that you're clean." More bare than not, he stepped right in front of her, cupped her head in one hand, and used the towel in the other to carefully rub over her hair.

The sweet scent of her shampoo mixed

with the warmth of her skin. He breathed her in — and felt himself reacting.

That wouldn't do, so he concentrated on not getting hard as he continued to towel-dry her hair. "Tell me if I hurt you." Very carefully, he touched the soft terry towel around her stiches.

When she said nothing, he looked down at her and found her eyes on his abs, her cheeks flushed. He would love seeing her like this more often.

"Feel good?"

"Yes." She kept her injured arm, wrapped up in the half cast and Ace bandage, tucked up close to her body. With the other arm she balanced herself. Her toes curled into the carpet. "Dash?"

He mimicked her soft tone. "Hmm?"

"Have you ever been married?"

One brow lifted. "No." And then he wondered . . . "You?"

"No." She looked up at him. "Ever been in love?"

"I'm thirty."

"Me, too. So?"

How to answer her? "I've had a few more serious relationships where I thought I was in love, but it never worked out."

"Why not?"

Apparently a drugged Margo was not only

more openly sensual, but also far more curious. "My mother says I'm too particular and too set in my ways."

Her cool fingers touched his ribs, drifted down to his abs, then hooked in the loose waistband of his jeans. "Particular how?"

He never should have started this ploy. It was difficult enough being near her, wanting to protect her, care for her, and then to have her looking at him with hunger . . . Yeah, difficult.

But if she planned to touch him, too, he was screwed.

Or rather, *not* screwed, given she was definitely out of commission for that.

"Why don't we have this conversation tomorrow, after you've gotten some sleep?" Not giving her a chance to object, he dropped the towel and used his fingers to brush back her hair, moving it away from her stitches. Her short, soft waves glided through his fingers. "Better?"

Her eyes sank shut. "Mmmm . . ." She leaned toward him again. "You have an incredible body. I especially like this happy trail, how it disappears down here —"

"Margo?" Time for another battle. "Hold up, honey." He caught her wrist and lifted her hand to kiss her palm. "Even warriors wear out every now and then."

"I'm not a warrior."

"But you are too hurt for me to take advantage of."

She snorted. "I wouldn't let you."

"You," he murmured, "are under the influence." He crouched down in front of her. "I'll help you get your clothes on, okay?"

She lifted her heavy eyelids to stare at his mouth. "No one has dressed me since I was three."

"I'm sure that's an exaggeration."

"No." She literally swayed. "My parents were strict about independence."

He didn't know her parents, but he liked them less by the minute. "Were they strict about other things?"

"About . . . everything really." She shifted, winced and went still again. "My family is all in law enforcement."

"Logan mentioned that once." Something about her being a fourth generation of cops. Her dad was some hotshot chief of police before he retired early with a medical problem or something.

"I was supposed to be a boy."

What did that mean? "I'm very glad you're not." He pushed back to his feet.

She gave a heavy sigh. "Me, too."

Needing a minute to get his head on

straight, Dash said, "I'm going to go grab the flannel shirt Logan brought me. It's big enough to fit over your splint and it'll be easier to get on you than the T-shirt you chose."

"The only button-up shirts I have are starched dress shirts."

He tipped up her chin. "Sit tight. I'll be right back." With long strides he left the room to get the bag Logan had brought to him. The cat snored from his bed, oblivious to Dash's presence. Outside, a weak sun tried to penetrate heavy clouds rolling in. Great, just what they didn't need — more lousy weather. Work at the current job site would stall for a day or two. Not a big deal since they were right on schedule — a rare thing in the construction business.

After automatically double-checking that he'd secured the front door, he snagged up the bag and dug out the flannel shirt on his way back to Margo.

He found her sitting exactly where he'd left her. Going to his knees again in front of her, he braced himself for what he'd do. "Let's get you out of this robe first, okay?"

"I'll be naked."

Dash put his hands on her hips, his thumbs brushing her thighs through the soft cotton of her robe. "I'll be as fast as I can."

"You'll want me."

He searched her face and didn't see a single sign of modesty or timidity. "Already do, but right now I just want you to be comfortable." He untied the belt.

"If you tell Logan or Reese, I'll castrate you."

Not so drugged that she couldn't threaten him. For absurd reasons, that made him feel better. "You think I would?"

"I don't know. I'm not a great judge of men. *Some* men," she amended.

"You can trust me." He eased the robe off her right shoulder and down her arm until she slipped her hand free.

His blood thickened, and it sounded in his tone when he added, "Believe me, Margo. I would never say or do anything to embarrass you."

Goose bumps rose on her flesh.

"Are you cold?"

"No."

Was being cold also considered a complaint? "I'm sorry." Quicker now, Dash pushed back the material and, except for where the terry cloth draped one thigh and still covered her left arm, she was bare.

His gaze naturally went to her body. *He was sympathetic, but not dead.* Her uniforms and business suits did a great job of hiding her generous rack. Full, pale, with dusky mauve nipples. Only the bruises painted over her collarbone and shoulder kept him from touching her.

"Easy now." Breathing more deeply, he stood to gently free her left arm.

Margo said not a word, but her face tightened, her brows pinching together, her lips compressed.

"You can groan, you know." Dash hated seeing her suffer in silence. "You're allowed."

She gave one sharp shake of her head, composed to the bitter end.

To hell with that. "A groan or two won't make you less sexy, especially when I can see your nipples."

Nothing.

"They're very pretty."

She stiffened.

"And those dark curls between your legs —"

She jerked her head up to stare at him — and groaned in discomfort.

"That's it." The way she affected him was so strange, and so appealing. "No reason to hold it in."

Groaning again, deeper this time, she said, "Damn you."

The bite in her tone almost made him

smile. "Be yourself with me, honey."

"I am!"

"No, you're manning up and it's stupid. You aren't a man, and you aren't impervious to pain." He picked up the flannel shirt but made no attempt to put it on her. *He was a freaking saint, standing there before a gorgeous naked woman and still remembering his altruistic motives.* "Or is that another family rule? No female attributes allowed?"

"It's a weakness and there's no point in advertising it."

"Huh. Well, if it makes you feel better, I would be groaning."

She shocked him by pushing to her feet and leaning into him, her splinted left arm caught between them, her right hand flattening on his chest, her fingers in his chest hair. "Kiss me."

*Whoa.* He hadn't expected such an aggressive assault, given her state. "I don't think so."

"It'll make me feel better."

But it'd kill him — since she couldn't do anything beyond a simple kiss. "Not a good idea."

"You don't want me?"

"You already know I do —" When her hand snaked down his body to cup him through his jeans, he froze.

"Yes," she said with purring satisfaction. "You do."

Dash groaned as she cuddled him.

"Better," she murmured. "Why don't *you* groan and I'll continue manning up."

Jesus, even boggled with meds she was doing him in.

It took a lot to step back from her exploring hand, but Dash managed it. "I said no." Her mercurial mood swings had him braced for anything.

But not for her to snuggle up against him. "You're right, I am cold."

A perfect segue. He allowed his arms to go around her, his hands to stroke down her silky back to that lush little bottom — *God, she had a great ass* — before he got it together and raised his hands to her waist, which really was still sexy enough to make him cramp. "Let's get you dressed and in the bed so you can sleep."

"What about you?"

"I'll make use of a quick shower, too. Okay?" Without meaning to, he dropped his hands to her hips.

*One day soon,* he promised himself.

He should win some type of award for restraint under extreme circumstances. "The doc said I only needed to check you every three hours. Hopefully that can be accomplished without disturbing you too much."

"And what will you do?"

"I'll kick back on your couch and watch some TV." Dash summoned his most serious expression. "Now, what do you say we get the shirt on you, then I'll help you to step into your panties, then your bottoms."

Her heavy eyes watched him with suggestion. "The drawstring yoga pants will be easy enough."

"Good." He wasn't really in the habit of dressing women. Undressing them, sure. But never while worrying about causing pain.

"One thing."

"What's that?" *Stop stroking her, damn it.* He ordered his hands to be still.

"Instead of going to the couch, why don't you stay with me? After your shower, I mean." Her gaze went smoky. "My bed is plenty big enough."

*Shoot me and get it over with.* "I can if that's what you want."

"Thank you."

When was the last time he'd slept with a woman without having sex? *Never.*

"Now just stand still and I'll do everything." Trying not to move her arm at all, he inched the sleeve up and over her swollen hand, her bent elbow encased in plaster, and up to her shoulder. He pulled the shirt around her back and helped her ease her right arm in.

Logan's shirt swam on her. Dash pulled it together in the front. It was almost as loose as the robe had been.

Aware of his knuckles brushing her body, he started at the bottom, near her thighs, and buttoned it up — past the springy pubic curls, her taut belly, that narrow rib cage and her heavy breasts. "Better?"

Oblivious to the growl in his tone, she said, "Yes."

"We need to get your sling on you, too."

"It's uncomfortable."

"It'll keep you from hurting your —"

"No." She turned away, heading for the top of the bed.

Dash stared for a second before asking, a little desperately, "What about your panties and yoga pants?"

"Too tired."

*Torture.* He moved up past her. "All right, then. Let me help." He folded down the bed, plumped her pillow. "Sit down."

"You're awfully bossy," she complained around a yawn, but she sat and let him help her ease back. Stark pain darkened her expression until she got situated, then she let out a shaky sigh and closed her eyes.

Dash sat on the bed beside her. He brushed back her bangs to see her stitches, and realized she was already falling asleep.

It was a dangerous game to play, but he did it anyway. "What about your family, Margo? Are they glad you weren't a boy?"

"We don't complain."

He had no idea what that meant.

"We're strong and independent," she whispered, her voice fading. "You're expected to do things right. And if you do things wrong . . ."

She sounded like a lost little girl, and it broke Dash's heart. "What if you did it wrong?"

She was quiet for so long Dash thought maybe she'd gone to sleep. He stayed still, unwilling to leave her yet.

Her eyes opened. "They didn't complain when they got me instead of a boy."

*Bastards.* It wasn't easy, but Dash kept the anger from his voice. "What did they do?"

She released a long breath and closed her eyes again. "Petersons accept what they cannot change, and they make the best of it."

Dash watched her fade away — and decided it was past time for him to learn more about Lieutenant Margaret Peterson.

The brush of Dash's calloused fingertips against her cheek woke her. Sluggish, she struggled to get her eyes to open. Her drapes were shut so only slivers of daylight filtered in, leaving the room dim.

Stretched out next to her on the side of her bed, Dash rested without a shirt. Nice.

"Hey, sleepyhead. Sorry to bother you."

She started to move, and pain coursed through her.

Dash's hands settled on her shoulders. "Shhh . . . be still."

Reality crashed in on her. "The wreck."

"You remember what happened?"

Using only her right hand, she touched her forehead where she'd gotten the stitches. "I remember." As long as she didn't move too much or too quickly, the pain abated.

"Good." He bent and put a butterfly kiss to her forehead. She didn't quite understand that, but it was nice so she said nothing. "I have to ask you a few things."

Right. The neuro test because of her concussion. She gave a very slight nod.

Voice husky and deep, Dash went to a series of questions, asking for her name, if she knew how she'd gotten home, the day of the week.

Lastly he asked for her birthday.

Odd, but whatever. She told him because she wanted to return to the oblivion of sleep.

He didn't let her.

He wanted to know if she'd gotten any gifts, how she'd celebrated . . . and she told him. She'd bought herself a car, and celebrated alone — as she always did.

Somehow, she knew that had made him sad. She felt it in how he touched her, the murmured words of "next time." Meaning . . . what? That he'd be around to celebrate her next birthday with her?

A nice thought.

When next he woke her, he helped her to sit up and insisted she take two aspirin.

"Do you need the bathroom?"

"No." She sank back to the bedding — with Dash's help — and closed her eyes.

"You know the drill, sweetheart."

He used an awful lot of endearments. When she had her wits again, she'd set him straight on that. Anticipating his questions, she said, "I'm Lieutenant Margaret Peterson. Thirty years old. I'm in my own home."

"Good." He brushed the backs of his knuckles along her jaw. "Favorite food?"

Sleep tugged at her, and she mumbled, "Mmm, maybe fried chicken."

She heard his smile when he said, "Favorite color?"

"Sky blue." Such odd questions, but the sooner she got through them, the sooner he'd let her get back to sleep.

"The last man you slept with?"

"I don't know."

Dash hesitated, then asked, "You don't remember his name?"

"Never knew it." She let out a long breath. "Names are a nuisance." When she hooked up, all she wanted was escape from the duty of her own choices. And thinking that, she faded into a dream about faceless men who served a distinct purpose, no strings attached.

Unfortunately, at the height of the dream, the multiple men morphed into one — Dash.

And not a single inch of her was numb.

# CHAPTER FIVE

On his back, his hands stacked behind his head, Dash stared at the ceiling. After scrounging for food in Margo's kitchen he'd taken a quick shower and changed into clean boxers and the borrowed athletic pants that Logan had brought him. Typical of Ohio weather, the day brought a big turnaround. Snow and ice gave into a slow melt beneath a blazing sun and milder breezes. The forecast claimed they'd be in the sixties tomorrow.

He'd awakened Margo twice now. An equal number of times Ollie had come to check on her. He wasn't the type of cat that Dash could play with. Older, slower, set in his ways, Ollie enjoyed a little petting, edible treats and plenty of time for napping in the sunshine.

Oliver was a sweet old guy . . . taken in by a very tenderhearted lieutenant.

She was such a fraud, charmingly so.

Who'd have ever thought it? He'd bet his last nickel that neither Logan nor Reese knew Margo owned an ancient blind cat who missed the cat box.

They also didn't know that, when her defenses were down, she was as soft and vulnerable as a woman could be.

The conflicts in her personality left him in turmoil.

He wanted to fuck her. Bad.

From the moment he'd laid eyes on her, all starchy and buttoned-up and in command, he'd wanted to break through her defenses with a good old-fashioned lay.

But he also wanted to make love to her. Endlessly.

He wanted to kiss her from head to toes, lingering at warm, damp places in between. He wanted to show her that she didn't have to be strong, not with him.

She could lean on him when necessary, and he'd support her, always.

He wanted their relationship to matter.

He wanted to leave an impact in ways both physical and emotional.

Locking his hands to keep from turning to her, touching her, he stared at that damned ceiling and planned his next move. It was going on five o'clock, and in a few more minutes he'd need to check her again.

She was so complex.

While drugged and exhausted, she'd tried to seduce him. He had a feeling that, now better rested, she'd wake with new determination to send him packing.

He was just as determined to stay, to pamper her. To have her.

*I don't know his name.*

How could she not know the name of a man she'd slept with? Delirium from her concussion? Forgetfulness because the encounter had happened so long ago? Or lack of caring, because sexual involvement didn't matter that much to her?

Or . . . had Margo indulged a one-night stand with a complete stranger? Dangerous, except that she wasn't a helpless woman. Far from it.

Did she often hang in bars looking to hook up?

He could accept that; she was a beautiful, smart, independent woman, and hey, he understood sexual urges — and the lack of interest in commitment. But his back teeth locked when he thought of her admiration for Rowdy. At least that was one interlude he knew would never happen. Rowdy Yates was many things — a good friend, a dangerous rebel, a terrific business owner.

And a loyal family guy. He would never

cheat on Avery.

Dash was still sorting through his thoughts when he heard the soft moan.

He went still at first, then turned his head to look at Margo. Was she dreaming?

In a sensual, lithe movement, she arched her neck a little.

Fascinated, alert, Dash went up on his elbow to better see her.

She made a soft sound, and her lips parted.

"Margo?"

She shifted, gave another throaty moan. . . .

A knock sounded on her front door.

Damning the interruption and determined not to wake her, Dash moved silently from her bed and out of her bedroom. He quietly closed the door behind him. Whatever Margo was dreaming, she'd have to continue on without his absorbed attention until he got rid of her company.

A big, rough hand touched her face, her ear, down her throat and to her shoulder. "Wake up, honey."

No, she didn't want to leave the dream. But even as she fought it, the sensation of Dash's mouth on her belly, her thighs, began to recede. She tried to hold on, and whispered, "Please." She needed a conclusion.

She needed release.

As if from far away, Dash's voice called to her. "C'mon, baby, open your eyes."

His voice was so compelling, so husky and warm. . . . "Dash?"

"I hope all those soft hungry sounds were for me."

Oh, God. His amusement cut through the last remnants of the dream. She cracked one eye open — and knew the pain meds had worn off. "You turned me down." Sunlight sliced through her brain and her arm felt like throbbing lead. She bit her bottom lip to stifle any wimpy sounds.

"Shhh, it's okay." He helped her to sit up, put a pill to her lips and tilted a water glass until she swallowed.

Discomfort engulfed her.

Dash caressed her shoulder. "How about you proposition me when you're not hurt?"

"Snooze you lose." But speaking of hurt . . . "Was I run over?"

"Close." He tipped up her chin. "And let's be clear here. I wasn't snoozing. I just want to know that it's *you* coming on to me, and not the drugs."

Margo dismissed everything he said when she saw his face. She knew immediately that something was wrong. She straightened, flinched as she readjusted her arm and asked, "What's the matter? Did I snore?"

"Yes, but I didn't mind." He gave her a grim yet sympathetic stare. "Actually, your relatives have come to visit."

*Unfair.* She barely had her eyes open. Before facing her folks she needed a little time — like twenty-four hours — to get it together. "You let them in?"

"Should I not have?"

Right. Like Dash could have kept them out. "Of course." She chewed her lower lip. "Oliver?"

"When he heard the knock, he ducked into the kitchen under the table. I checked on him. He's okay, just laying low."

"Thank you." She didn't trust her father alone with her cat. Actually, she didn't entirely trust her mother, either.

Curious, Dash watched her. "You're welcome."

She cast about for an idea on what to do next, but couldn't seem to get beyond the fact of Dash sitting there, shirtless, barefoot, loose drawstring pants hanging low on his lean hips, looking so . . . delicious. Especially after that stirring dream.

Her splitting head and the *thump, thump, thump* of her arm, coupled with a visit from

113

her mom and dad should have obliterated any and all carnal urges. Nonetheless, with Dash so close, smelling so incredibly good and watching her intently, she felt the burn of need.

What disturbed her most was that it wasn't all sexual need.

She'd been asleep for hours, but he had stayed with her, gently caring for her.

*Caring for her cat.*

Who did that? She should have been outraged because really, she didn't need anyone.

But some dormant female trait told her that it was nice to have the attention anyway. She couldn't remember the last time anyone had taken care of her.

She didn't know if anyone ever had.

Before Dash, before this particular moment, she wouldn't have let anyone.

Dash glanced at her closed bedroom door, then back to her. "Not that I don't enjoy a little banter with a sexy woman still in bed, but don't you think we should get a move on? Your father struck me as the type who wouldn't mind intruding."

"Perceptive."

"I am, but he's also as obvious as the hair on an ape." As if he hadn't just insulted her father, Dash reached an arm around her waist. "Let me help you up so you can at least get into your panties."

The realization that she was barebottomed almost leveled her. Lieutenant Margaret Peterson — naked except for a man's shirt. *With her parents only a room away.*

"Do you want to put on your yoga pants, too?"

She wanted a suit of armor. Or even her uniform. Right now neither was possible. Overwhelmed with the idea of her father waiting while Dash was in her bedroom with her, suggesting she put on underwear, she merely nodded.

Her world had turned upside down.

"Do you need a quick trip to the bathroom first?"

Now that he mentioned it . . . "Yes." Thank God she had a master suite with her own bathroom so she wouldn't have to go into the hall yet.

With her right hand she held on to Dash as he more or less lifted her from the bed then assisted her into the bathroom.

"The pain pill should kick in soon, and no, they have no idea I was giving it to you." He propped a shoulder on the door frame and gave her an insolent look. "I have the bottle in my pocket, so unless your dad or brother frisks me, we're good."

"My brother, too?"

"Yeah, imagine that."

Margo didn't understand the dark note in Dash's voice, and she was too frustrated to care. "They're all three here?"

"Yes." His gaze held her captive. "All three."

It got her back up, the way he sounded more abrupt by the second. "I can manage if you want to —"

He looked away from her, but said, "I'm waiting."

"Ooookay." Knowing her father's intolerance for tardiness, she didn't want to waste time. She closed the bathroom door in Dash's face, and came hobbling back out a mere half minute later.

As if searching for signs of distress, Dash looked her over.

On top of relieving herself, she'd also gargled and smoothed her hair one-handed. Neither had helped all that much. Though she felt more alert, she knew the truth. "I'm a mess."

"With good reason." Dash took her uninjured arm again and led her toward the bed, where she'd left her panties and yoga pants. He put her hand on his shoulder. "Hold on to me for balance."

Why not? In one day Dash had already seen her in a more pathetic state than anyone else ever had in her entire thirty years. "Right."

Going to one knee, he held her panties for her. Black panties with frosty pink lace as decoration. *Soooo* not the look for a feared lieutenant known for the ruthless demolition of corruption in the force, an ice queen who'd faced down enraged male officers with nary a flinch.

Dash looked up at her, his gaze dark and steady and somehow knowing. "It's okay."

Why was she still having sexual thoughts? *Because a gorgeous hunk is on his knees in front of you,* that's why. If he had her backed to a wall, this would be the perfect position for him to —

"Believe me, I know," he murmured low, sending a swirl of heat through her stomach.

"Do you?" She put her hand on his jaw, now dark with beard shadow.

"I'm trying not to think about it." His attention went down her body. "Yet."

Meaning later they could both think about it?

Obviously she needed to get laid, and fast. It no longer seemed to matter that Dash wasn't the right man. In fact, he was starting to look like exactly the right man. He was here, and she had no doubt he could get the job done, that he would probably be quite thorough.

The powerful relief of sex would help to counter the weak way she felt right now.

But would he be willing?

Leaning on him, Margo lifted one foot at a time. "This might sound egotistical, but I've never had a man refuse to kiss me."

"Think of it as a delay, not a refusal." With the same dispassion he might have used on a child, Dash pulled up her panties, and then her yoga pants.

"So if I hadn't just taken a pain pill —"

He sat back on his heels, his dark eyes filled with challenge. "I don't take orders, either."

"Orders?"

He straightened before her, so tall, so leanly muscled. And now he had a commanding air about him, something she'd never before noticed with Dash.

He cupped her face in his work-roughened hands. "You're so used to calling the shots, you probably think you can get by with it in all situations, with all people. But I'm not one of your detectives."

The steel in his tone gave her a shiver. Muscles going warm and weak, Margo leaned into his chest. "I have no idea what you're talking about." But of course she did. And of course . . . he was right.

The entire appeal of one-night stands was the opportunity to be someone else, someone unknown, a woman without a reputation for being so tough.

A woman . . . not so in control.

"All that aside," Dash said, "you need a few days to recover. And tasting you here —" he brushed the corner of her mouth with his thumb "— makes me want to taste you everywhere."

"Everywhere?" She hoped he meant what she thought he —

Obliterating her thoughts, he said, "Here," and brushed his knuckles over her right nipple.

How could she be so sensitive? In the back of her mind, she thought, *Because this is Dash.*

She breathed harder.

Watching her, he trailed his hand down her ribs and over her stomach, stopping between her thighs. "And here." His fingertips played over her ever so lightly.

Her bones turned to butter. . . .

Until he said, "But you're not up for that yet."

Wrong and wrong again. She wanted him and no paltry injuries would change that.

Persuasive arguments tripped to her tongue. "Dash —"

"No is no, honey."

How . . . *naughty* of him, to get her primed when he had no intention of following through.

And why did that just ramp up her excitement more?

Unfortunately, with her parents in the other room, she couldn't very well make him live up to the promise of his touch. "Because I can't keep the folks waiting, I'll accept that. For now."

"Good girl." Dash smiled, then took his hands from her body and shoved them into the pockets of the loose cotton pants. His lean jaw flexed. "Now that we've settled that, I have a question."

"Can it wait?"

"Afraid not." And with no pause at all, he demanded, "If they already had a son, why the hell weren't your parents happy with you being a daughter?"

His mom called him the carefree one. His dad praised him for knowing how to relax and when to laugh. True enough, when compared to Logan's serious persona, Dash was the cheerful, lighthearted brother.

But right now, his temper simmered near

a boil. Not only had Margo slipped out of the bedroom without answering his question — if she even had an answer for something so asinine — but now he also had to deal with her dysfunctional family.

Like detached strangers on a public bus, they politely tolerated each other. He was uncomfortable with them, so how would Margo feel?

At the edge of the couch her mother sat like an ice statue, back ramrod-straight, feet together, hands folded over the purse in her lap and her face as smooth and seamless as plastic surgery could make it. An expensive sweater and pleated slacks emphasized her still-trim figure. Her hair was lighter than Margo's and without the fun curls. In fact, her hair looked like a damned helmet it was so starched into place. And instead of Margo's beautiful blue eyes, her mother's eyes were a lackluster gray.

Her father deliberately took up space, brawny arms stretched out over the back of the couch, expression critical of everyone and everything. His only concern upon arrival wasn't whether or not Margo was okay. No, he wanted to know only why Dash was there.

*Surely not to help, as if such a thing were unthinkable.* The ass. Dash imagined the senior Peterson enjoyed cowing others; he had that smarmy type of personality prevalent in bullies. For now, because he was Margo's father, Dash would give him respect.

As long as the man didn't push him too far.

Her brother, as tall as the dad but leaner, had a more affable manner. He seemed equal parts amused curiosity and brimming anticipation. The jury was still out on him.

Margo did her best to stand straight and tall as she greeted her family. "Mom, Dad, you didn't have to come out in this nasty weather."

"If you hadn't been sleeping," her father said, "you'd know the weather isn't so nasty now."

"It wouldn't look right if we didn't," added Mrs. Peterson as she toyed with a single pearl necklace.

Focusing on Dash, his tone accusatory, her father said, "Is there a reason you wanted us to stay away?"

"Of course not. I just meant —"

"Damn, sis." Her brother stepped forward, blocking the father's view of Margo.

Dash waited, ready to level the guy if he wasn't gentle enough.

But her brother only inspected her, then

gave a half shake of his head. "I'm thinking you should have stayed in the bed."

"No, I'm okay. It was a late night, though." She tried a brave smile that made Dash want to leap to her defense. "Did Dash do introductions?"

"I tried," Dash said, and even he heard the antagonism in his tone. "But I was sent to summon you forth."

Expression tight, Margo looked away from him. "Of course. I'm sorry I kept you waiting, Dad."

Her father sat forward. "Let's hear it then. Who is he and why is he here?"

The first order of business should have been Margo's injuries, not her company. She wasn't an underage girl, and he wasn't the one who'd hurt her. Dash sawed his teeth together a little more, but seeing Margo's deer-in-the-headlights expression, he felt compelled to come to her rescue.

"My apologies. I'm Dashiel Riske." Forgoing their history together, he said, "I was on the road behind your daughter yesterday when the van rammed her car and —"

"Situational awareness, Margo," her father chided. "You weren't paying attention."

*Bastard.* It wasn't easy, but Dash said without inflection, "It was more a matter of the icy roads and zero visibility. No amount of situational awareness can prepare you for that type of sudden ice storm."

Lifting both brows, her brother watched him.

Apparently unused to being contradicted, Mr. Peterson bunched up as if he might attack.

Dash ignored his hostility, just as he ignored Margo's dismay. "When she crashed, she was temporarily knocked out but came around after I got her car door open. We took cover in an alley. Margo fought them off —"

"Physically?" her brother asked with mock awe. "Guess all that time in the gym is paying off, eh, sis?"

How was it a joking matter? Dash forged on. "She shot at them."

"Ah, a shoot-out." Her brother rubbed his hands together. "No doubt she was a crack shot, even with a dislocated elbow."

"And a concussion," Dash snarled.

Her brother said, "*Pfft*. Margo wouldn't let that slow her down."

Good God, they were all nuts. She was not superhuman. She was not invincible. Jumping past the reality of her pain, the danger and the hospital visit, Dash tried to wrap it up — so that, yes, he could get her back in bed. "She insisted I return here with her until we knew if it was safe for me to go home."

Margo gave him a wide-eyed stare.

As far as lies went, it sounded believable enough. He embellished on things with a shrug. "The goons saw my truck and probably read my plates. I'm involved now, so given Margo's expertise I didn't argue with her."

Now knowing that her daughter had been unconscious, that she'd been deliberately rammed, that goons had tried to murder her, her mother said, "Margo?" in an imperious way.

Dash didn't understand. "Excuse me?"

"You call my daughter 'Margo'?"

Given the woman's expression, he shouldn't have. Too late now, though. "Yes, ma'am." He glanced at her seething father. "I'm not an officer, and she's not my lieutenant."

"Damn. What are we thinking?" Her brother gestured for Margo to take the seat he'd vacated. "Sit down already."

Gingerly, Margo sat.

Dash went to stand on the left side of her chair, near her injured arm.

Her brother took up the other side — and offered Dash his hand. "Since we're on a first-name basis here . . ." He smiled. "I'm

West. My mother is Marsha, my dad Martin."

Mrs. Peterson added with bloated pride, "West is head of DVIU."

Taking his hand, Dash asked, "DVIU?"

Her father filled in. "Drug and Vice Investigation Unit."

Was that somehow more impressive than Margaret being a lieutenant at such a young age? He'd have to ask Logan. "Nice to meet you, West."

"The pleasure is all mine."

Dash noted that when West ended the handshake, which was friendly, not combative, he rested his hand on Margo's shoulder.

A show of support? After all that teasing? Maybe. He understood the way with older brothers. Logan often gave him shit just for the fun of it.

But never when he was already down.

"And you, Mr. Peterson?" Dash turned to her father. He looked a lot like Margo, with the same dark hair, but with silver at the temples. Where Margo was slight, the father was a beast. Powerfully built, seasoned, the type of man who liked to make his presence known — in one way or another. "I understand Margo comes from a long line of law enforcement."

The elder Peterson slanted a venomous

look at his daughter. "I'm retired."

Whoa. What was that about?

"Margo insisted," West murmured as if sharing an inside joke with Dash.

Margo, for her part, sat perfectly still without even blinking.

Her mother watched Dash with a sharp eye. "What is it you do, Mr. Riske?"

"I work in construction."

"You're a laborer?"

Said with a curled lip of disdain. Dash barely resisted the urge to roll his eyes. The inquisition wouldn't have bothered him if Mrs. Peterson weren't so condescending. "When it suits me, sure."

Margo spoke up. "He owns his own construction company, Mother."

That renewed her father's interest. "Is it a large operation?"

Dash shrugged. "Not really. We're local only, working within the tristate. I employ three crews, around forty-five guys."

"Commercial or residential?"

"Both."

"Don't construction workers spend a lot of time off?" Mrs. Peterson asked.

"Sometimes. But since we're a design-build firm with in-house design and planning services, we stay pretty busy."

Mr. Peterson eyed him. "Any plans to

127

expand?"

"Nope." He and Logan had inherited small fortunes from their grandparents, but neither of them was the type to laze around or serve on a committee. Logan loved the cryptic uncertainty of police work, and he was good at it. But Dash wasn't the suspicious type. He preferred the simplicity of construction.

With her parents still scrutinizing him, Dash said, "Actually, my brother and I are both pretty well set for life. Generous grandparents with trust funds and all that." He smiled. "They adored us."

Margo went wide-eyed.

"I work because I want to, because I enjoy it — not because I have to."

"But as the owner, you don't actually *work* in construction," Mrs. Peterson wrongly asserted. "You just run things."

"Running things is actually the hardest part. Paperwork is the bane of my existence. But more often than not, you'll find me side by side with my crew. I like getting sweaty, using my hands." He held out his calloused palms, flexed his fingers. "I take a lot of satisfaction in seeing a project come together, whether it's new construction or remodeling."

Suddenly Mrs. Peterson's attention dipped

down his body and roamed lazily over his naked chest. "Obviously you stay in shape."

West said, "I'm guessing his shirt is on Margo."

Being judicious, Dash said, "Her clothes were a bloody mess, so I played the gallant." Funny that he'd been so worried about Margo facing her family that he'd forgotten he wore only boxers and drawstring pants. "My clothes were ruined, too, actually. I borrowed a few things from my brother."

"I assume you're leaving soon?"

He met Mr. Peterson's hard stare with one of his own. If the abrupt statement was meant to throw him, it didn't work.

Before he could reply, Margo stood. "He's staying until I tell him to leave."

True enough, as long as she didn't send him packing anytime soon.

Margo smiled, and then, with her eyes growing a little glazed, she asked, "Anyone want coffee?"

Mr. Peterson left his seat, his attention narrowed at his daughter. "Did you take something?"

"Aspirin," Dash said.

"Her eyes look —"

"Jesus, Dad," West interrupted. "She has a *concussion.*" He turned to his sister. "And no, Margo, you are not making coffee."

129

"If everyone is staying, I am." Arm held close to her body, she turned to Dash. And smiled at him. "You want to come to the kitchen with me?"

He wasn't the only one to catch the suggestive way she put that. Dash didn't know what to do. Maybe giving her the pain pill was a bad idea.

West saved him. "No need. We're leaving now." He said to his parents, "Remember we have early dinner plans? Mother, you don't want to be late."

Mr. Peterson folded his arms over his chest and planted his big feet. "You'll return to work tomorrow?"

Forgetting her injury, Margo shrugged, froze with discomfort, then lifted her chin in defiance. "Likely. But I'll decide that later."

Surely, Dash thought, the department had restrictions on that sort of thing. Whether her parents realized it, or Margo wanted to admit it, she needed time to recover.

She and her father had a staring contest, and to Dash's surprise, Margo won.

It helped that Mrs. Peterson showed her impatience by going to wait by the door . . . without saying a word to her daughter.

Mr. Peterson made an ordeal of checking the thick watch on his thicker wrist. "We have plenty of time but since we're done here . . ."

"Thank you for stopping by," Margo sang. "So kind. So considerate."

Her brother smothered a grin and shuffled everyone out. He was almost off the porch when he turned back and came to the door, again offering Dash his hand. "Thank you."

Cold air prickled his bare skin, but Dash stood his ground. "For?"

"Your care, your assistance — and your discretion." He winked at his sister, and left.

# CHAPTER SIX

Margo stood in the doorway and watched as her meddling family drove away. She even waved — but as soon as they were out of sight she closed the door, locked it and turned to find Dash missing.

"Coward," she mumbled to herself. Yes, the pills made her less circumspect. She wasn't unaware of her own nature; she felt it necessary to be a control freak, an alpha, and aloof.

But that was for Lieutenant Margaret Peterson.

Margaret was unyielding and in charge. Margaret was cold and calculating. Margaret ruled with an iron fist.

Margo, however, enjoyed the contrast of being a smaller, softer woman — with a bigger, harder man.

*Oh, yes — hard.* "Dash?" she called, anxious now to see him, touch him and coerce him into returning her touch.

She heard water running in the kitchen and, smiling in anticipation, followed the sound. Wishing she'd put on the sling, she kept her arm and the heavy splint supported close to her body. "You can run, but you can't hide your big gorgeous self." She paused. Okay, sure, that was a rather uncensored comment. But who cared? Without the muscle-loosening pain pills she might have only thought it, not whispered it aloud.

And to say it about Dash? Logan's brother. Logan, one of her best detectives.

Again, who cared?

Dash was at the sink, Oliver winding in and around his legs, when Margo came in. The muscles in his broad back caused a deep furrow over his spine. His shoulders flexed as he filled a carafe with water.

She wanted to eat him up. "There you are."

"Making coffee." He glanced at her, did a double take on her expression, dipped his attention over her whole body, then looked away. "Take a seat."

Instead she propped a hip against the table and watched the play of muscles in his biceps as he got out coffee mugs. Visually she traced his gorgeous upper body down to his sexy tush. She couldn't help noticing the remnants of a tan, especially where the low-hanging soft cotton pants exposed a paler strip of flesh at the bottom of his spine.

One little tug on that drawstring and the casual covering would drop to his ankles. She warmed and her heartbeat accelerated.

Unfortunately he wore boxers, too. She slightly lifted her left arm, and winced. Still too painful for much use.

So he'd just have to strip all on his own. She could watch.

And enjoy.

"I figured you might want something to eat, too," Dash said, still not facing her. "Soon as the coffee is done I can —"

Moving forward, Margo caged him up against the cabinet and leaned into him, her cheek against his warm back and her right arm circling around him, her fingers splayed over his washboard abdomen, toying with that tantalizing trail of hair that went down, down . . .

Lord have mercy.

Dash froze. "Margo —"

Overwhelmed with need, she lightly bit his shoulder blade, licked his sleek, warm skin and felt him shudder.

"You shouldn't —"

"I can't resist." She kissed a path to his spine.

Very gently Dash turned in her hold. "You

have to stop that."

"No." She leaned into him again, brushed her nose against his solid, lightly furred chest. *Could a man possibly smell better than Dashiel Riske?* Impossible.

Her nerve endings sparked and a heavy pulse beat of heat settled between her legs. Knowing he didn't want to hurt her gave her the advantage. "Now, about that kiss . . ."

He threaded his fingers into her hair. "You're loopy again, lady."

Nuzzling her nose into his chest hair, she said, "Just a little. But if you'll recall I wanted you before the pain pill kicked in."

"You're not yourself."

"You have no idea who I really am, so how would you know?" No one really knew her. Not her family, certainly not anyone at the station. Only the few one-night stands —

"Time out." Frowning, Dash cupped her face, looked deep into her eyes. "What does that mean?"

Ignoring the discomfort of her elbow, she snuggled into him again. His chest was wide and solid. She gave a low sound of appreciation. "I want to touch you all over."

"Shit." He pressed back farther, put an inch of space between them.

"All this teasing," she told him, "just adds

to the urgency."

He rubbed a hand over the back of his neck, looked around the kitchen and asked suddenly, "What's up with your mom?"

Because she didn't want to talk about her parents right now, Margo used her good arm to wave that off. "She was past due for her cocktail, probably. Around five o'clock every day she needs a few drinks to keep it together. The longer she has to wait, the stiffer and colder she gets. Sometimes Dad insists she have a drink just so she won't crack." Closing in again, she put her nose to his neck. Ah, God, he smelled *so* good. She kissed a small path toward his nipple.

"Enough, Margo." He clasped her waist and stepped her back a little. "This isn't happening."

Oh, yes, it was. She *needed* it. "Will you help me with another bath?"

"No."

"Fine. Guess I'll have to take care of things on my own." With that threat made, she went down the hall to her bedroom, aware of Dash following along. She opened the closet door, and cringed at the loud creaking of the hinges.

Leaning against the wall, arms crossed, Dash tracked her every move. "That sounds like a horror movie."

136

"I've been busy," she explained. "I need to hire a handyman." That spurred her imagination and she turned to Dash. "Wanna play the handyman? You'd look pretty good in a tool belt . . . and nothing else."

He slowly shook his head. "No, I don't think so."

Something was different about him now. He no longer looked determined to avoid her. In fact, he looked . . . predatory.

She breathed a little faster. "Spoilsport," she said, but a shiver sounded in her tone.

"I didn't know you wanted to play." Eyes narrowed, Dash studied her. He must have liked whatever he saw, because he moved away from the wall. "I think I understand now."

Oh, how he said that . . . "Understand what?"

His tone changed. "I've decided you do need a bath."

"*You* decided?"

His jaw flexed and his gaze bored into hers. He held out a hand. "Come along, Margo."

His autocratic manner had her taking one step toward him before she faltered. Sudden nervousness — and excitement — held her in place. "Why the change of heart?"

He watched her just long enough to get her pulse tripping. "I've decided that you'll be easier to deal with after you're more relaxed."

Easier to deal with? "I thought you were worried about me getting the splint wet."

At her continued hesitation, his dark eyes glittered and a slight knowing smile curved his mouth. "You won't hurt yourself because I'm going to take care of everything."

A tsunami of heat rushed through her. "Everything?"

"Everything you need."

"Oh." She actually backed up a step. Surely he didn't mean what she hoped he meant. "I'm not sure . . ."

His eyes narrowed sensually. "You're only making this more difficult than it has to be." He kept his hand outstretched. "Now, come along."

Dark, hidden desire sparked into full-blown lust. She swallowed hard and meekly accepted his hand.

"Good decision," he praised, still in that firm voice. He gently led her down the hall and into the larger bathroom.

With every step, her heart beat harder.

Once inside, he told her, "Wait here while I get the bath ready."

That sounded entirely too close to an

order, but Margo stood there just the same, watching him, trying to contain her rioting emotions as he filled the tub with warm water, and got out two big towels and a washcloth. He put one towel on the side of the tub, presumably for her to rest her arm.

When he was satisfied with the arrangements, he turned to her. "Your arm isn't hurting?"

She shook her head.

"Is that a yes or no?"

"No."

"Good. Your head?"

"It's fine." Right now the only ache she had was sexual.

"I'm glad." He coasted his fingertips over her jaw, down her throat. "Stand still while I undress you." Slowly, with his lower body angled close to hers, Dash unbuttoned the flannel shirt. It was like a reverse striptease, and very effective. She tingled all over by the time he got all the buttons undone.

He opened it to expose her breasts.

For the longest time he stood there studying her in such minute detail that she almost couldn't take it. "Dash?" You'd think the man had never seen breasts before, he looked so intent.

"Shh." He brushed the flannel shirt over her shoulders and it dropped down to catch on her splint on one side, her elbow on the other. "I'm going to touch you now."

*Thank God.* The anticipation was killing her.

"I don't want you to move. Do you understand me, honey?"

She didn't, not really.

"Tell me you understand."

If that's what it took to get his hands on her . . . "I understand."

"Good." He cupped both breasts, lifting as if to measure their weight while letting his thumbs brush just under her nipples.

Margo locked her knees and tried not to gasp as her nipples stiffened.

With a dark look of satisfaction, Dash caught each nipple with his fingertips and lightly tugged. "You like that?"

"Yes." Her lips parted, her eyes grew heavy — and she leaned toward him.

"Ah, no, honey. Remember? You're to stand still." He pressed her nipples a little more tightly until she froze with a gasp. He searched her face with no discernible emotion. "Does that hurt?"

It felt too wonderful to bear. "No."

"Feel good?"

She managed a nod.

"I'm glad." He did a little more tugging. "You'll be still now." He waited, and when she didn't move, he smiled. "That's better. Now let's try this again." He went back to teasing, brushing the very tips, rolling, toying with her.

On a soft groan she closed her eyes.

He paused. "Your arm is okay?"

"Yes, yes." She nodded hard. "Absolutely fine. Just don't stop."

"Please."

It took her three breaths, and she said, "What?"

Very gently, he told her, "You forgot to say *please.*"

He looked so serious, watching her as he added more pressure to her nipples again. She licked her lips and whispered, "Please."

He didn't smile, but she saw the pleasure in his dark eyes. "That one word sounds so pretty coming from you." He bent his head. "Let me see if you taste as good as you look."

That was all the warning she got before he closed his mouth around her right nipple and started gently sucking.

"Ah, God . . . Dash . . ."

"What?" He moved to the other nipple, nipped with his teeth, tugged, then sucked her in. She felt the rasp of his velvet tongue, the heat of his moist mouth, and as he sucked the sensation went straight through to her womb.

Urgency mounting, Margo reached for the waistband of his pants . . . and Dash caught her wandering hand, then moved out of her reach.

While he seemed to contemplate some decision, his thumb coasted over the pulse throbbing in her wrist. "Maybe sitting in the tub will make it easier for you to stay still." He knelt in front of her, coasted his hands over the backs of her thighs, then her bottom, before hooking his fingers in the waistband of her yoga pants. He stripped them down her legs. "Step out."

The steamy tub kept the bathroom warm, but still her wet nipples puckered at the touch of air . . . and the touch of command in Dash's tone.

She stepped out.

Staying on his knees, he eyed her lacy panties. "Such a contrast." Using one finger, he traced tantalizing circles around the front of her underwear, dipping every so often to a spot that turned her knees to butter.

Margo was busy contemplating ways they'd be able to have sex with the clunky splint in the way when Dash said, his voice low and gravelly and sexy as hell, "I'm going to make you come."

She wanted to say, *When?* Instead she

held her breath.

"Twice," he added. "That ought to help take the edge off so you can settle down and rest."

Oh, definitely. That'd be a big help.

He eased her panties down to her knees and touched her again, oh, so gently, using only one finger. "But we're not going to have sex."

Wait a minute . . .

He brushed her panties down the rest of the way. "To ensure you don't make your injuries worse," he continued, helping her to lift first one foot and then the other, "you're going to do exactly as I say, exactly when I say it."

"But —"

Standing again, his body only a breath from hers, he cupped a hand over her sex and stared down into her eyes. "If you don't," he warned with enticing gravity, "I'll stop and instead of being satisfied, you'll have to sleep with your frustration."

She couldn't get enough air into her starved lungs. It was almost as if Dash knew her secret fantasies — fantasies she'd never shared with anyone, that no other man had ever picked up on, and had definitely never enacted.

But she believed him when he said he

would satisfy her.

The drugs stole her edge, but she wasn't completely without reason. When the sex games ended, Dash would need to know that they were *only* games — and they had a time and a place that could never infiltrate her real life.

Later she would explain it to him. Right now, she desperately wanted to see how things played out.

Her entire body warm and pulsing with need, she stared up at him, nodded and whispered ever so quietly, "Thank you."

Margo looked so sweet and so fucking ready, it took all of Dash's resolve to stick to the plan. She might not realize it, but he recognized her desire on a very basic level. He understood her, appreciated her sexuality.

She was a woman through and through.

Tough when she needed to be, strong always and incredibly intelligent. More than equal to a man in every way that counted.

But sometimes a woman enjoyed the innate contrasts of being smaller, gentler and physically weaker than a man. It worked for him because on occasion he enjoyed playing the dominant role.

With Margo, he liked it a lot.

His goal was twofold. First, he wanted to help her relax and deal with the discomfort of her injuries. Arousal blunted many things, including aches and pains. A mind-numbing orgasm could also relieve her of worries, of the many problems ahead.

Secondly, but just as important, he wanted to show her that she could be herself with him. That sexual need didn't detract from her strong personality and capability. Taking a more submissive role in bed — *with him* — wouldn't carry over into her everyday life out of bed.

Stepping back from the temptation of her nudity, her silky hair and fragrant skin, and especially her helpless anticipation, he studied her body while rubbing his mouth. She trembled with need; he couldn't leave her like that. She would rest better after getting off.

After *he* got her off.

But he also couldn't forget, not for a minute, that she was hurt. And that meant he'd just have to do without, torturous as it would be, until she was better able to reciprocate.

"You really are so fucking hot." He was going to love touching her, hearing her moan, feeling her come with his fingers pressed deep. Knowing how it would affect her, he said, "Let's get you in the tub so I can get started."

He held her right arm to keep her from slipping, then arranged her to his liking.

Breath held, she let him.

"Rest your left arm on the ledge." He helped her, ensuring she didn't get the splint wet. "Is that comfortable?"

She drew a breath. "Yes."

With a hand opened wide between her shoulder blades to support her, he said, "Lean back."

She did, and the water lapped at her nape, dampening her short dark curls. Liking that, enjoying the compliant picture she made, Dash sat outside the tub and used a cupped hand to pour water over her breasts.

"You are so incredibly stacked." He trailed a finger down her stomach. "Open your legs."

Anticipation kept Margo silent and unmoving, on the precipice of need.

"Did you hear me, Margo?"

She licked her bottom lip and slowly widened her feet apart.

"Nice." He studied her. "Know what I think would be even nicer, though?" He didn't wait for her to answer, knowing that she wouldn't. Coming up to his knees, he lifted one of her feet and rested it over the tub ledge. Yeah, he liked that. "Brace yourself. I know you have a tub mat, but I don't want to take any chances on you sliding."

With her uninjured right arm, she held on and nodded.

Carefully, Dash lifted her other foot to the ledge on the opposite side of the tub, leaving her exposed. "Stop tensing your knees . . . Yeah, that's better." He could see every inch of her soft pink flesh, swollen with need.

Her breasts rose with each quick inhalation.

Dash met her gaze. "Now I can really get to you."

With a vibrating groan, she bit her lips and struggled to stay still. Steam left her face rosy. Or maybe that was sharpening desire. She did seem to be as into the sex play as he was.

Trailing a wet fingertip up the inside of her thigh, he ordered, "Leave them there."

She closed her eyes, but only briefly. Lieutenant Margo Peterson was not a coward, ever.

Picking up the soap, Dash lathered his hands. "Since you insisted on the bath, I want to make sure you enjoy it . . . for a really long time." Her nipples were still tight, and got tighter still when he put his soapy fingers to her and teased.

She squirmed and Dash, knowing it wasn't her problem, asked, "You didn't want to get clean?"

Turning her head to the side, she made a hungry little sound of need, the muscles in her sleek thighs clenching, her feet flexing.

"Easy now." He paused, his slick fingers still on her breasts, but now only holding her. "Are you going to be able to stay still?"

Aroused color slashed her cheekbones. Her eyes were dazed. The bath water lapped at her breasts. "Yes."

"Is that a promise?"

Her gaze pleaded with him, and she whispered, "Please don't stop."

He smiled . . . and rinsed her breasts. She was sensitive here, and he almost thought he could get her off with just this.

But that'd be asking too much of him. He *needed* to touch her. All of her.

Everywhere.

"It won't be easy, I know." Leaving one hand to toy with her nipples, he lowered the other into the water, between her legs. "But you're not going to move, not until I tell you that you can."

"All right."

Dragging out the suspense, he slipped his fingers along her inner thighs, teased behind her knees, tickled over her hip bones and belly.

"Dash," she whispered desperately.

"Shhh. No talking, either." It took all his concentration to hang on, to remember that this was for her, only her.

She drew in a shuddering breath.

"All you need to do is rest there and let me have my fun." Knowing she couldn't, he said, "Now loosen up for me," at the same time that he cupped his hand over her again — this time with her legs sprawled wide.

A vibrating moan escaped her.

"You just can't keep quiet, can you?" He pressed two fingers into her, easily since she was already slippery wet and ready. With his other hand he toyed with her nipples.

She made another throaty sound of excitement, and Dash told her calmly, "You may as well get comfortable, because I'm not in any rush here." He eased his fingers back out of her. "We have all night."

She lifted her hips, his hand now loosely covering her, seeking the more intimate stroke.

"Shh. Rest back in the tub or I'll have to stop. I won't chance you getting hurt."

"I won't," she all but wailed, writhing against his hand.

"Your arm is okay?"

"Yes!"

He smiled. "Does your head hurt at all?"

"Damn you . . ."

"Cursing me?" He pretended to pull away.

"I'm sorry."

"Better." He held one nipple and despite how she squirmed, kept his fingertips just barely inside her. "You sounded sincere enough."

Two deep breaths . . . and she said, "I am."

"Then behave." He pressed his fingers deep again, slowly working her, using the heel of his hand to add friction to her clitoris.

Her teeth locked. She was already so close, and he'd barely done half of what he wanted to do.

"Keep your knees open."

Eyes closed tight, she nodded.

He watched her splinted left arm, making sure she didn't forget about it.

And suddenly she gasped, almost lost in a fast orgasm.

Surprised by her swift response, Dash eased up, saying softly, "No, not yet."

Ripe excitement left her entire body taut, rosy.

Dash touched her everywhere, her swollen sex, her breasts and her mouth and her plump little ass. "You are so sexy, Margo."

"I . . . I need to come."

"And you will," he promised. He saw the carnal desperation on her face . . . and he loved it. "After I've gotten my fill of enjoying your body."

One thing was certain: she did not feel any pain. He could tell by the way she moaned and moved and how easily she kept trying to spiral out of control.

Dash abandoned her breasts for the moment to concentrate between her legs. "I think you'll like this."

She caught her breath and waited.

"Two fingers in you, nice and deep." He watched the movement of his hand, his fingers sliding in and out of her tender body. "I have large hands, but still, it's not quite the same as when we'll have sex." His cock hurt, he wanted her so much. But he wouldn't veer off track.

She strained to remain still.

"And with my other hand, I can . . ." He touched her clitoris, and she gasped, her hips lifting. "Maybe we should put that off until later."

"Do it now." Her voice was high, thin.

"I don't want you to come yet."

"Dash . . ." Frustration made her frantic. "I don't know if I can wait any longer."

He said with certainty, "You can."

151

She moaned raggedly.

Maybe he should save that much teasing for her second orgasm. She was already drawn so tight that it worried him. He didn't want to add to her aches and pains. He wanted to alleviate them.

"I'll prove it to you. . . ." She was about to protest when he touched her again, saying, "Later."

It took him less than thirty seconds to push her over the edge, and hearing her cries, seeing the open, honest pleasure on her face, he damn near followed her.

As her orgasm faded, she slumped and he quickly pulled the drain on the tub to let the water out. "Relax, honey."

She gave a faint but honest laugh. "Now I can, definitely."

"I'm glad." Pleased with her, Dash shook open the towel. "Time to dry off."

"Forget it." She motioned him away with her right hand. "Just leave me here for a little while."

He grinned at her tranquil posture. "You know I can't do that. Come on now, you'll be more comfortable once you're dried and dressed."

"And fed."

"Exactly." He caught her under the arms. "Careful now." He helped her out, then said, "If you can stay on your feet, I can take care of everything."

"Yes, sir." She giggled.

Pausing with the towel to her belly, Dash stared at her. A giggle? From Lieutenant Margaret Peterson. "You are dopey as hell."

"I'm *boneless.*"

"Boneless, huh?" He kissed her, and wanted to go on kissing her. But that would test his control too much. "I like that 'sir' business."

"You earned it." She sobered as he bent to dry her legs. "But, Dash, you do realize —"

"That it's only in the bedroom? Or in this case, the tub? Maybe someday the kitchen table?" He sent her a quick smile of re-assurance. "Of course I do." He briskly dried her thighs, and more slowly between them. "I've never known a stronger, more independent woman than you. What we do together won't change that."

Margo put a hand on his shoulder, balancing herself.

He brushed the edge of the towel over her breasts, concentrating on her nipples. "But games are fun for everyone, so anytime you want to play . . ." He couldn't stop himself from bending to her nipple for one quick, soft suckle. "Just let me know. I liked it. A lot."

Maybe a little uncertain, she ran her tongue over her lips.

"It's all right if you admit that you liked it, too." Hoping to put her at ease, he teased her and said, "I won't tell."

"You already know that I did."

"You'll like it again in . . . oh, a few hours. Before we go to sleep." He smiled. "I did promise you two climaxes, right?"

She sighed. "And what about you? I'm more than happy to —"

"No. I won't take the chance of causing you pain." He kissed the bridge of her nose, her temple, and suggested, "Make it up to me when you get the splint off in a few days." He waited to see what she'd say, if she'd maybe deny the odds of being with him a few days from now.

Instead she lightly trailed her nails down his chest to his abdomen. "Count on it."

# CHAPTER SEVEN

Dash woke curled around Margo. She was on her right side, his knees behind hers, her splinted arm resting above his around her waist.

Her sweet little bottom pressed into his lap.

Even before his eyes opened he remembered yesterday and lust rushed through him. His arm tightened the tiniest bit.

After her bath, he'd cooked her dinner, held her and Oliver on the couch while watching a movie and then they'd gone back to bed.

Using only his fingers, he'd given her another climax. He'd badly wanted to pleasure her with his mouth as well, but hadn't trusted his restraint. Instead, after she'd come, he stayed with her, touching her softly, then with more insistence until she caught up, until the sensations began to build again.

He kept her going, loving the way she cried out, how she clutched at him with her right hand. Slowly the orgasm built and, body taut and breath ragged, she came a third time.

No wonder she'd slept through the rest of the night.

Lieutenant Peterson took to the submissive role with amazing heat.

All things considered she had incredible endurance, a wonderfully uninhibited streak and she was every bit as sexual as him.

Only he'd done without, and now he was in a very bad way.

Trying not to wake her, he lifted his head and searched for the clock. A little after ten. Not super late, not super early. Finally, they'd both caught up on sleep. Hopefully, now well rested, she'd feel better today.

He glanced at the window and saw plenty of sunshine coming in. Nice.

Tomorrow morning Margo would see a doctor about getting the splint removed. Never mind what she'd told her father, she'd need some physical therapy before returning back to work.

His lip automatically curled at the thought of Mr. Peterson.

God willing, her family wouldn't feel the need to visit again anytime soon.

Just as Dash finished the thought, a knock sounded on the door. Shit.

He let his head drop back with a groan.

Margo stirred, then clumsily sat up, almost clubbing him with her splint.

He dodged it. "Easy."

She looked around as if confused, zeroed in on Dash and . . . blushed.

Nice. How she could look so pretty with bruises and sleep-rumpled hair, he didn't know, but the blush only added to her appeal. "Morning, beautiful."

The heat in her cheeks intensified. "What are you groaning about?" She eyed him up and down . . . pausing on his morning wood. "Or maybe I already know."

Only half-awake and still she sounded interested. Damn, but he couldn't wait for her to be 100 percent again so they could really burn up the sheets. Dash shook his head. "You have a visitor."

"Who?" She glanced around as if expecting someone to be in the room with them.

Grinning, Dash said, "At your front door."

"Oh." That stymied her — until the knock sounded again. Face pinched in discomfort, she threw back the sheet and swung her legs off the mattress.

And froze at being naked.

She was so small, so trim and toned, that

157

even the sling couldn't detract from her sex appeal.

He trailed a finger down her elegant spine, all the way to her adorable fanny. "Maybe your folks have returned." After kissing her nape, Dash, too, left the bed to stand beside her.

Knowing she watched, he stretched lazily. Blasé, he asked, "Want me to get it?"

"It?" She stared at his dick.

He lifted her chin. "The door."

"Uh . . . no." With a nod at his erection, she said, "I doubt my parents would return this soon, but regardless, I don't want anyone to see you like that."

Possessiveness? He hoped so. Now that she was awake and clear-minded, he didn't try to insist on helping. "Give me a few minutes then and I'll come make coffee." He brushed a thumb over her cheek, down to her jaw. If he didn't go now, he might not go at all.

He turned without another word and headed into her private bath.

Wow. Things had changed dramatically overnight.

Margo raised her splinted arm to test it, and felt nothing, not even a twinge. Great. With her right hand, she touched her head near the stitches, but that felt mostly fine, too. She had only the slightest headache, and that might be a dire need for caffeine.

Time to get it together.

Knowing it would take her forever to get a robe on over her splint, she wrapped a blanket around her body and hurriedly headed to the front door. A quick glance out the peephole and she cursed softly. Just what she didn't need.

Reluctantly, she opened the door to none other than Rowdy Yates.

Bright sunshine turned his dark blond hair golden and added an interesting sparkle to his sexy bedroom eyes. He wore faded jeans, a black T-shirt under a zip-up sweatshirt and boots. He was so incredibly hot that Margo had to remind herself to breathe.

Though she wore only a blanket, his gaze never wavered from her face. "If we woke you, we can drop off the get-well package and let you get back to bed."

Watching his mouth move was a special treat. The man exuded raw sensuality on every level.

"Lieutenant?" One brow lifted, Rowdy glanced in past her. "Dash around?"

Avery stepped in front of him, her smile confident. "You have her tongue-tied." And then to Margo, "Don't worry about it. I understand. Every woman still reacts that way to him. I'm used to it."

Rowdy rolled his eyes — and that helped Margo to collect herself. She felt foolish, but hopefully hid it. "I'm sorry." Holding the blanket secure with her right hand, she nudged the door open wider in a silent bid for them to come in. "The pain pills — which Dash insists on me taking — keep me in a fog. I didn't mean to be rude."

"Not a problem." Rowdy's gaze dropped to her body, and quickly away. "We woke you?"

"No . . . Yes . . ." She did not want them to assume she'd slept — even in the platonic sense — with Dash. "You mentioned a get-well package?"

Rowdy lifted the loaded bag with a shrug. "It's what Logan and Pepper did when I got cut."

"We enjoyed it," Avery said. "So we figured you would, too."

Rowdy searched the room. "We saw Dash's truck out front and assumed you were up and about."

Her mouth firmed. It was already happening, the intrusion into her private life. "Yes, he's here. He brought me home from the hospital and insists on staying to play my nurse." He'd also insisted on making her

160

insane with lust. Three times.

Now that she'd given in, she couldn't wait to get back to it again.

As if she thought nothing of it, Avery said, "Of course he did." She set her purse aside and slipped off a jacket. "You shouldn't be alone."

The protest came without her permission. "I can take care of myself."

"If you had to, sure. But why not let Dash help out?" Sotto voce, she added, "Men love playing caregiver."

Not all men. Her father had certainly never shown any signs of caring for anyone.

"You don't have a car yet," Rowdy pointed out. "And it can't be easy accomplishing much with that bulky splint."

Margo looked down at her wrapped arm and shrugged. "Hopefully I'll get it off tomorrow." She mostly had to wear it until the swelling went down and the doctor confirmed she could start physical therapy. Not that she'd need a lot of PT. More than anything she just wanted to get back to work.

Rowdy lifted up a stuffed bag. "We brought coffee and Danish for now, and chili for later."

"From your cook?"

"The chili is, yeah."

"Bless him and you, then." The chili was terrific, one of her favorites.

He looked around her living room with interest. "Nice place."

Never had she thought to have Rowdy in her home. Oddly enough, while she still admired the sight of him — as Avery had said, what woman wouldn't? — Margo didn't feel that usual bone-melting liquid heat, a response that Dash had so easily engendered.

"Thank you." She nodded toward her kitchen. "Make yourself at home while I get dressed." Before she could exit the room, Oliver poked his nose around the corner and hissed.

Both of Rowdy's brows shot up this time. "You have a cat?"

His reaction was nearly identical to Dash's. Was it really so unheard of for her to have a pet?

"That's Oliver. He's blind." Dash strode into the room. Surprising her, he'd taken the time to don the loose athletic pants, a T-shirt and socks. Hair combed and face shaved, he didn't look as if he'd just awakened at all.

But he did look good enough to eat.

And damn, there was that bone-melting heat again, making her legs feel like noodles.

Had he dressed and cleaned up to help hide the fact they'd slept together? So considerate.

Margo started to explain further about Oliver, but Dash marched forward as if on a mission. His intensity was such that she backed up one step before she caught herself and stood her ground.

*What in the world —*

Winding an arm around her waist, Dash lifted her chin with the edge of a fist, and kissed her full on the mouth.

Rowdy and Avery were silent.

It wasn't an extended kiss, but it sure wasn't a simple peck, either. As he slowly lifted away his tongue moved over her bottom lip.

Margo went mute.

For a few heart-throbbing seconds, he just looked at her. "Do you need help getting dressed?" His voice was deep, rough.

Possessive.

She glanced at Rowdy.

Impassive, he said, "It's not a surprise, Lieutenant, so don't look so sheepish." He turned his astute gaze on Dash. "He's been obvious enough for a while now."

Oh, dear God. "Obvious about *what?*" If he'd already blabbed somehow —

"How interested he is." Avery smiled at

163

her. "You were the unknown, but I'm glad to see you're softening toward him."

Dash gave Margo a one-arm hug. "You see? They're rooting for me."

Rowdy made a rude sound. "Wouldn't matter to me one way or the other except that I hate to see a man suffer."

Dash put a hand to his heart. "You are such a good friend, Rowdy."

Margo elbowed him hard. She was used to his teasing, his nonstop amusement and carefree attitude about life. But she didn't want to be the brunt of a joke.

Holding his ribs, he said, "Maybe she hasn't softened that much after all."

Avery snickered. "You need someone as strong as you, so be glad she's not one of those moony-eyed girls that falls at your feet."

"No," Dash said, "she's not that."

Done with the nonsense, Margo said, "I'm going to get dressed — and yes," she added, eyeing Dash, "I can manage on my own."

"Would you like me to play host until you return?"

She no longer knew what she wanted, so she simply nodded.

He kissed her again before she could stop him. "Take your time." Leading the way, Dash had Rowdy and Avery in the kitchen before the enormity of his familiarity really hit her.

Why didn't he just beat his chest and brand her? Eyes narrowed, stomping as much as a woman could in nothing more than a blanket, Margo exited the room.

But damn it, she knew Oliver would be concerned with others invading the kitchen and she had no idea what Dash might tell Rowdy, so she hurriedly struggled into the big flannel — she really did need to find something else to wear — and a pair of leggings.

God, doing things one-handed took forever.

She slowed down long enough to clean her teeth and wash her face, but one look at her hair and she knew that was a lost cause. She finger-combed it, and bypassed any efforts at makeup; nothing would hide the bruises anyway.

How was it that Dash looked more gorgeous after their night of chaos and she just looked a wreck? Unfair.

Barefoot, furious about the possibility of gossip, she rushed back into the kitchen.

They were all seated at the table and Dash, with Oliver in his lap, regaled them with tales of her heroism during the debacle. Oliver didn't look the least bit upset by the company. Even from the doorway Margo could hear his rumbling purr.

No one seemed to notice her.

Dash said, "She didn't let on that her elbow was dislocated until after it was safe."

"Wow," Avery said. "I knew she was tough, but that's amazing."

Rowdy sipped his coffee and kept silent.

Dash continued to stroke Oliver's back while talking. Though he sounded grim, his touch on the old tomcat was gentle. "I'm glad it wasn't her right arm. Not that I think that would have slowed her down, either. Even injured, she's deadly when she has a target."

Margo's face heated. What she'd done wasn't all that extraordinary. She was a lieutenant, trained to act, and so she had.

"Logan and Reese have nothing but good things to say about her," Avery added. "They trust her completely. I mean, not just to make the right decision, but to back them up when necessary. I think it's awesome that she's as lethal and controlled as they are."

"I give major props to Logan and Reese for being badass cops," Dash agreed, "but Margo has them both beat."

Rowdy dunked a doughnut into his coffee and murmured without looking at her, "Margo is embarrassed by the praise."

Avery and Dash both twisted in their seats — and chagrin showed in their expressions.

Dash pushed back his chair and stood, the cat held close to his chest. "Rowdy and Avery brought us coffee." He searched her face. "I already fixed a cup for you."

Oliver's continuing purrs overrode the awkward silence.

Rowdy turned his head and looked at her. "The right focus can mask pain when you need it to. But after things settle down, the pain settles in, and it sucks."

Because Rowdy would know that first-hand, Margo just tipped her head in a nod.

"I'm guessing," he said thoughtfully, "that like me, you were more pissed than anything and that helped to put the injury on hold."

"You guess right." Sure, the pain had been there, but overriding it was the fury that she'd been attacked, and even more, that Dash was in danger. "Luckily, Dash wasn't a slouch."

"You thought he was?"

Dash said, "Compared to her . . ."

"He's a cop's brother," Rowdy argued with a frown. "He understands the risks. Hell, we've both seen him in action and he keeps his cool."

Dash saluted him.

Margo didn't want to think about the time

167

a perp had gotten the jump on her, hand-cuffing her to a bed with Reese while another goon aimed a gun at Rowdy.

Thanks to Reese's wife, Alice, Logan had been notified and he and Dash had taken control of the situation. They'd all escaped unscathed. "Dash wasn't in the thick of that."

"He'd disabled a goon out front."

Avery chimed in, saying, "Since he works construction he's pretty fit. I can't imagine him being a slouch at anything."

Margo rubbed her temple. "He's a civilian. We were pinned down in an alley and people tried to shoot us."

Dash sat forward. "It was *you* they wanted dead. I was just in the way."

She ignored Dash and said to Rowdy, "I assumed he'd be more rattled by it all than he was." Grudgingly, she admitted, "He handled himself well, though. It's in large part due to him that we survived."

Rowdy looked at Dash's grin and shook his head. "If you two are done with the mutual admiration, I'd like to make a suggestion."

Already knowing what he'd say, Margo shook her head. "No."

"It wouldn't take me any time at all to check into things for you."

She should have known he hadn't made the visit just to drop off food. "No."

"I could ask my contacts on the street."

Margo came forward in a rush, her scowl fierce. "Do *not* involve yourself." Not in that way. It was bad enough that Dash was now likely a target. She didn't want Rowdy in danger, too. "I can handle it."

Dash held out a chair. In contrast to her tone, he sounded like calmness personified when he said, "Come sit down. Drink some coffee."

He said it more like a request than an order, and she needed that coffee, so she agreed. Her splint clunked on the tabletop, making her wince. She grabbed the coffee with greed. "Perfect. Thank you."

Dash went to the refrigerator, got a pre-made bag of ice and a hand towel, and gently layered them on her arm.

Margo said nothing. She needed the ice, but she hated the weakness.

Rowdy waited until that was done, but he didn't let it go. "I never said you couldn't handle things, but you know I can't resist lending a hand."

"*Try.*" Flustered anew, she gulped more coffee. Dash, damn him, had fixed it exactly as she liked it.

Did he have to be so considerate, so annoyingly perfect, as well as a scorching sex partner?

"It was bad enough when we thought they'd moved on, that they were out of reach." Folding his muscular arms on the tabletop, Rowdy gave her his most intimidating stare. "The fact that they made a grab for you proves the opposite, that if anything, they're more brazen and more dangerous than ever."

"We don't know for sure that it was the same group. I'm a cop. I make enemies." Inside the department and out. "That's a fact."

"They're still here, still a threat, and I could —"

Imbuing as much command into her tone as she could muster, Margo rejected him. "Absolutely not. This is a matter for the police."

He replied with a very rude snort.

"I mean it!" Losing her aplomb, Margo pointed at him. "This is no concern of yours."

"Bullshit, Lieutenant."

Dash started to protest but Margo silenced him with a touch to his wrist. The last thing this conversation needed was Dash acting territorial. To her relief, he didn't press it. In fact, other than that familiar kiss, he'd been as respectful and gentlemanly as always in front of Rowdy and Avery.

"You told me months ago that you thought my bar was involved." Rowdy paid no attention to Dash at all. "That makes it my concern."

"Not involved precisely. Only that we'd found some of your cocktail napkins and a matchbook at one of the crime scenes."

"There you go." Rowdy sat back in his chair. "They've encroached on my territory."

"But," Margo said with emphasis, "you know I gave up on any probable link when no one from your bar approached me."

"That doesn't prove jack shit. Could be it went down right outside the bar. Maybe someone followed women home." He scrutinized her. "Tell me what you have and *maybe* I'll agree there's no connection."

Avery rolled her eyes. "Yeah, right. Like that'll happen."

He gave her a look of censure. "Avery . . ."

"She's a capable professional, Rowdy. You heard what Dash said. She knows what she's doing — and she knows if she needs your help. Respect her authority."

"I do respect her. Like her, too, and that's why I want to help."

Now Margo felt guilty. She refused to look at Dash as she tried to explain. "It's personal now, so I'll handle it."

"My brother-in-law is a freaking cop," Rowdy said, as if she needed the reminder.

"So?"

"So thanks to that connection, I'm determined to walk the straight and narrow."

Dash coughed a laugh.

A grin breaking, Rowdy admitted, "At least whenever possible." He crossed his heart. "If I find out anything, you'll be the first I tell. And then you can *personally* decide what to do with the info."

Margo considered it. Short of locking him up, stopping Rowdy probably wasn't possible, so maybe it made sense to have him working with her. "You won't act without me?"

"Not if I can help it."

For Rowdy Yates, that was an enormous promise. "You won't put yourself in danger?"

He took longer to reply to that one — until Avery shoved his shoulder. He looked at his wife, his expression softened with obvious love, and he drew her out of her seat and into his lap. "I'm not allowed to endanger myself anymore. Avery forbids it."

Dash grinned. "Good for you, Avery."

Margo was willing to bet that Avery's idea of danger varied greatly from Rowdy's, but she kept that to herself. "What do you think you can do?"

"Running a bar comes with its own challenges, especially when the place used to be such a dive. So I've maintained my contacts on the streets. Nothing gets by them, and for a few bucks they'll spill their guts on anyone and anything. I'll ask around — discreetly — and see what I can come up with."

"I have street contacts, too, you know."

"Maybe." While hugging Avery, he gave Margo an indulgent smile. "But these people will talk to me when they refuse to say shit to a cop."

Avery slid a hand over his shoulder to the back of his neck. "Rowdy knows things about the city, but Cannon knows about the neighborhood. You should probably talk to him, too."

Slowly, Rowdy nodded to acknowledge that. "True enough. And he's trustworthy."

Cannon Colter was Rowdy's newest hire, as well as an MMA fighter. He was in his early twenties, unassuming, with a shredded body, a gorgeous face and quiet competence. Margo had seen him a few times, and if he weren't so young, she might've been interested in him.

Then again, he worked at Rowdy's bar, and that close association made him off-limits regardless of his age.

Suddenly, under the table, Dash's hand slid over her thigh. She blinked at him, and his eyes narrowed.

Had he read her thoughts?

"Can I make a suggestion?" Dash asked of everyone at the table. "Maybe it'd make more sense for Rowdy to coordinate with Cannon and then share with Margo their collective info."

"I can do that," Rowdy said. "No problem. As long as the lieutenant agrees to my help."

"Can I stop you?"

He grinned. "No."

She waved her hand. "Fine. Then have at it. But understand me, Rowdy. You will not overstep. You will not break any laws on my behalf. And you will not, under any circumstances, get yourself into risky situations."

After saluting her, he stood and picked up Avery in his arms. Still holding his new wife, he eyed Margo from her hairline to her injured arm. "You'll be okay?"

"What? My elbow?" She detested being the source of concern. "Yes, it'll be fine."

His dark gaze moved over her. "And your head and the rest of those bruises?"

Backbone stiffening, she assured him, "I'll be back to full speed in no time."

"Don't push things, okay?" He set Avery back on her feet but kept an arm around her. "And try letting Dash help out."

Oh, the way Dash had helped . . .

"If you need anything," Avery told her, "please let us know."

It was another couple of minutes before she and Dash said their last goodbyes and they were finally alone again.

Dash closed the door, set Oliver down to the floor and gripped her shoulders. "Was I quiet enough?" His thumbs massaged her shoulder joints, easing her tension. "Did I stay properly in the background?"

"Is that what you were doing?" She wondered why he'd been so quiet.

"As much as I know you don't need it, as impressed as I am by your capability and resilience, not pampering you was tough. Mostly because I enjoy it so much." He bent to press the gentlest of kisses on her forehead. "I see these bruises on you and I'd like to hold you the same way Rowdy held Avery."

The same way . . . with love? Or just being a protective male? "You were very restrained . . . except for that initial kiss." Which had felt so incredibly intimate.

"Except for that," he concurred. He traced a fingertip down her injured arm to the splint. "It's so hard to see you like this and not be able to do anything."

"You did something." She'd slept like the dead after he'd left her so utterly replete.

His smile was slow and knowing. "Anytime I can be of service, let me know. But I'd also like to help you out with everything else if that won't hurt your pride too much."

So he understood it was her pride?

"This steel backbone of yours is admirable, honey." His hand went down her back to her behind, then up again. "Leaning on me a little won't change that."

He could be so charming — and seductive. She knew she shouldn't, but Margo rested against his strong chest, her forehead on his sternum. "Want to tell me why you did it?"

"That kiss?" When she nodded, he said, "Just making sure you didn't forget me."

As if she could after the incredible way he'd made her feel. "Well, other than that, thank you for behaving."

He hugged her a little closer. "I would never do anything to embarrass you."

"It's not that you embarrass me exactly. . . ."

"You want to keep your private life private.

I get it."

More like she wanted to keep her sexual preferences private, but she wouldn't nit-pick.

"As long as you don't shut me out, I'm good with that." His big hand moved over her head to her nape. "So what's first on the agenda today?" And just to make it more difficult, he put his lips near her ear and whispered, "Want me to help you relax before we get started on everything else?"

Yes. Definitely yes. Right now, she could use another dose of his special brand of painkiller. But preferences aside, she had to take care of business. Still . . . "What exactly did you have in mind?"

"Ah, no. I'd rather surprise you." His tongue touched her ear, his breath was warm, soft. "Just know that you won't be disappointed. In fact, I'm thinking I'll make you come until you're too exhausted to do anything but rest — as the doctor ordered."

She believed him. And she was so tempted; already her body felt sensitive in key places, tingling with awareness, with eagerness.

But it was because she believed him, because she already knew exactly how easily he could get to her, that she had to decline. "Sorry. We should put that off for later. I have too many arrangements to make, and I can't make them if I'm numb."

# CHAPTER EIGHT

She hadn't refused him, and already Dash could feel her quivering, the breathiness in her voice. Amazing, but it seemed they both stay primed around each other. He'd never experienced anything like it before.

The near violent way he wanted her, to fuck her, to talk with her, just to be with her, was fast becoming familiar.

His hand went down her body to her flat belly. "I could give you just a prelude if you want." Fingers spread, he spanned her from hip bone to hip bone. Visualizing it even as he said it, he rasped, "I wouldn't mind going on my knees for you."

"Dash . . ." She gave a sharp inhalation. "That would be —"

"Incredibly hot."

"— so unfair to you."

"Not true." He looked into her beautiful blue eyes. Voice rough and filled with lust, he whispered, "I would enjoy eating you."

Involuntarily, her hand fisted in his shirt. She drew two deep breaths, and shook her head. "If you did that I would want more. A lot more."

"Like me inside you? Sliding deep. Riding you hard." Jesus, he was turning himself on. "Tell me you want it." *Tell me you want me.*

"Yes." Her fist loosened, smoothed his shirt, over his pec muscle. "I'm dying to feel that."

"Soon," he promised her.

"But I need to focus on my life first."

Putting his forehead to hers, Dash concentrated on breathing. "Got it." He wouldn't pressure her. More than anything he just wanted to alleviate some of her burden. The next few days — probably the next few weeks — would not be easy on her.

"If you offer again later . . ."

"I'll insist." He couldn't wait to kiss her everywhere, to taste her all over. *Stop,* he told his overactive imagination. He couldn't very well take her on her errands with a perpetual boner. "For now, do you want a pain pill?"

"Better not." She stepped back to look at his body, her expression concentrated. "God, you are sexy. I always thought so, but now . . ."

"You always thought so?" She'd sure hidden it well.

"Don't be coy. You know you're hot."

He smiled, and the smile turned into a laugh. "I don't think anyone would accuse me of being coy. And thank you. I'm glad you think so."

"The thing is, it isn't always about looks." Ah. "I see." And he did. "It's more about me understanding you, recognizing what you like, what your body likes and what you need. Because I understand you, you know I can get you off, and you know that you love it."

"Do you understand me?"

In bed . . . and out. But she might not be ready to hear that yet.

He tucked a short curl behind her ear. "I can make you scream in a dozen different ways. Later, I'll show you just a few."

Eyes heavy, she looked up at him. "When I'm one hundred percent again, I want payback."

His heart skipped a beat and his gut tightened. "Meaning?" he asked with a raised eyebrow.

Coasting a hand over his chest, she asked, "Have you ever been tied up?"

"No." His level of trust didn't quite stretch enough to put himself at anyone's mercy. But maybe this was a test. Maybe she needed to know he'd play along before she could completely let loose. Tightening at that possibility, he asked, "You?" Because if that's what she wanted, he was in, 100 percent.

She chose not to answer him. "Would you let me tie you up?"

*Hell, no.* "Guess that depends." This conversation would not help him keep a boner at bay. "For what purpose, exactly?"

"Right now I can't get my fill of you, not with only one hand, and not while this damn splint is in the way. But after I'm cleared by the doc, or before that if I can manage it, I'd like to have all the time in the world to look at you, touch you and taste you everywhere."

An image of her riding him, her body holding him snug, her face taut with pleasure, nearly stole his breath. "You don't have to restrain me for that. Just say the word and I'll play along."

"You say that now, but —"

He bent and took her mouth in a hot, wet, tongue-twining kiss. "Let's see how it goes." And hopefully he'd turn that idea around on her. He had a feeling Margo would love being totally at his mercy.

"How what goes?"

"You can try me first, and if it doesn't

work out the way you want, then maybe — *maybe* — I'll let you tie me up."

The idea stirred her, he could tell.

What he'd do to her, with her, would stir her more. "But until then, until you're able to take full advantage, you're still mine to play with. And I enjoy playing a lot."

Closing her eyes and with a slight groan, she put her hand over his mouth. "Enough. I need to be totally clearheaded for a while and if you keep on teasing, I'll be a muddled mess."

Dash caught her wrist, kissed her palm and then lowered her hand. "I'll be all business, I promise." He, too, needed to get the fog of lust off his brain.

"You're very considerate. Thank you." She pushed back from him, her smile warm, teasing — and damn it, that turned him on more than the sex talk.

She rarely looked at him like that, and he relished it, seeing it as a sign that he made progress. "I understand skipping the pain pill." For a woman like Margo, being totally clearheaded would be very important. "How about some aspirin instead?"

"Probably not a bad idea."

And now being reasonable, too? He didn't know what to think. They went into the kitchen together. Oliver had already retreated to a sunny spot in the living room. Dash put the makeshift ice pack away and got her the aspirin while she filled a glass with water.

He watched her take the OTC meds and knew she must be feeling a lot of discomfort for her to be so agreeable, given her aversion to all meds. "How's your head?"

"It's fine." She went back to the table and sat with her coffee. "I need to call the insurance company, arrange for a rental car, and I should probably get hold of my commander." She looked disgruntled over that last task.

"Any way I can help?"

"You've already done so much."

"I want to be with you. Nothing I've done has been a hardship, believe me. In fact, I already took the next few days off. My foreman can handle anything that comes up, and when he can't, he can reach me by phone."

"Well, then, if you're sure . . . would you mind playing chauffeur today?"

"I was hoping you'd ask." Honestly, keeping it together this morning hadn't been easy. Not kissing her — especially with the way she looked at Rowdy — had been impossible.

Yeah, he wasn't blind, and by her own

admission he knew she considered Rowdy Yates prime material for fantasies. Rowdy seemed unaware or uncaring; he was probably well used to it, the likable bastard, and Avery didn't appear threatened, either.

So why was he the only one on edge about it? It left him disgruntled all over again.

While he had the opportunity, he wanted to make an impression on Margo. Not just sexually, but in every way.

Surprising him, Margo propped her chin on her fist and let her gaze move all over him. "It might take me much of the day to get everything taken care of, but knowing what comes after will make the time pass more quickly."

Meaning he'd be spending much of the day with her — and hopefully beyond. "Your appointment tomorrow is early and you're still not supposed to drive."

. She gave him a hot look. "Angling to spend another night?"

"Absolutely." And just to ensure he got the answer he wanted, he added, "Unless you'd rather have someone from your family, or Logan or Reese."

She wrinkled her nose. "I'd call a cab first. Or take a bus. Or walk —"

"Then consider me at your service."

Still in a rare teasing mood, she said, "I

like the sound of that." After finishing off her coffee, she used her cell phone to call her insurance adjuster. She knew where the station usually towed cars, so she shared that info while also making arrangements to pick up a rental tomorrow.

Dash enjoyed watching her in business mode. She was one of those women who, depending on the circumstances, could be a no-nonsense professional, a hard-nosed supervisor, or a soft sex kitten.

And if she knew his thoughts on that one, she'd probably kick him to the curb.

He started a small load of laundry so he'd have clean jeans to wear while she made a few more calls. When she finished half an hour later, he was just putting the clothes in the dryer.

Margo stood to indulge a one-arm stretch. "Guess I'd better go find something appropriate to wear, too. It won't be easy. My wardrobe is not set up to accommodate this dumb splint."

"Maybe I can help."

"Now you're good at women's wardrobes?" She held up a hand. "No, never mind, don't tell me. I assume you're good at everything."

"Let's say *adequate* and leave it at that." Dash followed her into the bedroom and went to her closet. When he opened the door, it again screeched. "Maybe while we're out, if you're feeling up for it, I could pick up some oil for the door."

"Sure." She stood next to him as he eyed her button-up blouses. "I need a few groceries anyway."

Moving aside her clothes, he reached to the back corner of the closet and produced a pale blue blouse that looked more worn.

"That's an older one," she said. "It's a little too tight now."

She wore her work clothes and uniforms so tailored to a perfect fit that they almost completely hid her curves. It'd be nice to see her in something both businesslike and sexy. "So you won't mind if we cut off the sleeve?" He turned to her. "That way it'll go over the splint."

Giving it only a moment's thought, she nodded. "I have scissors in the bathroom." She walked off but returned half a minute later.

Dash cut the sleeve for her, then helped her to dress. He enjoyed the intimate task. He enjoyed *her*.

So far, everything with Margo had been different. In some ways more intriguing. In most ways better.

She certainly never bored him.

Now that she was ready, he had to get dressed too. When he'd run them through the wash earlier, the blood had come out of his jeans, but he had to wear the flannel shirt Logan had brought him. At some point today he'd need to stop by his place to pick up more clothes.

Convincing Margo of that might be tricky, so he'd spring it on her later.

They had both just finished dressing when her landline rang.

Taking her time, Margo adjusted her sling, then searched out earrings.

"You're not going to answer that?"

"I don't want to get stuck on the phone. We have too much to get done this morning."

We. Nice that she now included him, never mind that if the situation had been with any other woman, he might have been put off by the implied responsibility.

But Margo wasn't any other woman, and it had been so tough to find a weakness in her walls, he wanted to take advantage of every toehold he could get.

Expertly, she slipped studs into her ears, but when Dash saw her struggling with the backs, he stepped up to help her. "What if it's important?"

She held still while he fastened the earrings. After tidying a few of her short silky curls, she said, "The machine will pick up."

As if on cue, Margo's taped voice announced that the caller should leave a number and message.

A male voice said with suggestion, "Lieutenant, where are you? You're supposed to be at home resting."

Her rank was said with affection, almost as if the caller had said "honey" or "sweetheart" instead.

For a single heartbeat she went still, but just as quickly she shook it off. Striding to the safe, she rapidly touched the keypad entry with practiced ease and it opened. She withdrew a magazine-handcuff case combo that clipped onto her belt. After double-checking that it was loaded and ready to go, she slid a Glock into place.

While the caller on the line said her name again, waiting, maybe hopeful that she'd pick up, Dash approached her. "You're not —"

"Leaving here unarmed? Of course not." She slipped an expandable baton onto her belt also. "Usually my jacket conceals the weapons, but I'm not about to cut the sleeve off a suit coat."

"Margaret?" The caller's exasperation grew. "If you're there, pick up damn it."

Seeing her set expression, Dash said, "I take it the two of you are familiar?"

With a deliberate shrug in her voice, she said, "He's my commander."

Whoa. "And he curses you?" Not real professional. Unless they were also friends. Or more.

"As the commander, he thinks he can do whatever he wants."

Before Dash could dig into that, the commander spoke again. "If you're there and just not picking up, well, I hope you're not avoiding me."

Margo snorted.

"I prefer to think that you're resting, but I have my doubts on that."

"Smart man." At Margo's glare, Dash shrugged then said, "Are you resting? No."

"I need you to understand," the commander continued. "You're off work until you get a doctor's clearance. Period. I assigned Detectives Bareden and Riske to run the attempted murder/assault charge. And yes, we're going to assume it was attempted murder, so don't bother arguing with me."

Her eyes narrowed.

Voice changing, the commander got more intimate. "If you need anything, you know you can call me. Not as your commander, but as a . . . friend."

*Friend, my ass.* Slowly, Dash's brows drew together.

"I'm serious, Margaret," the commander went on, his tone as soothing as warm honey. "*Anything* you need. Anything at all."

Trying to hide his temper, Dash said, "He sounds desperate." And no wonder. The man had called her Margaret, not Margo, so he obviously hadn't made much headway getting personal.

"I'll be checking on you, Margaret, so try to behave." The call ended.

"Condescending ass." Margo walked over to the phone and deleted the call.

Dash noted her stiff shoulders, the compression of her mouth. "I think I heard him salivating."

"Probably. He takes great pleasure in annoying me."

Yeah. Not exactly what he'd meant.

No matter that the commander had run up against a brick wall, Dash felt pretty damned territorial again. "Annoying you isn't what he was after. Was that a relationship gone sour that I just heard?"

"What? No. Like I said, he's my commander. That's all."

"Then is it appropriate for him to hit on you?"

Her gaze shot to his. "That's what you

thought?" She laughed with contempt and headed to the kitchen. "You misread things."

Dash followed. "You're not naive, lady. He wants you." Hell, who wouldn't?

"No. He wants to grind me under."

"Under him, yeah, I know."

She rolled her eyes. "He wants to remind me at every opportunity that he's a superior. That I answer to him." She gathered steam. "Most of all he wants . . ."

When she fell silent, Dash grew suspicious. "What?"

She shook her head. "He knows my father."

So? What did that have to do with anything? "He's older, then?" If he was her father's age —

"Twelve years older than me."

That'd make him early forties. Not old at all. "Married?"

She looked away. "He divorced a few years back."

And Dash would just bet he'd gone after Margo right off. "Unattractive?"

Oliver wrapped around her ankles and she knelt to give the cat some attention. "You're being tedious, Dash. It doesn't matter that he's dropped in unannounced a few times, that he's ingratiated himself into my home — which is why I didn't answer, by the way.

192

If I had, he would have asked to come visit and I'd rather not have to deal with him. That, or he'd know I wasn't home and would come to lay in wait on me."

"He's done that before?"

She didn't answer. "Since I didn't answer, he probably thinks I'm sleeping and that's for the best."

"He already said he knows better." Dash folded his arms. "And he wouldn't want to come visit you so badly if he wasn't a man personally involved."

"You're wrong. The commander is not interested in me that way."

"Bullshit. I know a come-on when I hear it."

"All right, fine. You want the nitty-gritty?" Since she couldn't lift Oliver, Margo sat on the kitchen floor and leaned back on a cabinet. Oliver moved into her lap with a rumbling purr. "He's actually considered a good catch. Silver hair, dark eyes. Tall, lean . . . he stays in shape. And he's financially set enough to be flashy about it."

Dash sat beside her. It was odd, sitting on the kitchen floor with a fat blind cat moving between them. Quietly, to help hide his sudden and uncomfortable jealousy, Dash asked, "Have you fucked him?"

She half choked. "God, no."

Only a little appeased by her repulsed re-action, he pressed her. "Because you don't want to mix work with pleasure?"

Watching the cat, she shrugged as if the reasons didn't matter. "He's friendly with my father, he's autocratic and sexist, and he cheated on his wife."

"That's why they divorced?"

She shrugged. "All I know is that he inherited a nice vacation home and a lump sum of cash from his parents a few years back. Suddenly he started thinking he was Huge Hefner or something." She tickled under Oliver's chin. "Before that, he wasn't such a bad guy."

It was the cheating that ruled him out, Dash figured. "Definitely not your type." The cat moved back into her lap, arching up to snuggle the top of his head to her chin. She kissed his bent ear, then hugged him.

Dash liked seeing her like this, comfort-able, soft in her attentions to her pet, at ease with him.

Needing to touch her, he cupped her cheek and tipped her face up to his. "I guess we don't need to go to the station now?"

Determination sparked in her eyes. "Oh, I'm still going."

"You'll ignore his orders?"

"You bet. Now forget the commander. I plan to." Surprising him, she leaned in to give him a quick kiss. Before he could take advantage of that, she gave Oliver one more luxurious stroke from nape to tail, set him aside and pushed to her feet. "Let's get going."

Because he didn't entirely understand the workings of the station, Dash didn't debate it with her. He'd ask Logan later, and try to get an understanding of the pecking order. Obviously the commander had some clout, but enough to rein her in?

Apparently not.

Or, knowing how her mind worked, maybe Margo had a valid reason for ignoring the commander — and enough dirt on him to keep from getting in trouble for it.

Going through the station with Margo, Dash noted the attention she got from a dozen different officers and a few detectives. Some asked after her, others made a point of not staring too much. Seeing her injured must have been a real aberration for them.

Did they, like Logan and Reese, see her as Superman, impervious to hurt?

At that moment, his brother and Reese came around the corner, heading down the hallway together.

Their reactions were priceless.

"Damn." Logan winced theatrically. "Either you bruise easy or you should be in the damned hospital still."

Reese whistled. "You're all psychedelic, Lieutenant."

"Be quiet," Margo said without heat, cutting off any real sympathy for her darkening bruises. "Where are you off to?"

Logan, holding a file, said, "I was just going to do some desk work."

Reese checked his watch. "I was heading out, but I've got a few minutes."

"We weren't expecting you." Still holding the file, Logan folded his arms over his chest. Suspicion sharpened his expression. "Should you be here?"

Giving him a dead-eyed stare, her tone clipped, she said, "In my office. Both of you."

Dash couldn't help but admire her. When necessary, the woman knew how to crack the whip.

"What the hell are you smiling about?" Logan demanded.

Dash quickly tried to wipe away his amusement.

Eyes narrowed, Margo glanced at him. "I won't be long."

"Take your time." Since his brother

worked here, Dash was familiar with the station. Finding his way around was a piece of cake.

All three of them watched Margo walk away, her step as strident as ever. Once she entered her office, Logan shot Dash a questioning look.

He held up the truck keys. "I drove."

"Well, aren't you handy to have around?" Reese elbowed Logan, but said to Dash, "She's not supposed to be here."

Dash rubbed the back of his neck. He didn't want to betray a confidence, but he was pretty sure Reese and Logan were already aware of the situation. "The commander called her."

"Dan Ford." Logan stepped closer to keep their exchange private. "He said she was off the case until the doc releases her."

"Yeah, she, ah —"

"Ignored him," Reese filled in, his own words as quiet as Logan's. Lifting both fists, he bumped them together and pretended they exploded. "That's how well they get along."

"Do you know why?"

"She's stubborn, that's why." Reese smiled. "Stubbornly righteous."

"And a damn good cop," Logan added.

Meaning in a pinch, they would side with Margo?

"She's also impatient," Reese said, "so let's go."

Logan looked plenty displeased with Dash, but said only, "Find something to do. This might take a while."

"I have a few calls to make, so I'll park myself on the bench over there." He started in that direction, but added over his shoulder, "If she needs me, let me know."

Logan drew himself up. "Why the hell would she —"

Laughing, Reese hauled him away.

If things went as planned, his brother would just have to get used to the idea of him and Margo together. Pulling out his cell, Dash was about to put in a call to his foreman when he saw Cannon Colter walk in, accompanied by a young female officer. He stowed the phone back in his pocket and intercepted the pair.

"Cannon. What's up?"

As if stalling, Cannon said, "Hey, Dash. Didn't expect to see you here."

"I drove . . ." Dash caught himself before using her first name. "Lieutenant Peterson. You know she was in a wreck?"

"Yeah, I heard." He glanced at the female officer. "Actually, that's who I came to see."

Dash had a very bad feeling. "She's in a meeting with Reese and Logan. Want to wait with me?"

He thanked the officer, and after the woman had walked away, he pulled off a stocking cap, ran a hand through his overlong hair, then over the back of his neck. "So . . . you're with her?"

"Margo? Yes." He wanted no misunderstandings about that.

Frustration palpable, Cannon nodded. "Then you may as well hear it, too."

Rather than sit behind her desk, Margo shrugged off the coat she'd draped over one shoulder, tossed it to a chair and paced the room. Reese and Logan tracked her every step before sharing a male-inspired, conspiratorial glance.

She wouldn't have it. "I know Dan put you two on the assault the other night."

"Attempted murder," Logan corrected. "Yeah, he did."

Reese propped one shoulder against the wall. "I take it he was incorrect in saying you were off the case?"

"Very."

"Figured as much," Logan said. "Also figured you'd want your involvement kept quiet."

199

"Which is why," Reese added, "we put everything into a file."

Logan lifted the folder he carried in a salute.

"Nice work." Margo took it from him.

Before she could open it, Reese said, "We had planned on dropping by after work to share that and answer any questions you had."

"But since one and all already saw you walk through the station, the cat's out of the bag now." Logan dropped into a chair, his long legs stretched out, his body relaxed as he scrutinized her. "Hadn't figured on seeing you up and about already. Especially here."

Margo was doubly glad she'd made the trip to the station. If they had come by in the early evening, they would have interrupted things between her and Dash. And given how eaten up she was with wanting him, that just wouldn't do.

Even now, in her office at the station with her two top detectives in close proximity, a low hum of need kept her entire body tingling.

Most saw her only as a professional, as a tried-and-true ballbuster. With reason. She'd earned that cred. But she was also, deep down, a complete hedonist. She wallowed in her sexuality, enjoying her own pleasures — pleasures that, as a lieutenant, she'd kept hidden from the rest of the world.

Except for Dash.

Already he knew more about her than any other living soul.

She eyed Logan. "Did you really expect me to skulk around?"

"One can hope," Reese said for him.

"Wish for a unicorn if you want, but don't expect me to shirk my duty." She propped her hip on the edge of the desk. "I'll study the file and if I have any questions, you'll be hearing from me. And just so you know, Rowdy will also be checking into things using his less respectable connections."

Logan surprised her by nodding. "I was going to suggest it."

Given how Logan had fought Rowdy's involvement in the past, Margo stared at him, astonished.

Reese shrugged. "He's good. He has great instincts and he's reliable. It makes sense."

Their combined cockiness nettled her. "Then why do I need the two of you?"

Rather than be insulted, something close to amusement altered Logan's posture. He glanced at Reese. "She sounds testy."

"Must be the discomfort," Reese agreed. "She's usually so . . . collected."

Eyes narrowing, Margo said, "You're pushing your luck."

Neither of them looked threatened, and she realized she was losing her edge with them. Damn it, were they becoming . . . friends?

"Seriously." Logan sat forward, looking her over with concern. "How are you?"

"As you can see, I'm fine."

"I'm not buying it." He pushed to his feet to stand in front of her. "You look like a herd of elephants stomped on you."

Great. Just the image she wanted in her head. How would she convince Dash she was up for full-go sex if she looked so mangled? Somehow she had to convince him, because no way could she wait another day.

"It's all superficial," she claimed, and wondered if that argument would work on Dash.

Tipping his head, Logan surveyed a bruise on her cheek, then the stitches on her head. "Sorry, Lieutenant, but I've had concussions so I know better."

"Me, too," Reese said. "Your head wants to explode."

"And the headaches last for days, sometimes even weeks." Logan gave her a sort of big-brother look that caught her off guard.

"If you push too hard —"

"Enough!" Frustration brought Margo away from her desk in a rush. Finger in Logan's chest, she snapped, *"They tried to kill me."*

Full of sympathy, he clasped her hand and gently lowered it. "I know."

Of course he did, because the attempt to kill her had also left his brother in the crosshairs. She jerked her hand away. "Damn it."

Reese joined Logan. "At least you're admitting it *was* attempted murder. And in admitting it, you know you're too close."

"Being emotionally involved," Logan said quietly, "screws with your perspective."

"The hell it does." Her perspective was that they needed to be caught, arrested and prosecuted. Period.

"If you're too closely involved you lose your edge," Logan reasoned. "You know that."

That bit of sage nonsense nearly made her hair stand on end. "Oh, my God, are *you* actually saying this to me?"

Logan scowled.

"She's got you there," Reese agreed. "Even when I tried to get you to pull back, you jumped in feetfirst with Pepper and that enormous cluster-fu—"

"And you!" She rounded on Reese. "You have no room to talk because you're just as bad as he is."

"I was taking your side!"

She shoved past Reese to pace. "Just because I'm a woman you think I have less ability to push through an injury."

"You're not supposed to push through," Logan chided her.

She tuned out his nonsense. "And, of course, being a woman means I can't logically sort out the facts. Only men can be cold enough, levelheaded enough, to stay professional under duress. I guess you expect me to break down in tears, to look for some big macho guy to —"

Rolling his eyes, Logan interrupted and said, "Speaking of big macho guys . . ." He put himself in her path. "Is Dash staying with you?"

She almost plowed into him before taking a stance. "What are you talking about?"

He and Reese shared another look before Logan said, "I'm not prying."

"We're concerned," Reese added, then held up a hand. "And before you shoot us for being so audacious, may I say that I understand completely."

Tension crawled up her spine, turning her voice into a growl. "Understand what?"

"You're a cop, Peterson, through and through. Tough as nails, no one doubts that."

"All that other stuff you spouted," Logan said, "is absurd. We know damn good and well you fire on all cylinders no matter the situation."

Why she wanted to smack them both, Margo couldn't say. But the temptation was there, making her palm itch. "Your point?"

Shouldering Logan aside, Reese faced off with her. "For a cop, especially a cop in your rank, it's difficult to admit to any weakness."

He was so big all over that he damn near left a shadow on her. Eyes narrowed, Margo squared her shoulders and tipped her head way back to glare up at him. "Do you have weaknesses, Reese?"

He ignored that. "I still remember how Logan was when he got himself shot in the arm. Pepper had to sit on him — although I think she actually enjoyed that. She has this hidden nurturing streak — very hidden, in fact — but it's there and she coddled Logan back into health."

"Fuck you, Reese." No real heat accompanied Logan's words.

Reese grinned. "Don't mind a little pampering myself now and then." And to Margo he said, "I'm just saying . . . you might want to give it a try."

"It does have its advantages," Logan admitted. "From one badass cop to another, lighten up and enjoy the opportunity."

The two of them turned to walk out — without her dismissal, damn them. "Don't. You. Dare." Her whispered words were more lethal than a shout.

With a lot of exaggerated impatience, they turned. Logan asked, "Is there more?"

Yes, but at the moment, she didn't know what.

A sharp rap at the door saved her. She barked, "Come in."

And to her surprise and displeasure, Dash stuck his head in. He looked past his brother, past Reese, to meet her gaze. "Sorry to interrupt, but this is important."

Grateful for the reprieve, but determined to maintain her status, Margo strode forward. "It damn well better be."

# CHAPTER NINE

Recognizing her volatile mood, Dash kept his distance while ushering in Cannon. He had no idea what had set her off, and he regretted the intrusion knowing she wouldn't like the familiarity of him inserting himself. But for this, it couldn't be helped.

He glanced at his brother. "You and Reese should hear this, too."

Expression sardonic, Logan crossed his arms. "Not a problem, since I wasn't going anywhere anyway."

He knew his brother wasn't thrilled with the idea of him and Margo hooking up. *Too late, big brother,* Dash thought, then he gave his attention to the seriousness of the situation. "Cannon has some important info."

"All right." Margo's gaze met his — and she held the door open. "Thank you, Dash."

No fucking way. Did she actually think to dismiss him? Given the expectant way she watched him, Dash realized that was exactly what she wanted to do.

Defiant, he gave one small shake of his head and went to a chair to sit down. If she wanted him gone, she'd have to spell it out.

And then maybe drag him away.

Reese's gaze ping-ponged between them and he grinned, the mammoth ass.

On an exasperated sigh, Logan eased the door from Margo's hand and closed it with a click. "He's staying with you, he's in it up to his neck, so he may as well be informed."

"That is not your decision to make!"

"He's my brother," Logan said, as if that gave him certain rights. He came to stand behind Dash.

Nice. He could always count on Logan for support when needed.

"What happened to you?" Margo asked Cannon. When Dash appeared confused, she nodded at his face. "Black eye, bruise on your cheek —"

"Oh, yeah." Cannon touched his face. "I had a fight."

"About what?"

His mouth lifted in a crooked smile. "Who was the better fighter."

"Right. You compete in MMA."

"He's good, too," Dash said. "Not that I'm a judge or anything. Just going by his

208

record."

"I'm making headway."

Gesturing grandly to the remaining chair, Reese said, "Cannon, you may as well get comfortable."

"Right. Comfortable." Stocking hat twisted in his hand, Cannon dropped into the straight-back chair, relaxed his spine and glanced around Margo's office.

"First time in a police station?" Margo asked.

"Yeah." He rolled one shoulder. "No idea why, but it makes me a little nervous."

Dash laughed. "Rowdy feels the same. I can almost see his skin crawl whenever he's here."

Half-smiling, Cannon said, "Yeah, well I think our reactions are based on very different circumstances." He looked up at Margo. "My mother would have skinned me if she'd ever had reason to visit the police on my behalf."

"Good for her."

"That's one of the biggest differences." Cannon shifted again, clearly uncomfortable. "I had a mom, and Rowdy never did."

"She passed away?" Reese took up his usual posture as he rested a shoulder against the wall.

"A few years ago. Cancer."

"I'm sorry." Margo tipped her head. "Your father?"

"He used to own a bar a lot like Rowdy's. He got murdered when I was eighteen."

"Robbery?" Margo asked.

Cannon shook his head. "Street thugs tried to extort money from him in exchange for 'protection.' Dad refused to play along. One night when he was closing up they came in and beat him to death."

"Damn," Dash muttered. He'd known Cannon had some deep motivations for protecting the neighborhood, but he'd never heard why.

"Mom almost worked herself to death to keep things afloat, but when Marissa got cornered one day coming home from school —"

"Marissa?" Dash asked.

"My little sister. Well, not so little now. She's nearly as tall as me, but a hundred pounds lighter." His pride showed in a soft smile. "Really pretty. And smart."

"Was she hurt?" Logan asked.

"Scared mostly. She was only sixteen then. A bunch of guys told her . . ." In a silent struggle his expression darkened and his hands fisted. "They said they would do things to her if mom didn't sell."

"And so she did," Dash concluded for

him. "Damn, man, I'm sorry."

"I found them." Sitting back, Cannon shook off the tension. "The bar was already sold by then, but I found them and I gave them the beat-down they deserved. Thing is, I knew I couldn't be there 24/7." He looked at Margo. "It's not a good thing to feel helpless."

"No," Dash agreed. "It isn't."

"The cops didn't help you?" Logan asked.

"Didn't ask them to." Almost apologetic, he looked away. "They knew the area businesses were getting squeezed and they didn't do anything about it. Most knew not to bother going to them. Some even figured the cops were in on it."

Margo rubbed her temple. "Possibly. Corruption had wormed its way in pretty deep here."

Dash said what Margo wouldn't. "She took care of that, though, so if it ever comes up again, know that you can trust her."

"And Reese and Logan," Cannon added. "Yeah, I know. That's one reason I'm here now. My mother gave up the family business but she refused to give up her home. It had sentimental value to her. Now my sister lives there and she's as stubborn as my mom ever was."

"Huh." Logan nodded as if just figuring

out a puzzle.

"As Rowdy can tell you," Cannon said, "little sisters are big motivation."

Dash smiled at that statement. Far as he could see, they were big motivation to honorable men. He included Rowdy and Cannon both in that category.

"So yeah, I sort of keep a watch on the neighborhood."

"Big brother to one and all?" Margo asked.

"I grew up here." Cannon shrugged as if that explained it all. "I know just about everyone. Most of the business owners, the local guys who go to the same gym as me, the elders who've been around for a while." His eyes narrowed. "The troublemakers. The thugs."

"It's like a network," Reese said.

"Pretty much." Cannon tugged on his ear. "But the info I have now came from some kids, so I don't know how reliable it is."

"I appreciate it that you came to me so we could sort it out." Margo went to her desk in front of Cannon. She propped her sweet behind on the edge, crossed her ankles and waited.

Was her head hurting? Her arm? Her expression was now so enigmatic, Dash couldn't tell.

To get things going, he offered up a brief explanation. "Cannon started a gym as part of a community project to help get some of the at-risk kids off the street. It's sort of a supervised rec center with a lot of coaching and direction thrown in."

"Yeah." Uneasy with the credit, Cannon shifted. "I just got it organized. Rowdy and Avery footed the bill."

"Thanks to Avery's inheritance from her stepfather," Reese explained to Margo. "Rowdy didn't want the guy's money —"

"So they decided to put it to good use," Logan finished.

Cannon narrowed his eyes on Logan, then Dash. "I've also had some anonymous donors who've helped in a really big way."

"Cash only goes so far," Dash replied. "You're the one who puts that money to good use and keeps the place running . . . along with a few other projects." Like working at a bar, staying on track with his MMA training and engaging in actual competition.

"A lot of guys pitch in."

"Guys like you?" Margo asked.

"If you mean other fighters, yeah. Some who are doing really well, some just starting out, some who are also looking for a little guidance." He shifted yet again. "It's a good mix, having the youths in there with the more experienced guys. They pick up a lot just by watching, every guy volunteers a little help to the kids, to show them the way. There's an overall camaraderie that makes the kids feel involved and wanted, and gives the men a chance to contribute."

Impressed, Dash decided to make yet another generous donation. Again, anonymously. He had no doubts that Logan would do the same. They'd both been blessed, and they knew it.

"Out of curiosity . . ." Margo again checked out Cannon's bruised face. "Who won that last fight?"

"I did." For once he didn't look uncomfortable. When it came to his ability, he had no reserve. "TKO."

"I suppose the other guy looks worse."

Cannon laughed. "These were just a few taps. He didn't hurt me."

She shook her head, seemingly enthralled. Dash understood because he felt the same way. Professional fighting? He loved it.

At least she wasn't looking at Cannon with personal interest. Dash could tell the difference.

She didn't look at Cannon the same way she looked at him.

"How old are the kids you work with?"

Margo asked.

"Anywhere from ten to eighteen." Cannon sat forward. "It was a couple of boys, fourteen and fifteen, who came forward after I asked around. They're brothers, lousy home life but still good kids. Just . . . energetic."

Dash grinned at the judicious way Cannon phrased that. "Meaning they've been in and out of trouble with juvie?"

"Minor stuff," Cannon defended. "Stealing beer, fighting, skipping school. That sort of thing."

Perspectives, Dash thought. If he'd have tried any of that, his parents would have grounded him for eternity. But then, he'd had everything given to him. He had no reason to search for escapes, not when his life had been golden.

How had Margo's life been growing up, especially given her folks hadn't wanted a daughter . . . ever?

"I understand," she said to Cannon. "I'm not looking to go after any kids. Just tell me what they know."

"First, I need your assurance they won't be drawn into anything. I don't want them in danger just because they tried to do the right thing."

"You have my word."

Her word must've been good enough, because Cannon did finally relax. "I fudged things a bit, saying you and I are friends and that I was worried about you after the wreck. I mean, most of these kids are at best suspicious of the law, at worst, scared to death of anyone official. If you weren't a personal friend to me, they wouldn't give two thoughts to what happened to a cop."

"Understood." She smiled at him. "And I like to think we are friends."

Despite the assurances he'd just given himself, Dash went on the alert — until Logan "accidentally" thumped his ear while stepping forward. "Promises aside, it's possible Reese and I might need to talk to the boys. Will that be a problem?"

"Not as long as you make it low-key, keep it quiet and take it easy on them. They're tough little nuts — but they've been through enough." Cannon nodded at Reese. "I know you understand."

Because he'd adopted Marcus, Reese had firsthand experience with troubled kids. "Only too well."

Margo stepped away from her desk. To Dash, she seemed antsy — or sore. "Both of my detectives are great in dealing with kids. Rest easy on that."

"Thanks." Cannon glanced at Dash,

cleared his throat, rubbed his chin. "There's a hit out on you. Apparently the bastards that want you dead have offered up a grand to anyone who can make it happen."

Even though Cannon had already told him, Dash still reacted. The urge to hold her, to somehow shield her, crashed through him.

Unfazed, Margo asked, "How are they to collect?"

*Jesus,* Dash thought. *She took that without a single flinch of emotion.* But then, neither Reese nor Logan looked all that shook up about it, either.

"Once the deed is done, they're to spread the word on the street. The right goons will find out and be in touch. That's all I know."

Reese frowned thoughtfully. "How did the kids know this? Where did they hear it?"

"They were approached on the street. Because of the snow they were off school, hanging out front of a liquor store, and a car pulled up and called them over. There were six of them in the group, but I don't know the other boys." Cannon pulled out a photocopied news article with Margo's face shown. "They were given this, so they'd know for sure who you are."

Reese took it from him, holding it so Margo could see, too. "This is the write-up when you made lieutenant."

She barely gave it a glance. "What liquor store?"

Cannon shared the info and Logan wrote it down.

"There's more," Cannon warned them.

Knowing it all had to be shared, Dash curled his hands into fists.

"The thing is . . ." Cannon cleared his throat. "If they take you alive, the price jumps up to five grand."

"Alive?" Logan asked.

"So that . . ." Cannon worked his jaw. "So that she can be used."

Hearing it again ramped up Dash's killing mood. No way would he let anyone hurt her, but he was counting on his brother to find the men, and to put them away for good.

Reese no longer looked so relaxed. "Did the kids give you a description?"

"Older — which could mean just about anything since they're kids. The driver had dark hair and a goatee. The passenger was big and bald. There was a third man in the backseat, but they didn't get a good look at him."

"The car?" Logan asked.

"Black sedan. That's all they noticed." He cleared his throat again. "They gave me something, though."

Everyone waited.

Cannon reached into his pocket and pulled out a flash drive. "It's . . . well, a video. Explicit stuff. Not something the boys should have seen."

Logan started to reach for it, but Margo took it instead. On the way to her desk, she asked, "You watched it already?"

More uneasy by the second, Cannon nodded. "I don't know if it's acting or real. A naked woman tied to a display case, two guys . . ." Revulsion roughened his voice, and he gestured. "You get the idea. The woman is drugged I think. At least she looked it to me."

Logan cursed. Reese growled.

"The driver gave it to the kids as . . . prepayment for helping out. Told them they'd like it and there was more where that came from."

Margo reached her computer and inserted the flash drive. When no one joined her, she scowled. "Well? You have to see it whether you want to or not. It's evidence. There could be a clue here."

Cannon came to his feet but turned away. Dash was the first to reach Margo, not because he wanted to watch, but because he insisted on being by her side.

Reese and Logan, their moods thunderous, flanked them.

Logan said, "We could watch this later —"

"Now," Margo said.

"I'm not a meek schoolboy," Reese told her. "But this is awkward."

"Grow a pair, why don't you?" The file loaded and, with only a heartbeat of hesitation, she clicked it to play, straightened and waited.

More than ever, Dash wanted to put his arm around her, to offer support in any way she needed. She was so damned indifferent, so distant and contained that it bothered him on an elemental level.

At the same time, he accepted that this was her job, that she was good at it. Seeing her like this filled him with pride.

So he stayed silent . . . but close.

Cannon remained well out of the viewing area, his face averted, his body set in angry lines of disgust.

If it weren't for the possibility of it being, as Cannon had said, "real," it would have been regular, poor-quality, run-of-the-mill porn. But they all knew that rather than being an actor, the woman in the film could be a victim, and that not only kept it from being sexually exciting, but it also made it revolting and enraging.

"All we're getting is the back view of the bastards," Reese said, "but one has dark hair and the other is —"

"Bald," Logan finished. "Could be the same guys the boys spoke with."

Quietly, above the sounds of bodies slapping together and the woman's faint moans, Cannon said, "I think I recognize the place."

Logan looked up. "It's a business?"

"Local. A family-run pawnshop."

"Pawnshop?" Logan gave his attention back to the video, his brow knit as he studied the scene.

Dash looked, too. "That's a display case," he pointed out, referring to the image to the right. "I see watches, rings, bracelets."

"And behind that are some older guns and knives." Logan searched the scenery as the men continued with their sexual escapades. "Damn. I think you're right, Cannon."

"I went by there before coming here, but it's closed up. I don't know why. Usually Tipton Sweeny, the guy who runs it, is there from sunup to sundown. His granddaughter, Yvette, helps out but I didn't see her, either."

Everyone looked at Cannon. Margo spoke first. "Do you think it's her in the video?"

He shook his head. "It's not."

"You sound so sure."

"Yvette just graduated last summer. She's small, with a different build. Just turned nineteen, I think. That woman is older and heavier than Yvette."

Margo glanced at the images again. "You can't see her face very well, and the guys are mostly covering her body —"

"Still," Logan confirmed, "she's definitely older. I'd say late twenties."

Peeved, Margo started to argue.

"She doesn't have the figure of a kid," Dash explained. As a woman, Margo might not see the nuances and probably didn't have the same perception of the female body. "No one can be certain, especially with the light so dim, but Logan's right. It's a good guess that she's older. I'd say even early thirties."

Reese concurred. "Somewhere in there."

Bracing her hand on the desk, Margo leaned in for a closer look — then used the mouse to pause the screen so she could study it in more minute detail.

Recognizing her in cop mode, Reese and Logan went on the alert, too.

"You see something?" Logan asked, crowding in closer and shouldering Dash aside.

Reese, being so big, looked over their shoulders.

"There." Margo pointed to the glass front on a large display case. "A reflection."

In a rush, Cannon came around the desk to join them.

Dash stepped farther back, giving them all room. "Do you recognize him, Cannon?"

He shook his head. "I don't think so. Hard to tell with the image so blurred." He leaned in. "He's white, though. Wearing glasses."

"I can see that the prick is smiling," Reese growled.

"Smug." Logan studied the image. "Light-colored hair. Polo shirt or some other casual button-up collared shirt. He looks heavy."

"Could be our man from the backseat." Margo looked at each man. "Maybe the one in charge."

Cannon stepped away. "I can ask around, see if the description rings any bells."

"Discreetly," Margo warned. "We don't want the public stalking all the overweight, blond, spectacle-wearing men in the area."

Cannon nodded. "I can be discreet, no worries."

"In the meantime . . ." Margo pushed a notepad forward. "Write down the address of the pawnshop."

He accepted the pen she offered. "I have their home address, too, if you want it." Worry kept his voice tight. "No one is there, either — I already checked."

Jesus. Dash hoped a nineteen-year-old girl wasn't caught up in this mess.

"Got a phone number?" Margo asked as Cannon jotted on the paper.

"No, sorry."

"It's all right. You've been a huge help." Taking the notepad from him, Margo started out around her desk. "I'll check it out and —"

"No." Reese stood in front of the door, cautiously barring the way. "All respect, Lieutenant, it'll be better if Logan and I go."

To Dash's surprise, she didn't argue. Rubbing her forehead, her frustration palpable, she nodded. "Yes, of course, you're right."

Logan took the notepad from her. "We'll report back as soon as we know something."

Cannon turned to the detectives. "Mind if I go along? I'm . . . worried."

"Sure." Reese held the door open for him. "Long as Logan doesn't object, I don't mind if you show us the way."

"Why not." Mockery twisted Logan's mouth; they damn well didn't need a guide. "You know their routine and we don't. Can't hurt to have you along."

Once everyone was out the door, Margo looked toward Dash. He saw the dark thoughts reflected in her blue eyes; he knew exactly what she was thinking . . . and why.

He wanted to reassure her. It ate at him, the need to gather her close and offer comfort. With any other woman he wouldn't have hesitated. But this was Margo, a woman so extraordinary that she'd become the youngest female lieutenant in the city's history. So he held himself still, unsure of the right move for a woman like her, in her position, with her injuries —

"God, this is so frustrating," she growled, and then she took the steps necessary to come up against to him, to lean on him.

*She trusted him.*

Staggered but inordinately pleased, Dash slowly put his arms around her, holding her closer as he weighed the significance of the moment. "What can I do?"

"There's nothing."

A world of difference existed between playing games with a man of her choosing — him — and a victim being forced into an abusive situation by rapists.

But Dash suspected that didn't stop her from reacting to the similarities.

"Margo." His mouth brushed her temple. "I want to help."

She pushed back a little to see him. "You already are. Being here. Understanding."

Because it was so important, because he wanted her to acknowledge it, he asked, "Not interfering?"

"That, too." The weight of her responsibility reflected in her blue eyes and still she teased him. "I appreciate your restraint."

He cupped his big hand to the side of her face, brushed his thumb over the warm downy skin of her cheek. "Why would I interfere? Clearly you know what you're doing or you wouldn't be the lieutenant, right?"

"Yes, of course."

For her job, her rank, the duty assigned her, she was more than competent. In so many ways, Dash thought that might be the source of her personal demons.

"And only a very intelligent woman, an astute woman with a lot of intuition and logic, would be trusted with that rank."

"I suppose." Suspicion brought her slim brows together. "Where are you going with this?"

Not kissing her proved a great trial. But this was too important to skimp on, and a kiss would have easily sidetracked him. "Just pointing out the obvious — which I'm already sure you know." But just in case . . . "What we did —" *what he hoped to do again with her* "— and what is on that video are night and day."

Her breath left her in a long exhalation. "Games versus reality."

So she had already been thinking about it, just as he'd assumed. "One is for pleasure, honey."

Her eyes closed. "My pleasure."

Did she think her desires were so twisted? So dark? Silly woman. After he'd taken her a few dozen times, she'd learn that anything between them was special, and oh-so-right. "*Mutual* pleasure. And the other is all about abuse, about a lack of consideration or even feeling."

She swallowed hard. "Still, I can't help it that it . . . it disturbs me."

"Because you enjoy giving up control every now and then?"

"It makes me weak."

He laughed, and when her flashing blue eyes slanted his way, he wanted to pick her up and kiss her silly for her misplaced anger and guilt. "Enjoying a few sex games no more makes you weak than it makes me abusive." He drew her closer. "And honest to God, Margo, I do enjoy playing with you."

She let out a sarcastic laugh. "You enjoy being a man."

"And I enjoy you being a woman." And

before she could misinterpret that, he expounded on it. "You're complicated. So strong at times you leave me in awe, so rock-solid and steady when you need to be."

"That's part of my problem, you know."

He pretended disbelief. "A woman as perfect as you has problems?"

"I intimidate men."

"Not me." From the first moment he'd seen her, he'd wanted her. The want had grown stronger every day.

Lifting a hand she indicated the station full of department personnel on the other side of her closed office door. "In one way or another I've competed with most of the men here."

"And you always win?"

"Whenever I can." Her chin went up. "Men resent that. They resent me."

Chiding, he corrected her. "Not Logan and Reese. They respect you."

"And in no way see me as a sexual being."

Thank God. He and his brother shared many things, but no way in hell did Dash want to share lust for Margo.

She paced away from him, a nervous habit that Dash had noticed whenever she tried to sort her thoughts. "My job is my life. And that means the men I have time to know, the men who know me, see me only one way." She drew in a slow breath. "And it's not as a woman who wants to get down and dirty in the bedroom."

Hearing her say it made him want it all the more. He approached her again, closing the space between them. "But now you have me." Let her muse on that reality. "I think your strength is sexy. Your intelligence is sexy. But I'm just as drawn to your sweet little body, and your vulnerability."

"I'm not —"

He hushed her with a finger to her soft lips. Those lips . . . well, they could inspire a few fantasies, too. "You're small and soft and *human,* and like the rest of us you sometimes need a shoulder to lean on."

She tried an uncertain smile, accompanied by a sensual stroke to his upper body. "Maybe it's just that your shoulders are so wide and appealing."

Dash would not let her distract him. "Luckily for me, you're also confident enough in what you enjoy to indulge a few fantasies."

She looked away, but Dash brought her face back so she had to meet his gaze. "That's normal and healthy and a huge turn-on. You have no reason for comparisons to a victim."

Still a little worried, she said, "Can I be

totally honest?"

"With me, always. About anything."

She nodded. "Before you, there was no one I trusted to . . . know what I like."

Dash doubted she knew everything she'd enjoy — but he planned to show her.

She looked away from him. "I've had sex for the sake of sex."

His gut clenched, but he did his best to keep that reaction from his tone. "With strangers?"

"That was the only safe way."

Nothing safe about it. "You expect me to judge you on that?" Determined to be honest, too, he put his hands on her shoulders. "I've done the same." Especially while nursing his ego after her rejection.

"Most think it's okay for a guy to —"

"But not for a woman?" He bent to kiss the side of her neck, inhaling the scent of her skin. "Would I be that sexist?"

"Yes."

He hugged her tight. "Okay, I admit it. But could we call it protective instinct?" Another kiss, this one just behind her ear. "It worries me to think of you with some nameless asshole that may or may not be respectful of you as a woman."

Drolly, she said, "Yes, well, I wasn't exactly after respect."

Shit, she knew how to turn him inside out. "Respect comes in all shapes and sizes, honey, and you know it. It includes caring about boundaries, about desires and demands. I've played a lot of games myself, but only when I know the woman I'm with will enjoy it, too. That's respect." With his chin on top of her head, Dash emphasized the differences in their sizes. "Without that respect, you could end up seriously hurt."

"I can take care of myself."

He continued to hold her, his long arms wrapped around her, gently because of her splint. "You have more ability, definitely better aim when it comes to a shoot-out, than most anyone I know." In a shoot-out, he'd bet on her winning. "But one-on-one, my size and strength alone would overpower you — if I was ever intent on harming you."

Defiant, she whispered, "Don't you see, Dash? That's part of the thrill."

Never had he had a conversation like this. He loved sex. He loved the antics of females. But the women he'd known had played and laughed and driven him crazy in bed. Some were kinky, some traditional. All of them reveled in their sexuality.

They did not fight their own inclinations, or suffer shame over them.

Margo was the strongest, and yet the most

fragile woman he'd ever known. "You're talking about the thrill of being physically weaker."

"Yes."

"You liked having your weaknesses exposed. Being just a woman with a man, not a superior, not a boss." He turned her to him. "But that was before you knew me."

She waited.

"Before you let me in." He didn't want her to deny him.

"Yes. Before that."

He hadn't even had her yet, but he wanted things to be exclusive. "Here on, for as long as it lasts, anything you want, anything you need, you get it from me."

Searching his face, she frowned. "What are you saying?"

"That I don't want you with anyone else."

For the longest time she seemed to be weighing his audacity. Then her chin went up. "That goes both ways."

Hell, he hadn't wanted another woman since meeting her. He'd only played the field in an attempt to cleanse her from his mind.

But it hadn't worked. He had a feeling she was in his head, in his heart, for good.

"No problem on my end."

Heat replaced the disquiet in her gaze.

She touched his chest, trailed her fingertips down to the waistband of his jeans. "All right then." Stepping closer, she stretched up to kiss his chin. "Game on."

# CHAPTER TEN

Sensual possibilities bombarded Margo —
but she still had a workday to get through.

Dash kissed her, a sweet kiss that felt
amazingly like acceptance. "We'll figure out
the game rules tonight."

Insane, given the circumstances, but she
almost grinned. Dash was proving to be
more fun than she'd ever imagined.

Hard to believe she'd once discounted
him. Now she felt the urgent need to experience him in every way. "Tonight," she
agreed.

"Until then, what's next on the agenda?"

"I'm sorry, but I want to watch the video
again, at least a couple more times. Reese
and Logan will do the same. It's always possible we missed something, or that a puzzle
piece might fall into place. You just never
know."

Admiration showed in the way he agreed.
"I had no idea how heinous your workload

could be."

Might as well be honest with him, she decided. "It gets incredibly ugly far too often. Children murdered. Women raped. Men beaten to death. You have to grow a thick skin to do this job." Only her skin would never be thick enough to keep the brutality from hurting her. Far too often she brought her job home with her.

Far too often, she tried to drive it away with strangers in seedy motel rooms.

But for now at least, that was over. Who needed a hotel room when she had Dash in her home? Or . . . wait. She looked up at him. "Tonight . . . what exactly are we doing?"

"I was thinking I'd run to my place and grab more clothes along with a few other necessities while you do your thing. Maybe meet you back here in a couple of hours."

"That should give me enough time." On top of watching the video she had some phone calls to answer, some emails to catch up on.

"Whatever works for you." Dash toyed with one of the short curls at the nape of her neck. "Then we can head home."

Home. Together. She liked the sound of that more than she should have. "Okay."

Both hands framed her face. "Even tomor-

235

row, after you see the doctor, I'd like to stay with you."

Her pulse tripped. "Dash . . ."

"Or you could stay with me. What do you think?"

She thought that sounded an awful lot like a relationship. "You have to understand. I'm first and foremost a cop."

His slow smile reeked of male confidence. "No, you're first and foremost a woman. A beautiful, take-charge, sexy piece of work who handles the duties of being lieutenant with ease."

That was . . . the nicest compliment she'd ever received.

"You want balance in your life? Start with me. You can be both a woman and a cop. Let me show you that one doesn't detract from the other."

Talk about dangerous. A real relationship with Dash scared her half to death. It was the unknown, and she could end up devastated.

Her heart punched so hard that it hurt. But the idea of ending things with him, not knowing what it would be like to have him, hurt far more.

"Since I have Oliver, my place is better."

As if a weight had just been lifted, his shoulders loosened and the corner of his mouth curled up. "Works for me." He touched his teasing thumb to her bottom lip. "Would it be inappropriate of me to kiss Lieutenant Margaret Peterson, *really* kiss her, here in her office?"

"Very inappropriate." She leaned into him. "But your brother and Reese are the only cops impertinent enough to barge in without knocking — and they're not here."

The smile widened into a grin. "So is that permission?"

More like a plea; she needed to lose herself a little in his touch, his taste.

No reason to always make it so easy on him. "You are in my office so maybe we should call it an order."

The heated way he looked at her did amazing things to her mood.

"Yes, ma'am." And with that he took her mouth, not in a timid peck, but in a kiss of possession guaranteed to fill her with a new type of tension.

Holding her face, he sealed his mouth to hers until her lips parted, until he could tease his tongue over her bottom lip, the edge of her teeth, then deep in a hot, damp consummation.

The reality of the danger remained; she never lost sight of her duty. But Dash's touch, his effect on her, made it easier to deal with and gave her a more grounded control of her emotions.

At least where the job was concerned.

When it came to Dash, her emotions were all over the place.

As he eased away again, ending the kiss by small degrees, little pecks and gentle licks, he groaned. "God, I need you, Margo."

She felt the same — times ten. "Tonight."

Gently chiding, he shook his head and reminded her, "There's plenty we can do tonight, but not that. Not until your splint is off."

"We'll see." She had plans to change his mind on that proviso. She blew out a thick breath. "While you're out, would you want to stop at the grocery, too?"

"Sure, why not? The sooner we get done, the sooner we can head back to your place." He glanced at his watch. "I might run by the job site, too, but there should be time for everything. Write me a list of what you want."

He hadn't even blinked an eye. In fact, she had the feeling it amused him to be sent on errands. "You're sure you don't mind?"

"Anything I can do to help. I already told you that."

"All right then." Taking him at his word,

Margo wrote out a short list.

When he left her office, everyone in the vicinity was agog. Dash either didn't notice or didn't care. Either way, seeing him stride away, his body tall, strong, his smile contagious, she couldn't help but be proud.

The women watched him with covetous envy, the men with ripe speculation.

And they all realized he was there for her.

Wearing her own smile, Margo turned away and shut her door. Maybe, just maybe, she could be both a woman and a lieutenant. Then she thought of that awful video, and went into full-blown cop mode.

Dash and all his appeal would just have to wait.

Luckily he didn't seem to have a problem with that.

Cannon knew he was lucky that Logan and Reese trusted him, otherwise he'd be left on the outside, wondering what was going on. This was his neighborhood. He cared about it — sometimes too much. Not being involved now would make him nuts.

Again he knocked on the front door of the pawnshop, harder this time. He had a very bad feeling about things.

Hands to the glass, Logan peered in through the front window. "I thought I saw something move."

From somewhere inside, a noise sounded, like something hitting the floor, then . . . absolute stillness again.

No lights came on and no one called out.

Tension welled up, churning, expanding. Cannon started around the side of the building. "Something's wrong." He knew it. He *felt* it.

Logan and Reese followed.

Near the trash bin, Cannon found a large chunk of fallen brick. He hefted it in his hand.

"Whoa." Logan scowled at him. "Just what the hell do you think you're doing?"

"I'm going in."

"You can't do that." Hands on his hips, Reese pointed at Cannon. "There's a process, and it doesn't involve busting windows."

"Look away then," Cannon told him, and he hit the pane on a low window. Glass shattered.

"Shit." Reese gave up without much fuss. "I have to call this in."

"Do what you gotta do." Pulling off his thermal shirt, Cannon wrapped his hand and wrist, then reached in and opened the lock on the window. It pushed open and, as he started to crawl in, something came crashing down near his head.

He barely managed to duck back in enough time to avoid having his brains scattered. A heavy wooden ball bat reverberated off the linoleum floor.

Both Logan and Reese were suddenly armed with big black guns in their hands.

"Take it easy," Cannon told them. And then, in a softer tone, "Yvette?"

Her face appeared, ravaged from tears and smeared makeup. "Cannon?"

"Yeah." Christ, she was a mess. He kept his tone gentle. "Open the front door."

"Oh, God." She hugged the bat to her chest while her gaze pinged here and there nervously. In a hush, she asked, "What are you doing here?"

He said again, more firmly this time, "Open up, honey. Or should I come through the window?"

She knuckled one eye, further spreading the mess of her makeup and tears. "I'll . . . I'll open the door."

Going around front, followed by the silent detectives, Cannon waited with vibrating impatience. The second the lock opened he pushed his way in.

The smell of kerosene assaulted his nose. "Yvette?"

A sob bubbled up and her shoulders

shook. She hugged herself tightly.

Cannon did his best to ignore the presence of two top-notch detectives looming behind him. He knew they were giving him some leeway, so he didn't want to waste the opportunity. "Shhh. Take it easy." He relieved her of the ball bat, setting it aside. "It's okay now."

"No — no, it's not."

Surprised that neither Logan nor Reese attempted to take over, he lifted Yvette's chin. He'd found that making eye contact with a friend often soothed frazzled nerves. "Where's Tipton?"

She swallowed hard, turned and headed toward the back of the shop.

The men followed.

Usually Yvette walked tall, shoulders back and chest out, confident of her sex appeal. Right now she was so curled into herself that it worried Cannon.

Her clothes were stiff and dirty, her tank top ripped near the neck. Barefoot, her flared jeans dragged the floor. At the door to a small room she stopped. "Grandpa? Cannon is here."

Cannon pushed in past her. On one side of the room, pawned items of every variety, some large and some small, lined metal shelving. Opposite that, cleaning supplies were stacked alongside a mop bucket and broom. Against the back wall was one utility sink and a toilet. The harsh overhead fluorescent light showed spots of blood on the floor and in the sink.

There in the corner, bruised, bloody and battered, Tipton sat, his legs out and his back against the wall.

"Damn it." Rushing in, Cannon went to a knee beside him. He found a head wound that didn't look too awful but had bled considerably given the mess on Tipton's shirt. His eyes looked clear, though swollen. He had a vicious split lip. "What the hell happened?"

Tipton barely shook his head, but looked up to his granddaughter. After a long, painful hesitation, he whispered, "Tell him."

Yvette twisted her small hands together. "Grandpa . . ."

"Tell him, Yvette."

"First," Reese said, his voice gentle, "I'm going to call for an ambulance, okay?"

That he asked pleased Cannon.

Tipton nodded. "You're here, so I guess it don't matter anymore."

Reese turned his back as he made the call.

Logan knelt down by Cannon. "You weren't supposed to call the cops?"

"Or move, or leave the shop," Yvette said,

her voice filled with defeat. "Not until Monday."

Another entire day? To Cannon, it looked like they'd tried to clean up. They had water, a little food, but no change of clothes. And Tipton needed medical care.

Maybe Yvette did, too.

Covering her face, her slim body quaking, she dropped back against a wall. "If . . . if we left before then, he said he'd know, that he'd come back." Her voice cracked. "And next time he'd go ahead and . . . and light us up!"

The kerosene. Cannon fought back his rage now that the permeating smell made sense.

Logan reached out and carefully touched the edge of Tipton's shirt hem. "He doused you in kerosene."

Tipton drew a cautious breath through his nose. His gaze darted to his granddaughter. "Both of us. Stuff eats on your skin, so Yvette rinsed out our clothes the best she could."

It wasn't enough, Cannon could tell. The clothes had dried stiff and they still smelled.

"He . . ." Yvette swallowed again, choking on her tears. "He held a lighter over us." Fresh panic drove her voice higher. "He said if we made a sound or moved, he'd watch while we burned."

Cannon carefully clasped Tipton's shoulder to let him know things would be okay, then he stood and went to Yvette.

Slumped against the wall, her head down and her shoulders hunched, she quivered from head to toes. There was fear, shock and maybe a little relief now that she wasn't alone.

So many times she'd flirted with him in outrageous ways. Because she was so young, because he respected the neighborhood business owners and because he had bigger goals in life that didn't include an entangled relationship with an innocent girl, he had never expected to touch her.

Now everything was different. "Yvette?" She looked ready to come apart, so he didn't want to approach her too quickly.

Big green eyes, swollen and red, looked up at him, and she sniffled pathetically.

Never had he seen a more wretched sight. Pity almost choked Cannon as he slowly reached for her. "Come here."

On another broken sob, Yvette shot up against his bare chest, her slim arms squeezing tight around him, her face wetting his skin as the sobs came full steam. Her petite but stacked body — a body he had always ignored — pressed as close to him as she could get.

Cannon just held her, trying not to breathe in the remnants of kerosene fumes while noticing that her long dark hair was still oily with it. "You're safe now."

"No," she wailed. "He said he sees everything. He told us not to talk to the cops until tomorrow — or else. But you brought them here *now*! He said if we didn't follow directions, he'd make us pay. He said . . ." She shuddered, her voice choking. "He said he'd use me like he did that other lady."

"He'll never touch you." Already Cannon made plans on how to find the bastard, how he'd make him pay. "Do you know the other woman?"

"Oh, God." She shook her head hard. "No. But it was so awful!"

Reese interrupted those dark thoughts. "We'll take care of everything, Yvette." He held out a hand. "I'm Detective Bareden, by the way."

Without releasing Cannon, Yvette stuck out one small hand. Reese took it in a calm greeting. The second he released her, she snuggled in close to Cannon's chest again. He kept one arm around her shoulders, the other around her waist, giving her his heat, his strength, his comfort.

Over the top of her head, Cannon met

Reese's gaze. They were both grim.

"You said he told you to wait until tomorrow to call the cops." Logan stood, then looked around at the small room. "How long have you been here?"

"Since yesterday afternoon," Tipton said. He held his side and tried to sit up a little more, but gasped in pain instead.

"Your ribs?" Logan asked.

"Bastards kicked me."

Yvette shuddered again, so Cannon said near her ear, "Shh, shh," while rocking her a little.

"Can you tell me how many men? Can you give me descriptions?"

"I can try." Tipton caught his breath, let it out in a measured way that showed a lot of pain. "Three men. One had dark hair and a beard. A goatee. Other two weren't as dark. They were both heavy, one bald and the other thinning."

"Two of them . . . they raped her," Yvette cried, her breath against his now damp skin. "She was so out of it, I don't know if she realized what was going on. But it was horrible. She made these little sounds, like . . . like she wanted loose but couldn't fight —"

Again Cannon rocked her. "It'll be okay."

"What about the third man?" Logan asked.

"He made us watch with him,". Tipton said. "After they soaked us with kerosene. He — the one in charge — said he used kerosene 'cause it'd burn hot but wasn't combustible like gasoline."

"They said they'd burn us to ashes and no one would ever know what happened."

Absently, Cannon stroked her. The top of her head barely reached his shoulder. Usually whenever he'd seen her she'd been wearing heels. He hadn't realized she was so short. "Are you hurt, too?"

Keeping her face pressed against him, she shook her head. "No."

"They slapped her," Tipton said, " 'cause she cried when they were kicking me."

Cannon leaned back and tried to lift her face, but she clung to him like a vine. "Come on, honey. Let me take a look."

"No." And then, in an absurd show of vanity, she cried, "I'm a mess!"

Cannon looked around and found Reese, Logan and Tipton all watching them. In their gazes he saw the same pity he felt. No wonder Yvette wanted to hide.

Holding her a little closer, he asked Logan, "You've got this?"

Logan nodded. "I'll get the descriptions. Go take care of her."

"Ambulance will be here shortly." Reese

joined Logan at Tipton's side. "I told them to come in quietly."

Cannon accepted all that. No lights or sirens was good. "Then Yvette and I are going to the other room."

Tipton watched him with a lot of suspicion and concern. "What for?"

"To talk."

Logan spoke quietly to Tipton, and the older man nodded. "All right."

Before he got out of the room, Tipton said, "Cannon?"

With Yvette held close, Cannon looked back. "Yeah?"

"Thanks." He looked at his granddaughter. "For everything."

Cannon acknowledged that with a nod, but as he walked out of that room, he felt like he was taking a giant step into new responsibilities.

And into . . . trouble.

Petite, stacked, young trouble.

# CHAPTER ELEVEN

Afternoon sunshine had melted away all the snow, leaving behind a mild springlike day. After running several errands, it was almost dinnertime before Dash returned to the station. He'd called over an hour ago to see if Margo was done yet, but she'd needed more time.

Not a problem for him.

He wanted her to know that a relationship with him wouldn't get in her way.

But he also wanted to be a priority for her — because she was a priority for him. Now more than ever.

Knowing someone wanted to hurt her sent a rush of determination clawing through him. Somehow, someway, he would be near her, offering protection.

The fact that she could protect herself didn't matter, not to his emotions, not to his instincts. He was a man and, cop or no, she was still a woman. In the most basic way known to nature, he wanted to protect her.

The easiest way to help her figure out the balance of life and work was to show her that he considered her work as important as she did, and intimacy with him beat indiscriminate sex any day. It heightened every sensation, making it better, hotter, more consuming than a random encounter with a stranger.

The argument was a reversal for Dash. Other than sexual relief, he hadn't wanted anything from a woman in a very long time. But women, in his experience, wanted sex to mean something. They thought of it as a show of affection and caring, a prelude to love.

Not Margo.

Nope, she just used it as a carnal tension reliever from a very emotionally stressful job.

As Dash parked out front of the station, he saw Margo, Logan and Reese speaking together. Margo spotted him, too, and waved him over.

Interesting. Why weren't they in the building?

Leaving his purchases behind on the seat, he exited the truck. Even from the distance separating him from her, he saw the anger on Margo's face. She stood there without her coat — not that she'd need it with the sun shining down and the temps hitting the low sixties.

In several long strides Dash reached them, just in time to hear Margo give Reese an order.

"Get hold of the rest of your guys. I want them watched at the hospital, at home and at the shop."

"Already took care of it."

She paced, rubbing her injured arm, though Dash doubted she realized it. "I need this kept quiet. We're not taking any chances."

"My guys can be trusted." Reese took a few steps away, still on the cell.

"Reese has guys?" Dash asked.

She looked up at him in a distracted way. "Men he trusts. Officers who have proven themselves loyal to him, and therefore loyal to the letter of the law."

With a shrug, Logan said, "The crew was necessary before Margo took over."

She did some more pacing. "They still come in handy when I want to make sure details are kept as private as possible."

"And you have something you want kept private?"

"Everything." She gave him a meaningful

frown. "I don't like taking chances." All business, she added, "And speaking of chances, you need to park your truck somewhere safe. Away from where you live."

She seemed so urgent, he agreed without question. "All right."

"I mean it, Dash, you . . ." She frowned, finally realizing that he hadn't questioned her. "Do you have good security?"

"On my house? My brother is a cop, so yeah, the place is kept secure." He looked at Logan, hoping for a few answers.

As if to work off anger, his brother flexed his shoulders. "We checked out the pawnshop. The owner and his granddaughter were there when they shot the video."

Oh, shit. "What do you mean they were there?" Dash watched Margo rub her shoulder, then her wrist, above and below the splint. "I thought Cannon stopped in and they —"

"Three men with a drugged woman in tow broke in and used the place. To control the owner they doused him and his granddaughter in kerosene, then the head guy threatened them with a lighter the whole time they were there."

Reese disconnected his call and rejoined them. "I think the sick fuck enjoyed tormenting them. From what they said, he took as much pleasure in terrifying them as he did in videotaping the rape."

"Damn," Dash whispered. And these were the same people who wanted Margo? He wanted to haul her close and somehow insulate her from it all — but her job kept her at the forefront.

"A couple of Reese's guys are with Mr. Sweeny at the hospital. I'm guessing he has a few broken ribs at the very least." Logan stepped closer to Dash. "Cannon knows the granddaughter so he stayed with her at the hospital. She's pretty shook up."

"Margo?" Because he needed to touch her, Dash put a hand on the back of her neck. "What now?"

"They threatened that girl, told her they would use her next in a video if she talked to the police."

Dash searched her face . . . and saw iron resolve. "That's not going to happen."

"No, it's not. We won't let it." Wearily, Margo leaned into his side.

Dash put his arm around her.

Logan stared.

Reese raised his eyebrows.

Dash was about to call them on their idiotic behavior, but Margo beat him to it.

"Put your eyeballs back in your heads, boys. I know it strains your boundaries of belief, but I enjoy a little human contact every now and then, same as anyone else."

"Yeah, no, I wasn't . . ." Logan transferred his bemused gaze to Dash.

Reese coughed . . . and clapped Margo on the shoulder, just like she was one of the guys. "Glad for you."

She staggered into Dash, but laughed. "It doesn't require applause, detective, so stow it."

To Reese and Logan, Dash said, "You're both idiots."

Still leaning on him, Margo smiled at Logan. "He said it, not me." Then she got serious again. "We can pick up the rental on our way home —"

Logan and Reese did more asinine staring at that disclosure.

"— and then you can stow the truck somewhere safe."

"There's only one problem with that. I can't drive my truck and the rental, and you're out of commission until the splint comes off."

Logan checked his watch. "Leave your keys with Reese. He can store it and I'll drive you both to get the rental."

"You have time for that?" Dash asked.

"Sure." His eyes narrowed. "That way I can be positive no one follows you."

Disconcerted, Dash looked around the area. "You think we're being watched?"

Margo nodded. "I feel it, too." She took Dash's hand. "But stop being so obvious, okay?"

Her show of affection surprised him enough that he looked at her instead of checking for signs of surveillance. He curled his larger hand around hers, holding her securely. "Sorry about that."

Logan pretended not to see. "If Margo was driving she could lose a tail easy enough, but —"

"Yeah," Dash agreed with a grin. "I haven't exactly had a lot of practice at that."

"You'd do okay," Logan assured him, ever the loyal brother. "But I'll feel better if I drive."

Done discussing it, Margo started to walk away. "I'm ready if you are."

Since she didn't even try to let him go, Dash went along with her as she took the few steps to a nearby brick retaining wall to pick up her purse and coat. Taking advantage of the moment of dubious privacy, Dash asked, "Have you taken any aspirin lately?"

Shaking her head, she said, "I'm fine."

"Bullshit." He took her items from her and hauled her along with him to his truck, where he fished aspirin from his glove compartment and handed them to her with a half-empty bottle of water.

For only a moment she looked defiant, then grateful. "Was I that obvious?"

"Only to me because I'm paying very close attention."

A smile flickered over her lips before she tossed back the aspirin and washed them down. Nodding to the bags on the passenger seat, Margo asked, "What's all that?"

"Groceries, dinner, the clothes and stuff I grabbed." He hauled the bags out, holding them all in one hand.

The amount of clothes he'd packed in his overnight bag — enough for a week — seemed to throw her, but all she said was, "Dinner?"

"I figured I'd cook tonight. Fried chicken." *Your favorite.*

That left her momentarily mute. "You cook?"

Didn't everyone? Dash said only, "I'm a man of many talents."

"And you want to cook *tonight*?"

He smiled, knowing she'd had other plans — plans to thwart his determination to wait until she had the splint removed. But he had a surprise on that score, too.

Bending to her ear, he whispered, "I've

been thinking about that, about the care we need to take with your arm."

"My arm is fi—"

"About making you scream with a killer O. And you know, I just might have come up with an idea that'll work."

Eyes darkening and cheeks flushing, Margo went perfectly still. Even the comically interested stares from Logan and Reese didn't reach her.

"I can make you crazy with pleasure, but you have to trust me. You have to let me lead. And you —" his lips touched her ear "— will follow my directions . . . no matter what they are."

Her breath shuddered in; she let it out in a soft groan. "Okay."

Knowing he had her, Dash's smile warmed even more. "Come on then. Let's get the damned rental car so I can get you home alone and start on this very long, slow process."

"Long and slow?"

"Agonizingly long. Excruciatingly slow." He glanced at her breasts and saw that her nipples were stiffened points against her blouse. "Foreplay that I guarantee you're going to enjoy."

She shivered and Dash put his arm around. But she didn't move.

"Margo? Logan and Reese are watching. One foot in the front of the other, honey." He urged her forward and she finally got with it.

"How you can distract me like this when usually my brain would be eaten up with work —"

"You won't slide on work. You're better than that. But this way you can tackle it with a clear head." He kissed her temple. "You're every bit as primed as I am, aren't you?"

"Well, I am now." But then she let out a long sigh and admitted, "Yes, I was plenty twitchy before your little tease, too. God's truth, Dash, you plague me."

Logan and Reese pretended to be busy, but they didn't fool anyone.

With her coat folded over an arm, Margo hid herself as she approached them. "The second either of you hears anything, I want to be told."

Reese took the keys that Dash offered him. "They're releasing Mr. Sweeny from the hospital tonight, so I'm going to run by there myself before I head home for the day, just to make sure everything is set. I'll let you know how he and the girl are doing."

Still worried, Margo thanked him.

"After I drop you two off I'm going to meet up with Cannon at the sports center to talk with the boys just in case I can find out anything else."

"Pepper allows you to be out late?"

Logan started to reply, realized Dash had baited him, and instead glanced at the fading sun. "She understands the responsibilities of my job."

"Yeah, Pepper is great." But he enjoyed taking part in the running joke. Pepper could be noticeably demanding when it suited her, and despite all earlier indications, she was a true mother hen when it came to worrying about the people she loved.

Margo seated herself in the back of Logan's car. "Cannon might not be comfortable leaving Tipton and Yvette. I got the feeling he's taking responsibility for them both."

"For the entire neighborhood," Dash said. "At least that's how it seemed to me."

Rather than get in the front seat as Margo had probably expected, Dash squeezed into the back beside her, forcing her to scoot over, and then he put an arm around her before she could move all the way to the other side.

Smiling at her disgruntled expression, he helped to fasten her seat belt.

"We talked about that." Logan got behind

the wheel, denying her the opportunity to switch things around. "I convinced him they'd be safer once we found the guys responsible, so for now, he's willing to trust Reese to help see to their protection."

"We'll definitely get them," Margo decreed. "Sooner would be better than later."

"We're on it." Logan started the car. "But until then, watch your ass."

"My words to you, Detective." Margo got comfortable against Dash. "But yes, we'll be careful." She glanced up at Dash. "Both of us."

Pulling his stocking cap a little lower, Curtis ordered, "Follow them."

Toby, who'd also worn a hat and kept his back to the scene, glanced over his shoulder. Two vehicles headed in two different directions. Without looking at Curtis, he asked, "Which one?"

"The car." Curtis took off his glasses and polished them on a sleeve. "I want to know where they go, what they do — I want to know where she lives, if she's alone or if he stays with her. I want to know . . . everything."

In that inscrutable way of his, Toby said, "No problem," and in two long strides he reached his big muscle truck. He'd catch them at the next light and because he was good, Saul knew he wouldn't lose them.

Curtis held back, looking at the police station, at the truck the big cop drove, and then at Saul.

Feeling like an anxious puppy hoping for affection, Saul waited. Ever since the cluster-fuck where the cop had gotten away, Curtis had been more glacial than usual — which was saying something given Curtis's aloof manner. Saul was used to him being that way to others. And to some extent he froze Saul out, too.

But never like this.

Taking in Saul's ball cap, his aviator sunglasses, Curtis smiled.

And Jesus, that scared Saul more than anything else. He'd been told to disguise himself and so he had. He'd left the morning whiskers on his face, dressed down in an old corduroy jacket and worn jeans. Should he have worn a fake mustache, too?

Very uncertain of his brother's mood, he asked, "Everything okay, Curtis?"

"It will be." He approached Saul, his expression indulgent in that big-brotherly way. He cupped his face. "No more fuck-ups, Saul."

His thighs actually felt shaky. "No — no, there won't be. I swear."

"You like spending my money, don't you, Saul? You enjoy the house I supply, the clothes. The playtimes?"

"Yes." It was thanks to Curtis that Saul never had to work a legitimate job. Curtis was a genius at making money, and even better at entertaining.

"Very soon," Curtis continued, as if Saul hadn't spoken, "you'll get the opportunity to right your wrongs, to make up for the extra trouble you've caused me." His fingers tightened, squeezing into Saul's face, deliberately painful. "You will not disappoint me again."

As Curtis walked away, Saul stood there, working his jaw, awed by his brother's strength . . . and hating him just a little for it.

Margo couldn't believe how affected she was by the promise of getting alone with Dash. Never had she experienced such a level of anticipation. And here she'd thought he might not be exciting enough.

She'd missed the mark on that one by a mile.

Dash's muscular thigh pressed against hers and his long arm kept her close. Logan continued to talk, probably just to make conversation, but Margo didn't bother try-

263

ing to follow along. When necessary, Dash replied.

He also kept his fingers teasing her arm. The sunny day had warmed his skin, amplifying his scent, making her blood surge. She wanted to put her nose in his neck, but not with Logan continually glancing in the rearview mirror.

Hopefully on the outside she looked impassive because on the inside an inferno of sensation and need burned. She kept thinking about Dash naked, running her hands over all that solid muscle, rough hair, warm flesh. . . . She could almost feel the wet heat of his kiss, his hard fingers on her, in her. . . .

She closed her eyes, but that only made her picture him over her, his biceps bulging, his hair-roughened thighs spreading her more slender legs as he slid deep.

Drawing in a shuddering breath, she tried to compose herself — and instead drew the attention of both men.

Gaze dark and knowing, Dash watched her.

Logan asked, "You okay?"

*Get it together, Margaret.* "I'm sorry. I . . . It's not easy for me to . . ." The stammering didn't help. She straightened away from Dash. "No offense to you or Reese, but I'd rather be handling things myself."

"I know." Sympathetic, Logan said, "I'd feel the same, so I get it. But don't worry about it. You'll be plenty involved."

"I'd better be."

"And," Logan said, ignoring her tone, "that's why I'm telling you that we're being followed."

She frowned, then grabbed Dash's thigh when he started to look out the rear window. "Don't." Leaning forward, she asked Logan, "You're sure?"

"Whoever he is, he's good, staying just far enough back that it's not obvious. But yeah, he's been on us almost since we left the station."

No longer distracted by Dash, Margo's blood surged for a whole different reason. "Can you lose him?"

"If that's what you want."

She considered things. "If Dash wasn't staying with me, I wouldn't mind laying a trap for the bastard. But —"

Dash spoke over her, saying, "Fuck that. Don't change things because of me."

At least he hadn't objected to the trap part. In so many ways, Dash proved that he trusted her ability, her instincts and her position.

Oh, he was still a guy with a guy's instinct

265

to protect the little lady. But he didn't downplay her own skill.

"No," she said, thinking it through. "It's never a good idea to leave a trail to your home. If we knew he was the only one involved —"

"But we know he isn't," Dash interjected. "There are at least three."

"And maybe more," Logan said. "So if I can make a suggestion . . ."

"Let's hear it." Margo leaned forward to look through the side-view mirror but she didn't see anyone suspicious.

"How about I draw him out?" Already making the decision, Logan turned away from their destination. "I can lead him on a winding chase until he's forced to get closer. At the very least we can maybe pick up the plates."

Appearing fascinated by it all, Dash asked, "Do you think they might match the plates from the van?"

"Doubtful. We'd have to be dealing with morons. Plus it's a truck following us, not a van." Margo opened her seat belt and moved into the window seat — away from Dash. Her Glock had a fully loaded clip and she had another weapon in her purse. It bothered her that Dash was along for the ride, and it bothered her more that she cared.

Making up her mind, she met Logan's gaze in the rearview mirror and gave a nod. "Let's do it."

# CHAPTER TWELVE

As rock-steady as Logan with the same lethal look, Margo said to him, "Don't interfere."

"Wouldn't think of it." But Dash couldn't help but look — repeatedly — for their tail. He saw several trucks but none seemed more nosy than the others. As always the mind of a cop intrigued him.

He wanted to tell Margo not to hurt her arm, but knew better. Instead he asked his brother, "Is there anything I can do?"

"Yeah." Logan took a right, then an immediate left, but he drove without haste — as if he didn't know a killer followed them. "Be cool. Stop looking around."

"Okay." He sat forward, but damn it wasn't easy.

"He's good," Margo complained.

"Meaning?"

Logan said, "He's not getting close enough for me to see anything. He might be on to us."

"The bastard is even dropping back," Margo said.

Dash thought about it for a second, then said, "Is he far enough back that you could let me out without him seeing?"

Logan shot a sharp look over his shoulder. "No."

But Margo took it differently. "It might be possible." And then to Logan she said, "There's no reason for him to be involved in this."

Laughing, Logan stated the obvious. "He's not dodging out to avoid the danger, Lieutenant. He wants out so can lay in wait for the bastard to go by."

Incredulous, Margo twisted to face Dash.

Dash tried for nonchalance. "If I'm just a bystander on the road, I could get a good look at him, read his plates, get you a description —"

"No!" But that shouted word must not have sufficed, because she pressed her anger forward and said not two inches from his face, "Are you out of your mind?"

Was she incensed from worry, or because she didn't want him butting in? "How could it hurt?" Gently, Dash touched her chcek, but she jerked away. "I seriously doubt he's twisted enough to shoot me on the street

corner. And look, there's a park up ahead
—"

"No and no!" She turned her face away,
grumbling to herself about male stupidity.

"Actually," Logan said, "it's not a bad
idea."

"Absolutely not." They turned another
corner, and Margo cursed. "We're losing
him anyway. He's so far back I can't even
see him anymore."

"If we can't see him, he can't see us,
right?" Dash pointed to a small convenience
store. "Pull in there, around the back. We
can watch to see if he shows up."

"I was thinking the same thing," Logan
said, already maneuvering into the lot. "You
will remain in the car, Dash. Got it?"

"I already said I wouldn't interfere."

Surly, Margo gave him a narrow-eyed
stare. "You're having way too much fun,
damn you."

"I like watching you work." Especially
when she wasn't in any real danger. Dash
stretched out an arm along the back of the
seat, but he didn't quite touch her yet. He'd
confused her enough for one day. "More so
this time since no one is shooting at us and
you aren't bleeding."

The angle Logan used kept the car hidden, but if anyone drove past, they'd be able

to see. Margo kept watch out the back just in case their tail had the same idea about pulling over.

Thirty seconds later — which felt like an eternity to Dash — the big truck drove past.

"There he is," Logan murmured.

"Are we going after him?" Dash wasn't sure of the protocol for this sort of thing.

"No." Margo answered since Logan was busy putting in a call. She sat back in frustration. "We'll have the plates checked, see if we can find out anything."

"Couldn't you have someone pick him up?"

"For what?" She holstered her weapon. "We don't know for certain that he's done anything wrong."

Logan finished a call. "They'll run the plates and get back to me." He started another call.

"Who now?" Margo asked.

Without answering her, Logan said into the phone, "Rowdy, hey. Sorry to bother you, but I've got a plate number and a description for you, just in case you find out anything."

Margo rolled her eyes. "I forgot we brought Rowdy in on this."

"That he forced his way in, you mean?" Dash grinned. Damn, but Rowdy led an exciting life. If being a bar owner wasn't enough, he also managed to get enmeshed in more conspiracies than anyone else Dash knew.

Rowdy was more domesticated now, but deep down, he still relished life on the edge.

Logan relayed some details to Rowdy, adding, "It was a big black muscle truck all tricked out. Light bar over the front bumper, a silver toolbox in the bed. The driver wore a ball cap and sunglasses, but I could tell he has a dark mustache and goatee." Logan nodded. "Yeah, right. If you find out anything, do not —" He listened, and his frown eased. "Good. I'm glad you understand."

While Logan and Rowdy talked a little more, Margo seemed lost in deep thought.

Dash touched the soft curls in her hair — such a stark contrast to her iron determination. "What are you thinking?" Not about him this time, though he knew earlier she'd been daydreaming about sex, about what they would do tonight, about what he would do to her.

She'd been so flushed, so soft and aroused and trembling, he'd gotten semihard just looking at her.

Now, though, sex was far from her mind. She had that calculating, concentrated look about her that showed concern and cunning and an indomitable will to take charge.

Margo kept her attention on the street. "I'm betting he had fictitious plates, that he and his cronies are too inept to kill me, but too cunning to be easily caught. I'm thinking that this is going to take longer than it should." Her gaze flickered to Dash. "And I'm thinking that once I get them, I'll make damn sure they never again have the ability to hurt women."

"Castration?" Dash asked, half teasing, but with the way she looked he just wasn't sure.

"Life in prison." She turned away again.

By-the-book Margo. She was as honorable as she was sexy. A nice combo. "Will you share the info with Cannon also?"

"Yes." She stewed a moment more, then leaned forward to speak to Logan. "I think Dash was right."

Having just finished his call with Rowdy, Logan disconnected and put the phone back in his pocket. "About?"

"Stepping out. Waiting." She opened her seat belt. "Our perp isn't an idiot. He'll circle back looking for us. I want to be there, where he can see me."

Gut clenching, Dash froze. Logan, damn him, didn't react at all.

Margo continued. "You stay here. I doubt

he'll stop, but if he tries to grab me —"

"Or *shoot* you," Dash interjected, already forgetting that he'd said himself how unlikely that would be.

Logan only spared him one dismissive look before addressing Margo again. "I'll be on him."

She opened her door — and Dash cracked. "Wait."

She didn't. She stepped out, so Dash slid across the seat and followed.

Margo rounded on him. "Back in the car, now."

He was not one of her lackeys to be ordered around!

But damn it, at the same time, he knew her mindset was different from many women. Tamping down on his basic nature, Dash drew one breath, then another.

As calmly as he could, he asked, "What if we underestimated him and he does something stupid?"

From the driver's seat, Logan let out an exasperated huff. "Before he could shoot her he'd have to show a gun. He can't shoot through the damn car door. He'd pull his weapon, and we'd see it."

"And I would react," Margo told him, still bristling. "And if I couldn't shoot fast enough to defend myself —"

"Then I would," Logan finished for her.

Standing over her, Dash looked down into her stern face. Such a beautiful face to him. "All right."

"It isn't up to you!"

"Yeah, I know." Strung tight with frustration and worry, he ran a hand over his hair. "I meant I'll stop being an annoying ass and let you get to it."

Margo lightened up, but not much. "I know what I'm doing."

"Obviously."

"If she doesn't do it now," Logan grumbled, "we might miss our chance."

Dash framed her face in his hands, kissed her hard and quick and turned back to the car. He didn't watch her walk away because, damn it all, he couldn't.

"You are being an ass," Logan said while keeping his gaze on Margo. "You know that, right?"

"Yeah." He slumped in his seat. "I know." He pulled out his cell phone.

"She's a damn fine cop. More competent than most."

"Yeah." Opening the phone to access the camera, he prepared himself.

Logan's tone went acerbic. "I'd have made myself the sitting duck except that with her arm in the sling she can't be the driver, and using a civilian could fuck us on regulations."

So Logan wasn't any more thrilled with the scenario than he was? That made Dash feel better. "She'll be fine."

"Of course she will." Logan had his weapon in his hand, his senses on high alert. "Now be quiet and let me concentrate."

Toby pulled over to the curb a good distance away. The sun was behind him, aiding him because it highlighted her, but would make it difficult for her to look toward him.

"Do you think I'm an idiot, sweetheart?" He watched the woman make herself available at the curb, watched her look around in casual disregard, then lean against a light pole.

Toby snorted. She didn't blend in any more than he would have. She was too alert. He saw it, felt it.

Lifting the cell phone, he called Curtis.

"Is she home already?" Curtis asked after only one ring.

"They took a scattered route, and then pulled over. The woman is standing on the curb. A trap, I assume."

"Meaning they saw you."

"Guess so." He wouldn't apologize when he knew it took someone really good to spot him. "I think she expects me to make a grab for her. Probably has a few cop buddies waiting in the wings to close in on me if I do."

"She's appealing to your vanity. She expects your male ego to demand you confront her. That, or she thinks you're an idiot."

Curtis always admired wit. "Yeah, she's a real clever bitch," Toby said with dry impatience. "Want me to pop her?" He had a clear aim from a good distance away. It'd draw a lot of attention, but with Curtis's influence, he could —

"No. We don't need that much heat coming down on us." For the longest time Curtis thought things over. With a smile in his voice, he said, "Here's what I want you to do instead."

Toby listened without interrupting. Curtis was a spoiled, entitled, twisted fuck, but sometimes he was funny, too. "Consider it done."

Thoughts of Dash divided Margo's concentration. Men, she well knew, could be prickly when their pride took a blow. Dash, like other men, had wanted to play the superiority role. He wanted to do her job even though he had zip experience and even less authority to do so.

Anger again sent her pacing along the curb, her eyes squinted against the low-hanging sun. Where was that damned truck? Did they want her enough to risk taking her off a crowded street? She wanted them to try.

She wanted that a lot.

She also wanted Dash. Tonight. Every part of him. She wanted to feel his tall, hard frame over her, his muscles straining in pleasure, his breath hot, his thick erection sliding in, filling her up. . . .

Something flashed in her peripheral vision and she took closer notice. But no, it was nothing. A woman pushing a stroller. Not a threat.

Would Dash be annoyed with her for ordering him into the car, for so totally discounting his concern — concern that had insulted her because he'd shown it toward a woman. Not a cop. Not a lieutenant.

Just a woman.

A woman he . . . cared about?

One of the things she enjoyed most about being with Dash was that he didn't treat her differently. Right? So why start nitpicking with him now?

Rubbing her temples, she strode to a bus bench and circled it, too antsy to sit.

Yes, the fact that Dash saw her as a woman thrilled her.

*But not when she was working.*

Not when she needed utmost respect from all those around her. She'd fought too long and hard to gain that respect to give it up for anyone. She'd even fought her own father, for God's sake. But with Dash, everything was wonderfully different.

Would he still want her tonight? He seemed pretty annoyed. Maybe he, like most men, would use an excuse to punish her.

He could even be put off enough to leave her tonight instead of staying over. That possibility caused an invisible fist to squeeze her heart. . . .

Another flash of light drew her away from her personal problems. This time when she looked up she found the truck slowly rolling toward her. Being so close, she noticed things she hadn't before. Like oversize wheels and customized, colorful rims unlike any she'd ever seen before. Those rims had to have cost plenty, so maybe he was a man of means.

Or underground porn paid well.

The driver wasn't surprised to see her, and didn't bother trying to hide from her. No, he smiled at her, a smug, obnoxious tilt of his mouth that dared her to react.

In an instant Margo knew she wasn't in peril. He wouldn't try to nab her, or shoot her. No, he just wanted to mock her.

Bastard.

Well, two could play that game. Wearing her own cocky smile, Margo held out her right arm and took a step closer to the curb — offering herself. *Come and get me, you miserable fuck.* She even used her fingertips to beckon him forward.

When he rolled closer, his truck directly in front of her, she mouthed a single word — *coward.*

Thanks to his reflective sunglasses she couldn't see his eyes, but she saw his smile tighten, saw his jaw lock and his mouth compress.

And that made *her* smile.

When the traffic stopped, he had to brake hard to keep from rear-ending the vehicle in front of him. That finished off his provocative expression really quick.

Displaying her own arrogance, Margo gave him her most intimidating stare without blinking. He flexed his hands on the steering wheel, turned to her again and jerked off his sunglasses to show her flashing black eyes — and a fresh bruise on his cheekbone.

Talk about a look of hatred.

He wasted it on her.

She took another step into the road. "What?" One more step. "You want something, big boy? You want me? Come on, then. Come and get me."

The light changed, traffic moved. He said nothing, but he did give the slightest nod.

Margo felt a rush of power. "I'll be waiting."

Elbow resting on the open window frame, he drove off, not speeding, not even looking at her again.

And it infuriated her because there wasn't a single thing she could do about it.

When she could no longer see him she turned to head back to Logan and Dash.

Dash. She'd almost forgotten about him. But now, thinking of him added to her smoldering annoyance. She reached the car just as he pushed open the door for her. And blast the man, as she moved into the backseat and faced him, she saw that he looked admiring.

"That was a bust," she grumbled, trying to hide her mounting fury and concern.

Logan kept watching the road. "Oh, I don't know about that. You daring him like that will maybe get them to make a move sooner rather than later."

"Maybe." She refastened her seat belt.

"Any news on the plates?"

"Soon."

If the search on the plates had come back wrong, they'd have had a reason to pull him in.

Dash put a hand on her shoulder, drawing a questioning look from her. As if nothing else had happened, he asked, "Getting hungry?"

"Yes." But not so much for food. What she wanted, what she needed, was Dash. Every inch of him. Hot, grinding sex would do a lot to improve her mood and take the edge off.

Looking at her mouth, he gave a small sexy smile. "Good, because I'm starved."

Well, damn. Maybe he wasn't still peeved.

"Logan?" Dash kept his arm around her. "We headed back now? The rental place might close soon."

"Up to the lieutenant."

"Let's call it quits," she agreed. "But make sure we're not followed."

They had just pulled into the rental office when Logan got his return call. The plates on the truck belonged to a stolen SUV. He twisted to see Margo in the backseat. "I'll call it in. If he's still on the road, someone will spot him."

Sinking into a bad mood, Margo jerked

open her seat belt and got out. The odds of spotting him now were slim. *Damn it.*

She heard Dash say to Logan, "Thanks for the lift."

"No problem. Stay prepared, okay?"

"Will do."

Seconds later Dash jogged up to her. When he reached her he put his arm around her waist. "You're tense."

"I'm pissed."

"Understandably."

God, how did he roll with the punches so easily? She wanted to ask him, to know his thoughts, but she didn't want to invite his criticism.

His hand opened on the small of her back. "Seeing you like that, swaggering and so authoritative, really got to me."

Unsure of him, Margo pushed the door opened to the office. "Got to you how?"

He leaned down to whisper in her ear. "It turned me on. I had to fight off a boner."

No way. She pushed him back. "You were afraid for me."

With a shrug, he said, "I'd have felt the same about Logan or Reese. Crazy people do crazy things, and there's no controlling that regardless of how badass you might be, so don't crucify me for caring."

Caring. Did he?

Teasing her, he said, "So yeah, I was worried. And turned on. And I fucking can't wait to get you alone." His hand dipped down to her hip. "You want to know what I'll do to you?"

How did he always manage to keep her off balance? Margo slowed her step, swallowed, licked her lips. "Yes."

His gaze burning, Dash stared down at her. "I'll give you a few clues in the car on the ride home."

That was all the incentive she needed to take care of the paperwork in record time. Within fifteen minutes they were on the road in a sporty little Ford Escort. Her heart thumped heavily, her thighs quivered and tingling heat swirled low in her belly. Arousal. With Dash, it happened so easily, so overwhelmingly, that she stayed in a damned fog.

Dash kept his attention on the road — and one hand on her knee.

She was just about to moan in frustration when he said, so very calmly, "I want you to part your legs for me . . . and then leave them that way."

Cannon stood in the waiting room facing a window, watching the people come and go from the hospital. Only minutes ago a woman and her husband had left the room, ready for a tearful visit with a relative.

He relished the moment alone to think. Hitting a heavy bag would have been nice. Or a long jog.

Or prolonged, sweaty sex.

But at the moment, he had no way to work off the tension.

*What would he do about Tipton and Yvette?*

He had enough friends in the neighborhood that he'd already called in reinforcements. As long as Yvette and Tipton stayed indoors, or told him if or when they had to go out, he could ensure someone kept an eye on them.

He figured for at least a few days they'd be home, locked in and safe. But after that?

Sometimes it sucked that he couldn't be everywhere at once.

For such a long time he'd felt territorial about his neighborhood. He especially felt protective of those who lived there.

And for a girl like Yvette, someone so close to his sister's age —

"Cannon?"

With his hands in the back pockets of his jeans, he braced himself and turned to face her. She looked so damned small, so defenseless. Her dark, freshly washed hair hung in long wet hanks over her shoulders.

The ghastly makeup had been removed, but her cheeks were still blotchy, her eyes swollen and red-rimmed from crying. She looked painfully young.

Young, innocent, scared . . . and full of hero worship.

Shit. He drew a breath and tried to relax, but for some reason that proved impossible. He felt strung tight in ways he definitely shouldn't.

The stench of kerosene was gone, along with her ruined clothes. She wore a pair of scrubs . . . and no bra.

He shouldn't have noticed that, but damn it, he did. The girl had an impossible-to-ignore body. "How's Tipton?"

"The nurse said he'll be okay." She bit her lush bottom lip to still the fine trembling, drew a deep breath and blew it out slowly. "I should be able to take him home in a few hours."

Though she tried to hide it, her nervousness over that prospect was plain to see. She probably felt safer at the hospital around so many people. "Come here, Yvette."

Hugging her arms under her breasts, she slunk in.

It used to amuse him how she'd strut her stuff, slim hips swaying, firm breasts thrust forward as she tested the boundaries of her sex appeal.

Now she looked utterly cowed and it bothered him. A lot.

He waited for her to choose a seat, her eyes averted, her hands twisted together. Once she did, perching on the edge as if she might bolt at any minute, he sat next to her — nearby but not *too* close. "You won't be alone, you know. One of Reese's guys will make sure you get home okay. The locks on your doors and windows are good, right?"

"Grandpa says they are."

"Tipton would know. He won't take chances with you." But Tipton was hardly in any shape to console, much less protect her. Cannon bent to see her face behind the fall of her damp hair — and committed himself. "I'm going to make sure someone keeps an eye on things."

That had her big green eyes wide on his face. "Someone?"

"Me, when I can. Friends that I trust when I'm not available."

Dropping her gaze again, she fretted. Cannon took her hand, and was surprised at how she gripped him, her hold tight, desperate.

Screw it. He moved closer still and put an arm around her narrow shoulders as he told her what he had planned. "Forget their threats, okay? They won't get to you again."

She didn't answer — maybe because she didn't believe him.

"You're safe inside. But I'll need you or Tipton to always let me know when you go out." To ensure she understood, he put his fingers under her chin and lifted her face.

When she looked up at him, it hit him like a punch. Her lips were soft and pink, her eyes once again liquid. Her breath low and fast.

*Get a grip, Cannon.* "Do you understand, Yvette?"

She swallowed, nodded. "Grandpa said we won't be able to open the shop for a while."

Relieved to hear that, Cannon put his hands back on safer ground. Like her elbow. "I'll talk to Tipton, too, but don't worry about the shop right now. I'll go over and get it cleaned up. Okay?"

"You . . . what?"

Yeah, he could understand her confusion. He knew her grandpa, but they weren't related, weren't all that close really. "It's not a big deal. I'll round up some friends and we'll clean it up. It won't take long. Then when Tipton is ready, he can go back."

Her attention went from his eyes to his

mouth. He stilled, on the alert . . . until more tears welled up and that damp bottom lip started to quiver again. "You are so nice."

Her soft voice unnerved Cannon. "Friends help friends," he told her gently, and he hoped she accepted that.

Her face flushed and she looked down at her hands. "You mean my grandpa."

Without intending to, he smoothed back her hair. "We're friends, too."

"No," she said in a tiny voice that crumpled at the end. "You don't even like me."

The last was said almost as a sob, ripping at his heart. If she hadn't spent so much time flirting with him, he'd . . . what? Hold her closer? Touch her more? Cannon shook his head and tried to think of her as his little sister.

Right.

"Don't be silly," he whispered, his voice gruff. "I like you fine."

"I'm sorry." She sniffled. "I know I should stop crying like a baby —"

"You're upset. Anyone would be." He sat back from her a little. "But I don't want you to worry. Reese said he's going to have cops patrol the area for a while, and my friends and I will keep a watch on things, too. You'll be protected."

She nodded, but covered her face. "Nothing is ever going to be the same again."

Lost, Cannon gave in, pulling her into his lap and cradling her against his chest, rocking her a little. She leaned into him, saying over and over, "I'm so sorry."

He felt her rounded bottom on his thighs, her breasts against his chest.

He felt himself sinking.

Hugging her closer, he lied and said, "No problem." It was a big problem — but somehow he'd deal with it.

Determined, he kissed her temple, smoothed her hair. Somehow he would make everything okay. It wouldn't be easy, but few things in life ever were.

# CHAPTER THIRTEEN

The slow, almost resistant way Margo moved her knees apart fired Dash's blood.

"A little more," he insisted softly.

Staring straight ahead out the windshield, she bit her bottom lip — and pressed her knees farther apart. "This is silly."

"You with your legs open for me?" He stroked her slender thigh, feeling the muscles taut with expectation. "That's as sexy as it gets."

"You can't do anything in the car while driving."

"I can get you primed." And himself, as well.

She stilled, then admitted, "I already am." She glanced at him, her eyes dark and mysterious and heated from within. "It seems that with you, I always am."

Progress. Soon she'd realize that she needed him, only him. "I'm glad. I like seeing you like this. Open to me. Ready." He skimmed his fingertips up the inside of her thigh, but didn't touch her between her legs. Not yet. "You are ready, aren't you? Tell me you're wet."

Embarrassment heated her face, but she gave one faint nod.

With the backs of his fingers, Dash touched her warmed cheek. "Remember something, honey. When you're with me like this, you're not a lieutenant. You're not the boss. And you're definitely not holding the reins."

She trembled . . . with excitement.

Pushing her, Dash whispered, "I know what you need, and I know when you need it."

Being in control was important to her. Dash knew it, and that was the main reason he wanted her to trust him to do what was best for her. He wanted her to let go completely.

With sex, *with him,* it was the only time she'd ever let that happen.

She shifted slightly. "What if someone sees us?"

"What if they do? You're a woman enjoying the touch of a man."

"In a car, in the open —"

"And that's not proper?" He lowered his fingers to her breast, lightly brushing over her nipple before resting his large hand around the very top of her thigh. "I don't want you to be proper," he told her, keeping his voice low, cool. Commanding.

"Then what should I be?"

Dash didn't hesitate. Clasping her thigh firmly, he drew her legs farther apart still. "Carnal." Damn, he loved seeing her like this. "Honest. Open and real."

Her eyelashes fluttered, her lips parted with fast breaths.

"Before we're done tonight," Dash promised her, "I'll make you sweat and cry. And come. I'll touch every part of you and taste you all over." He gently cupped her mound. "Especially here."

With her right hand, she gripped the door handle as if to ground herself. "Dash . . ."

Keeping his attention on the road wasn't easy. "You're too stiff. Relax your spine a little." Hell, he was the stiff one. No way could he do this and not get hard. "That's better," he told her as she exhaled and relaxed her shoulders back against the seat. "I'm wondering about something."

In a small voice, she asked, "What?"

"Will you be as agreeable without the drugs?" He trailed his fingers back and forth along the seam of her slacks. Even through the material, he could feel her softness and heat.

"I don't know." Still resting back against the seat, legs open, she turned her head to see him. "Maybe. Depends."

He glanced at her, then back to the road. "On what?"

"On whether or not you leave me hanging."

His smile quirked. Even now, with her legs sprawled and her eyes dark with need, she tried to wrest control from him. He understood that instinctive reaction; it was in her nature to always push. "I already told you that I'll give you an orgasm. More than one. In fact, I'm going to enjoy making you come again and again."

A low groan escaped her, and for only a moment she closed her eyes. "I want you inside me, Dash. I want to feel your weight on me, feel you sinking in." She stared at him. "I want you filling me up."

Damn. She said it and he saw it, him over her, her legs around his waist, or maybe on his shoulders. His gut knotted with the need to take her, but losing to her now could mean losing her forever.

As a strong woman, she needed a stronger man. He intended to be that man.

"It's going to happen." Her eyes flared,

and he added, "Eventually." Then, chastising her, he added, "Not tonight, though."

She started to close her legs, but Dash pressed his hand against her more firmly. "I'll have my fingers in you." He waited two heartbeats. "And my mouth on you."

Reluctantly, she settled back with another groan of impatience. "God, I can't wait."

"But you will, because I'm going to feed you first."

"Damn it, Dash!" She caught his wrist, but didn't push his hand away. "You're talking hours from now!"

"One hour, that's all. I bought boneless chicken. It cooks quickly." He kept his smile contained. "You need to eat, honey. And you need some aspirin."

Sizzling frustration made her voice high. "Then why start teasing me now?"

That particular tone was all woman without a single sign of badass cop in sight. "I like touching you and teasing you. I love knowing you want me." He cupped his hand over her. "And you like it, too."

Chest heaving, her face flushed, she finally released his wrist and, in a sign of surrender, stopped straining away from him.

"Plus," Dash said softly, his fingers once again exploring, "you've forgotten all about your work and worries."

Her lashes lowered over her eyes and she shifted uneasily. "So you're making me wild to *help* me?"

"Oh, no, honey. I haven't even started yet on making you wild." Picking up again as if she hadn't interrupted, he said, "After dinner, we'll take a bath. Yes, we. I want to sit behind you with your back to my chest. I have long arms, Margo. Long arms and big hands and I'll be able to reach every inch of you. You can trust me to be thorough."

Eyes dark as midnight and full of sultry expectation slanted his way. "You'll have to be naked, too."

"Naked and nestled up against your sweet little ass." His testicles tightened just thinking about it. He squeezed her thigh. "It'll be torture for me, but I'm looking at it as a character builder."

She shook her head and, surprising him, gave a tense, breathless laugh. "You are so nuts."

No, he was in love — but she wasn't ready to hear that yet. So instead he'd win her over with sex and the freedom she'd have around him, and he'd ease her into the idea of more. A lot more.

Like everything. And forever.

"After our meticulous bath, where I promise to pay special attention to certain areas

—" he bobbed his eyebrows at her, making her groan with excruciating need "— I'd like to have you on my lap. Facing me."

The smile faded. "Still naked."

"Yes. You're beautiful, Margo, always. But never more so than when I can see every sweet inch of you." He pressed his fingers more firmly to her sex. So much heat. He couldn't wait to have her, all of her, in every way. "Your pretty thighs will be wide open around me so I can look at you and touch you as much as I want." *As much as she needed.* He lifted his hand and brushed his knuckles repeatedly over her left nipple. It stiffened, making her catch her breath. "And with your breasts right there, even with my mouth, it'll be easy to —"

"That's enough." Trembling a little, she straightened, drew a long broken breath. Like a threat, she said, "Tomorrow when I get this sling off —"

"Then all bets are off," Dash agreed, "and I'm going to fuck you senseless."

With an explosion of heat, Margo stared at him, bit her lips again and nodded. "Okay."

Dash's hand slipped away from her body — and didn't return. He had ratcheted up her need to the point she knew it wouldn't take much to have her begging for release. It was diabolical the way he pushed her only so far, then retreated, only to get her going again. With every touch her body thrummed more insistently, the heat building, the sweet tension coiling tighter.

Dash gave a low curse, and that prompted her to finally open her eyes. "What?"

"Company."

She followed his line of vision and . . . Damn.

It was a nasty trick of fate to find her father and brother in her driveway as they started down the street to her house. Disappointment overwhelming, Margo groaned long and low. The last thing she wanted or needed was another delay.

Face set in lines of regret, Dash said, "I'm sorry, baby."

"Are you?" No way could she temper the accusation. "Because it's thanks to you that I'm on fire over here."

His hands worked on the steering wheel as he slowed the car. "They won't recognize the rental so I could maybe slide by without them —"

"Yeah, nice try." Dash was the funniest man she'd ever known — and by far the sexiest. "They'll just wait forever. My dad is pigheaded, and West is probably worried."

Straightening, she drew three deep breaths that didn't even come close to abolishing the lust. "God, this is awful."

"I know." His hand smoothed over her thigh, this time comforting more than inciting. "We'll get rid of them as quick as we can."

"My dad goes only when he wants to go."

Dash glanced at her. "It's your house, honey. Tell him you have plans — which you do — and he should understand and book."

She snorted. "That's not how it works."

Speculative, Dash asked, "So he doesn't respect your wishes?"

There was a wealth of interest in the question, much of it unrelated to the current untenable situation. She didn't want to admit that her dad didn't respect anything about her. Instead she shrugged. "Hopefully he has his own plans and won't be able to stay long."

He withdrew his touch. "You and West are close?"

How to answer that? In some ways they were extremely close. In other ways — because of her — they were galaxies apart. "I've always competed with him."

Dash frowned. "And him with you?"

She gave him a "yeah right" look. "You saw him. He's bigger, stronger and more intimidating than I could ever be."

Slowly, Dash approached the driveway. "Intimidating how?"

Poor Dash. He kept wanting to protect her when she didn't need protection.

She just needed him to live up to the sensual promises he'd made.

"Not to me, if that's what you're thinking." She smoothed her hair, wondering if the lust churning deep inside her showed in some way. "West always treated me like a typical little sister, and I probably drove him nuts trying to keep up with him. What I meant is that he intimidates others when necessary. He looks at people, and they fall into line."

"And you crack the whip to make it happen."

It wasn't really funny given how hard she'd had to work to earn the respect she deserved in the department, but still she found herself smiling. "Something like that. West, well he's one of those guys that even while he's putting you in your place, you still like and respect him. But whenever I had to reprimand men, they hated me for it."

"Sexist jerks hated it." He put the car in Park. "Anyone with an ounce of sense would know you deserve your position, and they'd like and respect you for it."

"A position on your lap, naked, facing you?" As if that didn't tease him enough, she added innocently, "And if you're still naked, too, well just think what my hands can be doing."

He went still — and Margo opened the door and got out. After a few seconds, Dash rushed to join her, but she saw him adjust his jeans as he did so.

Good. *Take that, you tormentor.*

"Dad, West." Even she heard the lingering breathlessness in her voice. Usually that'd be enough to level her. She didn't fear her father, but she always strove to make the best possible impression on him.

Now . . . well, Dash had her distracted enough that she just didn't care. "I wasn't expecting you."

West's expression went from her to Dash and back again. Rubbing the back of his neck, he gave a chagrined smile. "I know. Sorry."

Dash stepped forward and held out his hand. "West."

Her brother accepted the shake, and Margo heard him whisper, "Sorry."

Dash glanced at her, but only smiled at West. "No problem."

Her father wasn't nearly as welcoming.

301

"You're still here?" He folded his thick arms over his thicker chest.

"Yes." Dash stepped away from him. "She's not supposed to be driving yet."

Margo felt the animosity swelling in the air and badly wanted to defuse things. "Dad, is everything okay?"

He looked at her arm. "Still wearing the brace, huh?"

"I see the doctor tomorrow. I assume he'll remove it then."

Grunting, he eyed her. "You were at work."

"Yes." She assumed he would approve of that at least.

"Dan said he put you on leave."

Yes, of course the two of them had conspired. Unwavering, Margo stared him in the eyes. "I haven't spoken to Dan."

Gaze narrowed and nasty, her father took a step closer. "You're calling him a liar?"

Used to this idiotic game, Margo lifted a brow and asked mildly, "Are you calling *me* a liar?" Rather than give her father a chance to admit he was, she tipped her head. "I've been gone since early morning. Perhaps he called and left a message."

"Personally," West said, "I think he'd be better served letting you work as long as you're up to it." And then, in a deliberate jab, he added, "Even if you weren't the most qualified — which you are — after routing out so many dirty cops, it's not like you have an overflow of available bodies to fill in for you."

Her father rounded on West. "That's bullshit and you know it!"

Dash stepped closer to her.

"It's a fact." West, unmoved by the riled expression on their father's face, grinned at Dash. "Margo swept the place clean. All the trash has been kicked to the curb, and if you know my sister at all, she's meticulous when it comes to replenishing the ranks."

That statement infuriated her father. "She threw out good men!"

Confused by the sudden contretemps, Dash slid his arm around her. The gesture wasn't missed by her already fuming father.

To sidetrack him from making Dash his target, Margo said, "Good men don't accept bribes, Dad. They don't steal evidence, don't coerce witnesses and don't cover for so-called friends who do. Good cops," she added, "put an end to that behavior."

West literally applauded her.

Going florid, her dad started forward — and suddenly Dash was in front of her.

*Oh, no,* Margo thought, her heart shooting into her throat. Her dad could be unpredictable at the best of times. She tried to face her father but Dash held her back.

"Martin." Dash's voice, calm and undaunted, rose above the sound of the blood rushing in her ears. "Obviously there's something personal going on here."

"Damn right," her father said. "It's personal — so none of your goddamned business."

"Margo is my business," Dash corrected him, still in that mild, unaffected tone. "I'm sure you would never hurt your daughter —"

West made a rude sound, earning a glare from her father. Dash never wavered at all.

"— but I think it would be better if you finished this conversation later, when everyone is a little cooler."

*Oh, God,* Margo thought. She did not need this happening right now.

An uneasy breeze stirred the turbulence in the air. The seconds ticked by in a blanket of smothering silence.

Finally, his voice edged with disgust, West said, "Thanks, Dash. Of course you're right." Tone hardening, he added, "And, Dad, we had to go anyway."

When Margo managed to peek around Dash, she saw West had moved close to their father while Martin continued to stare laser beams through Dash.

Relaxed, unconcerned, Dash remained in front of her — a living, breathing shield.

Teeth locked, Martin said, "I wasn't ready to leave."

No one spoke to him as Dash just had.

No one but her.

"Yeah," West confirmed. "You're leaving. Now."

Unlike his relationship with Margo, her brother never had to butt heads with their father because he often showed deference to West.

Lip curled, Martin gave Dash an ugly look, then smoothed his hand over his head. "Fine, but I need to hit the john before I go. Open up your door, Margo."

Margo would have told him to hold it, but Dash said, "I'll do it," and it was clear to one and all that he didn't want her that close to her father.

Did Dash honestly think he could run interference for the rest of her life? She'd learned to deal with her father; she knew his limits, where and when he'd draw the line — especially when it came to public spectacles that could lead to witnesses observing his boorish behavior.

Turning his back on her father — which, under other circumstances, could be a gigantic mistake — Dash gave her a reassuring smile. "Keys?"

She didn't like this, how he wrested even this control from her, leaving her to look like the clichéd little woman. It was especially bad in front of her father. She just knew her dad would give her hell about it later —

Dash touched her chin. "Margo?"

Knowing he meant well and anxious to get the dramatics over so she could have Dash to herself, Margo huffed and said, "Fine." She dug out her keys and dropped them into his extended hand.

He winked at her and, assuming her father would follow, turned away and headed for the front porch. Her father curled his lip . . . and followed.

Amazing. Margo kept her gaze on the men. It was shocking enough that her father hadn't kicked up more of a fuss, but when Dash followed him in, she wanted to groan.

"Ballsy," West said.

"You have no idea," Margo agreed.

Before she could get too worked up about it, Dash was back — with Oliver in his arms. The cat arched in bliss, rubbing himself against Dash's chest, his chin. Margo felt herself softening.

He was protecting her cat. How could she

not love that about him?

Though he stayed near the front door, at least he didn't go so far as to follow her father to the bathroom. Still, his positioning made it plain that he didn't trust the elder Peterson.

Mumbling to herself, Margo started to go to him — and West gently touched her shoulder.

"Wait up, will you?"

"Dash is pushing his luck."

West gave her a look. "Oh, I don't know." He glanced at the front porch and waved. Margo looked, too, and found Dash keeping an eye on her while he petted the cat. "I have a feeling your boyfriend can fend for himself."

Her face went hot and she sputtered, "He's not my boyfriend."

Typical of big brothers, West mussed her hair. "No use lying to me, sis." With a devilish grin, he tsked at her. "You two were fooling around in the car. Bet it was an unwelcome surprise to find us in the driveway, huh?"

More heat burned her cheeks. She wanted to kick West, but she'd probably just hurt her foot. Lifting her chin, she tried for a dose of defiance. "Yes, so?"

"So I'm happy for you." Carefully, because

of her splinted arm, he pulled her in for a brotherly hug. " 'Bout damn time, too. I like him. Not many guys would face off with Dad like that, especially when he's being such a prick."

"West!"

"Come off it, Margo. You know he's a bastard. Hell, most people know it. Thing is, you're one of the few who had the guts to stand up to him." Going somber, he smoothed the hair he'd just ruffled. "I'm proud of you."

Such an outpouring in her damned driveway only left her more flummoxed. There was no denying her dad could be a grade-A jerk. But the rest?

Trying to figure him out, she eyed West. "Why now?"

He rolled a massive shoulder. "I've always been proud."

"Baloney." The way she remembered it, West had been plenty pissed at her when she'd "stood up to" their dad.

Another breeze stirred, bringing with it the scent of rain.

Hands in his pockets, West looked up at the darkening sky, then to Dash and the cat. "You've got it wrong, you know." That quiet, too serious tone settled around her. "I just wasn't crazy about your timing."

"Things happen when they happen." With her dad, well, there had been no putting off the inevitable. Not if she hoped to keep a clear conscience.

Not if she was to live up to the standards she set for others.

"The timing could have screwed you over more than anyone else." He kept his voice low but some rough, anomalous emotion filled every word. "I should have known to trust you to work it out, though. And I'm sorry that I didn't. You blow it off as just doing the expected, but the way you've risen through the ranks is nothing short of impressive. The rest . . ." West again glanced at Dash standing vigilant on the front porch — while also staying very focused on Margo. "Well, let's just say you did what was right. I know it. Even Dad knows it — though I doubt you'll never hear him admit it."

A compliment from her father? Yeah, right. Compliments were for the weak needing validation. And she was never weak.

But the praise from her brother . . . it filled her like a sweet bubble. "I don't need anything from Dad. But from you . . ." What could she add to that? She shook her head. "It means a lot. Thank you."

"You're more than welcome." He nodded toward Dash. "I don't think he trusts me any more than he does Dad."

She turned her head — and found Dash staring at them.

Again.

*Still.*

Knowing the truth, Margo twisted her mouth and gave her attention back to her brother. "He trusts you or he'd have dragged me along with him to the porch, rather than leave us alone."

West cocked a brow. "You would allow that?"

The brisk, fresh air filled her lungs. So many weighty problems occupied her thoughts, yet with Dash, she felt more lighthearted than she knew was possible. "It's funny. He has this protective, almost gallant streak that somehow . . . flatters me."

"No kidding?" West grinned, showing his beautiful teeth and that undeniable charm that could win over Satan himself. "I never figured you for being that female. Even as a little bug you were pugnacious as hell, always determined to do everything I did, by yourself, without any help from anyone. Even a hint of assistance offended you grossly."

"I'm not a little girl anymore."

"No, but from what I could tell you've only grown more independent with age.

Hell, Margo, you make grown men shake in their boots."

"Don't be ridiculous."

He put a hand over his heart. "Swear. You do understand that's the reason most of them give you such a hard time, right? You intimidate the hell of out of them."

She laughed and shook her head. Sure, they resented her authority, disdained her rank, but she didn't know of any men who feared her.

"Laugh it up, but I'm not telling you a tale." Undecided for only a moment, he stepped closer and said, "Last week I had to threaten to deck a guy. I caught him running his mouth about you to two of his idiotic buddies."

"I don't want you fighting for me!"

A slow grin spread. "You see what I'm talking about?" He leaned down to face her and enunciated clearly. "I'm your big brother. Grant me the right to defend my little sis, will you?"

He sounded so silly, Margo's smile went crooked. Indulging him, she gestured for him to continue. "Okay, let's hear it. What heinous things did the knucklehead say about me?"

"He called you a ballbuster. Said you were always breathing down his neck, demanding perfection." West shrugged. "That's me prettying it up a little for your ears, by the way. No way will I repeat his exact words. But I'd like it to go on the record that your reaction is typical for you. You brush off their dumb insults like they're nothing, like the men giving them are nothing. And that, as much as anything else, really neuters a guy."

"So what? You think I haven't heard it all before?" But then curiosity got the better of her. "So what did you say to him?"

West rubbed his ear. "Well, first I told him to take out his tampon and stop PMSing."

"West!" The sexist remark should have annoyed her, but instead it had her laughing. And that, too, was another of Dash's influences. The gravity of her existence had been lightened by his presence.

West shared her amusement, even looking pleased by it. "I also told him you asked no more of others than you were willing to do yourself and if he couldn't keep up, then maybe he wasn't much of a man."

"Wow, bet he took that well."

"He's lucky all he got was a verbal slap because I really wanted to stomp him — and he knew it. The clincher, though, was when I told him I just might report his behavior to you. He apologized real quick and went on his way."

Smirking, Margo wondered if gratitude was in order or not. She settled on a shoulder bump and said, "Thanks for sticking up for me."

"If it's any consolation, his two buddies weren't impressed with him. They both told me they haven't had any problems with you. They said they're glad you're tightening things up."

Who were they? She badly wanted to know, but refused to ask. "Glad to hear it. But you have to know that's an isolated incident."

"Not."

"Dash has never been intimidated." Just the opposite. He took great pleasure in showing her how soft and small she was in comparison to his strength and size. And thinking that made her shiver anew. She needed to be alone with Dash. *Now.*

Looking over her head, West missed her reaction. "Given how Dash is scowling at Dad, I'd say it'd take a lot to unnerve that one."

She jerked around, and sure enough Dash and her father were headed toward them. Her father led the way with Dash close behind him. He must've put Oliver back in the house because he no longer held the cat, and the front door was again closed.

"Took him long enough," West observed.

"He probably made a private call." Maybe even to Dan. It wasn't beyond her father to tattle on her to the commander. "You know Dad and his . . . allies."

"Not as well as you do, obviously." West scowled. "If you need me to run interference —"

"I can deal with Dad."

"How you deal with him seems to have taken a sudden change. Should I credit Dash with that?"

He could credit overwhelming lust for the transformation; she needed to be alone with Dash and didn't mind angering her father to see it happen. But she wasn't going to explain any of that to her brother. "It's probably just your imagination."

"It's not, but I'll let it go for now." Leaning closer, he said in a low voice, "Before they get here, I want you to know that I'm done keeping quiet about things. It hasn't helped and in fact has only made matters worse." His hand touched her chin. "After that damned wreck . . . Well, we could have lost you."

"West," she said, letting him know she was fine.

"Just thought you should know, I'm here

if you need me."

*What in the world did that mean?* Margo wanted to ask, but her Dad already stepped between them.

"You said you see the doc tomorrow?"

Cautious, unsure of his motives, Margo nodded. "Yes."

"When?"

"A morning appointment." As Dash stepped up close to her, he slipped his arm around her waist — and even that inflamed her. "I should know something by noon or so."

He ignored Dash. "You'll go into work after that?"

"I'll probably come by here first to dress in appropriate clothes." *And molest Dash.* She straightened her spine. "And then, yes, I'll go in to the station."

As if he'd expected no less, he nodded. "I heard about your newest case."

How much did he know? Did he know that someone had offered a reward for her? That some very twisted individuals wanted to punish her? She hoped not. Given her father's mercurial mood swings, she didn't know if he'd smirk, expect her to single-handedly find the men . . . or maybe even offer herself as bait.

Refusing to give anything away, Margo

asked, "What case is that?"

Annoyed by her obvious evasion, Martin waved a hand. "This kerosene business. Sick shit."

"Yes." Very sick.

"But you shouldn't be involved." He pointed at her. "Dan told you to take time away, and that's what you should do."

Good, he didn't know. She felt Dash watching her, felt his presence beside her. It was comforting, but also unnerving because she shouldn't want or need his comfort. "I would only be off duty until I got clearance. Tomorrow the doctor will give me clearance."

"Maybe." Her father gave her his patented glare of censure. "Who's your doctor?"

Did he hope to butt in, to maybe influence a medical specialist? She wouldn't put it past him. But if so, why? One minute he badgered her about not working, and now he acted as if he wanted to prohibit her from it. "You don't know him, Dad, but don't worry. He has an excellent reputation."

"Great," West said. "I expect to hear from you tomorrow, okay? Let me know what he says."

"Sure."

West opened the passenger door, holding it for Martin. "Let's go, Dad. I have a

316

hundred things to do yet today, and we've interrupted enough."

In lieu of reassuring either of them that they hadn't interrupted at all, Margo dismissed them by saying, "Drive carefully."

Her father didn't ask for a call. He didn't say anything. He just mean-mugged Dash a little, turned and settled his large frame into West's car.

Margo watched as they backed out. She watched as they drove up the street, as they started around the corner.

Dash watched her. "Your family doesn't know about the bounty put on your head?"

"God, no. Trust me, we'll all be better off if my family stays out of my business." Even West, who claimed to want to support her, would complicate things if he knew.

"You and West talked for so long, I assumed you told him."

Oh no, she wouldn't get sidetracked with lengthy conversations. She knew she was in over her head when even a visit from her father didn't dilute her physical need for this one specific man.

Grabbing Dash's hand, she started for the front door. "You've made a lot of promises," she told him. "Now it's time for you to pay up."

# CHAPTER FOURTEEN

Dash planted his feet and refused to budge. "Slow down, Margo. I need to grab our stuff from the car."

Looking frustrated enough to attack, she jerked around to blast him — and Dash took her mouth in a devouring kiss that quickly had her subdued. Little by little he lightened up, teasing with his tongue, tasting her, pushing her closer to the edge.

Turning her on turned him on, too. But he knew what would happen and when — and she didn't. That gave him a much-needed advantage.

He eased away from her lush mouth and panting breaths, then had to untangle her fingers from his shirt. Lifting her hand, he kissed her knuckles and felt the tension quivering through her. It wouldn't take too much more, and she'd be wound so tight, he'd have her screaming with an orgasm with very little effort.

Keeping his tone controlled, he stated, "I want you to go on in. Take a few minutes with Oliver. I'll be right there."

Her beautiful dark eyes searched his face. "And then?"

"And then you're going to take off your clothes and wait for me while I get dinner started."

Her lips parted on a protest, but she said nothing.

Dash could see the simmering excitement in her wary gaze. Making it clear he assumed her agreement, he asked, "Will you need any help?"

Uncertainly, she shook her head. "No," she said in a very small voice.

"Wear the sling if you need it, but nothing else." He cupped the side of her face, let his thumb brush her jaw. "Once I have everything cooking, I'll see to you."

Her breasts shimmered with a shakily indrawn breath. Again she started to speak, but didn't. Three more deep breaths later, she turned and headed for the house.

Dash watched her go, his muscles drawn tight, his chest restricted. He was so hard he could be lethal, and he knew it wasn't the game.

It was the woman. *His* woman — once she realized how perfectly suited they were.

When she stepped into the house, Dash turned and went to the car. Yes, he wanted to cook dinner for her; as he'd told her, she needed to eat. But this was about more than food and they both knew it.

Deliberately he'd bought boneless chicken so he could cook it more quickly, though at the time he hadn't seen this particular scenario playing out. He definitely hadn't planned to be sidetracked by her brother or father.

Her father. Jaw tight, Dash shook his head. Something was going on there, something personal and difficult and, at least for Margo, emotionally troubling.

Today she'd made him so proud, standing up to her father, unblinking when most people would quail under the big man's disapproval. He thought about calling Logan to see if his brother knew of any family issues between them, but that felt disloyal and he couldn't make himself do it.

Later, after he had her soft and replete, he'd ask Margo himself and hopefully she'd confide in him.

When Dash walked into the house, loaded down with his bag and the groceries, Margo was on the couch still giving attention to Oliver. He smiled toward her, and she reciprocated with defiance. That made him grin.

"Do you like oven-fried chicken?"

Her expression faltered. "Yes."

"Good. It'll take me about twenty minutes to get it in the oven and get the potatoes boiling. Then I'll have about thirty minutes before I have to do anything more to it." Thirty minutes that he'd spend on her.

He went on past her, down the hall first to drop off his bag in her bedroom. He'd brought a few changes of clothes — and plenty of condoms. Best to leave those in the overnight bag for now, though. He didn't want to tempt himself.

With that done, he left the bedroom and went up the hall and into the kitchen. Margo hadn't yet moved, but he didn't worry about it.

She was struggling with things, slowly coming to grips with the depth of their relationship. He cared enough to give her all the time and attention she needed until she completely accepted him.

First he set the oven, and then Dash found flour in the cabinet, an egg and butter in the fridge. In the bottom oven drawer he located a thick cast-iron skillet.

He felt more than heard Margo's approach and glanced at her over his shoulder.

Her dark eyes were huge, her face flushed.

Her nipples were tight points against her blouse.

He loved seeing her like this. *He just plain loved her.* "Everything okay?"

Her gaze moved over his back, down his spine to his ass and then his thighs. "If I get naked, are you going to get naked, too?"

He wouldn't lie to her. As he cracked the egg into a bowl, he shook his head. "Not just yet." Next he put the flour on a plate.

"Why do I need to be naked?"

Was that a note of worry?

Maybe apprehension over what he'd do?

Margo was one of the bravest people he'd ever met, but she didn't like the unknown.

He, however, liked it a lot because it gave him the advantage in dealing with her. He wanted everything; she wanted sex. It would take patience to show her how perfectly suited they were.

Without looking at her, he said, "So I can make you come."

Silence.

Without changing his demeanor, Dash turned to face her. "And so I can enjoy looking at you, and you can get comfortable with me."

Her chin lifted. "I'm comfortable."

"Then what's the problem?"

The seconds ticked by. Closing her eyes, she leaned back on the wall and groaned. "I don't know how you do this to me!"

So that neither of them would misunderstand, he said, "Make you hot?"

*"Yes."*

Dash studied her for a moment, then put butter in the cast-iron skillet and slid it into the oven to melt. Wiping his hands on a dish towel, he approached her. "We have a lot of chemistry between us."

"Then why aren't you just as turned on as I am?"

"You think I'm not?" He took her right wrist and carried her hand to the front of his jeans — against his straining erection. His breath caught at the first touch of her small fingers. "I'm dying to get inside you, honey. But I'm also determined to make this as good for you as it can be. And that means indulging the things you like, paying attention and really ramping up the pleasure for you."

"If you ramp it up any more, I'm going to lose it."

Her hand touching him made it difficult to stay on track. "Good."

Her fingers squeezed him through the denim. "I would like it if you'd just —"

"Shh. No." For the sake of his own control, he lifted her hand away. "You might think you'll enjoy taking over, but you'll like submitting more." It was the use of that particular word that really got to her. *Submit.* It was such an alien concept for such a dominating woman.

Dash waited.

She chewed her lower lip, looked away from him and whispered, "Is this what you do with other women?"

"I don't want other women." He needed her to understand that. Since meeting her, no one else had held his interest.

"In the past then. Is this some favorite game of yours?"

Touching her became a living, breathing necessity. He wedged his hand around the sling and cupped her right breast, then used his thumb to abrade her stiffened nipple.

On a soft moan, she closed her eyes again and shivered all over. Her reaction gratified him.

"I'll admit this — taking charge is a favorite of mine. But if you want to try anything else, you just need to let me know."

Her eyes narrowed on him. "Has any woman ever told you no?"

"Over a preferred fantasy?" He shrugged. "Of course."

"What?" Curiosity replaced some of the

324

heat. "What did you want to do that she didn't?"

That particular look in her eyes almost made him laugh. He could tell she was imagining a dozen wrong scenarios. "I think I'll save that confession for another day." He bent and kissed her nose. "Right now, I'd rather concentrate on you, with me, and how right this all feels. Okay?"

"Tomorrow, when I get cleared —"

"If you get cleared." He hated the thought of her pushing herself too hard.

"Tomorrow I just might switch things up."

She said it like a threat and his smile broke free. "Then I'll look forward to your efforts. But for now, tonight, trust me to know what you need." He punctuated that by plucking at her nipple, tugging, twisting the smallest bit.

And even that, such a simple thing, nearly pushed her over the edge.

Dash withdrew. He let his hands hang at his sides and just watched her, enjoying how the sensual fog cleared from her gaze, how she struggled to bring herself back from the brink.

Using her hand to push away from the wall, her gaze evasive, she nodded and turned away. "Forget your torturous bath. I'll go wash up all by my lonesome."

"You don't need any help?"

"Your idea of help will kill me."

"Spoilsport." Dash patted her backside. "Tomorrow then."

She looked at him over her shoulder. "When you're ready, I'll be in the bedroom."

That particular tone from her nearly sent his heart punching through his chest. God, he had it bad, and he was staking everything on sex games. He had to be good, better than good, because he had a feeling she'd use any excuse to end their relationship.

Oliver strolled into the kitchen, wound around Dash's ankles and brought him out of his ruminations. A second later he heard the water turn on in the bathroom.

Quickly Dash finished preparing the chicken, put it into the cast-iron skillet and closed the oven door. In record time he peeled a few potatoes, cut them up and put them on to boil.

To keep the cat busy he filled Oliver's food dish and drinking fountain, then washed and dried his hands. He'd given Margo twenty minutes — more than long enough.

Anticipation riding him hard, he tossed aside the dish towel and headed down the hallway to find her. As he passed the bathroom he peeked inside, but wasn't surprised not to find her there. She'd left behind a damp towel on the floor, and a wet tooth-brush on the sink. He grinned and decided it wouldn't hurt to do his own freshening up.

In the bathroom he glanced in the mirror. He should probably shave again to keep from scratching her, but the idea of her waiting, naked, in her room kicked that idea to the curb.

In under two minutes he stepped into the bedroom doorway and saw her seated at the side of the bed, bare except for her panties. Her small feet were together, her right hand resting on the mattress at the side of her hip, her splinted left over her lap. She kept her back ramrod-straight, her chest rising with deep breaths.

More excited than he'd ever been with a woman, Dash stepped inside, closing the door quietly behind him. "Margo."

She glanced up, then stood.

Dash stayed near the door. "Why aren't you naked?"

She came to him, breathing fast, her gaze heated. She flattened her right hand over his chest, dragged it down over his pectoral muscle, down to the waistband of his jeans, then lower still to his throbbing cock. "I was waiting for you."

Hiding her smile, Margo took in the added signs of arousal in Dash's face, how his nostrils flared, the color that rose on his high cheekbones.

Good.

One way or another, she was determined to push him. Yes, she enjoyed him being gently dominant. Actually, she *loved* it.

But even more than that, she wanted him. It was an odd realization, and the usual turn-ons still applied, but . . . *anything* with Dash was thrilling. Too thrilling.

She couldn't take much more teasing, but he had a lot of catching up to do.

Dash caught her hand, pressing it hard to his erection. Still soft-spoken and far too composed, he said, "Take the panties off now."

"You take them off for me."

His lazy smile sent her stomach into a somersault. He touched her cheek, her lips. And suddenly he turned her so that her back was to his chest. His hands came around her, one at her breasts, the other at the front of her panties.

"Did you enjoy your bath?"

"All three minutes of it." Breathing wasn't

easy. She leaned back into him. "I kept thinking about what you wanted to do, and I want that, too. But tonight I just can't take it."

"As strong as you are?" His tongue touched her ear, then she felt his warm, moist breath. "You could take it."

Oh, God. His fingertips teasing her nipple was arousing enough, his erection against her backside was enough to level her. "You're too good at this."

"This?"

"Foreplay."

Still near her ear, he whispered, "Let me see for myself."

Hot fingertips moved over the crotch of her silken panties, exploring, stroking. Putting her head back to his hard chest, she stiffened her legs and gave in to his touch.

"Mmm," he murmured low. "You're nice and wet. Were you in here thinking of me?"

"Yes." As an invitation, she deliberately widened her stance.

Dash kissed the side of her neck, her shoulder. "I love you like this, Margo." As he said it, he pressed his cock to her rounded backside and at the same time he carefully pinched her nipple.

For so many reasons, she stiffened. *Love?* The use of that word sent panic into her heart. And the tantalizing tug on her nipple . . .

"You like that, don't you."

*Very much.* "Yes."

He put his hand into her panties, his rough fingertips moving over her, opening her, testing her. "Do you think you can come standing up?" Not giving her a chance to answer, he added, "Let's find out."

Margo assumed he'd use his fingers, now damp from her, but instead he again turned her — and went to one knee.

Oh, God . . .

Without haste, he pulled her panties down her legs but didn't give her a chance to step out of them. They remained around her ankles, hobbling her, making her somehow feel more exposed than if they'd been completely removed.

His absorbed gaze moved all over her. "Damn, I love it that you're so small. It makes everything easier to reach." Leaning forward, he licked her nipple while his fingers returned to playing between her legs, parting her, teasing back and forth in her slick moisture, then slowly pressing two fingers deep.

She couldn't help but react, stepping back from the intense pleasure.

"No, none of that," Dash whispered.

Opening his other hand on her behind, he kept her close and pulled his fingers free, now glistening wet, to touch them to her nipple. "You want this, so don't fight me."

His breath brushed her skin seconds before he drew her nipple in, sucking gently but insistently. At the same time, he wedged his hand back between her thighs, then twisted his fingers deep again.

She was already so ripe with need that, between his mouth on her breast and his stroking fingers rasping her sensitive flesh, she felt the start of a climax building. She tightened, her body clamping down on his slippery fingers. *"Dash . . ."* she groaned.

"So soon?" Dash asked with sympathy and a bit of awe. "I guess I'd better get right to it, then."

Margo didn't know for sure what that meant until he began kissing his way down her body. Expectation held her breath; she knew he'd use his mouth on her and she was so very anxious for it she almost couldn't stand it.

"You are so soft," he said between open-mouth love bites down her ribs, over her belly, her hip bones. Sliding one arm around her waist, the other splayed over her backside, he held her still — and nuzzled between her legs.

Crying out, Margo locked her knees and held on to him. His hot, rough tongue stroked repeatedly over her, in her, then came up to curl around her clitoris with a hungry growl.

He gave only the slightest tug and she lost it, the orgasm crashing through her, stealing her breath and strength with an explosion of scorching sensation. She cried, and didn't care. She clutched at him, and didn't care. She pressed closer to his mouth, begging, and didn't even realize it.

Seconds, maybe minutes later, she became aware of Dash lowering her boneless body into his lap, cuddling her close and kissing her hair, rubbing her back. Beneath her hip she felt the very solid rise of his impressive boner.

Astounding. Almost shocking. And *so* wonderful. She would have laughed if she'd had the strength.

Instead all she could say was "God."

"Yeah," Dash murmured, lust keeping his voice rough. "You're fucking amazing." He continued kissing her, his touch both affectionate and tender and hot.

Trying to catch her breath, she said, "That was . . ."

"I know." He curved a big rough hand around her breast, his palm to her galloping heartbeat. He kissed her again, leaving his mouth pressed to her temple as he hugged her close.

"It was even better than before."

"Good." He kissed her neck, her shoulder.

"And to think I expected sex with you to be boring."

Dash froze.

Margo realized what she'd said, knew she owed him an explanation, but at the moment she still struggled for air.

Levering her back a little, Dash studied her. "Boring?"

Damn her postcoital babbling. "Not boring exactly." Her brain had a hard time catching up. "I didn't mean that." But never, not at any other time, had a sexual encounter left her so limp or affected her so strongly. She leaned in, but Dash turned his head.

"What *did* you mean?"

Putting a hand to his jaw, she brought his face back so she could kiss him — and tasted herself. She tucked her face into his throat, overwhelmed by his scent, his warmth. "I . . . You realize . . ."

"Tell me." He scooted to sit up a little higher against the door, Margo held secure in his lap. "You thought I was a two-minute man? You thought I was a selfish pig? What?"

"No, none of that." She tried to keep hidden against him but Dash didn't let her.

Holding her shoulder, his expression enigmatic, his tone devoid of emotion, he said again, "Tell me."

"I assumed you would be . . . competent —"

He laughed without humor.

"— but conventional, and maybe not up to my . . . preferences." Preferences that she now realized didn't matter, not with Dash. He could go for plain-old missionary and she thought she'd probably go wild with enjoyment.

He seemed to be considering that while studying her breasts. With one fingertip, he circled her nipple, then, still in that flat way, asked, "Your arm is okay?"

"Yes." The change of subject felt evasive, but she wanted to stay on track, to reassure him, to . . . What? Keep him interested? Was she really that insecure? That pathetic?

The possibility annoyed her enough that she scowled. "Stop asking already. I'm a big girl. If something hurts, I'll take care of it."

As if her acerbic attitude didn't faze him, he looked at her quivering belly, then down between her damp legs. "Your body is still flushed."

She didn't understand him at all. "Like I

said, it was an amazing climax."

"So you feel better now? Less wired? More relaxed?"

Damn him and his impersonal interrogation. "Yes. I'm fine."

"Good." Suddenly he rearranged her, moving her off his lap and onto the floor as he stood. "I need to check our dinner."

Her jaw loosening, Margo stared up at him. *"Now?"* He was still hard. And though she'd found release, she was far from done.

He touched his hand to the top of her head. "Yes — now. Get dressed and then come to the kitchen."

Margo gasped. How dare he give her an order?

How dare he leave her sitting naked on the damned floor!

She had to scoot out of the way when he opened the door and walked out of the bedroom.

At first she felt hurt — and then her temper ignited.

Enough already. No way would she let him get away with this.

*Why did he have the ability to leave her so befuddled?*

Shoving to her feet, she snatched up the quilt from the bed and stalked after him. Voice raised and mean, she spoke to his retreating back. "What is *wrong* with you?"

Several feet ahead of her, without haste, Dash entered the kitchen and used a pot holder to remove the chicken from the oven.

Brows drawn, she stared at him. "Damn it, Dash." She wanted him to react. She wanted to get a rise out of him.

"Stay back," he told her as he set the heavy cast-iron skillet on the stove top. "I don't want you to get burned."

Because her legs were still shaky and weak, she dropped back to the wall. "You're being impossible."

Nothing.

She watched him turn the chicken and return it to the oven, then put on vegetables to steam. "Chicken is one of my favorites."

"I know."

Vaguely she remembered him questioning her during his routine check of her concussion. And now, knowing her preferences, he'd been considerate enough to cook for her.

She felt like the bitch others often called her. "I didn't mean to insult you."

He turned to her. "Dinner will be ready in ten." His gaze went over her. "You going to eat in that?"

Would it bother him? Unlike her, he hadn't yet gotten his jollies. "Why not?" He might be pissed, but still her body kept drawing his notice. She liked that enough that she even let the quilt droop lower on one side until a nipple almost showed. "With this stupid splint it's difficult to get a shirt on."

When Dash pushed away from the stove, his own expression unreadable, a new thrill danced up her spine. Even now, with him obviously disappointed in her early perceptions of him, she knew he was determined to make her hot.

As he approached, she resisted the urge to back up. "What are you doing?"

He stopped in front of her and his big hands took hold of the quilt near her breasts. "If you want to turn me on, it's working." The way he curled his fingers over the material meant his knuckles brushed her skin. "But you know what would work better?"

She shook her head.

With a small smile, he slowly pulled away the quilt, leaving her naked. "God, you have a kickin' body."

The way he looked at her made her feel sexier than she'd ever imagined.

His hands went over her, stroking her breasts again, caressing down her belly. One hand moved over her ass and then up between her legs. He bent and kissed her, a slow, thorough kiss with plenty of tongue that made her legs weak all over again.

He kissed her until she clung to him, her breath rushing, her skin hot.

Gently he pulled away. "Let's see how we're progressing here." He stared into her eyes while the fingers between her legs examined her, then his eyes darkened with satisfaction. "Nice. It seems we're both in the same shape again."

"What . . ."

"I'm still rock-hard. It only seems right for you to be bothered a little, too, right?" Pulling off his shirt, he dropped it over her head, easily working her splinted arm through first, then her other arm.

It smelled of him, hot and delicious, and cocooned her in his scent.

So unfair. Now she was covered, but she had the view of his solid shoulders and wide chest.

He pulled out her chair as if he expected her to sit. "I hope you're hungry, honey. I made plenty."

Margo didn't know what to do. He just stood there, waiting oh-so-patiently, his gaze unwavering, so damn hot that she wanted to jump him.

He was right. Carnal need again racked

her body.

"Trust me," Dash whispered as he held out a hand to her, and the gesture was so sweet, a way to help her give in, that she blew out a breath and did as he asked.

Gratified, he bent and kissed her forehead — then went back to cooking as if the standoff hadn't happened at all. And damn it, that turned her on, too.

It seemed Dashiel Riske had her completely figured out. The man had the most diabolical way of turning her inside out, making her nearly frantic to have him. Margo didn't know if that was a good thing, or very, very dangerous . . . for her heart.

# CHAPTER FIFTEEN

Dash felt her watching him as he put two aspirin next to her plate and filled her glass with iced tea. "You can ask me anything, you know that, right?"

Confusion kept her brows pinched down. She tossed back the aspirin. "The chicken smells good."

"It's my grandmother's recipe. Mom is an okay cook, but my grandma could put twenty pounds on anyone." He smiled as he served first her, then himself. "But we both know that's not what you want to talk about." He joined her at the table.

It was the oddest thing, watching Margo screw up her nerve. She was a fearless woman who would put herself in the line of fire to save someone else, but now, with him, over chicken dinner, she seemed so uncertain.

Dash sat back. "Out with it, honey. Then we can both enjoy our meal."

Predictably enough, her chin lifted and she met his gaze. "Fine." It took a second as she seemed to search for the words. "You said . . . you said you loved it when I was . . ." More searching, and she settled on, "Passive."

Now what was she thinking? Dash crossed his arms over his chest. "I love seeing how turned on you get. So?"

"So I'm seldom like that. It's not really me, it's just —"

"It's you," Dash corrected her. No way would he let her deny how good the sex was between them.

That she'd once thought him boring . . . yeah, that burned his ass big-time. Hopefully he'd already disabused her of that notion. But it bothered him enough that he thought about giving in to her tonight. He worried for her injured arm, but he could take extra care — and utilizing that care would, in itself, be another form of foreplay.

"You know what I mean, Dash."

"I do." He knew her far better than she realized. "Occasionally enjoying a submissive role during sex is only a small part of who you are. But it's honest, and important." Catching on to her concern, he sat forward, his arms folded on the tabletop. "I love seeing you all warm and aroused, waiting for me to take care of you. But I also love it when you're cocky like you were today with that idiot in the truck. Much as it scared me, it also impressed me." He grinned at her. "I even like it when you're all prickly, giving me a hard time."

She shook her head, maybe in disbelief, maybe in confusion.

Dash reached for her hand. "And I love how you are right now, uncertain but straightforward with me, determined to draw some boundaries in our relationship."

"Is it a relationship?"

His gaze narrowed. "Yes."

She searched his face for the longest time. "And if I'm ever not in the mood to be docile?"

He grinned. "Then bring it on. I guarantee I can handle it." *Because I can handle you, every fascinating part of your personality.* But he decided not to voice that confidence just yet.

"You wouldn't mind?"

"I'm sure we'll enjoy ourselves all the same." Because being with her could never be less than mind-blowing.

She gave it a lot of thought and then with a slight smile, she released his hand and picked up her fork. "All right."

That was a mighty easy capitulation. "I'm

not boring?" He wanted to hear her admit it.

"Ha! No, definitely not boring." She eyed his chest. "You're so exciting, I'm not sure I can take much more."

Maybe she shouldn't have to. He'd see how she felt after dinner — and make up his mind then. It was that "boring" comment that made him want to prove himself, he knew, but what the hell, he was only a man and he had his pride.

It amazed Dash to see her dig into her dinner. "Mmm, this is good."

Fickle woman.

They were halfway through dinner when Margo got a call from Rowdy. She heard her cell ringing from the bedroom, where she'd left it in her purse, and started to stand.

Dash waved her back to her seat. "I'll get it for you."

"It could be the station," she said, getting up to follow him anyway.

Dash had no intention of breeching her privacy. He just picked up the purse and carried it back to her, meeting her in the hallway. Quickly she dug out the phone and answered on the sixth ring.

"Hello? Oh, Rowdy, hi." She gave Dash a quick glance and headed back to the kitchen. "What's up?"

Dash silently followed her. Unlike the last time he'd seen her with Rowdy, there was no inflection in her tone other than mild interest.

Jealousy was a bitch. He fucking hated it.

*She'd thought he would be boring — but she had wanted Rowdy.*

Hiding his feelings on the matter wasn't easy. Definitely, tonight, he would have her.

When she reached the table he held out her chair and she smiled at him as she seated herself. "When was this?" she asked Rowdy. And then she said, "I'll have Reese and Logan check it out." She listened, then scowled. "So I'm finding out last?"

Dash reseated himself across from her.

Her discontent intensified and she stiffened. "Damn it." She listened, shook her head. "Yes, you do that. And next time call me first." More listening, and then a sigh. "No, I would have sent . . . Well, yeah. All right, fine. I understand. Call me if you find out anything else." She closed the phone, looked ready to toss it and instead set it carefully on the tabletop.

"Trouble?" Dash asked.

She forked up some veggies. "Rowdy got a lead on where the firebugs might've been hiding out. He told Logan about it, and he and Reese went to check it out."

*Ah.* So Rowdy had bypassed her. "He went to them first because they were already out and about?"

"That's what he says. I still think he should have told me first. There's a proper order to the way things should be done."

Dash saluted. He, himself, had a proper order in mind . . . for winning her over.

Margo's eyes narrowed on him. "I guess it doesn't really matter. By the time the boys got there, the place was toast."

The boys. Funny that she would refer to two such competent detectives that way. "Toast how?"

"Burned down. It was an abandoned garage and someone torched it."

Thinking of the threat against her, Dash stiffened. The ones responsible proved more dangerous by the hour. "It was empty? No one else was hurt."

"Thankfully." She ate a few more bites. "I'll call your brother in a minute to find out the rest of the details, and of course we'll still check for evidence since Rowdy insists his informant was solid, but it's doubtful we'll be able to find much. Rowdy is going back to his snitch to see if there's anything new."

"Was it burned with kerosene?"

Before she could answer, a knock sounded on her door. Margo groaned. "It's like Grand Central Station around here."

Dash left the table again, pausing to pull out her chair. "You might want to get a housecoat or something. I'll answer the door for you."

Grousing, she grabbed up one more bite of chicken on her way out.

Oliver awoke with the knock and he darted into the kitchen to hide under the table. Dash sympathized with him, gave him a few quick treats and went to the door.

Logan and Reese stood there. The sky had darkened and it smelled like rain, but so far the skies remained dry. "Hey."

Giving him a disgruntled frown, Logan pushed his way in. "Where's Peterson?"

Margo appeared around the corner. "Is something wrong?"

Logan and Reese both froze comically, their gazes going all over her from her tiny bare feet to the tightly cinched belt on her robe, to her tousled hair and makeup-free face.

Logan's widened gaze came back to Dash and stayed there.

Reese looked at the ceiling, the floor, his own feet.

Fighting a grin, Dash said, "Come on in.

We were just having dinner."

"Fried chicken," Logan said while sniffing the air. And then to Reese he added, "He makes it just like our grandma does."

"Damn, that smells good," Reese told him. "Don't suppose you have any left?"

"A little. You want to —"

Margo cleared her throat loudly. "Why. Are. You. Here?"

Reluctantly, Logan turned to her again.

Dash almost laughed at the resolute look on his brother's face as he tried to keep his gaze north of Margo's breasts beneath the soft terry robe.

"Rowdy said he called you about the fire?"

"Yes."

Logan rolled a shoulder as if to relieve tension. "Yeah, well, we have some news. Rowdy was going to call you back, but I figured since we were out I might as well give it to you in person."

"Less chance of plans being intercepted that way," Reese told her.

Dash realized they were all still worried about controlling things, and the possibility of any residual corruption left at the station.

"Why don't we sit in the kitchen?" Dash asked. "They can eat while they talk."

"Fine." Margo led the way.

Reese glanced at her ass in the robe, then quickly away. He looked guilty as hell about it, too.

Glaring at Dash, Logan fell into line behind Reese.

It was too damn funny how they both continued to see her in such a one-dimensional way, which, in part, probably contributed to the difficulty Margo had in coming to grips with the different facets of her personality — facets he'd brought to the fore. If everyone else saw her only as a severe authoritarian, how hard must it be for her to show her softer, more vulnerable side?

While Dash divided the rest of the food on plates for his brother and Reese, Logan pulled out a chair and dropped into it. "A few hours before the fire started in that building, some neighborhood kids found kerosene dumped everywhere. They called Cannon because they thought it looked suspicious. Cannon says the kids claimed it was tossed on the walls, all over the floors and on some old tires."

With grave reservations, Reese sat next to Margo. "Cannon, of course, called us. Before we could get there, though —"

"Fire?" Dash filled in.

"The rear door had been pried open —

the boys said they found it like that. They cut through that back alley on their way home from shooting baskets down at Cannon's rec center."

"Good thing they didn't stumble into whoever set the fire." Dash could only imagine what might have happened to the kids if they had.

"That's what Cannon said," Logan confirmed. "He plans to talk to them about *not* going that way anymore."

"They need to avoid all alleyways, in my opinion," Reese added. And then to Margo, "I was going to talk to some of the unis about patrolling along that way a little more often, especially around the time the rec center closes up."

"Good idea." Margo fidgeted a moment. "How long before the fire marshal has a report?"

Dash noted her quiet, lethal manner now. Despite her lack of proper clothing, she was back to being a lieutenant, chillingly furious, probably over the fire and the possible danger to the kids. Not giving a damn what Logan or Reese thought, he reached over and took her hand.

Brows raised, she looked at his hand, nonplussed, and her gaze crawled up his arm to his face.

He didn't smile, but he didn't look away, either.

Relenting, Margo accepted the contact and curled her fingers with his.

It took Logan a second to shake off his discomfort. "Chief Williams said there were a series of small explosions that he assumes were tires blowing from the heat. He hadn't yet determined exactly how the fire ignited, but he's leaning toward deliberate vandalism."

Margo stewed in silence a moment. "No one knows we didn't find evidence. Whoever started the fire didn't expect kids to call it in so quickly. They probably assumed the building would burn to the ground. But it's still standing?"

"It is," Reese said. "The firemen got it under control right away, but everything is a mess."

"None of the other buildings — also vacant — were affected," Logan said. "Except for some external smoke damage."

"So . . ." Margo looked around the table at each of them. "We could let word out that we found a few leads. Yes?"

"Tell a few lies?" Logan slowly nodded. "Might push the bastards to show themselves."

Reese grinned. "Want me to put the word out?"

"No." A sly smile eased away her frown. "Given their connections, I think it'd be better if Cannon and Rowdy put the word out on the street."

"Hell of an idea."

"And if that doesn't work . . ." Margo drew a deep breath. "I could make myself available."

"You already did that," Dash said, starting to feel uneasy.

Logan scowled at her. "She means to set herself up as bait."

Ice ran through Dash's veins. "No."

"It's not up to you," she said mildly. "And, no, it wouldn't be my first choice."

Dash sat frozen, his gaze drilling into his brother — but Logan wouldn't meet his eyes. Because he agreed with her? Fuck.

"Let's try this first." Logan stood, his cell phone in hand. "I'll get hold of Rowdy right now."

Reese also moved from the table. "I'll talk with Cannon. I was going to stop by tonight to check on the kids who saw the whole thing anyway."

With satisfaction plain on her face, Margo watched them get started.

His brother would just have to make it

work, Dash decided.

Margo looked at the tabletop for several heartbeats before lifting her gaze to his. "I'm a damn good cop."

"I know." He really did.

"You can't interfere."

That fact made him all the more anxious to bind her to him somehow. He forced himself to nod. "Okay."

Her smile flickered over her face. "The lie might work. Right now the goons are smug, thinking we're lost — which we are. But if they start to worry, they'll make a mistake."

"And then you'll have them."

"Yes. And then I'll have them."

Logan spoke to Rowdy, updating him on the plans. Reese was on the phone with Cannon, making arrangements to drop by.

"Promise me you'll be careful," Dash said.

"Always." Somber, she said, "If I screw this up, another woman could be hurt."

And she'd never allow that.

Now, more than ever, Dash couldn't wait to get her alone.

Oliver sat in her lap through half an hour of a boring sitcom. Dash, who could have worked the inquisition, insisted on tidying the kitchen — shirtless — while she relaxed. Or rather, tried to relax. Instead, though, her gaze repeatedly sought him out as he moved around in the other room, giving her occasional glimpses of his magnificent body through the doorway.

Whenever he happened to look up and catch her watching him, he smiled. A few times he even asked her if she needed any-thing.

*Sex,* she wanted to say, but he already knew that and she saw no reason to keep belaboring the point.

Normally, on a night like this, she would have been stewing over the case and feeling the futility of trying to locate scumbags before they committed another crime. That frustration was there, but other frustrations trumped it and in some way, it helped her to keep a clearer head where work was concerned. It never made sense to obsess over a case. Doing so kept someone from seeing the obvious.

Right now, on top of the regular due diligence, she could only wait and hope that the tale Rowdy and Cannon would spread would force the bastards to react in a way that left them less protected.

Pans rattled as Dash put them away, and then water ran in the sink. That was enough to, again, distract her.

No one, ever, had pampered her like this.

Even as a child she couldn't recall anyone telling her to sit and relax.

Not that Dash was a martyr. She had no doubt that once she was 100 percent again, he'd enjoy her help in . . . everything. Cooking, cleaning, caring for Oliver.

Sex.

As he exited the kitchen, her eyes ate him up. She wanted to see him naked, to touch him all over —

He paused in front of her, a small knowing smile making him sexier than ever. "I'm done with the kitchen so I'm going to jump in the shower. I'll need about twenty minutes so I can shave, too." He rubbed his bristly jaw and some rough emotion darkened his voice. "You're so soft all over, I don't want to risk giving you whisker burns."

Margo's eyes widened. But with that cryptic comment, which made her stomach tumble over, he walked away.

She twisted to watch him go — and saw he was grinning. How could he give her whisker burns if he refused to have sex with her? Or — oh, God — did he plan to make her insane again while denying himself with another of his superhuman shows of control?

When he disappeared into the bathroom

and shut the door, she dropped back in her seat. Oliver, disgruntled, resettled himself over her lap.

For the next few minutes her imagination drummed up every sensual possibility known to man. She could hear the shower going, and in her mind she could see him naked, his hard, muscled body wet and glistening, how the water would trail through his gorgeous body hair, over his chest, his abs, down that tantalizing happy trail —

The water shut off and her heart missed a beat. An invisible ribbon pulled tight deep inside her. She realized she'd stopped petting Oliver, that her hands were still and her gaze staring off at nothing in particular.

Oliver stretched, yawned and made his way off the couch — with her help — to go to his bed. He turned three circles, pawing a blanket this way and that before dropping down and stretching out flat, his front paws off one end of the bed, his back paws off the other, his little furry face relaxed.

Margo smiled at him. He was still the sweetest cat ever. No one in her family, not even West, liked to pet him.

But Dash did. He was as attentive to the cat as she was.

She let out a sigh.

"Feeling melancholy?"

Twisting around again, she found Dash standing there, his hair still damp, finger-combed back from his freshly shaved face. He wore only drawstring lounge pants that hung low on his lean hips.

No shirt.

Mercy.

Mouth going dry, Margo stared as he looked toward Oliver. "Is he out for the night?"

"Yes." Oh, God, she sounded like a frog. A weak frog. Clearing her throat, she said more forcefully, "Yes. I'm surprised, too, because it's starting to rain and usually that spooks him."

"Maybe," Dash said, going to the front door to check that it was locked, "he's comforted by me being here."

Because she sure enjoyed having him around, Margo agreed, "Maybe." And wasn't that a kicker? She'd been alone so long, she would have sworn a man of Dash's size and presence would crowd her house, her lifestyle, her way of doing things.

Instead, it was so nice to have him there. Even now, as he took her hand and drew her up from the couch, she could breathe in his intoxicating scent and that, too, was so, so nice.

His thumbs rubbed her shoulders. "I haven't asked you in a while, but how's your head?"

She'd actually forgotten about that injury. "It's fine." With his chest right there, she had to touch. His chest hair was crisp, not superthick but definitely supersexy. "No more headache."

"And you said your arm isn't giving you any problems."

Oh, she hoped this was going where she wanted it to go. "I want the splint off, that's all. But no, there's no pain."

Standing there in her living room, he let his gaze wander from her face to her chest. Very intent, he lowered his hands and opened the belt on her housecoat. "Logan and Reese almost lost their eyeballs, seeing you like this." He spread the terry cloth wide. "But I understood."

"In a ratty old housecoat? What dull lives they must lead."

"It's soft in a way they've seldom seen with you. And comfortable." He pushed it off her shoulders. "There's no denying your curves in this thing."

As he looked at her "curves," she inhaled. His gaze was so tactile she felt it.

"If it had been any other guys, I don't know. I think it would have pissed me off."

His eyes met hers. "But my brother, Reese . . . I know they were just taken off guard. Again. With you hurt and us together, they've had to see you differently. It's entertaining. And now that they see you as a woman, there's no going back. Not that I want you to start flaunting yourself at the station or anything."

As if that would ever happen. "It would be grossly inappropriate for me to wear revealing clothes at work."

"I'm not talking about anything revealing. But what you wear is like a suit of armor." He cupped her left breast — and just held her.

She loved his hands, how big they were, how strong they looked in comparison to hers. His fingers were long, his knuckles big, his forearms and the backs of his hands dusted with hair. So masculine. So sexy.

"I've been to the station enough times to see other women in their uniforms." Dash lifted her a little as if testing the weight of her breast. "There are little things women know to do to make even a burlap sack look attractive. Except that you never do those things."

"Never?" Slowly, so he wouldn't object, she trailed her hand down his body, over those firm abs and that narrow line of crisp hair that disappeared into his sleep pants. His skin was so warm, so sleek. She curled her fingers over the drawstring waistband, then had to resist the urge to tug them down. "I dressed differently at Rowdy's bar."

His smile went crooked, maybe over her sneaky caress, or maybe over what she'd said. "Yeah, and Rowdy recognized right away that you were up to something. We both know he's different from Reese and Logan. You could walk up to Rowdy buck naked and while he'd no doubt enjoy the show, he wouldn't miss a beat."

True. There was little a woman could do to take Rowdy by surprise. He was the most sexual man she'd ever met. Or rather, she'd thought so . . . until she and Dash got involved. "And what about you?"

"What about me?" He cuddled her breast and finally his thumb came up to coast over her nipple. Once, twice — until her nipple tightened. He watched as if fascinated. "You already know how I enjoy seeing you."

"Do you 'miss a beat,' as you said?"

"Yeah, that and more. Seeing your sweet little body almost levels me. But honestly, honey, your attitude is every bit as sexy as your body." He turned her, taking his time as he stripped the housecoat off her shoulders, down her right arm and then down her splint. Instead of letting her turn again, he tossed the housecoat to the couch and kept her facing away from him, one hand splayed over her belly, the other stroking her backside under the big T-shirt he'd given her. "I wanted to wait," he told her. "I hate the thought of maybe hurting you. But damn, Margo, I can't."

She shouldn't sound so anxious, but it felt like she'd wanted him forever. "You mean —"

"Touching you today," he whispered near her ear, "tasting you, that was enough to obliterate my good intentions. But then seeing you in cop mode with Logan and Reese . . . Intelligence and cunning are so damn sexy."

Would Dash always surprise her with his odd observation of things? "What I suggested wasn't all that cunning, really. It's just —" Her voice dropped off when he cuddled both breasts.

"Let's go to your bedroom."

*Hallelujah.* "All right." She wanted to forget everything except Dash and how he made her feel and the fact she would finally get to experience everything with him. But she couldn't be that irresponsible. "Let me grab my phone from the kitchen."

"Sure." He picked up her housecoat. "Do you think Rowdy or Cannon might have news tonight?"

"I don't know, but your brother and Reese would also use my cell if they had any news." Phone now in hand, she passed him on her way to the bedroom. "Come along, Dash."

"Yes, ma'am."

Margo heard the amusement in the way he said that, but so what? Erotic need hastened her steps to the bedroom. Once inside, she put the phone on the nightstand and began stripping off the T-shirt.

Dash stepped into the room, closed the door and leaned back against it to watch her. His gaze burned over her, but he didn't offer to help, didn't move away from the door, didn't say a word.

Margo threw the T-shirt at him. It hit his stomach and fell to the floor. Not feeling the least bit modest, she faced him with her shoulders back, her chin lifted. She felt a little awkward in the splint, but not enough so to hesitate when what she wanted was so close at hand.

He took his time looking her over, his gaze lingering at the notch of her thighs until she wanted to squirm.

The prolonged, intense silence got to her.

"Take off your pants," she told him.

"Not yet." He looked into her eyes, letting her see the stunning lust in his. "You don't seem to realize it, but I'm hanging on here by a thread. I don't want to rush through this, so leaving them on for now is a safeguard."

"You promise they will come off?"

"Yeah. Soon." He stepped up to her, his hands — fingers spread — moving from her shoulders, over her breasts, down to her waist and thighs.

She trembled.

He opened his mouth on her throat, up to her jaw, below her ear. In a gravelly rasp, he said, "I want to eat you again."

Margo's knees went weak. She wanted that, too, but more than that, she wanted him, all of him. "I need you inside me."

"Come here." He drew back the covers on the bed, sat down with his back to the headboard, his legs stretched out, and patted his abs. "Sit."

Beneath the soft flannel sleep pants, his erection stood at attention making her heart pump in slow heavy beats. Yes, she would sit, gladly.

He helped her climb up into the bed, arranging her left leg over his hips so that she straddled him. She tried to sit lower on him so that her hands could play, but with a chastising, "Behave," Dash moved her up higher. He bent his legs up and let her rest back against his thighs.

She tried to reach back, but he caught her hand and instead placed it on her thigh.

"Relax, honey. You'll get your turn, but we don't want this over with before it even gets started. If you start playing touchy-feely, that's exactly what'll happen."

No, she didn't want that. But relaxing was out of the question. "Kiss me."

"All right." He took her shoulders and drew her forward, but instead of her lips, he drew her nipple into his hot, wet mouth, his velvet tongue lathing, his teeth teasing.

There seemed to be a direct link between her nipple and her womb. Breathing harder, she sank the fingers of her right hand into his hair and held him close.

He suckled for a very long time, leisurely, tirelessly. Even when she squirmed on him, pushing her bottom back to his erection, he continued to draw on her. When he did finally let up, it was only to move to her other nipple. He gave her a peck, licked, circled with his tongue. "This isn't uncomfortable for your arm?"

Breathlessly, she whispered, "No." It was so stirring she didn't know if she could take much more. With each soft suckle, her muscles drew tighter, the lust sharpened, pushing her ever closer to the fall.

"Good." He caught her hip and said, "Scoot forward again. Now lean down. That's perfect." And again he drew her in, his tongue curling around her, his teeth occasionally closing carefully for a gentle, tantalizing tug.

So lost in those wonderful sensations, at first she didn't notice when he smoothed a hand over her hip, along her bottom and down. "Tip forward, honey. Mmm, that's it." And he sank two fingers into her. Before again latching on to her nipple, he said, "You can sit again."

But sitting pushed his fingers deeper and she just naturally rocked against him. The spiraling pleasure escalated, growing sweeter, making her more desperate. It was a little unnerving, having Dash work her so easily. But it was also so wonderful that she didn't want him to stop, even whispered, "*Please* don't stop," in a ragged plea.

"No, I won't." He went back to her nipple, so gently now that the contrast of his fingers buried deep proved her downfall. She clenched around him, tightened her hand in his hair and cried out as a climax shook her.

Slowly, Dash lessened the intensity of his

touch until she almost melted against his chest.

Instead he eased her back against his bent legs. They both breathed hard.

He ran a hand over her. "Your nipples are so wet and stiff." He strummed one with a fingertip. "So damned sexy."

Sensitive now, she flinched away.

"Too much?"

Unable to drum up words yet, she nodded. She couldn't get her eyes to open, couldn't get enough air into her lungs.

Dash parted her thighs more. "You're beautiful."

And easy. At least for him.

While Dash idly touched her in various ways, she concentrated on recovering. Once she'd regained her wits enough to speak, she looked at him and murmured drowsily, "Now, finally, it's your turn."

# CHAPTER SIXTEEN

When Dash said, "Not just yet," she wanted to insist. She really did. But already he worked his magic, his fingertips lightly stroking over her collarbone, her breasts — while avoiding her nipples — over her ribs and along her trembling thighs.

"No more, Dash." And then, almost whimpering, she added, "I can't."

Too seriously, seduction personified, he whispered, "You can." He brushed his open palms over her stiffened nipples, lightly abrading them.

This crazy insistence he had of her tolerance made her frantic. "No, I . . ."

"Shhh." He cupped her breasts in his hands and stared into her eyes, his demeanor hot but measured. "Show me how strong you are, honey. Show me that awesome control."

Oh, God, a challenge — one he knew she'd feel compelled to accept. "It's too much."

"Not possible with you." His thumbs moved over her tightened nipples. "With us."

There he went again, saying things that sounded so serious, hinting at a future —

"I want you to relax back against my thighs. Let your arms rest." He snagged a pillow and tucked it next to her to support her splinted elbow. "Now," he whispered, "let's try this." He drew her knees up and eased them out, so that her feet were flat beside his hips. With rapt attention, he looked at her exposed sex. "Damn."

Margo groaned.

"You see," he said, still in that soft, almost awed tone. "You're almost there again, aren't you, baby?"

She tried to deny it with a shake of her head, but his attention remained between her legs.

Again, his fingers played with her, *so expertly,* and she knew he was right. She could, and she would.

With Dash.

No other man could be like him. So cocky but also incredibly caring. Sweet but surprisingly dominant. Carefree yet responsibly settled in a way she'd never expected for a player like him.

And focused. God Almighty, the man had

extreme focus, especially when it came to pleasuring her.

She was fast falling in love with the way he touched her, with how he made her feel, his touch.

*With him.*

But twenty minutes later, she crumbled. Tirelessly, he had teased every inch of her until her skin tingled all over and a fever invaded her muscles and she desperately needed to come. *"Dash —"*

"I love the way you say my name when you're so close to letting go."

His repeated use of the *L* word no longer alarmed her. She could feel his erection against her bottom, his muscles all rigid as he teased her.

"I love the way you look, how you smell, how you feel, those sexy little sounds you make when you're so close to coming." He watched her face as he tipped her back farther, worked his hands under her to push down his flannel pants. "I love watching you wait, hearing that anxious little catch in your voice when you tell me you need me."

"I do." She groaned, and managed raggedly, "I need you so badly. Right now."

"I know." He leaned forward and the kiss to her mouth was sweet and easy. "But waiting only makes it better."

The thought of waiting was too much and her legs just naturally tried to pull together.

"Hey, hey . . ." Dash gently parted them again, then touched her in a way that kept them open — and had her gasping. "Just a few seconds more, honey."

Carefully, he moved her back so that he could free himself.

Margo didn't know what new torment he had planned, but she couldn't bear it. She wanted him more than she wanted her next breath. More than she could remember ever wanting anyone, or anything.

He'd done that to her, deliberately. He'd brought her to this fevered, mindless state of need, and she finally had to admit it — she couldn't take it. Couldn't control her reaction. Couldn't withstand his sensual torment. Not anymore.

Desperately, not giving him a chance to stop her, she wrapped her fingers firmly around him and was rewarded with the catch of Dash's breath, his utter stillness.

So smooth and hot and hard. He flexed in her hand, a drop of fluid escaping him. In a daze of lust and . . . *love,* she stroked him.

Breathing with her, Dash said, "Baby . . . wait."

"I can't." She used her thumb to spread that drop of fluid around the head of his erection, and with a deep groan Dash gave up fighting her. "I want to taste you, too."

He clenched his jaw. "Later." His eyes were heavy-lidded, dark color high on his cheekbones. He breathed harder.

Deliberately, she licked her lips. "You promise?"

His hands contracted on her thighs. "Yeah," he rasped.

She moved against him, lost in the moment, and he let her, even helped her.

"This is dangerous," he warned.

"You're dangerous." Unable to wait a second more, Margo lifted up, positioned him. Dash let his hands rest lightly on her pelvic bones as he labored for breath. They looked at each other for a suspended moment of time.

With an excruciatingly slow purpose, Margo worked against him until the head of his erection had penetrated. She paused, relishing the moment. She could feel him pulsing, and the unwilling grasp of her body around him.

"Jesus." Dash strained, his fingers flexing on her thighs. He never broke eye contact.

Neither did she.

She licked her lips, and took a little more, sliding down, then back up again.

A guttural groan rumbled from deep in

his chest. "Tease," he accused, and then added, "I love it."

Heat mounted between them. She released his erection and instead braced her hand on his rock-solid shoulder.

"More," he ordered, his eyes glittering.

She nodded . . . and sank down. This time Dash held her hips and lifted up into her with one steady thrust that penetrated her completely.

Her thighs strained.

His jaw locked.

Margo slumped down over him until her forehead touched his, their noses bumping, their breath mingling.

Nothing had ever felt so good, so right. It was almost too much. He filled her up and then some, stretching her, touching her womb, but that wasn't the best part. It wasn't just the intense physical pleasure. It wasn't just the extreme talent he had for heightening her every sense until she felt drowned in pleasure.

It was Dash. The complete and total connection with him.

"That's it." He cupped her face, keeping her close to kiss her, lingering as if he enjoyed sharing her breath.

*How could he talk?*

His fingers tangled in her curls. "You are

so hot and wet. Do you know how you feel to me?"

She gave one small negative shake.

"Perfect. Fucking perfect." He lifted into her, and she moaned with the extreme enjoyment of it. "Do you feel in control now, baby?"

*How?* How did one simple movement send fire licking along her nerve endings?

"I know you," he said, as if he'd read her thoughts, knew her confusion and uncertainty. "Every inch of you." His hand went over her neck, down her back, down, down . . . and then in, touching her intimately. Eyes narrowed, he smiled. "I know what you like. I know what you need."

It could almost be scary, being so sexually dependent on someone who had so much physical influence over her.

"And this." He touched her nipple with just the right amount of pressure, in just the right way.

She almost came. *Almost.*

Margo knew he so easily judged her response by the broken sounds of pleasure she made, so she tried biting her lip and keeping still and quiet.

With Dash firmly planted deep inside her.

Dash laughed softly. "That won't do you any good, you know." He flexed his hips, sending new tingles spiraling through her already sensitized body. "I pay attention, sweetheart. There are so many ways I can gauge what does it for you, even if you deny it."

She shook her head, still trying to deny the overwhelming way he moved her.

"Yes. Like how pointed and stiff your nipples are." He touched each one, and his voice lowered. "How hot and wet you are." His thumb strummed her clitoris. In a nearly soundless whisper, he added, "And how you're squeezing my cock like a fucking fist —"

Riding against him, Margo came. Loudly. There was no holding back. No tempering what she felt or the explosive way she expressed it. Her body went taut, her back bowing, her thighs trembling around him.

Gripping her hips, Dash met her frantic rhythm, his own urgency finally making him lose control. She was still twisting with her orgasm when he gripped her down tight to him, his chest and shoulder muscles harshly defined. He growled out his release, and Margo felt it all.

Everything.

Because they hadn't used protection.

Her fault as much as his.

Fading down against him, feeling those

gorgeous muscular arms of his wrap around her, she just couldn't care.

Yet.

Tomorrow, though, would probably be a different story. But right now, with Dash pressing tender kisses to her temple, his big strong hands coasting over her back, keeping her close, it just didn't seem that important.

The storm woke her. Nestled against Dash, her cheek on his shoulder, one of her legs over his, she slowly opened her eyes.

It almost alarmed her, how entirely right it felt, how safe and comfortable, to be entwined with him. His heat surrounded her, his scent filling her head like a drug.

Outside the window, lightning flashed.

Her next thought was of Oliver. But as she listened, she didn't hear any scratching at the door.

Carefully she lifted her head to see the clock — 3:00 a.m.

Going by what she could feel, she and Dash were both still naked. Vaguely, she remembered him moving her to her back, going to the restroom and getting a cool washcloth to bathe her. She remembered the gentleness of his touch, his caring as he handed her more aspirin and then kissed her before crawling back into bed beside her, drawing her into close contact with his very fine physique.

Still raised up, Margo looked at him. A little in awe, she studied the breadth of his shoulders, the fine hair under his armpit, the bristly hair on his lean jaw, how utterly beautiful he looked in sleep.

Such a devastating man in every way.

She knew she'd stupidly fallen in love with him. Until she'd felt him coming inside her — without protection — she hadn't realized just how much she cared. But apparently along with her rigid persona, he'd also stolen her common sense.

Never, not even once, had she ever forgotten to be careful. She was on the pill, only . . . she hadn't taken it since the night of the wreck.

Dire repercussions tried to seep in, scrambling her thoughts and destroying her lassitude. She was now wide-awake.

Slowly she drew a calming breath. Maybe it'd still be okay. No reason to borrow trouble yet.

Her attention returned to Dash's stretched-out body, then his stunning profile. Sexual activity, her fingers and sleep had left his hair badly rumpled. Another burst of lightning showed the shape of his narrow nose, his cheekbones.

That incredible and clever mouth.

Emotion thickened in her chest, pooled in her lower body. There were so many small details about him that appealed to her. She could spend hours just looking at him —

A sudden thought crashed into her and she sat straighter.

Dash stirred, turning away from her and resettling with a deep sigh.

*Details.*

Taking only a moment to admire Dash's wide back, the furrow of his spine and how it curved down to lean hips, she slipped out of the bed. Feeling around on the floor, she located the T-shirt he'd given her to wear, and then her housecoat. When she opened the door, it squeaked a little, but he slept on.

Maybe finally getting release had exhausted him. God knew the man was tireless otherwise.

She slipped out of the room and made her way in the dark down the hall. Oliver slept on. The storm had brought a steady rain that seemed soothing more than disturbing. The lightning came without thunder, so it must've been far off.

After ensuring the cat wasn't disturbed, Margo slipped back to her office. She stepped in and eased the door closed behind her before flipping on the desk lamp.

Even now, with work on her mind, she couldn't completely set aside Dash's effect on her. Little reminders got in her way, like his scent on her skin, the unfamiliar ache of muscles she seldom used.

The smile that kept trying to play over her mouth.

Sitting in her desk chair, she turned on her laptop and pulled up the internet for a search of car-part dealers in the area.

She recalled seeing the brightly colored, expensive-looking rims on the truck they'd followed. They were unlike any others she'd seen — that had to mean a custom job, right?

If she could research them she could maybe find out where the creep had bought them — and ultimately where he lived. Concentrating, she tried to remember exactly what they looked like. Time ticked by unnoticed.

The search was made more difficult by her stupid splint. Typing was awkward and she had to resort to one-finger pecking to avoid typos.

Later, after the sun rose, she'd also check with Yvette to see if the guy who showed up had those wheels then.

With single-minded focus, she checked every possibility.

For as long as she could remember, she'd had great gut instinct — and right now she had a feeling that something monumental was about to happen.

She would solve this case — or maybe irrevocably lose her heart to Dashiel Riske.

Either way it went, it would be on her terms.

Dash saw the light under her office door. How long had she been up? He stood there a few minutes, undecided, before finally approaching. The rain came harder and flashes of light continually split the dark sky. The once distant storm moved closer.

Only the sound of muted tapping on a keyboard came from inside her office.

He didn't knock, only opened the door and saw her sitting there in deep concentration, the blue glow of the computer screen reflected in her dark eyes. Her lashes, long and curling, left shadows on her high cheekbones. He loved her hair, how the wispy little curls touched her cheeks, her forehead, the nape of her neck.

Was she upset that he hadn't used protection? He still couldn't believe it. He never forgot. Never.

And truthfully, with Margo, he still hadn't. He'd known he should stop her, that he should take over and move her aside so he could roll on a condom.

But even before her small hand had wrapped firmly around his dick, he'd been resenting the need for protection. He wanted nothing between them, and so . . . he'd just given in.

He'd conveniently pushed aside his responsibilities and taken her bareback, and God, nothing had ever felt so good. Electric, hot, emotional and physical and consuming.

Concerned, feeling a little guilty — and oddly horny — he stepped up behind her, putting one hand on her shoulder. "Couldn't sleep?"

For only a brief moment she rested her cheek against his hand, without losing her focus. "I slept — until the storm woke me." She glanced back. "You're like a powerful drug. That's the best rest I've had in a long while." She turned back to the computer.

Relief, that she wasn't angry or upset, eased some of his tension. He looked at the screen. "What are you doing now?"

"Researching those rims."

"From the truck that followed us?"

"Yes. I can't remember the exact design,

but I know they were colorful and unique."

He'd noticed them, too. "It's important?" *Important enough to drive you out of the bed in the middle of the night?*

"If I can find the exact rims, I can maybe find out information on our guy." Again she looked at him over her shoulder — then down his body, focusing on his semi-erection. "Whoever sold him those rims might have his address."

Not much he could do about getting hard. He was near her, and that was pretty much all it took. But he could offer some help.

Dash tipped up her chin, bent to kiss her and said, "Be right back."

She watched him go. He felt her gaze until he'd completely left the room.

A few seconds later, after pulling on his boxers and grabbing his cell phone, he returned and showed her the photo opened up on the screen.

"I took a pic," he explained with a shrug. "Just in case."

Eyes widening, Margo took the phone. She kept staring at it with disbelief.

Dash couldn't resist smoothing his hand over those dark curls, rumpled from sleep. She looked so pretty like this, and damned adorable, too. Not at all intimidating. Maybe . . . gentle. Cuddly.

It was a good look for her.

But then, he also liked it when the shrewd gleam came into her eyes. "You, Dash Riske, are a genius."

Her enthusiasm made his heart feel full. "I was worried. I wanted to make sure we could find the truck again if he managed to nab you."

"For once I'm glad you worried." She quickly emailed the photo to herself so she could see it on a much bigger screen. Once there, she zoomed in, looking at the rims in better detail.

Dash took her arm. "Why don't you let me type for you?"

"What?" she teased. "You want to be my naked secretary?"

"I put on boxers."

With a playful frown, she said, "I noticed. Such a spoilsport." She stood and indicated the chair. "Okay, be my guest."

Dash seated himself, but hesitated before typing. "About earlier —"

Leaning over his shoulder, she kissed his ear. "You're a stud. But for now, let's deal with this."

"I didn't use anything."

"I know." Her breasts rested against his back and shoulder. "Open that tab on the right. Check out their rims."

Avoidance. Okay, he could deal with his slipup later, when she wasn't so focused on work. He opened the tab and clicked to see a special customizable rim. Going back and forth from the photo, he used site settings to create a rim that looked exactly like those on the truck.

"So it's possible." Calculating, she straightened again. "Print out the name and number of that place."

"It's close," Dash told her. "Totally within range."

"Good. Print out a few copies of the truck and rims, too. I want to make sure Rowdy, Reese and Logan all have —"

Suddenly Margo went still, then alert. She kept her gaze on the wall, but Dash felt her sharpening vigilance.

"What is it?"

She breathed in, her eyes narrowing. "Probably nothing. It's just that —"

They both heard the awful screech of her bedroom closet door.

*Someone was in her house.*

Dash was out of his chair in a heartbeat, but Margo caught his arm above his elbow. Motioning him to be silent, she opened a desk drawer and retrieved a gun.

Realizing she meant to go out of the room ahead of him, Dash struggled with himself

382

— but only briefly. "Sorry, honey," he whispered. He bodily moved her aside and stepped out.

Margo said not a single word, but he felt the anger pulsing off her as she followed right on his heels. Putting a hand back, he signaled her to wait, prayed that she would, and began inching toward the bedroom.

He'd only take two small steps when they heard the abrupt thunk — and smelled the awful scent of . . . kerosene.

They were both flattened to the hallway wall, and Margo had to admit, Dash utilized as much stealth as she did. For a big man he moved without making a sound. But he wasn't armed, or trained, or official. *She* was, and no way would she let him play the caveman.

"Call 911."

Instead, he started forward.

In a low hiss, she said, "Damn it, Dash," and everything seemed to happen at once. Oliver screeched as he shot out of the bedroom, his fur clumpy and wet. Another crash sounded in her bedroom, accompanied by a whispered curse.

And Dash charged in.

Gun in hand, Margo followed, but it was too shadowy to see until the lightning flickered. At the same time the bodies stumbled into her before falling out into the hallway.

Her splinted arm banged into a wall, making her clench with pain. Furious, she snapped on the hall light, took aim . . . and saw that Dash had completely subdued a masked, armed man. The panicked fellow's gun lay a few feet away on the floor, and Dash — who was much taller than their intruder, and far more muscular — had the man pinned on the ground with a knee in his back. He'd taken the thug's right arm and twisted it severely back and up, levering it almost to his shoulders.

"Move," Dash said low, "and I promise she will shoot you."

Behind the stocking mask, wild eyes widened more. "I ain't movin'! I ain't movin'!"

Dash jerked off the man's mask, revealing a pasty-faced middle-aged goon with faded blond hair and loose jowls. Doing a quick search of the man's pockets, Dash found a lighter, but nothing else.

Retrieving the other gun, Margo dropped it into her housecoat pocket. Never did she shake over doing her job, but she was shaking now. Suppressed rage made it difficult to speak normally. "Can you hang on to him?"

Dash gave her a longer, searching look. "The prick isn't going anywhere I don't want him to go."

"Okay." She located her cell phone and, keeping an eye on Dash and the intruder, called it in.

Right after that, she dialed Logan.

He answered with a grumpy, somewhat breathless, "What the fuck?"

Hmmm. It was five in the morning, and yet she'd interrupted . . . something. "Your brother has detained a masked man who broke into my house and dumped kerosene in my bedroom."

With a new surge of energy, Logan asked, "Anyone hurt?"

Margo lowered the phone. "Dash," she said, hoping he didn't hear the quiver in her voice, "were you hurt?"

He snorted.

"No," she said to Logan. "Not hurt." Her jaw ached from grinding her teeth. "I already called it in. I just figured, with Dash here, you'd want to —"

"Definitely. Reese, too. I'll pick him up on the way." She heard the rustle of hurried movement, presumably Logan dressing. "And Margaret? I'd have wanted you to call whether Dash was there was not."

She'd just disconnected the call when sirens sounded nearby. "Hold him tight, Dash. I'll be right back."

"No worries."

So damned cocky. Her heart thumped painfully against her ribs. The intruder had a gun. He could have shot Dash. He could have killed him.

She might have lost him — after she'd just realized how much she cared for him.

At the door, she closed her eyes for just a moment to regain her aplomb. It helped only the tiniest bit.

Forgetting her state of undress, her messy hair and lack of makeup, Margo opened the door and let the officers in.

They were drenched from the downpour — and agog at her attire, but she just didn't care. She needed to find Oliver, needed to relieve Dash of their intrusive thug, and she needed to figure out how she'd been tracked down.

Because not for a minute did she think this was a random act. The porno-happy firebugs had somehow found her. She had a price on her head.

And Dash was more involved than ever.

They'd rattled the bushes with false claims of leads from the abandoned garage fire,

and look what happened.
Now what?

# CHAPTER SEVENTEEN

Arms folded, shoulder against the wall, Rowdy made sure to stay out of the way while the cops finished up — but he observed everything. Dash, he realized, was head-over-ass in love. It was there in his face, in the set of his posture, in the overall possessive way he tracked the lieutenant's every movement.

Margaret, however, didn't seem to realize it. Right now, in the center of the crime scene, she was focused on dictating every step of the process — while wearing that soft robe that emphasized her figure, her face clean of makeup and with her cute little feet showing.

When she'd decided to send out false reports of evidence found at the garage, she probably hadn't expected a direct attack. In fact, he was damned surprised, as well.

It didn't . . . fit.

Dash shouldered him, drawing his attention. The crusty old cat Dash held, now wrapped in a towel, complained with a rusty meow.

Contrite, Rowdy tickled the cat's chin. "Something on your mind, Dash?"

"You're staring at her. Again."

"Hate to break it to you, but every guy in the room is stealing looks at her."

Dash cursed low, but didn't deny it. "It's the way she's dressed. They're not used to it."

Rowdy acknowledged that with a nod, but added, "And it's intriguing, how she's dressed — or undressed — contrasted to her barking orders and verbally kicking everyone's ass."

"Yeah."

Rowdy leaned in to taunt him. "Thanks to you, everyone is seeing her differently."

Demeanor growing grumpier, Dash worked his jaw and kept silent.

That only left him open for more harassment. "They know you two have been hitting the sheets and that has all those male minds churning with speculation —"

Dash rounded on him. "You?"

Enjoying that reaction, Rowdy shrugged. "I'm not immune to imagination." And before Dash could deck him, even while holding that mangled cat, he added, "But you know me better than that, so why don't you get it together? It's almost embarrassing."

"Shit." Dash rubbed his eyes. "Yeah, sorry."

"No sweat. Falling in love is hard on a guy."

Dash shot him a look, but didn't bother denying it.

"She's more prickly than ever."

"Her house reeks of kerosene." Dash went back to scrutinizing the lieutenant's every breath. "I'd say she has reason."

"Yeah, but I don't think that's it." Again, Rowdy stroked the cat, this time using two fingers. He wanted the animal to warm up to him, but he recognized the signs of wariness. "I think it's you."

"Me?"

"You scared her."

Dash frowned.

"She's used to running into hostile situations. To seeing Logan and Reese and all those boys in blue confront danger. But she's not involved with any of them."

"Like she's involved with me."

"Right."

As if Dash had already concluded as much himself, he grumbled, "I'm a man, damn it. Not a kid. Not a —"

"Woman?" Rowdy gave him a grim smile. "Don't let the lieutenant hear that sexist comment."

"I can take care of myself."

"Not in question. My point is that she hasn't had to deal with that before."

"With what?"

"Seeing someone she really cares about caught in the middle of danger." Unfortunately, Rowdy had plenty of experience with it. He understood the sickening feeling all too well. "You get this clench in your gut, a cold sweat and a brain-numbing fear when you realize someone important to you could have been lost."

Dash stared toward her. He still frowned, but his voice softened. "I was never in danger."

"You're not that dumb, Dash. A man with a gun, kerosene and bad intent is a threat to everyone."

Dash chewed on that idea. "It did seem like something was off. I figured she was pissed at me for interfering."

"Yeah, you probably have that coming yet." He watched two officers pull on clear rain slickers in preparation for leaving. "But you know women as well as I do."

That had Dash coughing.

Rowdy didn't take the bait. "You specifically know her better."

"Yeah."

"So figure it out."

Dash started to speak, and Margo's voice drew both their gazes.

"Run him through the system," she commanded. "See what pops." And then, more disgruntled, she barked, "Who the hell called the press?"

They both turned to see a lady reporter and a cameraman trying to get in the front door. A uniformed officer held them back.

"Seriously?" Dash complained.

Rowdy frowned. "This feels like a fucking setup to me."

"I don't like it, either."

It was another ten minutes before Margaret finished up, and by then, the reporter had taken a fair share of notes.

Things were quickly getting complicated, and it wasn't just the complexities of Dash's intimate relationship with a top-notch, well-known lieutenant.

There was more at work than what met the eye.

Rowdy knew it, and because Margaret was so sharp, he was pretty damned certain she had figured it out, as well.

Even with so many jumbled thoughts and

emotions plaguing his mind, Dash enjoyed seeing Margo like this. There was something innately sexy about a confident, take-charge woman. Given the attentive way Rowdy watched her, he agreed.

Icy fingers knotted in his gut. True, he knew Rowdy was in love with Avery, that he was honorable and would never cheat.

But knowing it only helped a little.

With her right hand fisted and her brow pinched, Margo approached. She stared at the cat instead of Dash. "How's Oliver?"

"Nervous." *Like you.* Dash shifted the cat to the other arm. "I had to wash him twice to get all of the kerosene off him. He didn't like his baths, and he's still pretty shaken up."

Uncertainty had her nibbling on her soft bottom lip. "I'm sorry I wasn't there helping —"

"You had your hands full with other things. Oliver and I managed just fine."

"Maybe I should take him to the vet."

Dash switched so that now it was Margo he petted — her jaw, her neck, her shoulder. It helped that she didn't seem to mind, even leaned into his touch a little. "It's not quite seven. They won't open for appointments for a couple more hours and by then Oliver will have calmed down." And hopefully the time would also give Margo a chance to come to grips with his intrusion. "Besides, the vet said as long as he didn't ingest the kerosene, it wasn't a worry. You already had the dish liquid she recommended for cleaning, so he'll be fine."

She surprised Rowdy by cooing to the cat, kissing its wet head and in general babying it.

Dash smiled. Eventually everyone would know what a warm, sweet and caring woman she was. There was so much more to Margo than her innate ability to lead.

Suddenly her eyes narrowed on Rowdy. "Why, exactly, are you here?"

Rowdy seemed to have difficulty taking her rude tone to heart when she looked so . . . feminine. "Pepper called me after Logan took off. She knew I was helping out with things and that I'd want to know."

"So she informed you. I would have done that myself. But it doesn't explain why you're here."

"To see your intruder." Rowdy had no problem with her knowing his motives. "There's always the chance I would have recognized him."

"But you didn't?"

"Nope." He leaned in, his voice lowered — because while he didn't have reason to hide anything from the lieutenant, Logan or Reese, he clearly didn't feel the same about the rest of the cops in attendance. "I'll ask around, though. Show his picture to my snitches — specifically the snitch that knew about the garage fire, the same snitch that I told about our fictitious evidence. Someone, somewhere, will know him."

Her dark eyes widened marginally. "You photographed him?"

Damn. The sneaky bastard. Dash hadn't noticed Rowdy taking any pictures, but then, he'd been consumed with watching Margo. "Is that a problem?"

"No," Rowdy said. "It isn't."

Logan and Reese approached as the last of the cops filed out. The intruder had already been put in the back of a squad car. The reporter had reluctantly retreated.

Thankfully, the storm had mostly blown over and dawn approached with only a gentle rain.

Logan looked beat, and that concerned Dash. "You okay?"

"What? Oh, yeah." He rubbed the back of his neck. "Fine."

Reese threw an arm around Logan's shoulders. "I think Pepper awoke him extra early, and then forced him through a workout." Reese raised a suggestive eyebrow.

"Before he could recover, he got called here, so —"

Logan and Rowdy said together, "Shut up, Reese," making Dash grin.

Yeah, right here, right now, with the cat shivering in his arms, the stench of spilled kerosene burning his nostrils, there wasn't much to laugh about. But Logan had been a cop a long time so Dash knew well how morbid humor often covered darker emotions.

Of course, Reese didn't dial it down. If anything, he ramped it up now that he'd gotten a rise. But this time he aimed his sarcasm at Margo. "You sure threw everyone for a loop. Those poor guys, they kept tripping over their own tongues."

Dash started to say something, but Margo beat him to it. "You're so disgustingly chipper, Detective, how would you like some extra paperwork?"

Reese just smiled at her.

Indignation stiffened her spine. "You think that's funny?"

" 'Course not." But the smile turned into a grin.

Rowdy shook his head, then laughed. Wagging a finger around the circle of people, he included them all, but spoke specifically to Margo. "Things have changed, you know."

He tugged at her lapel. "Thanks to you and Dash hooking up, these two clowns now feel free to drop in on you, and to make jokes, and to treat you —"

"Like family," Logan said defensively.

Whoa. Dash would have said only "more familiar." But *family*? Yeah. That covered it as far as he was concerned. Nice that his brother understood it, as well.

He just hoped the teasing didn't scare Margo off. At the moment, she looked a little frozen.

"I sympathize," Rowdy told her. "I felt the same way at first myself. But you might as well get used to it."

Dash pulled her closer, pleased that the guys all understood what Margo hadn't yet accepted. "And as long as you're adjusting to that . . . I'm sorry if I worried you."

She sucked in an angry breath, ready to blast them all . . . but deflated. "It's difficult."

Reese laughed at her. "Lighten up, Margaret. He's a big boy. He can handle himself."

"You —"

Logan cut in. "You have to admit, the dynamics are different now."

Instead, she shifted her gaze from Logan to Reese and back again — and changed the subject. "We need to know if Cannon leaked our story about evidence, and to whom. Same with you, Rowdy."

"Sorry, but I already checked. This doesn't connect back to me. In fact, I'm not convinced it's even related."

Dash wasn't surprised when Margo agreed.

"Our visitor is no more than a local yahoo, a dime-store thug who someone paid to come to my house — specifically, *my* house — to set a kerosene fire. He claims he doesn't know or care why."

"Who hired him?" Rowdy asked.

Logan filled him in. "A man in a dark car gave him the kerosene and twenty bucks and told him he'd give him two hundred more after he caused the vandalism. He never got a name."

"Vandalism, huh?" *What a schmuck,* Dash thought. "Is that what he called it?"

"Yes."

"He said he thought the house was supposed to be empty." Rubbing her forehead, Margo drew a steadying breath that every one of the men noticed.

Dash bristled again.

"The thing is," she continued, "Oliver startled him, and once he'd run through the kerosene, our intruder didn't want to light it."

Reese, too, gave Oliver a few affectionate pats. "Luckily, the little worm is pet-friendly. He doesn't mind burning down a house, and possibly two sleeping people, but he drew the line at frying an animal."

"Thank God for small favors," Dash said, holding the old cat protectively closer. In a very short time he'd grown fond of the cat — and not just because Margo so clearly loved him.

"I suspect he's telling the truth, that he doesn't know anything more. But you two," Margaret said to Logan and Reese, "will of course question him further."

They agreed.

"The idea of the 'dark car' . . ." Reese shook his head. "I don't know. A lot of people drive dark cars. That part could be pure coincidence."

"That reminds me. Hold up a second." Margo went to her office. They all heard the hum of the printer, and less than a minute later she returned with several sheets of paper. She gave one to Logan, one to Rowdy. "Dash and I were doing some computer work when the firebug showed up. Notice the unique rims on the truck? We located a local dealer who sells a customizable rim identical to them." She handed out more papers with the name and address of the dealership.

"Could lead to an address for the driver."

Margo nodded. "I want you two to check out the dealership."

Reese checked his watch. "Soon as it opens."

"Rowdy, I thought maybe you could do some more asking on the street."

"Consider it done."

"The way things are heating up, I need everyone on their toes — and reporting back promptly."

Over Margo's head, Dash shared a look with his brother. "I think the biggest problem now is that your address is out there. I mean, not only did someone send that bastard here, but that reporter asked a lot of questions and took some pictures. It's probably going to be on the news. Everyone will know where you live."

"Why the hell was a reporter here anyway?" Rowdy wanted to know. "They sure as hell don't chase down every cop car that pulls onto a scene."

"Someone had to have alerted them . . . of something." More or less herding them all, Dash got everyone into the living room. Reese leaned up against the wall. Rowdy sat at the edge of a chair. Margo settled into the center of her couch and immediately reached for Oliver.

Taking the seat next to her, Dash handed over the big cat. He was now more dry than not and began grooming himself.

Logan went to her other side. "Someone wanted us to assume the perp was hired by the same men who visited the pawnshop."

Margo shook her head. "I don't like assumptions."

"It does feel off," Logan agreed. "The thugs from the pawnshop wouldn't care about a cat."

"Agreed. So what are you thinking?" Reese considered things. "We all agree it's not part of the underground porno operation, but because of the kerosene, it was made to look as if it is."

"Someone," Rowdy said, "is conveniently using one thing to instigate another."

That cryptic comment could have been confusing, but Dash knew exactly what he meant. "Someone on the inside track is working against you."

It gave him a very bad feeling, but Margo only seemed thoughtful.

He didn't want to voice the possibility, but more than that he wanted Margo protected — even if that meant protecting her from those closest to her.

"How did the guy get in?" He knew he would have heard the crash of breaking glass, but if someone picked a lock . . .

"Through the bathroom attached to her bedroom," Reese explained. "The window was jimmied open. He must have crawled in after you two were already in the lieutenant's office."

Margo stared down at the cat as she stroked him. "The window locks securely. There's no way to 'jimmy' it open."

"The lock wasn't broken," Logan said.

Rowdy couldn't understand the ramifications as he pressed her. "Lieutenant?"

She glanced at Dash, then away.

Did she want him to keep quiet? Was that her way of saying to stay out of it?

Like hell.

"If you two have something to share," Logan said, "now would be the time."

"I have to wonder," Margo said, all business again. "Any chance you two were followed when you came to visit?"

Immediately Reese and Logan objected.

"Definitely not."

"Hell, no."

She held up a hand, silencing them. "I didn't really think so. Even if you had been, it wouldn't explain the open window." She took a really big breath — and turned to Dash. "When my dad was here . . . which bathroom did he use?"

He should have known she'd have the same suspicion. Margo wasn't a dummy. She was, unfortunately, tough as nails, in part due to her father's never-ending hostility.

"I didn't follow him in." Dash wanted to hold her, but she'd hate that. With the others present he knew she'd insist on showing her strength. "I just waited at the door."

Logan sat forward, his elbows on his knees, his hands hanging loose. "Your father was here?"

"He and West came by to . . . check on me."

Cursing softly, Reese pushed away from the wall.

Dash and Rowdy were left in the dark. He wouldn't ask her now, not in front of everyone.

Rowdy didn't have the same reserve. "Someone want to fill me in?"

Silence. Dash felt the tension mounting — until Margo shook it off. She faced Rowdy with cool composure. "This goes no further."

"Who the hell would I tell?"

She smiled as if she saw the humor in that.

"My father was chief of police before he retired."

"I knew that."

"But you probably didn't know that I forced him to retire. And unfortunately, he's never forgiven me for that."

Breathing hard, excitement making him clumsy, Saul ran down the polished hallway and into his brother's posh office. It had taken him thirty excruciating minutes to get there, the drive feeling endless. He'd wanted to speed, but Curtis was strict about things like that. Other than their playtimes, which they deserved — and the occasional need to snuff someone who got in the way — they were to live as law-abiding citizens, the same as the good, ordinary, insignificant people.

As slow as the drive had been, the elevator to the twenty-sixth floor seemed more so. By the time Saul got to the posh office that encompassed the entire floor, he forgot the general rule about always knocking first.

Curtis was on the phone behind his massive mahogany desk when Saul literally fell in through the doorway with a lot of noise and fanfare.

Toby, sitting on the couch with a cup of coffee, lurched forward, his gun already drawn. Seeing Saul, he scowled and put the gun away, then cursed over the coffee he'd spilled everywhere.

"I'll call you back," Curtis said into the phone. Frowning, he stood as he placed the landline phone back into the cradle. "What is it?"

Trying to catch his breath, Saul hung on the doorknob. This was his opportunity to redeem himself and he almost pissed himself in his excitement. "I know where she lives."

Curtis circled around his desk. "She who?"

"That nosy cop. The one that got away." Why couldn't he ever remember names? It infuriated Curtis when he had to dance around without details. "The one Toby tried to follow today."

Toby narrowed his eyes. "The one *you* let get away!"

Curtis raised a hand, silencing them both. "Get in here and shut the goddamned door."

Saul slammed it behind him, wiped the sweat off his bald head, then pressed his damp palms to the front of his slacks.

Curtis rested a hip on his desk, studying Saul. "You're talking about Lieutenant Margaret Peterson."

"Yeah, her. Someone broke into her house. Someone acting like us!"

Curtis's frown darkened more. "Calmly, Saul, tell me what you mean. Who acted like us? How?"

Saul drew a deep breath and slowly blew it out. "Someone tried to burn her house down with kerosene, but she and the dude stopped him."

Curtis and Toby shared a look. "You're not making any sense."

God, why couldn't Curtis ever understand him? He took another step forward. "The cops *arrested* him. I was watching the TV and I saw the whole report. They said some masked guy broke into her place and dumped kerosene everywhere."

"But he didn't light it?"

"No. Something about there being a cat and he didn't want it hurt —"

"Jesus," Toby interrupted, glancing worriedly at Curtis. "What the fuck?"

Looking very unhappy with the information, Curtis asked through his teeth, "Was *anyone* hurt?"

"No, I don't think so." Why did Curtis care about that? He wanted the bitch dead anyway. "They said the dude staying with her restrained the guy until the cops got there and arrested him. But it had happened at the bitch's house. They showed her picture! It's her!"

Toby stood. "I don't like it. First the cops say they found something at the scene of that damned garage —"

Curtis slashed a hand through the air, making Saul duck in reflex. Curtis wasn't within striking range, and still his heart lodged in his throat and refused to budge.

Quietly furious, Curtis said, "We didn't leave any clues. The kerosene was everywhere. Regardless of the rumors we're hearing, I know it all burned. Every last single shred of evidence."

Often they had to get rid of evidence. Saul and Toby both knew Curtis's preference for burning it. After that damned druggie had let him down with the driving the night he tried to get the bitch, Saul had no choice but to kill him. He'd dumped the body at a current construction site where it would end up buried. Everything else had been burned in the garage.

Toby didn't look convinced, and that worried Saul. He didn't want to go to jail. Just the thought of it gave him nightmares for a week. It wasn't enough to discourage him from taking part in playtime. But close. "They found something at the garage?"

"No!" Curtis bunched up in that dangerous way of his. "I just fucking told you they couldn't have."

Still worried, he glanced at Toby, who gave one small shake of his head.

"I was on the phone when you burst in here," Curtis explained, "verifying that there was nothing but ash."

"Oh." Saul swallowed hard, but his throat felt restricted. "Well, I just wanted to let you know. About the break-in at her place, I mean. And . . . and that they arrested someone."

Eyes narrowed and mean, Curtis turned to Toby. "Find out what the fuck is going on."

"Right." After giving Saul a pitying look, Toby walked out of the room.

Staring at him with laserlike intensity, Curtis said, "You came here, to my office."

"Well . . . yeah. I didn't think you'd want me to use the phone. I mean, in case it was —"

"You burst in here, drawing notice. You know how important it is to keep business separate from pleasure."

"Yeah, I do." Saul didn't understand. "But I thought you'd want to know where she lives."

Curtis turned away. "I would have found the woman eventually, at the right time, when it suited me. But now I know that someone is daring to copy me, to *mock* me."

"Oh, well . . . I guess." Saul chewed the side of the mouth, backing up a little. "I can see where that'd piss you off."

"And now." His voice went gravelly and deep. "Now that bitch will be watched more closely. She won't stay at her house or travel freely, giving me the opportunity to get to her. No, she might even go into hiding somewhere. It's going to make everything very difficult."

Saul looked behind him, but unfortunately Toby had pulled the door shut again when he left.

No escape.

Curtis's hand curled around a heavy paperweight on his desktop. "Now, thanks to some fucking copycat, she'll have protection all around her." He turned suddenly and threw the weight with precision.

Gasping, Saul tried to cover up, but it bounced off his hunched shoulder, a solid hit that felt like it broke a bone. Better than hitting his head and cracking his skull, but still he cried out, cowering, closing in on himself.

"I know how to get to her, though. *Because I always have a plan.*" As Curtis advanced, he seemed deaf and blind to Saul's panic, his pain. *"The fucking whore is going to pay for causing me so much trouble!*

*Do you hear me?"*

But Saul couldn't hear anything.
He was crying too loudly.

# CHAPTER EIGHTEEN

Reliving the shame all over again, Margo forced herself to face one and all during her admission. "My father, along with a few others in supervisory positions, was involved in a nasty little game of using female informants for more than information."

Logan and Reese, she knew, had heard the rumors. Who hadn't? But true to her word, she'd kept quiet about those involved — as long as they left the force. None of them could be trusted to protect the public.

Not when they'd already breached that trust in the worst way possible. Not when they'd already taken advantage of vulnerable women under their protection.

"I knew there was some bad blood. . . ."

She gave Logan a humorless smile. "You always know when something is happening. And no doubt Reese gleaned the whole story through his different sources."

Reese didn't look happy, but he shrugged

an affirmative.

"I should have had them all prosecuted," she said, struggling once again with her conscience. "Unfortunately, for some of them, it would have been very difficult to prove."

"For your father?" Rowdy asked.

"Far as I know, he didn't actively involve himself, but he did turn a blind eye to what was happening. That's just as bad. I should have —"

"No," Logan disagreed. "An investigation would have just dragged it out and divided the department more. The locals already had enough to chew on."

"We'd all but lost their trust," Reese added. "You took care of it without stirring up the muck more than necessary. And by doing so, you protected everyone else in the department."

What they thought of her mattered, she admitted. It always had. They were good cops, good men, and as such she wanted — craved — their approval. It made her heart feel better to know they didn't judge her harshly.

But what Dash thought mattered most of all. So many times he'd told her how she impressed him, how he admired her. She didn't want to now see disappointment in his eyes.

She didn't want to let him down.

It wasn't easy, but she faced him.

He surprised her by taking her hand, then kissing her knuckles.

He said nothing, but then, he didn't really need to. She let out the breath that had caught in her lungs and finally felt a little of the strain ease from her shoulders.

Earlier, when she'd realized how easily she could have lost him . . .

Rowdy interrupted those dark thoughts. "So how many got the boot? Besides your dad? Who else was involved?"

Leave it to Rowdy to take it all in stride. But then, he never had much faith in the police to begin with.

Dash didn't give her a chance to answer. "You're thinking someone else could have a vendetta against her?"

"It's possible," Reese agreed. "An ex-cop would make more sense than anyone else, because he'd possibly still have ties to people at the station. That'd give him access to current information. He'd know how to attack her in a way that just tied in with another case."

"The world is overrun with idiots who do wrong, then blame others for busting them." Rowdy realized what he'd said and turned to her. "Not to call your dad an idiot —"

Margo waved that off. "To this day, he doesn't see the big deal in taking advantage of women who were trying to get their lives together. Believe me, I've called him worse."

"So many people were shuffled around," Logan said. "I'm not sure who retired, who left under duress, who was implicated."

She remembered well. "My father, serving as the police chief, two sergeants, a lieutenant, a dozen officers and a civilian crime-lab tech."

Rowdy whistled. "That's quite a haul."

In a protective gesture, Dash moved closer to her. "How many female informants were there?"

"Five." It sickened her still. "One of them was only nineteen." When she'd given her father his ultimatum, she'd been completely alone. Her department, as well as her family, had turned on her. Even West hadn't entirely understood her position. Oh, he'd known it was wrong, and he was all for shutting it down. He even agreed that some reprimands were in order.

But to kick out "good" officers? Their own father?

No, that he hadn't supported. After all, to him the women were criminals, prostitutes who'd been busted.

He hadn't been alone in that opinion. Most everyone had seen them as "less" than the men involved. It didn't matter that they'd been coerced into sexual situations, that they'd possibly been raped, demeaned. . . .

She pulled in a deep breath, calming herself.

This time she knew she wasn't alone. As she'd retold it all, she had Dash with her. And she knew 100 percent that he backed her — whatever she wanted to do — because he trusted her to do the right thing. Somehow that made it all so much easier.

But it was more than that. She now knew Logan and Reese well enough to know they would never turn away from that type of injustice, the abuse of others. They were honorable cops, through and through.

And Rowdy . . . No, Rowdy would have defended the women, the same as she had.

Reese folded his arms over his chest and studied her. "From what I've heard, the commander had some say in how it all went down."

"Yes. Dan insisted on keeping things quiet," she confirmed. "He and my father were close. Together, they had a lot of influence."

"They pushed for you to take the lieutenant's position?" Rowdy asked.

"Yes." She shook her head. "I even had the mayor breathing down my neck. I think they had some misguided notion of controlling me through a promotion."

Logan's grin went crooked. "You'd damn well earned the promotion and you know it."

Dash said, "That was probably just their way of getting you on the inside circle."

"The boys' club," Rowdy added with disdain.

True, all of it. Except . . . "It didn't work."

"No," Dash said, confident. "I'm sure it didn't."

She wouldn't sugarcoat the truth. "I suspected others of being involved, but I couldn't prove it. Not without going through an official, department-wide investigation."

"What you did was cleaner and quicker," Logan assured her.

Dash's thumb moved over her knuckles. "You remember the names of everyone that was involved?"

"Yes." She would never forget — and they all knew it. It was one of the reasons so much strife remained between her and the commander. And one reason she could ignore his edicts when she chose to.

"So now," Rowdy said, still in an analytical mindset, "you think your dad might've dicked with the window lock? You think he'd use the details of this current cluster-fuck to set you up . . . for what?"

She just didn't know. She couldn't imagine her father wanting her dead, but . . . "The window got open somehow."

Reese began to pace. "Maybe he just wanted to scare you off."

"Surely he never intended for an actual fire to be set," Logan added.

Dash pushed to his feet and stood in front of her. "You're not safe here."

But where *would* she be safe? "Only an idiot would try to strike twice at the same place."

"And we already confirmed we're dealing with idiots." He towered over her, so tall, so leanly muscled. "I think you should come away with me for a while."

*"What?"* Discrediting such a suggestion, Margo blinked up at him. Run? Is that what he wanted her to do? Abandon her job? Adamant, she shook her head. "No."

"Where to?" Reese asked, deliberately exacerbating Margo's overall mood. "Your secret cabin in the woods?"

"No." Dash held her gaze. "By now it's not so secret anymore. I have another place in mind."

With Oliver finally sleeping, Margo eased him aside and stood to face off with Dash. Before she got a single word out, he leaned forward and kissed her.

In front of everyone.

Not a wimpy little kiss, either, but a kiss of bold possession and honest caring.

As he straightened again, he looked far too serious. "The threat is real, whether you want to admit it or not. And I'm willing to bet Logan and Reese will back me up on that."

Logan and Reese both raised their hands.

"Agreed."

"Absolutely."

Seeing them, Rowdy, too, raised his hand. "Just for a little while, Lieutenant. Until we can sort this out."

She felt cornered, Dash knew, and he hated that. But if she was right, if her father was now trying to throw her to the wolves, then how much protection would be enough?

He rallied arguments to convince her. "Someone was in your house."

"Believe me, I'm aware of the significance." She started to turn away, but he brought her back around.

"The news has probably already shared the whole break-in. By the afternoon every creep out there will know right where you are."

"It's likely." She put a hand to her forehead.

Dash wanted to coddle her — but he knew she neither wanted nor needed that. She needed his support.

She needed his insistence.

"I'm not talking about your walking away from the job." He needed her to know that he understand the importance of what she did, and supported her diligence in doing it. "Just take a weekend." *With me.* "Let Logan and Reese do their thing."

"It's my thing, too."

It meant a lot to Dash that the others kept quiet and let him handle it. They'd back him up if he needed it, but he was hoping Margo would relent without their input. "I know that, honey, and you're damn good at that job. No one thinks otherwise."

"You don't have to placate me."

"I was shooting for honesty, actually." He used her experience against her. "Think about it from another angle. If another cop was in your circumstances, what would you tell him?"

Grousing, she again tried to walk away.

Dash again brought her back.

"Stop that!" Vibrating with agitation, she fisted her hand against his chest. "I need to talk to Yvette. I want to ask her about those rims. I want —"

"To know she's okay?"

In a bid to reclaim her calm, she breathed deeply. *"Yes."*

He could almost read her thoughts, feel her distress. She'd just experienced a fraction of what Yvette had suffered and her sympathy for the younger woman was a live thing.

He understood that better now after learning of her history with her father. That very understandable empathy interfered with her sound judgment, and showed her selflessness.

If they had any privacy, he'd calm her the best way he knew how — by loving her, by draining her tension through sexual release. But it would be a while before they had that opportunity.

Logan cleared his throat. "That can be arranged. Today even."

Reese spoke softly. "Maybe after your doctor's appointment."

They both sounded so ill at ease, it made Dash drop his head forward and laugh.

Not giving Margo a chance to get riled

over his misplaced humor, he put his hand over hers and grinned at her. "It is endlessly amusing to me how such a small woman can make such big cops so perturbed."

"Yeah, well," Logan grumbled, "she doesn't usually come off as 'small.' "

True, because Margo had the spirit of an Amazon. Dash cupped her chin, marveling again that a woman so strong could be so sweet and soft. "Your house is done for, honey. It's going to take a professional cleaner to come in here and get the floors cleaned."

"I know."

"Oliver needs a calm, quiet place to recover." Dash could just imagine the looks on the faces of the other guys. Using her cat as a lure was desperate — but he'd bet on it being effective. She loved Oliver.

Sighing, Margo put her forehead against his chest. "I agree. But your address was probably never well hidden to begin with, and as you said, this secret cabin of yours isn't secret anymore. I can't just take Oliver to a hotel —"

"I wouldn't ask you to."

She leaned back to see him. "So then . . . where?"

Shoving his hands into his pockets and resenting that he had to share here and now, in front of others, Dash said, "I have another place."

Logan, who had the same access to funds as Dash, thought nothing of that assertion.

Reese and Rowdy . . . yeah. They were more surprised.

"*Another* place?" Rowdy asked.

"Like . . . a third home?" Reese marveled.

Logan kept quiet. He understood that they could each buy multiple homes and not be strapped.

"Another lake house."

Her jaw loosened. "You have two lake houses?"

Feeling ridiculous, as he always did over excesses, Dash rolled a shoulder. "I was going to give the first one to Logan."

Logan perked up. "Really?"

He twisted to see him. "I know you guys have been looking. But Pepper has fond memories of my place, which is maybe why she hasn't been able to settle on a different one, right? So I figured you should have it."

"Right you are." Smiling, Logan stepped forward and took his brother's hand. "Thanks, man."

"You earned it." Dash would forever think of that rustic cabin as the place where Pepper sealed the deal with his brother — and in the bargain made him a very happy man. Even now, the very inventive and sexual way she'd tormented Logan made Dash want to laugh. "Anyway, the new lake house is a little more modern. Still private, though. Until I just told you guys, no one knew about it."

Margo stared at him hard. "Just how well-to-do are you?"

Deflecting, he said, "No more so than Logan."

Her gaze transferred to his brother.

Proving he didn't like talking about money any more than Dash did, Logan scowled. "We inherited a small fortune."

"Your parents are still alive!"

"Grandparents," Dash explained. "They were loaded, and they adored us."

Logan tried to downplay it. "It doesn't matter. Usually." He glanced at Dash. "But at times it comes in handy."

Like a junkyard dog, Margo found a new bone to gnaw on. "You keep this private place so you can take women there?"

"Not exactly, no." He hadn't taken women to either place. For Dash, the lakefront cabin had been an escape from everything and everyone else. But he wanted to share it with Margo.

"Is it far away?"

"An hour." He looked down at the cat.

"Does Oliver travel well?"

"No, he pukes."

Dash winced, but persevered. "So we'll put him in a carrier and hope for the best. Don't you think he'll be more comfortable without having to deal with cleaning people and cops coming and going and the stench of kerosene?"

"Yes." She glanced at the clock by the TV. "He's usually okay by himself while I'm at work, or if I have to be away a few hours, but you're right. Today is not a good day to leave him alone."

"I didn't say —"

"I think I should cancel my doctor's appointment."

Rowdy stepped forward. "Leave him with me."

Margo lifted both brows, but Dash nodded agreement. "You have time for that?"

"I don't have to be at work for a while," Rowdy told them. "And even if I'm late, Cannon can get the place opened up."

Still resistant, Margo asked, "Is there anything Cannon can't do?"

"Not that I've seen so far." Hands on his hips, Rowdy studied her. "But how long could the doctor's appointment take anyway? A few hours at most, right?"

"I assume no longer than that."

"Oliver knows me now and he doesn't hate me. I'll hang around, ensure no one comes in here that shouldn't and make sure the cat gets whatever he needs."

Margo's attention went from Rowdy to her sleeping cat and back again. "He's old and blind. . . ."

"And a real trouper, I know." Coming closer, he looked down at Margo. "I can even get hold of the cleaning people and get things set up. That way you guys can be gone for the weekend without any worries."

Logan said, "I'll make sure someone is here for the cleaners. No one will be in your house unattended."

"I'll call Mr. Sweeny right now and make sure he knows you'll be stopping by to chat with him and his granddaughter." Reese pulled out his cell. "Since you aren't sure how long you'll be, I'll just say sometime after your doctor's appointment. Will that work?"

Everyone watched her, and Dash could see she felt put on the spot. Usually that'd make anyone defensive.

Margo suddenly laughed. "It's absurd. All the big strong men arranging my entire weekend for me."

"Honey —"

"It's okay, Dash." The laugh faded into a

425

fond smile that encompassed them all. "Honestly, other than expecting me to abandon my job, I appreciate the effort. I'm not used to all this . . . fussing."

They all scowled over that. "Men don't fuss," Dash told her.

"Apparently they do — when they mean well. And yes," she said quickly, cutting off Dash's automatic objection, "I do understand that a weekend away might be smart. If for no other reason than just to regroup. But *only* for a weekend. If Logan and Reese can't make real headway by then, I'll be taking over."

"We'll be on it," Logan told her. "We've got plenty to work with now."

"Discreetly seeing what the senior Peterson has been up to, looking into the customized rims, interrogating the swine who broke in here." Reese rubbed his hands together. "Three days, counting today. I think we should have some answers by then."

Rowdy agreed. "Someone is going to know the guy who broke in. That's bound to be a lead of some sort. And by now it's all over the street that the department has evidence from the garage fire. Something will turn up."

Rather than be reassured, Margo looked unhappy to be missing all the police work.

"I want to be kept apprised of every single detail. I want to be updated at least twice a day. I want —"

"To run us like puppets, yeah, we get it." Logan clasped her shoulder. "You know damn good and well we can handle this, so stop micromanaging."

"But she does it so well," Reese said.

To forestall any fireworks, Dash smoothed down her unruly curls. "We've only got about twenty minutes before we have to leave." He kissed her forehead. "Are you hungry? Want me to fix you something while you get dressed?"

To his surprise, she leaned into him, her uninjured arm sliding up his chest as she . . . cuddled. "I'm not hungry, but thanks."

It took Dash a second, and then his arms went around her, keeping her close. Such a paradox. Near her ear, he whispered, "You're okay?"

"Yes." She rested there only a moment, and then with a sigh, she stepped away. "I can be ready in ten."

Knowing the turn of events wore on her, Dash watched her leave the room. She went into her bedroom to get clothes, then back into the hall bathroom. When he heard the door close, he turned, expecting his brother and Reese to once again act ridiculous.

Logan surprised him by smiling. "I think I'm getting used to seeing her like that."

"Easygoing," Reese said, agreeing. "I wouldn't have believed it, since she's usually hard as nails, but it suits her."

Unaccountably pleased, Dash nodded. "It suits her when she's with me."

"None of you should forget —" Rowdy went to sit by the dozing cat "— she's still an alpha female when necessary."

"Like your sister," Logan pointed out. "But I imagine Margaret will balance it as well as Pepper does."

"It occurs to me," Reese said to Dash, "that you're a lot like Logan."

Knowing where he was going with his comment, Logan said, "And you?"

Reese nodded. "You wouldn't be content with some sweet little bit of fluff no matter how cute or sexy she might be."

Rowdy looked up. "Luckily for him, Margo is all of the above."

It still nettled Dash to hear Rowdy speak so familiarly of Margo, and that got the others grinning. At least until the knock sounded on the door. They all looked up with menace. Oh, it would just be too perfect if that was her father, showing up to see the damage he'd caused.

Dash strode forward, followed closely by

Logan. He looked out the peephole, but didn't recognize the man there.

When he swung the door open, Logan said with a note of surprise, "Commander." He stepped back to allow him entrance. "We weren't expecting you."

Dan Ford, tall and fit, with silver hair and dark eyes, stepped in as if he owned the place. He scowled at the small crowd, sniffed the air with suspicion and narrowed his eyes. "Where the hell is Margaret?"

From the roof of a building a block away, flat on his belly, Toby surveyed the building where the girl and her grandpa lived. He had the side view, so he could see the front, back and south side of the aged redbrick building.

He didn't doubt that someone watched the front, where a security light lit the big wooden door. But around back, a narrow basement window left enough shadows to make entry accessible. There were no neighbors back there — just a noise-reduction wall that separated the old houses from the newer expressway. Tall trees grew up and around an old separate garage that looked ready to crumble.

That low-to-the-ground window didn't look real secure. And it was small, so it'd be a tight fit — but it'd probably work. Later, he'd check it out. Or maybe pay someone else to do that, just in case.

He wouldn't get locked up for Curtis, the crazy bastard. Sure, he enjoyed the pay, and the fucking wasn't bad, either. He grinned at his own humor.

Unlike Saul, he wasn't desperate to get laid. He could get some tail whenever he wanted. But there was something special about the depravity of what the brothers had set up, the thrill of the taboo. Nothing was sexier than a woman who fought hard — and lost anyway. Taking her against her will, recording all her mewling sounds, her desperation and eventual defeat . . . it made a man feel like a man.

Curtis liked to share his little creations with other rich assholes who craved the real deal instead of the absurd porn supplied by lousy actors.

They liked to see it, but were afraid of doing it themselves. The cowardly pricks.

Toby wasn't afraid of doing it, but he didn't want to get busted for it. And why should he? Moving to another area would be a piece of cake. Why fuck with problems when they didn't need to?

But Curtis . . . He could be blinded by determination. He often saw insults where none existed. Because of his wealth, he was spoiled, powerful enough that he felt authorized to do just as he pleased and to hell with the consequences.

At times, he was so violent that Toby knew he wasn't entirely sane. Left to his own devices, Curtis would get busted and they'd all go down.

But Toby planned to continue enjoying the game, so somehow he had to keep everyone protected. After meeting the little ponytail at the pawnshop, well, he wanted her. He wanted to tie her down and take his time, he wanted to hear her cry, feel her struggle, and he wanted it all recorded.

So he could enjoy watching it again and again.

Curtis and Saul could rape the crazy-ass cop if they wanted. Toby just wanted to kill her. Quick and clean.

Goddamn Curtis and his stupid, risky schemes.

For now, Toby had no choice but to do it Curtis's way. But someday soon Curtis was going to push him too far. Unlike Saul, he wouldn't just take the abuse and beg for more.

No, if it became necessary, he'd kill Curtis with his bare hands.

Sometimes he actually looked forward to it.

# CHAPTER NINETEEN

When she heard the raised voices, Margo finished tousling her damp hair and hurried from the bathroom. She'd quickly bathed and dressed as best she could in simple clothes that worked with her splint. So far, the shirt Dash had altered for her was the easiest. She paired it with slim jeans and ankle boots. A little mascara, a little highlighter and she'd considered herself prepped enough for the day.

Until she'd heard the arguing.

She was still adjusting her sling when she rounded the corner and saw . . . "Dan." Collecting herself, putting on her game face, she narrowed her eyes a tiny bit and gave a tight smile. "What are you doing here?"

He stepped around Dash and Logan. "I heard what happened, so naturally I came to check on you." His attention went all over her. "Jesus, Margaret."

She touched the lingering bruise on her cheek, but her hair covered the stitches on her forehead. The sling, well . . . "It's not as bad as it looks."

"It looks . . . Well, thank God you're okay."

Reese rested against the wall, a look of bored contempt on his face. "I made that call for you, Lieutenant. You're all set."

"Thank you."

As always, Logan remained professional, but she recognized the brimming anger in his bearing. What had happened?

"Why are you here, Dan?"

Encompassing everyone in his discontent, Dan cast a quelling glance around the room. "When you didn't return my call, I got concerned."

Dash stationed himself beside her. It was mean, and a little childish, but to annoy Dan she smiled up at Dash in a lover's welcome, then leaned on his hard shoulder. "Well, as you can see, I'm in good hands."

Dan took that on the chin. His jaw flexed and his lip curled. "Yes, well, I need to speak with you."

She took great pleasure in saying, "Oh, but I'm running late for my doctor's appointment." Narrowed eyes took any goodwill from her smile. "I get the splint off today."

"That's actually what I want to talk to you about."

For about five seconds she gave it thought, then turned to Dash. "Why don't you go finish dressing so we can leave? I don't want to be late."

To her relief, he didn't argue. "Be right back."

Next — tackling her detectives. "Well." She faced each of them, but knowing Logan would be the most difficult, she focused on him. "I appreciate it that you came by. Thank you for everything."

"They were doing their damned jobs," Dan barked.

"Yes," Margo agreed, anxious to know what had Dan so surly. Usually he took great pride in professional decorum. "That, and more."

He straightened, taking an imposing stance. To her surprise, he volunteered the info. "I demanded to see you when I arrived, and they refused to get you."

*Demanded?* She glanced at Logan in question.

Logan's icy respect left a chill in the room. "We explained to you that she was getting dressed."

Still shrugging into his shirt and carrying his shoes, Dash came back in. Wow, he'd dressed, washed and cleaned his teeth in record time. He hadn't bothered with a shave, but honestly, she liked the way he looked so rugged and rough. Even here and now, with her commander breathing fire, her home the scene of a crime, the stench of kerosene thick in the air, she wanted him.

The idea that she'd always want him scared her a little.

Maybe everything was starting to build up, but she gave a twittering laugh that sounded nothing like her usual starched self — as evidenced by the way everyone looked at her with wary concern.

Patting Dash's chest, she asked, "Did you run the entire time?"

"Yup." He hopped as he pulled on one shoe, and then the other. "And now I'm ready. You?"

Yes, more than ready. But she needed to clear house first. "Logan, Reese, thank you again. I look forward to hearing an update."

The detectives didn't like it, but they refrained from arguing.

Next she turned to the commander. "Dan, as you can see —"

"They won't be reporting to you."

That blunt statement landed like a slap. Margo never broke eye contact with him. He was a bully of the worst kind, and she knew it. She refused to blink. She refused to speak. Never would she show him a weakness.

The staring contest ended when Dan broke. "You're out of it, Margaret." He tried for a gentle tone that lacked validity. "Effective immediately."

Her smile let him know that wouldn't go unchallenged. "Detectives, I'll talk with you later. Rowdy, Dash, if you'll excuse me a moment . . ."

Rowdy stood and walked out front with Logan and Reese. Dash crossed his arms and stood his ground. By look and stance he made it very clear he wouldn't budge.

And again she wanted to laugh.

God, very little in her life right now was funny. But he so easily lifted her spirits and made stuff that would normally feel overwhelming seem very small and insignificant.

Dan gave Dash a burning glare.

"He can stay," she decided. "This won't take long."

That seemed to alarm Dan. And with good reason.

Margo stepped away from Dash and moved closer to Dan. "I have agreed — on my own, without your command — to remove myself for the weekend. If someone is trying to kill me, an innocent could get caught in the cross fire."

"Him?" Dan asked, nodding toward Dash.

"He can handle himself." True. She realized it, but that didn't make her any less worried. Love had that effect, she guessed.

"Who the hell is he exactly?"

*Mine,* she wanted to say, but settled on, "None of your business."

His lip curled with jealousy. "Meaning, it's personal?"

"Oh, yes." With a wealth of satisfaction, she said, "Very personal." Still walking, she circled Dan.

He turned so that she wouldn't be at his back.

*Smart.*

When she glanced up, she caught Dash smiling. "I was talking about pedestrians on the road who might catch a stray bullet meant for me."

"Jesus, you think someone would do that?"

She shrugged, embellishing since it served her to do so. "Why not? A few days ago someone T-boned me. During the night someone planned to barbecue me. I'm sensing a pattern. How should I know the limit of their sickness?"

He verbally pounced. "This is exactly my point —"

"No." With mock regret, she shook her

head. "Your point is, and always has been, to try to take advantage of me."

Alarm sharpened his tone. "Margaret."

"Don't worry. Dash already knows the sordid details."

Astonishment swung Dan around to snarl at Dash — which affected Dash not at all.

He continued to look insolent and stalwart. And sexy.

Definitely sexy.

"Why?" Dan asked through his teeth, his big hands curling and uncurling. "You agreed to never mention it."

"And you," she said in a raised voice, stepping up to meet his anger, "agreed to stay the hell out of my way!"

Dan breathed hard as they stared at each other, and before Margo even realized he'd moved, Dash inserted himself in front of her, then eased her back.

In an offhand, unconcerned way, he said, "Just to be safe, since he's sort of fuming there, and you're not exactly looking peaceful."

"This is bullshit." Dan turned away, but jerked right back around again. "You think I'd strike her?"

"I don't know you — but she does." Dash remained loose and relaxed. "I know she's fair and honorable, but she doesn't like you.

Sort of tells me a lot, ya know?"

Seeing he had a losing battle, Dan tried a new tack. "Margaret, you are too damn close to this case and you know it."

"Why?" She stepped from behind Dash. "Because it reminds me of another case?"

"No!" His gaze shifted nervously. "Damn it, don't put words in my mouth. This is completely different."

"There are definite differences — like the taping and selling of rapes on video."

Dan rubbed his forehead. "Sick."

"Yes." Funny, but that's almost exactly what her father had called it. "But women are still being abused. So you know I want to stay involved."

Snarling again, Dan knotted his hand in his silver hair and took three long steps away before turning to face her again. "I am still the commander."

"You should be satisfied with that." She went to the door and held it open and, having that settled, she said with amicable politeness, "Thank you again for stopping by, Dan. Your concern is appreciated."

Impotent fury showed in every line of his posture. "This isn't over."

"Yes, it is."

He stormed out, not bothering to speak to Logan and Reese, who loitered on the front porch, or Rowdy, who stood right by the door, his shoulder propped on the doorjamb.

Had he heard it all? She wouldn't be surprised.

She heard the squeal of tires as Dan sped from her driveway. Dash leaned down to her ear. "I am so horny for you right now." And he stroked her bottom suggestively. "The hottest thing I've seen in a long time."

Absurd . . . but damn it, she laughed. *Again.*

Every other man she knew would have called her a ballbuster, a tyrant, and much, much worse for how she'd dealt with the commander. But not Dash.

No, he liked it when she got autocratic. That complete and utter acceptance made her want him, too.

What had happened to her lethal edge?

But she already knew. Sexy, controlling Dashiel Riske had happened.

Would she ever again be the same?

It sucked that she hadn't invited him in to see the doctor with her. He understood — their intimate relationship was still fairly new, despite all the time he'd put in trying to soften her up. If it hadn't been for that damn wreck, she might still be shutting him out.

But he had made headway, damn it. Today, she'd accepted him as she'd faced off with her commander.

God, she'd been . . . incredible. Ballsy, yes; Lieutenant Margaret Peterson backed down from no man.

But she'd also been clever and righteous. And proud.

Could a woman be any hotter than that? More appealing? She was his. He'd make it so.

*Some sick fuck wanted to hurt her.*

Dash squeezed his eyes shut and said a few prayers. Sitting in the waiting room gave him too much time to think about all the problems, all the threats against her, and all the ways he wanted to keep her safe — while also supporting her in any way she needed.

Reese was right that he would never have been happy with a meek woman. But damn, Margo was a challenge.

Pacing didn't help much, but he did it anyway. He needed this current situation resolved so he could concentrate solely on loving her — and getting her to love him in return.

The receptionist kept smiling at him. Dash

nodded back and did more pacing.

A female patient, mid-twenties, tracked his every move. He ignored her suggestive staring.

Once he got Margo alone in his new cabin, where they could talk without interruptions, he would convince her to move in with him long-term. She'd be safer at his place. It was more secure — and she wouldn't be alone.

*Forever* would suit him, but he didn't want to rush her. At least, not more than he already had.

When the door leading to the patient rooms opened, Dash turned . . . and saw Margo striding out. It took no more than one look at her set face to see her distress.

The splint was gone, so what had happened?

He held back while she took care of paperwork with the receptionist, then held open the exit door for her when she angrily marched his way.

They were just leaving the building when he finally broke the silence. "Everything go okay?"

"No."

Whistling under his breath, Dash kept pace with her. "Bad news?"

Stoic, as always, she flexed *both* hands.

"Nothing I can't deal with."

Damn, he could guess the problem. The splint was gone, but apparently that wasn't the end of it as she'd hoped. He opened the passenger door to the rental. "You didn't get clearance?"

"No, I didn't. Not yet." She slid in and pulled the door shut, leaving Dash standing there.

Prickly. But he could deal with that.

On a sigh, Dash circled the hood and got behind the wheel. He didn't start the car. Not yet. "You plan to ignore the doc's orders." It wasn't a question.

"It's my body, damn it. I know how I feel and what I'm capable of."

He watched her for a moment, then decided to hell with it. She could be as disgruntled as she wanted. He wouldn't just accommodate her, though.

Smoothing back her hair, he checked her forehead. The stitches were out and the scar would be minimal. "You got the splint off." He brushed the back of his knuckles over her warm cheek. "Can't you take it one step at a time?"

"Of course I can." She half turned to face him, her expression speculative as she looked him over. "My next step is to go see Yvette Sweeny and her grandfather. I have questions that need answers."

"That's on the agenda." He'd already gotten directions from Logan on where the young lady lived.

"Afterward we'll need to go back to my house so I can get Oliver and a few necessities for the weekend."

Hearing her say it, knowing he'd have her all to himself for a few days, made his thighs tense and his gut coil. "Not a problem."

Hearing the huskiness in his voice, she smiled with sensual resolve. "And then . . ." Her hand slid inside the collar of his shirt so she could touch bare skin. She stared up into his eyes. "We'll go to this cabin of yours."

Damn, she seduced him so easily. But then, he'd been on a hair trigger for a while around her. "I'm looking forward to it."

"Mmm. Me, too." She leaned over to him, lightly kissed his mouth. "You have a few promises to keep and I'm going to see to it that you do."

"I promise to give it my best effort."

She shivered — and retreated to her own seat. "Let's go."

Smiling, he put the car in gear and drove out of the lot. Margo liked being bossy, Dash knew. She was trying to take control of this situation. And she had a lot of frustrations to work out. He could handle it. He could handle her.

Or so he thought.

Now that she had both hands, she used them. Continually.

Whatever teasing he'd done to her . . . she repaid tenfold.

She'd already touched him repeatedly — his chest, his abs, over his thighs.

But now, as her fingers slipped dangerously close to his fly, Dash gripped the steering wheel. He was so primed already it was all he could to keep from getting a boner. "I'm going to wreck if you keep that up."

"I'll worry about keeping it up later. Right now I'm more interested in getting it up." Her palm slid over him, once, twice.

He stiffened his arms, breathed a little faster.

She measured his length . . . and purred. "There we go."

Shit. He tried a deep breath but it didn't help much. His heartbeat punched. "We'll be there in under five minutes."

"I'll give you two to recover." She pressed lower, cupping his balls gently. "That gives me three more to play."

Oh, God. He shifted, but no matter what he did, she stayed with him.

"It's so nice that I have two hands now. Reaching you with my right wouldn't be easy. But my left?" She demonstrated, stroking over him as if the denim of his jeans didn't exist.

He locked his jaw until he thought he could speak coherently. "Your elbow doesn't hurt?"

As if to think about it she pursed her mouth . . . and continued the tantalizing movement of her hand on his cock. "No, not really. It's stiff, and I think I've lost some mobility."

"Then maybe you shouldn't be —"

"The doc said I should use it as much as was comfortable. No heavy lifting or anything like that. But this?" She brought her curved hand up to the head, using her fingernails to graze him, then teased her way back down to the base again. "This isn't uncomfortable at all. At least, not for me."

Stringing words together wasn't easy. "If that's so, then why didn't he clear you?"

"Who the hell knows?" Under her breath, she whispered, "I can't wait to get you out of your pants so we can try this again." And then, as if she hadn't just said something guaranteed to finish him off, she said, "The doctor wants to see me again in a few weeks and he said he could probably clear me then."

They were almost to the house, so Dash caught her wrist with utmost care. "That's enough, baby. You promised me two minutes."

She let out a sigh. "I suppose it's only proper. Can't very well interview a young lady with you sporting *that.*" She trailed one finger down his still-excited dick. "Then again, you could maybe wait in the car —"

"No." Once more, he removed her hand. "Behave."

"Or what?"

He did a quick double take, and caught on to her game. "Or I'll have to do my own payback. And it's guaranteed you can take a whole lot more than I can, so my payback would last longer than yours."

She grew quiet as they pulled down the street and Dash started watching the addresses to find the right house.

"Dash?"

"Hmmm?" He was slowly recovering, but it took a lot of concentration. Knowing she wanted him was as stimulating as her touch had been.

He spotted the right house just as she whispered, "I really enjoy this."

That got his attention. He slowed and

pulled up in front of the curb. "This?"

"Playing around with you. Teasing. The sex."

Damn, she knew how to throw him off guard. "You don't say?"

She nodded. "Even talking with you. It's all fun. And exciting."

So she enjoyed being with him. He smiled. "I love it, too."

She bit her lip, her gaze searching. He knew his repeated use of the *L* word kept her confused. Eventually, he hoped, she'd get used to it.

"Thank you for going to the doctor's with me."

"My pleasure." He meant that.

"Now that I'm out of the splint, I can do my own driving."

He didn't like that idea worth a damn, but she didn't give him a chance to say so.

"I know you have a job, your own life to live. But I wanted you to know . . ." She seemed to have a hard time coming up with the right words.

Dash just waited.

"I'm happy to keep seeing you. Even after this weekend, I mean. That is, if you —"

Dash leaned across the seat and took her mouth. He kept the kiss warm, firm, but not too consuming, considering they sat in front of a victim's house. He opened her seat belt, cupped her waist in his hand and finally eased up. One more peck, and he moved back to his seat. "I do." Definitely.

This weekend, he'd make sure she understood just how much.

Yvette didn't remember the rims. Or if she did, she didn't want to say so. She and her grandfather were literally holed up, the front door locked and barricaded, all of the curtains drawn.

Tipton, her grandfather, rested in an easy chair, still trying to heal. He was a tough guy, doing his best to give a show of strength for his granddaughter, but anyone could see that Yvette was still terrified.

She was a very pretty girl, Margo thought. Long dark hair, a very pretty face and a slender body with noticeable curves. No doubt she had her fair share of boyfriends chasing after her.

But now, after what she'd endured, the awful threat of rape, death, burning . . . would she ever be the same?

During her questions, Margo tried to be brusque, impartial, but she didn't have it in her. When Yvette said, yet again, that she didn't remember anything else, Margo sat close to her.

Dash, showing a lot of consideration, moved closer to the grandfather, conversing quietly.

Margo took the younger woman's hands. "I'm so very sorry for what happened, Yvette."

The girl nodded, her gaze averted.

"I'm sure Detective Bareden told you that officers will be doing more frequent drive-bys until we catch the men who terrorized you."

"Yes."

Clearly Yvette also knew that didn't assure her safety. And Margo, much as she'd like to, wouldn't make guarantees to the girl that she couldn't keep. "Detective Bareden is a man of his word. He and Detective Riske will be working very hard to get the animals who threatened you."

Drawing a slow, deep breath, Yvette freed her hands — and faced Margo. "I know. They're . . . nice men."

"Yes, they are." Folding her hands in her lap, Margo tried to put the girl at ease. "They're also very honorable and excellent at what they do."

Swallowing hard, Yvette dared a quick peek at Dash. "I wish there was something more I could tell you."

"Oftentimes, after things have settled

down, something will come to mind. It could be anything. No matter how insignificant, please share with us. You'd be amazed at what turns out to be important."

That made Yvette thoughtful. Chewing her bottom lip, she again peeked at Dash. Clearly men now made her nervous. She had seen things no girl her age should have to see.

Things no one human should have to see.

When the knock sounded on the door, Yvette almost came out of her seat. She gasped and her eyes rounded. Margo put a hand on her shoulder. "It's okay, Yvette. You aren't alone."

The grandfather narrowed his eyes and stared at the door as if he expected someone to break it in.

She nodded at Dash. He went to the front window, eased aside the curtain, and smiled. "It's Cannon."

The way Yvette reacted, going boneless with relief but also brightening, gave Margo pause. Maybe all men didn't worry her after all.

They could hear a quiet conversation between Dash and Cannon before both men appeared in the living room. Margo realized she was staring as openly as Yvette. Either of the men alone made an impressive sight.

Together . . . well, it was testosterone over-load.

Cannon was too young for her to look at seriously, and with Dash next to him, well, Margo could appreciate him — but she wanted Dash, and only Dash.

Yvette, however, looked as if the sun had just come out and shone specifically on her.

Mr. Sweeny struggled to sit a little more upright in his chair before Cannon waved him back and came farther into the room.

Hands on his hips, Cannon looked at grandfather and then granddaughter. "Have you eaten?"

Yvette watched him with big adoring eyes. "He ate some canned soup."

"And you?" Cannon came over and crouched down in front of her. "What did you eat?"

"Nothin'," her grandfather said. "She's still too upset to eat."

"Grandpa!" Blushing, Yvette said to Cannon, "We didn't know you were coming by."

"I called," Cannon told her with a frown. "Where's your phone?"

"Oh." She looked toward the kitchen. "I left it in there."

"Excuse us a minute," he said to Margo. He took Yvette's hand, pulled her up from the couch and led her into the kitchen.

Slowly coming to her feet, Margo watched it all with raised brows and a little disbelief. With Cannon, Yvette seemed more like a love-struck young lady than a recovering victim.

She glanced at the grandpa, and saw him smiling after them.

Near her ear, in a low hush, Dash said, "I wonder if Cannon knows what he's doing."

She hoped so, and decided to leave him to it. "We'll be on our way now."

Cannon returned, now holding Yvette's phone as he put in a number. "Speed dial," he told her. "You hit number one and it'll dial me. Got that?"

"Yes."

He said to Mr. Sweeny, "If anything happens, if anything doesn't seem right, call me."

"Those detectives told us the same thing."

Cannon nodded. "Sure, that'd work, too."

Twisting her mouth, Margo tried not to snort. "Gee, thanks, Cannon."

He still looked far too serious as he explained, "I mean, if someone actually bothers you, call the cops first." He tipped up Yvette's chin. "But if anything spooks you, even if you know it's not a real threat, well, then I can be here in no time."

"You'd do that?" Yvette asked.

His touch lingered. "Sure."

Mr. Sweeny pressed a hand to his ribs and nodded. "I appreciate it, Cannon. It's going to take a little while to stop watching shadows and jumping at every little sound."

"You make me sound like a baby, Grandpa."

Margo smiled. "Not so. Anyone would be jumpy after what you went through. I'd say you're handling it remarkably well."

"Especially," Mr. Sweeny said, "with them swearin' they'd be back."

Yvette shuddered.

Knowing she should go, Margo reached out for Yvette's hand. "Remember, anything at all, call. Okay?"

It took a minute, and then Yvette said, "There is one thing."

Everyone became more alert.

"It's probably nothing. And I . . . I'm not sure. But I think two of them were brothers."

Brothers? "What makes you think so?"

"They . . . I don't know. They looked a little alike, and the way they talked to each other. It was different from the other guy."

"Different from the man with the goatee?" Cannon asked.

"Yes. They . . . joked about what they were doing. The other man, he was darker and seemed . . . I don't know." She sucked in a shaky breath. "They were all disgusting. But the dark guy just seemed to be more serious about it."

Cannon slipped an arm around her shoulders and that encouraged her to keep going.

"He treated it like it was his job, but the brothers just did it because they could." She rubbed her forehead. "I know that doesn't make any sense."

"Actually," Margo told her, "it does. And if they are brothers, it might help us to track them down." She smiled, hoping to reassure Yvette. "Thank you for telling me. I'll share with my detectives and we'll see what we can turn up. You have my number, so if you think of anything else, call me."

"I will."

Cannon said, "I'll walk you out."

"You're leaving?"

The stricken note in Yvette's voice broke Margo's heart.

"No. I'm going to stick around for about an hour." Cannon pulled on a stocking cap. "I'll be right back in."

As they stepped out, Cannon pulled the door shut behind him, ensuring they could speak privately. Both he and Dash surveyed the area, on the lookout, cautious.

She'd already done the same herself. It

was an older neighborhood, the streets lined with sedans and pickups. Cracks split the aged concrete sidewalks and large oak and elm trees grew in every yard.

Similar redbrick houses lined this quiet suburban street. The backyards blended together without fences. At the back of each narrow property was a tall retaining wall, helping to block the sounds of a highway put in a few years ago.

Short of putting around-the-clock guards on the house, it couldn't be entirely protected. "As long as they don't open the door without knowing who's there, they should be safe enough."

"Convincing yourself, or me?" Cannon asked.

"Both, I guess."

# CHAPTER TWENTY

Bright sunlight made it feel warmer than it was. When the late March wind blew, the chill cut through Margo's clothes, making her shiver.

She pulled her coat tighter around her, and felt Dash step up to her back, his hands on her shoulders.

"I told them the same." Cannon shook his head. "They're supposed to let me know if they go out."

"You plan to trail them?" Dash asked.

"If I need to, yeah. Best way to catch a thug is to bust him in the act."

Margo couldn't believe the enormity of what he took on. "If you see anything —"

"I'll call." He squinted up at the bright sky. "Some of my friends helped me clean up the pawnshop today. It's not perfect yet, but the bulk of it's done, most of the stench gone."

Dash shifted in disbelief. "When the hell

do you rest?"

Cannon ignored that question. "When they're ready, they'll be able to get back to work. But I'm hoping you'll get the bastards first."

"I'm hoping the same." Margo sensed there was more on his mind. "You have something to share?"

"Sort of." He looked uncomfortable, hands in his pockets, shoulders up against the chill. "I know this all started with some weird black-market pornos, right? Videotaped rapes and stuff."

"And some women who were badly hurt, two of them killed. Yes."

His expression hardened. "Well, a friend knows a guy with a few of those type of movies."

Anticipation brought her forward and she put a hand on Cannon's arm. "Who? How did he get them?"

"I don't know the whole story yet, but I'm working on it."

"Tell me what you do know."

He looked out over the streets, watched an elderly woman walking with a grocery cart, an older man putting mail in the corner mailbox. "Most of the people around here are just average, hardworking middle-class folk trying to get by. But there are some others who want out and can't figure an easy enough way. So they try for short-cuts."

"By doing dumb things, you mean."

He shrugged, still not looking at her. "Often by working for someone with enough money to give a leg up. You prove yourself, gain some cred and you can temporarily change your circumstances."

Margo sighed. "You're talking about young men who get hired out as thugs. To do some rich guy's dirty work?"

"Yeah." He finally looked at her. "Money doesn't automatically make someone a good person."

"No," Dash agreed. "It doesn't. But it doesn't make him a bad guy, either."

Cannon grinned. "I know the difference — and I know you donated to the rec center. Appreciate it."

Margo twisted to see Dash, saw him flush and something like pride swelled inside her. She put her hand over his on her shoulder, and leaned into him.

"My point is that wealthier guys come trolling through here all the time. Looking for cheap sex or muscle for hire." He withdrew a slip of paper with a name written on it.

It was then that Margo noticed his busted

knuckles. She caught his hand. "This looks new."

"Yeah." He met her gaze without flinching.

"Another of your trained fights?"

"Not exactly, no." He gave her the paper, then tucked his hands away again. "There's a local guy who likes to make fast cash when he can. He got hired to buy drugs for a private party. When he delivered them, he said a movie like that was playing on a big screen. About six men and as many women sat around laughing about it as they watched."

Margo caught her breath at such callous inhumanity — and felt Dash squeeze her shoulders, his touch firm, caressing. Reassuring.

She looked at the paper and saw a name. "This is the address for the man who delivered the drugs, or the man who paid for them?"

"The man who paid."

"I guess you convinced your friend to give you that address?"

"He's not my friend."

And she supposed that was all the answer she'd get.

Dash pulled Margo closer. "You're sure it's the real thing?"

"No. I haven't seen them. But when the guy dropped off the drugs, he saw part of one and it turned his stomach. If you knew him, you'd know that's not an easy thing to do. He said it was obviously homemade, and that the woman was out of it."

Drugged. "The same woman in the other video?"

"I don't think so." Cannon shared the description he'd gotten — maybe through the use of his fists.

Margo braced herself against the hurt. "Sounds like one of the murdered women we found." Unsure how much Cannon knew, she explained, "Of the four women we know who were victimized, two made it to us, bruised and beaten up a little, scared and disoriented." The truth burned like acid in her throat. "Two were bodies we found that had similar marks of abuse."

"And then there's the woman in the last video," Dash growled. "They can't be doing this for money. They'd never make enough. So if a wealthier guy had a copy, then maybe he got it from one of his peers."

Margo wanted to grab Dash and kiss him. Of course she'd realized the enterprise couldn't be that lucrative, that the sick bastards did it to feed their perversions. But she hadn't thought about them being men of means, able to move around so easily.

Able to pay for immunity.

The buildings they'd used so far were disreputable, abandoned. But still . . . "I think you're right, Dash — and that gives us some direction."

He turned her to face him. "We're heading out of town. Right now."

"I know."

He literally lifted her to her tiptoes. "I hear it in your voice, honey. You're ready to jump in again, feetfirst. But you know it's not safe. They know you. Anywhere you go, any scene you touch, is a tip-off."

She put her hands to his chest. "I know." And just to reassure him, she gave him a quick kiss that startled him quiet. "Now let me go. I need to get Logan on the phone ASAP."

When she turned, Cannon wore a crooked grin. "I'll hold tight until I hear from you or Logan. But I'm willing to do whatever I can to get this done. Just so you know."

Margo held out her hand. "You're proving to be a very handy person to have around."

Grin spreading, Cannon accepted her gesture of gratitude. "Yes, ma'am."

When he didn't let go, Margo lifted her brows in question. "Is there anything else?"

"Not really." He held her hand in both of

his now. "I just wondered how you're do-ing. Rowdy told me what happened this morning with the break-in, the kerosene."

"We're fine."

He didn't look convinced. "Did you tell Yvette about it?"

"No." Margo would never do anything to alarm the girl more. "She doesn't need to hear about things that would only upset her."

Relieved, Cannon nodded. "This is so messed up."

"Very," Dash agreed. "That's why I'm tak-ing Margo away for a few days."

"Yeah." Finally releasing her hand, he tugged at his stocking hat, rearranged it. "I think it's smart."

Men, Margo decided, at least the good men, all tended to think along the same lines. "Logan will be in touch very soon, I'm sure. And Cannon? I'll tell you what I told Yvette. If anything else happens, any-thing at all, I want to know."

Flashing a grin, he said again, "Yes, ma'am."

After he went back into the house, Margo took Dash's hand and headed for the car. "Why do I get the feeling that he's a softer-edged version of Rowdy?"

After checking up and down the street,

Dash opened the door for her. "I think Cannon is his own man, different from anyone else I've known — including Rowdy. From what he said, he had a great upbringing."

"With loving parents," Margo agreed. And then, more quietly she added, "Until his dad was murdered." Childhood trauma had a way of molding a person. Sometimes it screwed him up, put him on the wrong path and he never found his way back.

But sometimes it made him determined to be better. With Cannon, she figured it was the latter.

With every minute that passed, Dash felt more urgent to get her away to someplace safe. With him.

Just knowing they were going wasn't enough. He wanted to be there, now.

It had always been difficult, knowing the risks that Logan took as a detective. But with Margo everything was amplified tenfold. He didn't like to think of himself as sexist. Yes, the fact that she was a small woman played into his uneasiness. Never mind her larger-than-life attitude and kick-ass authoritativeness. She was still a woman, slender in all the ways that mattered, without a man's muscle strength or bone structure.

He'd seen his brother fight, knew he could handle himself physically.

But Margo? If she didn't have her weapon, what would she do against a threat? He stewed over that concern the entire time they prepped to leave.

Putting the call on speakerphone so Dash could join in, she contacted Logan on the drive to her house.

"How are Yvette and Tipton?" Logan wanted to know.

"Nervous. Worried." Continually watching for a tail, she said, "You're on speakerphone. Yvette had some news to share, but Cannon stopped in, too." She explained about the possibility of the men being brothers, and the possible connection Cannon had exposed.

"I'll look into it," Logan said. "Give me the address."

She read the slip of paper, then went one further. "This could be nothing more than run-of-the-mill porn. But just in case, don't go in heavy-handed. If you start asking too many questions, you could spook him. Evidence will scatter and we'll never get answers."

"Yeah," Logan replied, his tone dry. "Because that's what I do. I just bulldoze in, no finesse, no common sense. I haven't

466

a clue how to work a witness or how to gather evidence, or —"

"Enough." Margo sat back, rubbing at her elbow.

Dash doubted she realized what she was doing. "Cut her some slack, Logan. The doctor didn't release her."

"Damn."

Margo gave him a dirty look.

"He'd have found out soon anyway, honey."

"Doesn't matter. I'm still returning Monday," she told him. "So don't get any ideas."

"You're worried," Logan said. "I get it. Try a little trust, okay?" As if he expected her to do just that, he changed the subject. "I've got news, as well. Reese just left the car shop and the owner was real helpful. Says he remembers the guy who ordered the rims because he's customized his truck in other ways, too."

"Paper trail?"

"Doesn't look like. The owner considers him a great customer — who always paid in cash. But he agreed to give a call if the man shows up again anytime soon."

"Damn."

They reached her house, so Margo finished the call. Dash stopped her from getting out.

"Your arm is bothering you?"

"No, it's just . . . tight."

"You don't need to do that." He leaned in, brushing a warm kiss over her mouth. "Not with me, okay?"

She didn't pretend not to understand. "It's not a big deal."

"So then take some aspirin for me, please." His plans for the night would include plenty of coddling mixed in with lovemaking, but he'd be damned before he hurt her.

Surrendering with a sigh, she said, "Fine. For you." Flexing her arm, she admitted, "It is sort of achy."

Dash had to kiss her again. With his hand on the back of her head, his fingers threaded through her dark curls, he held her close and moved his mouth over hers until her soft lips parted. Slowly, he licked her bottom lip, dipped inside to taste the warmth of her mouth, and when he felt his heartbeat thumping too hard, he put his forehead to hers.

He couldn't wait to have her alone. "Thank you."

"Just don't push your luck." Another quick kiss softened that order before she turned and got out of the car.

Smiling, Dash followed her to the door.

468

They found Rowdy sitting forward on the couch, Oliver curled up beside him, sleeping peacefully. Rowdy was on the phone, brows down, expression stern. He greeted them with a nod but kept on talking.

Rather than listen in, Margo headed to the kitchen. Toasting Dash with a glass of water, she downed two aspirin, then starting gathering up Oliver's stuff. She packed up a spare food-and-water dish, his favorite bed and blanket, several cans of food and a few toys.

Dash carried it out while Margo got the cat's carrier from her small garage. She left it by the front door.

As she retreated down the hall, he went along with her.

"You won't need much." He stood just inside the bedroom rather than step on the kerosene-drenched carpet. Luckily the cops had already taken a lot of photos, gathered evidence and given clearance for her to get what she needed from the room.

Still, she didn't disturb much as she tiptoed around the wet spots. "Now that my stupid splint is gone, I can barely wait for a long hot shower," she told him. Then thought to add, *"Alone."*

Dash noticed how she favored her arm, holding it close to her side. Icing it would be a good idea, too, but knowing how she felt about it, he didn't mention it again. Hopefully the aspirin would give her some relief. "Spoilsport."

"The next shower," she promised. And then with a hot look, "Or another bath."

*Hell, yeah.*

"But tonight I want to take a real shower, wash and condition my hair, use my lotion . . . all the things that have been difficult to do."

Did she want to pretty up for him? Dash could have told her it wasn't necessary. No matter what, Margo made him hotter than any woman he'd ever known. She could scowl at him and he wanted her. When she talked about showering, he had to fight off a boner.

"Can I help?"

"I'm about done." In the open overnight bag on her bed, she stuffed a few pairs of panties, a few T-shirts, a pair of jeans, socks. With another suggestive glance, she said, "I'm hoping a lot of clothes won't be necessary."

"If you want to stay naked, I won't object."

Without missing a beat, she replied, "I would hope not. When I'm naked, you have to be naked, too. And I expect you to be very agreeable to my turn."

God, was she trying to kill him?

One-handed, she carried the bag into her bathroom and loaded up with a few toiletries, a brush and a makeup bag.

Rowdy leaned in through the doorway. "Am I interrupting?"

"Nope." Dash nodded into the room. "She's just packing for the weekend."

Both men watched as she stepped back out, set the bag on the bed and turned to the safe. "Important phone call?" She removed not one gun, but two, with two boxes of ammo, and put them in the bag.

Knowing it'd be heavy now, Dash stepped in to carry it for her. It wasn't easy, but he avoided the wettest spots on the carpet.

"My snitch."

Margo took up her cell phone, a pager and her purse. "News?"

Dash and Rowdy followed her down the hall.

"My snitch knows the guy who broke in on you. Like you said, he's small-time." Rowdy ran a hand over the back of his neck and sent Dash a look.

Dreading the inevitable, Dash set her bag by the carrier and faced Rowdy.

Margo had already turned toward him. "I'm not that fragile, Rowdy. Out with it."

Dash knew she was far more fragile than

she wanted to admit.

Rowdy realized it, too. He didn't look very happy as he laid it out there. "The moron who broke in here has done his own snitching." Mouth flattened, he added, "For the police department."

The silence felt heavier than a wrecking ball.

"Well." Margo pasted on a false smile. "That doesn't really surprise me and yet . . . it does."

More than ever, Dash wanted to remove her from the entire situation. "Do you know what cops he reported to?"

"Not yet but I'm working on it."

"Logan or Reese will be able to find out." Margo jerked up the cat carrier, then winced at the pain in her elbow.

Neither he nor Rowdy mentioned it.

"I'd planned to call Logan." Rowdy watched her. "The cleaning crew is due here in a few hours. Logan said he wants to be here. I think he's bringing a few uniformed cops with him, too, just in case he gets called away."

Margo put a hand to her forehead.

Everything was as settled as it could be, so Dash took the carrier from her. "I'll get Oliver in. Does he fight it?"

"No." She went to her cat. "Poor kitty is

so worn-out, he might just sleep the whole way there."

Dash figured Margo was pretty worn-out, as well. Since getting rammed and dislocating her elbow, it had been one threat after another with little time to regroup.

They got Oliver into the carrier with little fuss. Dash and Margo stood to go. Dash held the carrier in one hand, her overnight bag in the other. "You ready, honey?"

Melancholy, she looked around the house one last time, and nodded. Her whole world had been turned upside down. The injury, the case, personal threats and the betrayal by her father . . .

Gently, Rowdy broke the silence. "I'm going to hang out until Logan gets here, just to be safe."

Dash thanked him.

It surprised him when Rowdy drew Margo in for a bear hug — but it obviously surprised her more. She didn't resist, but she remained unyielding, sort of stiff. Rowdy ignored her reaction. When he set her away from him, Margo was flushed.

"Well . . ."

Rowdy tipped up her chin. "You don't have to be badass 24/7, you know. You can kick back and give yourself some breathing room."

In a nervous gesture, she fussed with the curls on the back of her neck. "Yes, right." A little desperate, she cleared her throat and turned to Dash for help.

He had to grin at her. The high color in her face was not from arousal. A week ago, he would have hated seeing Rowdy touch her, even in an avuncular way.

Now it just amused him. "I'll see that she does just that." She'd rest — when they weren't burning up the sheets.

Either way, she'd get to focus on something other than the problems.

From what she'd hinted at earlier, he thought she just might want to focus on . . . him. He could hardly wait.

The sun was high in the sky when Margo awoke and stretched out the kinks in her neck and legs. Her arm, which had been resting over the center console, remained sore enough that she took care in moving it. When Dash pulled the rental car down a long drive to what looked like a very private retreat, she sat up and looked around.

She remembered watching for a tail after they'd left her house . . . until he hit the highway. Everything after that was a blur. "Did I sleep the whole way?"

"You and Oliver both — and I'm happy

to say neither of you barfed."

She poked his shoulder. "I said Oliver gets carsick, not me." She peeked into the backseat, where the carrier held her cat. Oliver had curled up, his head near his rump, and was sleeping peacefully. Poor baby.

Shielding her eyes, she studied the landscape as Dash pulled up alongside a curving drive that ended next to . . .

A cabin? She snorted. Though constructed of thick logs, the large, sprawling home was far from a fishing cabin. "This is it? You're kidding, right?"

"Why?" He turned off the engine. "You don't like it?"

Like it? It was . . . stunning. Margo opened her door and stepped out to the dew-wet grass. A distinct chill blew off the mist-covered lake. Here on the land, the sun played peekaboo through the leaves of tall trees, but over the lake it shone bright, mixing with the mist in an ethereal way. She inhaled — and filled her lungs with crisp, fresh air.

Dash got out of the car and, arms folded on the roof, looked at her. "It's always a little cooler here because of the shade and the water."

She shivered, but didn't want to pull on her coat. Moving forward, she ignored the house for the moment and instead looked at the large, peaceful lake. It wasn't that far from the house, the land leading to it almost flat with only the gentlest of slopes. Spring was in the air with wildflowers just starting to bloom all along the shore.

She saw no other houses, no other people. No sounds of traffic or conversation intruded, only the honking of geese, the trill of myriad birds, the chirping of insects. Even as she watched, a large fish did an impressive jump, splashing down again and sending ripples across the glassy surface of the lake, forcing the mist to part.

Tension seemed to seep away, when she hadn't even realized she was so tense.

Stepping up behind her, Dash put his arms around her. "I love seeing you like this."

He mentioned *love* so often that she barely noticed anymore. "It's beautiful."

"You're beautiful." He kissed the side of her neck, his mouth damp, hot. The familiar rise of his interest nudged against her backside. It was incredibly nice to be wanted so much.

Smiling, Margo stepped out of reach. "Let's get Oliver inside and settled. Then I want that shower." A thought occurred. "You do have hot water, right?"

"The house stays fully functional, even when I'm not here. I stocked up on basic groceries, canned goods and frozen meats, condiments . . . everything needed." He smoothed back her hair, checking her forehead where the stitches had been removed, then pressing a tender kiss there. "The whole point of a lake house is being able to escape at the drop of a hat."

In so many ways, he touched her heart, made her feel special and . . . loved. But she was afraid to think along those lines right now. Nothing in their relationship had been normal. She knew Dash was one of "those guys," the men who wanted to protect and care for others. He was alpha with a capital *A,* a natural-born leader. What had started out purely sexual had become so much more because of the threats against her.

Without those threats, would they have had a blazing affair . . . and then ended things? Dash was thirty years old . . . and single. That had to mean he enjoyed the bachelor life, and God knew he played the field. So why should she assume she was special to him?

Better to give it some time, to see where things went once the danger had ended.

If it ever did.

She remembered that their one and only time of actually consummating their attraction, they'd forgotten to use protection. Worries added up, too many to deal with at the moment.

To give her mind something else to focus on, she surveyed the house. It seemed to go on forever. Undisturbed trees grew up around it. A stone walkway led from the gravel drive to a side door. Green metal sheeting served for the roof while large, rounded stones climbed a very tall fireplace.

Dash unlocked the door, then pushed it open. "Go on in. I'll get Oliver and our stuff. The house has air and heat, but for today I'll build a fire to warm things up."

Curiosity kept her from arguing. She wandered in. The air smelled a little musty and a chill hung in the air. She wrapped her arms around herself.

The interior was even more impressive than the outside.

Natural wood . . . everywhere. The planks on the floor had been polished to a high shine. Lighter wood drew her attention to a cathedral ceiling broken only by multiple skylights and a few beams holding ceiling fans. A spacious, modern kitchen sat to the left and ran into an eating area and then a large sitting area, situated around that massive stone fireplace.

Dash came in behind her. "Main bathroom is the center door. There's a tub and shower. Bedrooms are on either side. There's a third loft bedroom up the stairs, with a shower. That's the one I like to use. The skylights up there make you feel like you're sleeping in the stars."

Because kindling had already been laid on the grate, Dash gave her Oliver's carrier, then went to the fireplace. In less than a minute, he had a fire started. "Be right back," he said as he went out the door again.

Margo freed Oliver and sat with him by the fire, soothing him so he would understand the new surroundings. He allowed that only a moment before he went to explore. She trailed him, making certain he wasn't afraid.

Once Dash brought in his bed and food dishes, she took care of setting them up near the fireplace. Oliver ate as if he hadn't been fed in days instead of hours, proof that his upset had waned.

The fire quickly warmed the interior and made everything cozy. She loved the crackling of the flames, the scent of aged wood burning.

Dash let her dictate the placement of the cat box, putting an old rag rug beneath it.

After the cat had finished eating, Dash showed him the box. "Try to remember, bud. But if you forget, we'll deal with it."

Sitting on the hearth, Margo watched Dash talk to Oliver as if he understood. He might not get the words, but the way Dash stroked him, his gentleness — *that* Oliver comprehended all too well. "You're so patient with him."

Dash smiled toward her. "He's family, right? And family is always important."

Family. Immediately she thought of her dad — and clearly Dash had, too. They looked at each other, Dash in apology, Margo in resignation.

"I should probably call him."

"No, let Logan and Reese do things their way first."

Of course he was right. It had never been easy for her to take a backseat when decisions needed to be made. Being so personally involved made it doubly difficult.

Letting that thought go, she stood and looked around. "I want to see the rest of the house."

"I'll show you around." Carrying her overnight bag, Dash approached. "Where do you want this? Up in the loft, or one of the rooms on this floor?"

Turning to look at the spiral staircase, she

said, "Let's start upstairs." She went ahead
of Dash, anxious for many reasons. Awareness of Dash, so close behind her, warmed
her as the fireplace couldn't. She could literally feel his gaze on her backside with each
step up.

Today, though, would be her day. She
wouldn't let him distract her. She would do
things her way — and they'd enjoy it.

"About that shower," Dash said, his voice
low and husky with arousal.

"Coming up next," she told him. "So
don't get any ideas."

"Too late for that."

She smiled. "Don't worry, I have ideas of
my own." She stepped into the massive
bedroom. It didn't disappoint.

An oversize bed dominated the middle of
the floor with four skylights overhead. A
wall of tall windows faced the lake, allowing
in the inspiring view.

"Wow."

"Yeah." Dash set down her bag and put
his hands on her shoulders. "I bought the
place because of the private setting, and this
room."

That had her slanting him a look over her
shoulder. "Planning to do a lot of seduction
here?"

Unlike her teasing tone, he sounded far

too serious. "Yeah." He kissed her temple. "I thought of you."

That would be so nice — if it was true.

Stepping away she went to the windows first to look out. It took her breath away. Across the lake, tall pines guaranteed privacy. She could see his dock, a rowboat tied to the side but a larger boathouse connected. Two benches lined the shore, complete with a kayak stand and bright yellow kayak.

"Do you have a bigger boat?"

"A speedboat, yeah. The other place — the one I'm giving to Logan — was fishing only. No need for anything fast. But this lake is bigger, without the restrictions. I bought the boat when I bought the house, but it's still winterized. Another couple of weeks and I'll get it in."

A door to the right led to a walk-in closet. She strolled to the bathroom off to the left. A pedestal sink, toilet and glass-enclosed shower — with another window looking out — filled the small room.

"The floor is heated. So are the towel bars." He stepped close, but didn't touch her this time. "Everything will be warmed up in just a minute if you want to take your shower."

"I do." She trailed her fingers over plush

towels hanging on the bar.

"I can fix us something to eat while you do that."

Margo turned to him. Yes, she wanted her shower, and food.

And then she wanted Dash.

Going on tiptoe, she kissed him. Then, drawn by his scent, the taste of him, she went on kissing him. Under her hands, his shoulders flexed as he planted both hands flat on the wall at either side of her head.

He didn't take over, just let her do as she pleased. She touched her tongue to his bottom lip, licked inside, tipped her head to better fit their mouths together.

His beard stubble was now even more noticeable. She brushed her fingertips over it, enjoying the rasp. Snuggling up closer, she brought her breast to his abdomen, her belly to his groin.

Breathing harder, Dash clenched his muscles and made a small gruff sound of encouragement.

Knowing she had to stop or she'd blow all her plans, Margo inched away. She kissed him once more, a short, damp kiss. Then another. Patting his chest, she said, "I won't be long."

It took a second for her dismissal to sink in. With a sound somewhere between a laugh and a groan, he stepped back. "You're wicked. I love it."

*Love.* God, how she enjoyed hearing him say that. "You have no idea yet how wicked I can be." She stepped around him. "But I'll enjoy showing you. Soon."

# CHAPTER TWENTY-ONE

With Margo busy upstairs, Dash put on soup then took his own quick shower, taking the time to shave, as well. Dressed only in jeans — unsnapped — he stood at the counter, making sandwiches when she came downstairs.

Like him, she wore very little, only a T-shirt and panties.

It fired his blood, seeing her like this, so sultry and on the make. *For him.*

It wasn't the first time a woman had taken the lead, but it was a first with Margo and because she was special, because he loved her, it ramped up his excitement to an acute level.

He turned, watching her come toward him. "Luckily the fire has warmed the floor. Otherwise your feet would be cold."

"No." She walked right up to him and, after a slow perusal of his body, stroked his chest, his shoulder, his chin. "I'm plenty warm."

Looping his arms around her waist, his hands meeting over her curvy backside, Dash kept her close. She wore no makeup and her naked mouth looked lush. He wanted to kiss her long and deep, but didn't want to steal her show.

She didn't need makeup to look good. With her dark brows and long lashes, her high cheekbones, she looked sexy as hell no matter what. The bruises that had marred her fair skin were finally fading. How long would it be before the memory did the same?

Trailing her fingers down to the waistband of his open jeans, she murmured, "I'm starving."

"A double entendre, I hope." Subtly, he let his hands drop a little more, and lazily stroked her ass. Firm, silky . . . He needed her naked. With him naked. No more reservations between them.

Smiling, she stepped away and went to the table. "How soon until we eat?"

So she wanted to drag out the inevitable? Good. He wanted to savor things, too. "It's ready now." More than willing to play the game, which only built the anticipation, he served her.

They each took their time eating, talking.

Oliver roamed the house, surprisingly at ease in the unfamiliar setting. He especially seemed to enjoy the fireplace and after a main-floor reconnoiter, he went back to doze on the hearth.

Seeing Margo like this made Dash want to know everything about her. "What were you like as a little girl?"

"I already told you." Done with her food, Margo sat back, her legs crossed, her posture relaxed as she sipped on her sweet tea. "I was competitive and stubborn and independent."

That much hadn't changed, but now, having met her parents, he wondered how they'd dealt with a headstrong little girl — that they'd apparently never wanted in the first place. "Were you a tomboy or a girlie-girl?"

She traced a fingertip in the sweat on her glass. "A little of both maybe. I wanted to do all the things that West did — but I also liked playing with the occasional doll." She tipped her head, thinking back. "I liked to dress like a girl, too, but it wasn't always appropriate."

The image in his mind was so adorably cute, he couldn't help but imagine how their daughter might look. He'd want her to have

Margo's features, her big blue eyes. "How so?"

"When competing, a skirt can be a problem. So more often than not I was in jeans or shorts. I remember that I seemed to stay dirty, either from tussling on the ground or climbing a tree or forever running and getting sweaty." She smiled to herself. "Mom stopped buying me shirts in pink and yellow and lavender and instead stuck with brown and gray because she said at least then the dirt stains didn't show."

It took all Dash had to keep his scowl hidden. "Did you like ribbons in your hair? Ponytails? Braids?"

Without any real deliberation, she touched the soft curls over her ear. "Maybe when I was really young. But my dad cut my hair when I was seven, and I've kept it short ever since."

"Your *dad* cut your hair?"

She looked up, her eyes meeting his. "Dad always cut West's hair. He'd use the clippers on him every other week it seemed. Then once, when West was about thirteen or fourteen, I followed him to the creek. He and some other boys were jumping from rock to rock, just looking at the fish and crawdads, screwing around like boys do. I tried to follow him, but I slipped and landed in the mud."

That familiar ache expanded in his gut again. "Your parents were mad?"

"Mom wasn't home when West took me in. He was afraid I was hurt, but I knew I wasn't. I just had a skinned-up knee and a few scrapes and bruises — and all that mud." She shook her head. "Dad ordered me into the bath, and when I was done, he made me sit in the kitchen chair while he cut my hair."

Thoughts churning, heart aching, Dash slowly sat forward. "With scissors?"

For the longest time she didn't answer, then she shook her head. "No. He used the clippers."

Dash wanted to kill him. Every muscle in his body went taut with the need to take the older man apart. She'd been a child, a little girl with scrapes and bruises and a need to fit in.

But her fucking father had humiliated her.

"You don't need to look so upset." Her gaze moved over his face. "I learned so much that day."

"You were only seven years old."

"And stubborn as a mule." Again she touched her hair. "Mom was furious when she saw me. She said we'd all be gossiped about. They had a big fight about it. It was one of the few times I saw her win. Even West was mad about it. Dad said he was wrong and I could grow it back."

But she hadn't. Comprehension dawned. "You cut it after that?"

His conclusion made her smile. "Every single time. I even got a whooping once for it, but I did it again the next time anyway. I figured Dad wanted it short, so by God, I'd keep it short."

She really had been a handful. And he was glad. That backbone had kept her safe, helped to protect her heart, and made her into the woman he now loved. "Clippers?"

"When they didn't hide them from me. Once when they did, I used scissors and it was so uneven, it was worse than just shearing it off." Her smile went crooked. "I was so bad."

"You were — are — so proud."

She didn't deny it. "Finally Mom gave up and started taking me to a salon so they could at least keep the short hair styled. They convinced me that some curls would be nice."

"Very nice."

"Before Dad cut it, the weight pulled it straighter. But no longer than it is now, the curl takes over."

"I love your hair."

"Thank you." She sat forward, her chin on a fist. "It's a reminder to Dad that I know how to win. In fact, he told me once that while he regretted cutting it, he knew I'd learned from it, that I had figured out how to turn the tables on people who tried to hurt me." She went quiet. "That's the closest he's ever come to giving me a compliment."

Nice insight from an abusive father. "Was he right?"

"Yes." Straightening, no longer so introspective, she lifted her glass for another drink. "With every step I took through the department, there were people who wanted to knock me down. Usually they ended up regretting it."

She'd tempered that fierce defense to opposition with extreme loyalty to those who deserved it. Like his brother, and Reese. Now Rowdy and Cannon.

"So." The ice in her glass clinked as she set the glass down. "You donated significant money to Cannon's rec center?"

In the normal scheme of things, Dash didn't like to talk about finances, and he especially avoided conversations about donations. But he wanted to know everything about Margo, and that meant she deserved to know everything about him.

He folded his arms on the tabletop. "I've donated a few times now. Logan also." His shrug didn't begin to cover how little the gesture meant. "I can afford it. It's easy to see how important it is to Cannon and to the kids who hang out there, so why not?"

"That's very generous of you."

This was where things got dicey, where he had to face his own shortcomings. "Actually, it's not." He didn't want to deceive her with misconceptions, so he tried for brutal honesty. "Donating money, especially when it doesn't even put a dent in my finances, is easy. Too easy. It's the people like Cannon, the ones who give their time and energy to a project, who really make a difference."

"Without the cash donations, Cannon couldn't do it." She continued to study him. "But you know, it's nice that you downplay it."

She'd totally misunderstood. "I'm not."

A smile brightened her eyes. "Sometimes, Dash, you're just too wonderful."

That made him scowl. "Damn it, I'm not. That's what I'm trying to tell you. Not only have Logan and I never done without, we always had the best of everything. Our folks are awesome. They're the ones who helped our grandparents set up the trust for us because they didn't need the money. Soon as each of us turned twenty-one, we got a substantial inheritance. Not that we'd been struggling before that. Hell, Margo, we were spoiled."

"And yet you work." Margo again sipped her drink. "You have your own business."

For some reason, it bothered Dash that she gave him qualities he didn't possess. "I told you, I don't do well with idle time. Plus I like the physical labor."

"Yeah, you sound like such a pampered, spoiled, rich kid."

Was she baiting him? His eyes narrowed. "I didn't say that exactly. It's just that I . . ." What? Frustration brought him out of his seat and he began clearing the table. "I've been really blessed."

"And look at how that negatively affected you. You are so lazy, so self-indulgent." Teasing humor filled the insults with irony. "You only ever think of yourself."

He closed the dishwasher and, staying near the cabinets — away from her — turned to scowl. "I am self-indulgent. Especially where my personal pleasures are concerned."

"Women have come easy to you, haven't they?"

Damn it, she still smiled as if the whole thing were a joke. "Yeah, they have. With good reason."

"Because you're so gorgeous," she mused. Her gaze dipped over his chest, then down to his unsnapped fly. "And such a stud in the sack."

That only annoyed him more.

"But I'm glad."

*Glad?*

With sensual intent, she left her seat. "Now I get to be the recipient of all that expertise."

He opened his mouth — then closed it. No way would he argue that, not when she'd once thought he'd be boring.

"But," she added, "I'm not so bad myself."

*Oh, hell no.* He did not want to hear about her with other men. She might be able to take it, but he couldn't.

He started to tell her so, but when she reached him, she only hooked a finger in the front belt loop of his open jeans and tugged him closer. "I think it's time I proved it to you."

Going on tiptoes, she caught his mouth — and damn, the lady knew how to kiss.

His heart threatened to punch out of his chest, and with her fingers right there, so close, his dick jumped to attention.

Flattening her left hand on his ribs, she stroked him, up to his chest, down over his abs. Her mouth continued to consume him, so much so that he barely realized what her hands were doing until his jeans loosened more.

Sliding both hands around to his back, and then down, she pushed the denim below his ass.

Freeing her mouth, she stepped back to look at him. She started with the top of his thighs, then slowly looked up to his erection, his stomach, his ribs and his chest, his throat. "You are so impressive."

Dash braced his hands on the counter behind him, his fingers curling over the ledge, bracing himself against the searing, suggestive heat in her eyes.

With a small purr, she stepped up to him again, but instead of kissing him, she . . . played. Using both hands. Over his nipples, his clenched abs, around to the top of his ass, back around front again.

Down to his dick.

He locked his jaw.

Her cool fingers moved over him, so featherlight that he couldn't help but twitch. She kept her head down, her attention on his nakedness.

Slowly, carefully, she wrapped one small hand around him. Squeezing.

"Ah . . . God."

Her thumb slipped over the head, making his balls tighten.

"You like that?"

"Yeah." He managed to free one hand so he could pet her head, teasing those silky little curls that she had fought so hard for. "I love having you touch me."

"And this?" She firmed her grip and started stroking with one hand while the other went lower, cuddling gently.

His eyes closed. "Yeah."

She kissed his chest. "I love how you smell, Dash." Her small tongue came out to tease, and all the while she continued to stroke him.

"Baby . . ." He fought back a wave of pleasure, swallowed hard. This would be over soon if she didn't lighten up, and he wanted, needed, to make sure she kept pace with him. "Maybe we should —"

"We will." She looked up at him, her eyes heavy, and licked her lips.

Dash nudged her forward. "Kiss me."

But as he started to lean down to her, she whispered, "All right," and sank to her knees.

Seeing her there in front of him damn near did it for him. Then when her breath brushed him, he stiffened even more. Brushing her cheek over him, she whispered, "You smell even better here."

"Ah . . . fuck." He sucked in air, but it didn't help. "Baby . . ." Sinking his fingers into her hair, close to her scalp, he rasped, "You're killing me."

"Mmm, maybe this'll help." Her hot little tongue flicked out and tasted him, almost stopping his heart. She did it again and again, licking over his shaft, holding him tight between her fingers, up to the head and over.

Trembling with restraint, Dash squeezed his eyes shut and locked his knees. He kept his hand on her head loose, gently encouraging. Not looking at her proved impossible, so he opened his eyes again and stared down at her.

What a sight. She looked so damned pretty sitting back on her heels, her nipples taut against the soft T-shirt, her small hand circling his cock.

Her hotly aroused expression made it clear she enjoyed teasing him.

Unable to stand it, Dash guided her closer, hoping like hell that she'd take the hint and —

Her eyes closed, her lips parted and she drew him into her mouth, her velvet tongue teasing as she took him deep, eased back, slid down over him again. With a humming sound of pleasure, her cheeks hollowed out as she sucked.

His spine made contact with the sharp edge of the counter when he moved both hands to her head, urging her to a faster pace. Insanity. If she didn't stop now, there'd be no going back for him.

Already he was on the verge of coming.

He hated to call a halt, but . . . "That's enough."

Her fingers tensed on the base of his shaft, squeezing to let him know she disagreed. Her tongue moved over the sensitive underside, then curled up and over the head, wrenching a deep groan out of him.

His testicles drew taut, signaling the point of no return. She held them gently in her palm as if urging him on.

He fought against it, growling, "If you don't stop, I'm going to —"

Pulling back, she looked up at him and whispered, "Do," before sucking him deep again.

That one small word, coupled with the way she looked at him, on her knees, his dick in her mouth . . . It was more than enough. Too much, in fact.

He clenched his fingers in her hair, holding her closer, breathing harder — and groaned out a raging release. She took all of him, everything, and even after the twisting pleasure waned, he heard the soft, hungry sounds she made.

Spent, he twitched as she licked along his length before finally releasing him. He got several more small, damp, teasing kisses, each one sending aftershocks through his now lax muscles.

He needed a hold on the counter now more than ever but he didn't want to let go of Margo. His legs trembled and he sucked in air, trying to regain his wits.

As she gradually rose, she cupped her hands behind his denim-covered knees, up to the backs of his bare thighs, then to his ass.

Walking her fingertips up his back, she kissed his hip bone, opened her mouth on his abs, lightly bit his left pec, then cuddled in close, nuzzling his throat, aroused and warm and sweet.

Could she feel him shaking?

He dropped his head forward, pulling her closer. Love left his heart full while a slow burn remained just under his skin. "Give me a minute or two."

"Take all the time you need," she murmured, still licking his skin, tasting him all over with open-mouth love bites — doing a lot to revive him. She snaked a hand back down to his crotch and gently held him.

It took some concentration, but Dash managed to string words together into a sentence. "You know what this means, right?"

She gave him an easy tug. "It means I'm in control now."

He smiled, cupped her cheek and leaned her back so he could see her face. By the second he recovered, now semisated and without the sharp bite of desperate need.

But she looked beautifully aroused. Dash glanced down at her breasts, at her stiffened nipples. At that very tempting mouth that had just pleasured him.

He touched her lips with his thumb, then had to bend down to kiss her. "Now that I've come — and I thank you for that, by the way — I can hold out longer. A lot longer."

Something passed over her features. Surprise. Sudden awareness. Hot excitement.

He nibbled on her bottom lip. Had she done it on purpose? Had she deliberately helped him release the sexual tension so he could take her through her paces again? It was a nice thought — one that did a lot to get him going again.

And since her hand still held him, she felt it when he flexed, thickened.

Eyes widening, she looked down at him. "Already?"

"You're here with me, in my house, and I'm thinking about everything I want to do to you. Everything you're going to love." He kissed her, moving his mouth over hers but keeping it gentle.

Controlling it.

Her hand released him, moving to his chest as she anxiously tried to get closer.

Raising his hands to her breasts, Dash closed his fingertips over her nipples. Very, very gently he teased, pinched, rolled.

Moaning, she broke away, bit her bottom lip and turned for the stairs.

Dash hiked up his jeans and followed. "In a hurry?"

"Yes."

The spiral staircase put her at a disadvantage as she climbed the treads ahead of him. He nipped at her bottom, managed to stroke her a few times, and by the time they reached the spacious bedroom she was gasping.

As soon as her feet hit the floor she turned to face him and whisked off her T-shirt, effectively making him pause.

Staring at him, she hooked her thumbs in the waistband of her panties and skimmed them down. Because of her elbow, because she still felt the effects even though she'd deny it, the striptease wasn't as smooth as it might have been.

Didn't matter.

Dash wanted to devour her, but he forced himself to stand back. "Lay down on the bed."

Without question she turned to do just that . . . and he added, "On your stomach."

He heard her soft groan as she went to her knees on the bed, almost stopping his heart with the tantalizing view, before stretching out. She kept her healing arm at her side, but folded the other under her head.

Never taking his gaze off her, Dash stripped off his jeans. Emotional overload, scalding lust — the combination left him devastated.

He walked around the foot of the bed, surveying her from each side. The sides of her breasts swelled out from under her, her back dipped down to a tiny waist, then flared up to that round, sexy rump. Shapely legs, crossed at the ankles.

She was sleek and smooth and strong as only a woman could be.

As he walked, she turned her head, keeping him in sight. "Do you have a condom?"

"A boxful." He was hard again, and he

knew he wouldn't be able to play as much or as minutely as he wanted. He needed her a second time, maybe even a third, before they could rest. But he wouldn't forget himself, not this time. Not ever again. "You don't have to worry about it."

He sat beside her on the bed, trailed a hand down her graceful back.

She purred, and said, "Wasn't all your fault. I know better." Without his direction, she turned to her side, propped her head up on a fist. "Odds are it'll be okay."

Would a baby be so horrible?

That thought stunned him, scared him a little, and made him feel desperate. Because no, for him, it wouldn't be terrible at all. Just the opposite.

Coming down over her, Dash took her to her back and covered her mouth with his. *A baby.*

He nudged her lips open and licked his tongue inside, going deeper and deeper. He didn't want to analyze his own reaction too much because it made no sense. He still didn't know how Margo felt about him, if she cared even half as much as he did.

Which would be tough, given he loved her more than life.

Cupping her face, he kissed her until he stole her breath while settling his body over hers, one knee between her legs, opening her.

She kissed him back, just as wild.

She lifted her belly up against him and he realized he was, in fact, on dangerous territory.

Time to get it together.

He raised up, not far, but enough to separate their mouths. "Does your arm pain you?"

"No." She tried to take his mouth again.

Staying out of reach, he caught her wrists and, watching her closely for any signs of discomfort, pressed her hands to the mattress. "Okay?"

She adjusted, moving her left arm to a more comfortable angle. "What are you going to do?"

"Kiss you all over until you come."

She drew in a shuddering breath. "My arm is fine."

"Margo." He opened his mouth on her throat. "I don't want to hurt you."

"Then hurry it up." Squirming under him, she breathed, "And please don't tease too much. Honest to God, Dash, today, right now, I just need *you.*"

He searched her face, knew she meant it, and pressed the gentlest of kisses to her mouth. "All right." And with that, he left a damp trail of soft biting kisses down her neck to her breasts, where he sucked softly — then not so softly — on each nipple. He didn't touch her between her legs, wanting the anticipation to build.

Leaving her nipples wet and tight, he moved down more, licking over her ribs until she twisted away, then over her flat belly and her cute navel, down to her hip bones. "Ticklish?"

"On fire."

He smiled, and nibbled his way to the inside of her thigh. She tried to part her legs, but with him still resting on her, she couldn't. He breathed her in, loving the heated scent of her excitement. Her skin was so silky, he couldn't stop sucking her against his teeth, marking her in various places.

When she breathed raggedly, shaking and moaning, he shifted, lifting her legs up and over his shoulders, holding her bottom in his hands, burrowing his mouth against her, his tongue seeking —

"Ahhh . . . Dash." She arched up.

He licked over her, past the silky wet lips, into her.

Her hands came down to tangle in his hair, holding him closer, stinging in her intensity. "Stop playing."

He licked again, this time up and over her clitoris.

She cried out, her heels pressing into his back.

Nice. He loved getting her like this, pushing her into a climax. Carefully he closed his teeth on her, holding her for the wicked flick of his tongue, a soft sucking, playing his tongue over her — and far too quickly she came.

He waited only until her shudders eased before raising up to grab a condom, rolling it on, then moving over her again.

Gathering her close, he kissed her parted lips, her dewy cheekbones, her temple. "Look at me, honey."

Dark, heavy lashes lifted, showing her slumberous, sated eyes. Smiling lazily, she focused on him. "That was —"

He pressed into her. There was no going slow, no building her need. He swept her away with him by sheer, raw sexuality. Each hard thrust rocked the bed, faster and faster.

He knew the second she caught up, when her own need escalated. Her knees came around him, high on his waist, her ankles locking at the small of his back. He felt her nails on his shoulders. She turned her face and, trying to muffle her cries, bit his chest.

God, yes. "Now, baby." He needed her

with him. Holding back became nearly impossible, even painful. *"Now."*

Her inner muscles squeezed him, milking him as her second orgasm overtook her, and Dash lost it. Going to his elbows, his gaze glued to her face, he joined her in a near violent release.

*How did it keep getting better and better?* As the wild thundering of his heart slowed and his clenched muscles eased again, he sank back against her.

With every breath he inhaled the combined scents of their bodies, the scent of sex and sweat and satisfaction. Slowly, he rolled so that she was on top, his hands cupping her ass, keeping her right where he wanted her — as close as she could be.

As if that suited her just fine, she sprawled over him, her hand on his heart. Around a yawn, she asked, "How do you feel about a nap?"

It took all of Dash's concentration not to crush her with a tight hug. It was even harder not to say aloud how he felt. Repeatedly he stroked her, kissed her shoulder, the top of her head.

He turned, putting her to her back again. Seeing her like this was such a gift. He kissed her. "Go ahead. I'll get rid of the condom and be right back."

She stretched, smiled and closed her eyes. "Don't take too long."

When Dash returned only a minute later, she was sleeping. But as he gathered her close, she snuggled in . . . right where she belonged.

# Chapter Twenty-Two

They spent the days having sex, talking, walking along the shore and enjoying the tranquillity of nature.

Margo couldn't remember ever being so relaxed. She got updates from Logan, Reese, even Rowdy and Cannon, but work didn't dominate her thoughts. The concern remained; nothing would make her not care. But she didn't suffer the near-frantic need to single-handedly resolve the problems.

With Dash as a buffer to her workplace persona, she was better able to compartmentalize the various duties of her life.

Her only regret was that the time passed too quickly.

It seemed in the blink of an eye, Sunday morning rolled around. Dash woke her with soft touches that turned into hot demands. Every time with him just seemed to get better.

They had lingered in bed until late morning and now a quiet lassitude left her pleasantly at peace. Yoga-style, she sat on the dock next to Dash. The bright sunshine glittered off the surface of the lake, but the temperatures remained in the mid-sixties and with the breeze off the lake, she couldn't help but shiver. Because she hadn't packed warm clothes, Dash had loaned her one his sweatshirts, then tucked a blanket around her.

She watched bubbles rise from a hungry fish, but Dash watched her. With the back of his knuckles, he touched her cheek. "In the summer, we can swim. It's deep right off the end of the dock."

Summer seemed a long way off. Would they still be together? She turned her head to look at him. "You really enjoy the water, don't you?"

"I grew up around it. My parents often took us vacationing at the beach. I can't remember a time when we didn't have a boat or two." He traced a fingertip along her jaw to her mouth. "Water has a way of draining away tension."

When he reached her mouth, he teased that one finger along her bottom lip. She opened, licked the tip, drew him in.

Expression arrested, Dash caught his breath. In the next second she found herself in his lap while he kissed her like a starving man.

Always, though, he used care with her, never forgetting about her injured elbow. She cupped his face. "Can I ask you something?"

"You can ask me anything." He kissed the corner of her mouth. "Shoot."

She was so curious about him, she wanted to know everything. "Is your home as big as the lake house?"

"Bigger. Maybe twice as big. Why?"

What could she say? That he fascinated her? "Do you really need that much room?"

He shrugged. "Mostly I choose it for the land. It's private, and secure." Looking abashed, he admitted, "It has an indoor pool."

And he loved water.

"When we get home, I'll show it to you. In fact . . ." He drew in a deep breath. "I was hoping to convince you to stay with me."

*For how long?* But she couldn't ask him that. She'd fought a lifelong battle for independence; giving it up in any way wouldn't be easy.

Dash went on as if he sensed her uncertainty. "I know your place has already been cleaned up, but I don't want you to be alone."

She smiled at him. "I can take care of myself." If that was his only reason for wanting her to come to his house, there'd be no need.

"What if you're caught without your gun? What if two men come after you?" He lowered her to her back on the dock, half covering her with his chest. "You're still healing from the last attack."

She touched his jaw. He hadn't shaved today, but she liked him with the rough whiskers on his face. "What if a man bigger than you attacked you? What if two men jumped you from behind?" She loved the feel of his weight, his heat and his incredible scent mixed with sunshine and fresh air.

"I'm a man."

Somehow his sexism felt more caring than insulting. "We're all vulnerable under the right circumstances, but I'm not helpless." She gave him a quick kiss. "When you were off vacationing at the beach, I was taking self-defense classes. True, I've got the bone structure and muscle mass of a woman. But it's not always about brute strength."

He didn't look convinced. "Margo . . ."

She lifted up to kiss him, then pushed at

his chest. "Come on. Let me show you."

Determination changed his expression. "Show me from here."

*Oh, a challenge.* "You want me to get away from you?"

"Yeah." He looked at her mouth. "If you can."

Fun. One thing about Dash, he never, ever bored her. Slowly she put her arms around his neck. Her elbow wasn't entirely comfortable yet, but she managed without a single flinch. "Maybe I don't want to." She kissed him again, this time making it more than a fast smooch. With her tongue she traced his bottom lip. Making her voice husky, she admitted, "I like being under you."

So much heat showed in his dark eyes, she almost felt guilty. But not that much.

When she invited his mouth to hers, he didn't disappoint. And honest to God, the way he kissed, she almost forgot her purpose.

Encouraging him with small sounds, wicked touches, she waited until he really got into it — in a sudden, fluid move she rolled out from under him and shot to her feet.

Confused, Dash was left grasping the air.

Margo stayed out of his reach. "Were you a real adversary, I would have stomped your balls, maybe kicked you in the chin."

Still stretched out at her feet, Dash stared at her. His smile came slow and easy. "A surprise attack?" He seemed mildly impressed. "Hate to break it to you, honey, but I was trying *not* to hurt you. Someone else might not be so considerate."

Margo gestured him up. "Playing the victim is a great way to get free." When he didn't stand, she cocked out a hip. "Up. I want to show you what I mean."

"I'm already up." He nodded at his lap.

Mmm, perfect. She could combine her two favorite things — defense and Dash. "We'll deal with that next. But you asked how I'd handle an attack, so let me show you."

In an impressive show of muscle and dexterity, Dash rolled to his feet without using his hands. "All right, I'm game."

Standing in front of her, he blocked the sunshine and she shivered.

He took her hand. "But not here on the dock. That damn water is still frigid and I don't want either of us to take an accidental dip." He scooped up the blanket and led her to the flatter, grassy area that sloped down to the shoreline. He tossed the blanket aside and pulled off the flannel shirt he wore over a long-sleeved T-shirt.

Margo gave a short laugh. "Stripping?"

All too serious, he said, "I'm warm."

And here she was chilled. Yes, major differences between a man of his size and a petite woman. In Dash's case, they were wonderful, tantalizing differences.

He pushed his sleeves up past his elbows, showcasing those awesome forearms. He had muscles . . . everywhere. Not bulky like a bodybuilder, but long and firm.

Hands on his hips, he faced her.

That he looked so serious gave her a little tingle of excitement. "We're just going to act this out. I won't hurt you, and I assume you won't hurt me."

"I'd rather lose a limb than hurt you."

The way he looked at her, his gaze so fixed, staring into her soul, sent a thrilling alarm up her spine. "Okay." She cleared her throat. "Just grab me and I'll —"

He reacted so quickly, she actually screeched in surprise. One second she was telling him what to do, and the next he had her spun around, her back to his chest, those long arms locked around her. Near her ear, he whispered, "Like this?"

Against her backside, she felt the solid rise of his erection. That, along with the way he'd snatched her up, had her heartbeat racing. Okay, so maybe he wanted a very real demonstration.

She rested back against him, saying softly, with a touch of fear, "Dash?"

He flattened one hand on her ribs, pressed down to the junction of her thighs. "What are you going to do, baby?"

She caught her breath, briefly struggled and didn't get even an inch of space between their bodies.

Pressing her heels into the dirt, she pushed back against him.

Dash laughed. He had his big feet planted and other than aligning her body more flush against his, she accomplished nothing.

"Do that again," he taunted. "I like it."

Oh, he was getting into his role, and enjoying himself in the bargain. She tried jerking forward, twisting.

He so easily controlled her that she found herself responding. Though it might be a demonstration on getting away, her body knew this was Dash, and only enjoyed the close touching.

His forearm brushed her stiffened nipples — probably on purpose — making it even harder for her to think.

"Dash," she whimpered, ready to end the game.

He lowered his head and she felt his smile when he nuzzled her cheek.

That was all the opening Margo needed. She dropped her weight, slipped through his loosened hold and turned, her knee coming up to within an inch of his crotch.

She stopped in time and stared up at him, triumphant.

Gazes locked, they watched each other.

"If I'd been serious," she said, "I would have headbutted you first."

His hand curved around her nape. "Before making me a choirboy?"

She knotted a hand in his shirt. "Yes."

"You're fast."

"You're hard."

He drew her close, pressing that hardness to her belly. "I'm still going to worry."

"Did you believe I was scared?"

"Uncertain maybe." He slid his other hand to her ass, keeping her in close contact with his erection. "It bothered me."

"And turned you on?" She rocked once against him.

"No matter what, when I'm touching you, it's a turn-on."

Maybe. But it was also more than that. "It might only be a game, but you like playing the dom."

He brought his hand from her neck to her breast, his open palm rasping over her taut nipple. "And you like being submissive."

517

Margo swallowed hard, pressed in closer, and gave him an emotional truth. "I do . . . with you."

His gaze searched hers, his eyes narrowed and he murmured, "Only with me."

Margo would have agreed, but it was hard to talk while he kissed her like that.

Margo dozed over him, her head on his chest, her legs draped outside of his, her body utterly limp.

He couldn't move without possibly waking her, but he didn't mind. He liked holding her like this.

He knew he'd worn her out, pushing her to a second orgasm before he took his own. God, how he loved to watch her come, listening to those incredibly sexy, rough little sounds she made, how she looked in the throes of intense pleasure.

Pleasure he gave her.

He lazily trailed his fingertips over her back, occasionally kissed her shoulder and ruminated on how to convince her to move in.

His first attempt hadn't gone well . . . unless you counted that impromptu lesson on self-defense that ended them back in the bed for vigorous lovemaking.

Overall, the weekend had gone great, and

he'd hoped to talk her into extending it . . . to forever. The thought of returning to reality and the threats made him more determined than ever to keep her close.

He was still constructing arguments in his mind, weighing all the options, when her phone rang.

Drowsily, she lifted up, looked at him in confusion for just a moment, then comprehension dawned. "Oh." She moved away — losing the sheet in the process — and stretched to reach the nightstand, where she'd put her phone.

She quickly cleared her throat and, in a businesslike voice that amused him, said, "Hello?"

Dash visually traced her body. Would he ever get used to seeing her? Would there ever come a time when her nudity didn't stir him?

He didn't think so. In many ways he felt addicted. When she was near, he wanted her. If he even thought of her, he wanted her. When he couldn't have her he at least wanted to touch her, kiss her.

Talk with her and be near her.

Fuck, he had it bad. She loved the sex — but did she love him?

"Yvette." Margo sat up. "You're okay?"

Dash became more attentive, now looking

at her face instead of her ass. He saw how her brows came together, how she nibbled her bottom lip.

"Of course." She leaned around, looking for a clock and finally finding one on his dresser. It was two o'clock. She said, "I can be there by —" She looked at Dash.

"Four is doable. That'll give us time to pack up, drop off Oliver and get back to her house."

She nodded. "Four o'clock." Listening, she shook her head. "I'm sorry, but I'm . . . away from my home. It'll take me that long to get back." And then, gently she asked, "Are you sure you're okay? I could send over Detective Riske or Bareden . . . No, it's okay. Don't worry. It'll just be me, I promise."

Dash put a hand on her thigh, then left the bed and started dressing. It seemed their weekend had ended abruptly, so he'd do what he could to help Margo make her meeting.

But it wouldn't just be her, because he was definitely going along.

After she ended her call she left the bed to rush into the bathroom, saying, "She wants to talk to me. I mean, me as a woman. Understandably, men make her a little nervous now. She almost panicked when I mentioned sending Logan or Reese."

Dash heard the water turn on and a little splashing. He walked to the open door and enjoyed watching Margo at his sink. "Do you know what she wants to talk about? Did she remember something?"

As she dried her face, she said, "She thinks so, but she wasn't really clear about it. Often witnesses worry that something will be too insignificant but it turns out to be a game changer." She hung the towel on the bar and dumped out her makeup bag.

Dash was already dressed, and he didn't need to pack a bag, so he asked, "How can I help you?"

"Could you get Oliver's stuff together?" She rapidly applied mascara.

It was a unique pleasure, watching her prepare herself. He wanted to spend every day like this, sharing with her, working with her. "No problem. I'll be ready when you are."

Five minutes later she came down the steps with her face freshly washed and a modicum of makeup in place. Dressed in trim jeans and a casual shirt, she dropped her overnight bag and quickly finger-combed her damp hair.

"Slow down," Dash told her. "We've got enough time."

521

She made a beeline for the coffeepot, saw he hadn't yet dumped it and doctored a cup with cream and sugar. She downed it in two long gulps.

Was she nervous? This was a new speed for her and he couldn't help but wonder. "Oliver is ready. I'll carry him out last to the car." The cat stared through the side of the carrier and meowed.

Still rushing, Margo washed out her cup and then the coffeepot, while Dash carried out her bag and the cat's belongings. She was on her knees beside the carrier talking to Oliver when he came back in.

Less than five minutes later they were on the road. This time, Oliver wasn't as accommodating. He meowed and fussed and demanded attention. Between calls to Logan and Reese, Margo had to spend a lot of time reassuring the cat to keep him calm.

Which meant Dash didn't have a chance to talk to her about moving in with him. The cat and Yvette's request to talk occupied her 100 percent.

"Will you call Rowdy or Cannon?"

"Not yet." She straightened in her seat and blew out a breath. "Not until I actually know something. Could be Yvette is right and what she's remembered isn't important. But yes, if it is, I'll clue them in."

They were only about fifteen minutes away from her house when Dash saw her rubbing her arm. Over the weekend, he had gotten her to ice her elbow regularly, to take aspirin when needed. Now, with the job at the forefront of her mind, she hadn't thought to take care of it.

One hand on the steering wheel, he reached past her and opened the glove box to retrieve the pill bottle. He'd put it there as a convenience for her, to ensure she had it when necessary. "Here you go."

She hesitated, then gave in and dug out two pills, drinking some water to wash them down. "Thank you."

Now that they were off the busy highway, he rested his hand on her thigh. "I like taking care of you."

Pausing, she gave him a hot look. "You do it so well — and I'm not talking about medicine."

If nothing else, he could use the enticement of sex as a reason for her to let him stick close. She'd been teasing when she said it, but it meant too much to him. "Just because we're away from the lake doesn't mean that has to change."

Her smiled faded. "Dash." She covered his hand with her own. "Now that I'm out of the splint, there's no legitimate reason for me to keep you under my roof. If you're there, it's going to open the door to all kinds of speculation."

His chest went tight. "You're a grown woman. You can do as you damn well please."

"Please understand." Sadness left her voice quiet. "I love spending time with you. I don't want that to end. But I won't be gossiped about at work. Going back after everything that's happened will be controversial enough."

"You're ignoring your commander's decision?"

"You already know I am." She stroked up and down his arm, before curving her hand over his biceps. "This case is important, and it's going to soak up a lot of my time. Plus the insurance company should be done processing my claim. I'll need to turn in the rental car, then buy something else. I need to get my house back in shape. And there's that whole mess with my dad and his possible involvement in the break-in."

She sounded overwhelmed. Dash wanted to point out that he could help her, but damned if he'd beg. "So we're going to catch the occasional date night — when your work schedule allows?"

Letting him go, she instead pinched the

bridge of her nose. "You knew my job came first."

Well, there was some plain speaking. If he pushed her for more specifics, would he find out he came in second — or even further down the line?

Did she plan to go back to one-night stands from seedy bars? A fist clenched his heart, making his chest ache, but he kept quiet.

"Dash . . ."

He waited, hoping she'd say she wanted him, that she cared. That he had a place in her life.

She reached out to him — and Oliver barfed.

The sound was wretched, and Dash winced. "Man. Poor guy."

Opening her seat belt, Margo turned in the seat. "Oh, no!"

Yeah, that didn't sound good. "Did it stay in the carrier?"

"Unfortunately, no. It's sort of . . . everywhere." Reaching back, she tried to soothe the cat. "It's okay, Oliver. I'll get you cleaned up real soon, baby."

Dash eyed her ass, reminded himself that he was annoyed and told his dick to calm down. *He would not be ruled by sex.*

Not with Margo.

Not when he wanted so much more. Like everything. "We'll be at your house in one minute."

She climbed into the backseat, her rump bumping him twice before she got settled. "Poor, poor baby. It's okay. I'll take care of you."

Hearing her baby-talk to the cat lightened Dash's mood. Sure, work was important to her. She might even think it came first, especially now with Yvette so shaken.

But she had other priorities, plenty of them. He'd just have to make sure he was one of them.

When they reached her house, he parked and said, "Let me carry him in for you. You can clean him up while I clean the car and carry in the rest of our stuff."

Margo tried to deny him. "I can handle it." She slid out of the backseat and hauled out Oliver's carrier. "There's no reason for you to —"

"You're not getting rid of me."

Surprise brought her around. "I wasn't trying to!"

"Bullshit. You're rebuilding those walls at Mach speed. But I guess you're forgetting that my truck is parked wherever Reese put it."

"Oh, yeah."

He smirked. "So like it or not, I'm going with you to see Yvette." When she started to complain, he relieved her of the carrier. "I won't intrude. I can even wait in the kitchen. But I'm going."

Scowling at him, she folded her arms over her chest.

Until Oliver gave a pitiful meow.

Dash chucked her under the chin and, knowing he had her, turned to head in with the cat. "We'd better hustle if you don't want to keep Yvette waiting."

She growled . . . but she also gave in.

Now as long as she didn't try to leave him waiting in the car while she talked to Yvette, he'd count the day as a win.

Cannon checked the clock on the concrete block wall. He didn't have to be at the bar until four today. He had plenty of time yet to pound the heavy bag. Wearing bag gloves, he threw a punch. And another. Mixing it up some, he kicked hard, then more punches.

Sweat trickled down his neck, over his bare chest, soaking the waistband of his shorts. He concentrated, clearing his mind of everything else while delivering several hard strikes that worked his shoulders, his arms, hell, every muscle on his body. He'd been at it about half an hour, steadily pounding away his tension.

Sexual tension.

But there was the quandary. He had choices, only none of them appealed to him. The woman he wanted . . . No.

He struck again, harder, faster, and followed with a kick.

"Looks like we got here just in time."

Pausing, Cannon turned at the unfamiliar voice, then felt his stomach drop. Holy shit. He put a hand up to slow the swinging bag, his thoughts scrambling before he caught himself and said, "Simon Evans and Havoc." Stepping forward, he dipped his head in greeting. "It's an honor."

Havoc clapped him on the shoulder. "You're Cannon Colter."

Evans added, "Your place, right?"

As if he'd never seen the rec center before, Cannon looked around. Gear was stacked everywhere. At the far end, youths sparred under the supervising eye of an older fighter. Toward the back, another fighter worked out while his friend spotted him. People milled in and around and none of them seemed to realize that MMA legends were on-site.

Getting it together, Cannon nodded. "Yeah. I set it up. I had sponsors who —"

"I should confess," Simon says. "Already know all about it."

"You do?"

"Saw your last fight." Hands on his hips, Dean Conor, better known as Havoc in the fighting world, looked around at the various activities going on.

"You watched me?"

"Wasn't the first time."

Cannon kept ping-ponging back and forth between comments from the two men. What did their presence here mean? Wiping a forearm over his face to swipe off some of the sweat, he looked at each of them. "Are you recruiting?"

Simon grinned at Havoc. "He catches on quick."

That only made Cannon's heart drum harder. He tried for a cavalier shrug. "You said you'd seen more than one fight. You're here now." *And I know I'm good.*

"We want to train you." Havoc stopped perusing the gym and instead studied Cannon. "You have a lot of skill, but I think it can be improved on."

"Always," Cannon agreed.

"Good attitude." Grinning, Simon rubbed his hands together. "This is going to be fun."

"What is?"

He held out his hands. "I've already

spoken with Drew and he's interested in signing you."

"Drew?" Cannon's brain cramped. "Drew Black?" *The owner of the SBC fight club.*

"There's only one, right?" Havoc said, and then as a joke added, "Thank God."

"So what do you say?" Simon waited, wanting an answer.

Cannon opened his mouth — and one of the kids came charging in the front doors.

"Cannon." Breathing hard, the kid stopped in front of him. "You told me to let you know . . ."

Forgetting the icons from the fight industry, Cannon knelt down. This particular kid was only ten, and short, and he looked like he'd run the entire way. "Take a breath, Leo."

The boy inhaled sharply, blew out fast and said, "There's a black car parked down the street from her house."

Ice trickled down his spine. His world closed in. "Four doors?"

Leo nodded hard.

Slowly, Cannon stood. "Did you see anyone in it?"

"No. It's empty." He rubbed his nose. "Looks like a 'spensive car, though."

With a hand on the boy's head, Cannon said, "Thanks. Leo. I'll check it out. Why don't you go tell Armie to give you a snack and drink? He's in back. Tell him it's on me. Got that?"

Nodding, Leo ran off to the back room to find Armie.

Cannon turned . . . and almost ran into Havoc. Damn, but he'd forgotten all about him. "Shit. I'm sorry. Seriously. But I gotta run."

Instead of looking insulted, Havoc asked, "Trouble?"

"Maybe. Not sure. But —"

"You have to check." Simon nodded and handed him a card. "Give me a call early next week. We'll work out the details."

Cannon paused long enough to say, "This is really happening?"

"Damn, I hope so." Simon had an inexhaustible humor. "If it's not, Drew will be pissed."

Havoc added, "And you definitely don't want to piss off Drew."

No, he didn't. "Thanks. I'll call first thing Monday." Already unlacing his gloves, Cannon broke into a jog. He had to change out of his sweat-soaked shorts, but he wouldn't take the time to shower. Uneasiness dug in and refused to go away no matter how he tried to tell himself that everything was probably fine, that there were probably plenty of black cars in the area.

After he stepped into his jeans, he pulled out his cell and called Yvette. No answer.

She could be showering. She might —

"Hello?"

Slowly, Cannon straightened. Damn it, he didn't know how, but he heard it in her voice, and that gentled his. "What's wrong?"

"Nothing."

God. His thighs tensed. "I'm coming over."

"No!" And then, more quietly, she said, "No, really. Grandpa is sleeping and I . . . I have stuff to do."

Bullshit. Yvette looked at him like he walked on water. If no one coerced her, she'd want him there.

Every fucking time, no matter what.

Trying for calm control, he said, "Yvette, now listen to me. I'm going to —"

"I need to go now. Thanks for calling."

The line went silent, sending the queerest sort of panic clawing through him. Shoving his feet into his shoes, Cannon called the bar. He knew he should get hold of Logan or Reese, but he knew Rowdy's number by heart. On his way out he snagged a jacket, but forgot to grab the stocking cap he often wore.

Rowdy's wife, Avery, answered the call.

He said only, "Get me Rowdy. Quick."

A second later, Rowdy said, "What's wrong?"

Cannon didn't bother with long explanations. "Something's wrong at Yvette's. I'm heading there now. Can you send Logan and Reese?"

To his credit, Rowdy didn't question him. "Will do. And Cannon? Watch your ass, okay?"

"Thanks." He shoved the phone back in his pocket. It would take him less than ten minutes to reach the house Yvette shared with her grandpa.

# CHAPTER TWENTY-THREE

Margo paused at the door without knocking. They were ten minutes late — a delay that couldn't be helped. She hated leaving Oliver after he'd been sick, so she'd spent extra time coddling him, ensuring he felt better and understood that he'd been returned home to familiar surroundings.

She especially regretted arguing with Dash.

The weekend had been so wonderful that the intrusion of reality seemed doubly harsh. It threw her off, making her testier than she should have been.

Right now, standing on the concrete porch with the hot sun overhead, her frustration level hit an all-time high.

Sensing a problem, she turned to gaze up at Dash. "Are you sure you don't want to wait in the car?"

Dark eyes direct, he said, "Positive." He stood very close to her back, reminding her of all they'd shared.

"Now stop stalling." To preempt any further discussion on it, he reached past her to rap on the door.

Disquiet growing, Margo chewed her bottom lip and looked around the area. "Something's not right."

Dash kept a hand on her shoulder. "What do you think it is?"

All the blinds were drawn, blocking the windows. Not unthinkable given what Tipton and Yvette had gone through and their desire for privacy. Shaking her head, Margo listened but heard nothing, no ruckus from inside, no whispered conversations. "I don't know. I just feel it."

Dash rubbed the back of his neck. "I thought maybe it was just me." His hand slid down to her upper arm, intent, she knew, on moving in front to shield her.

From behind them, Cannon said, "Why are you here?"

Margo turned in time to see him bound up the steps. Without his usual hat, his jacket open, he looked hot — in more ways than one. "Cannon. I didn't hear you."

"I didn't want you to." He'd obviously rushed, but still wasn't breathing heavy. "Did Yvette call you? What's going on?"

"She wanted to meet to talk."

His light blue eyes burned bright with anger. "Something's wrong."

Dash searched the area. "We were just thinking the same thing."

The door opened, and they all three turned, Cannon stepping up front.

Her face pale, a wild pulse racing in her throat, Yvette stood there in something akin to shock. "Cannon."

"Yeah, me."

It surprised Margo how furious he sounded when she'd never heard him even raise his voice.

"Tell me what's wrong."

Sickly, maybe even a little desperate, Yvette shook her head. "Nothing. I just . . ." She tried for a smile and failed. Looking past Cannon, she said to Margo, "I thought maybe you weren't coming after all."

Margo studied her and knew, down deep in her gut, that Yvette wasn't alone. Cannon was right; something was seriously wrong.

She could handle it. She was trained for this. But damn it, she did not need Dash or Cannon caught in the same trap.

Her smile was more successful than Yvette's, but then she'd had more practice. "I'm so sorry that we're late. My cat got sick in the car and we had a mess to clean up." Turning, she looked up at Dash.

"Yvette and I might need to talk awhile. Why don't you and Cannon —"

"Hell, no," Cannon said.

Dash was more subtle. He stared into her eyes, and she knew, *damn it, she knew* he understood what she was asking.

And still he refused.

He gave one small shake of his head. "Sorry, no."

Cannon said, "Let me in."

Yvette's eyes went glassy. "No. No, I'm . . . I called Lieutenant Peterson. I need to talk with her."

Cannon snorted, put a hand flat on the door and shoved it open to search the room. Arms around herself, Yvette stepped back and away from him.

Drawing her gun, Margo whispered to Dash, "It's a trap."

He tried to stay in front of her. "I figured." Ignoring Yvette, he, too, looked around. Voice as low as hers had been, he said, "Also figured you wouldn't leave her."

And that meant he wouldn't leave, either?

Cannon glanced at her gun, at how Yvette stood off to the side shaking, and murmured, "I'm glad I told Rowdy to send in the troops."

Margo was glad he had, too. She didn't see Tipton; his easy chair was empty. She glanced to either side of the narrow living room, but saw no place for thugs to hide.

The kitchen, then.

It opened both to a dining room and to the living room. You could literally circle from the front door to the kitchen, into the dining room, the living room and back to the front door again.

Cannon took a step toward Yvette but she backed up, farther and farther until she stood in the dining room. "I'm sorry," she whispered miserably. "I'm so sorry."

Tipton, holding his ribs, limped painfully out of the kitchen first. "She didn't have a choice, Cannon." Two men came out behind him.

They stood back, using Tipton and Yvette as shields. They each held lethal guns, but the darker man — the one who'd tailed them — also kept a big knife pressed close to Tipton's ribs. Judging by the renewed pain on the older man's face he'd already suffered a few fresh blows.

Margo studied both the thugs. Neither Dash nor Cannon said a word, but she noticed Dash separating a little, spreading out, dividing the target. She wasn't surprised. Dash had proven himself to be both intuitive and intelligent.

She prayed Logan and Reese would arrive

in time to keep them safe.

"Put the gun down, bitch," the dark man said. "Now, before I gut the old man."

She had another gun in her purse. Best to play it calm for right now. Finger off the trigger, she held up her hands and slowly lowered the gun to a side table — within easy reach if she got a single opportunity.

"You," he said to Dash, "that's far enough. Take another step and I promise I'll make you very sorry."

The bald guy cackled maniacally.

To keep them talking, and therefore distracted, Margo gestured between them. "You two aren't brothers, so let's see . . ." Finger to her mouth, she gave them each due attention, then pointed to the hulk with the goatee. "You were ordered to tail us, so you must be the hired muscle."

His flinty gaze never blinked. It was so probing, so icy, she could almost feel his hatred.

Ignoring that for the moment, she looked at the balding man, who couldn't stop snickering like a demented brat. "So that must make you a brother. But obviously you're not the brains behind this circus, so where is the other one?"

A laugh sounded — and kerosene flooded the floor, washing around Tipton's and

Yvette's feet.

The girl went rigid, making the balding fool snicker louder.

Out stepped the third man. He looked . . . inconsequential. Average. Like any other middle-aged guy on the street.

Until he smiled.

Why couldn't the loonies just look loony and make her job easier?

"That would be me." He held a lighter that he repeatedly flicked. With fumes in the air, that worried Margo. "I'm the mastermind, thank you."

She lifted a brow. "Right, if you can call a deranged sicko a mastermind." Just how combustible was kerosene?

Dash shifted — and from one heartbeat to the next, the main guy went ballistic. "Step away from her, right now!"

When Dash hesitated, the guy clubbed Tipton in the gut, making him groan and almost fall to his knees. Only the bearded guy kept Tipton on his feet.

"That's not necessary," Dash said. "You're giving me mixed directions. He told me not to move, and now you're telling me to move."

"I'm the boss."

"Okay, okay." Placating, Dash held up his hands and took a step away from her. "No problem."

So much anger radiated off of Dash that it worried Margo. To anyone who didn't know him, it might not be noticeable. He looked calm, collected, but alert.

Margo *did* know him, though, and she saw that he kept his composure with a strict and enviable discipline.

"Over there," the man said, gesturing toward a wooden dining chair that had been placed in the far corner of the living room. "Take a seat. Now."

His gaze constantly burning over the three men, Dash walked over and seated himself.

"Good, good." The bossy one handed nylon hand ties to Yvette. "You're going to fasten his hands behind him to the chair rails. But first . . ." Grinning, he poured more kerosene on her legs, her feet, soaking her jeans up to her knees.

Screeching, she struggled to move away, high-stepping, recoiling, but he locked an arm around her, holding her tight, the lighter in his hand pressing into her stomach.

The brother giggled and wiggled as if the terror excited him.

Only the muscleman stayed silent and deadly, his ebony gaze going steadily back and forth from Dash, Cannon and Margo,

541

his gun raised, his finger on the trigger.

That one, she decided, wanted a reason to kill. The gunshot, however, would draw notice. And if he tried it, well, she had her own gun within reach and —

"Toby," the main man said, "if she moves even an inch, shoot her."

Eyes narrowing in satisfaction, Toby nodded.

She had one name now. Margo wanted the other names. She wanted to be able to address them more casually. The more familiar she could make things, the better her chances.

The head guy pushed Yvette toward Dash, saying, "Hurry it up or your grandpa will pay."

Stumbling, trailing kerosene everywhere, Yvette rushed over to Dash.

"It's okay," Dash said softly. "You're doing great." He put his hands behind him.

It was a bad time for Margo's heart to expand, but that didn't stop it from happening. God love the man for reassuring Yvette.

"You see, bitch," said the head honcho, "I know you're still armed. I know you're a cop. I know everything about you."

"My name?"

"Lieutenant Margaret Peterson." He

posed, studying her. "I put a bounty out on you, didn't get even a nibble, and now, here you are." And then to Yvette he bellowed, "Hurry it up, damn it! Lash his hands together and then lash them again through the rails."

Biting her lip, concentrating hard, Yvette got Dash secured and jumped back, as if she might be punished for not finishing on time.

Margo was about to ask for their names in return when he ordered, "Saul, go and check that it's done right."

The idiot rushed to do just that — making certain he skirted the kerosene. Holding the gun to Dash's temple with one hand, he used the other to test the restraints.

Margo was deathly afraid that someone as unbalanced as Saul might accidentally shoot. Dash must've had the same thought, especially since Saul kept his finger on the trigger. Dash didn't even blink. He stared at nothing, staying perfectly still.

"It's fine, Curtis."

"Good. Good. Now get her gun."

At that, Saul hesitated.

Now she knew all their names. Margo gave him her meanest smile. "The women in the videos —"

"What about them?"

"Where are they?"

"The videos?"

"You don't need to play dumb. I'm already a believer."

His mouth compressed. "As long as they don't force us to kill them, we dump the women after we're done with them."

"Dump them where?"

He shrugged. "Anyplace convenient. They don't know us, are too doped up to remember anything, and usually aren't in a hurry to go blabbing about their exploits."

It gave her hope that perhaps the other women involved were still alive. "What constitutes forcing you to murder?"

"Usually that's an error." And with that Curtis glared at Saul. "If everything is handled correctly, the women are grabbed, drugged, used and dumped. Nice and neat. But Saul has been . . . messy a few times. And of course, we can't have women running around who know what he looks like." He grinned at her, making sure she knew that she was in that same category.

Luckily Yvette didn't seem to catch on. She could still have hope that they'd get away.

"Damn it, Saul, get her gun!"

Margo turned to the brother. "Come on, Saul. Be a good baby brother and do as you're told."

Toby snarled. "She's trouble. We should take care of her now. I could drag her to the basement and shoot her down there. No one would hear a thing."

Dash stiffened.

"Oh, no," Curtis said. "I'm going to enjoy watching her beg."

*Well, hell,* Margo thought. *That wouldn't do much to help calm Dash.* She stole a quick look at him and saw his eyes narrow, his shoulders bunch. But otherwise he kept quiet.

When he looked at her, she gave an almost indistinguishable shake of her head.

"You and Saul will enjoy her," Curtis continued. "And once she's broken, after she's sobbing and desperate, then we'll kill her. But not before."

Proving he was smarter than the others, Toby curled his lip and shook his head. "Saul can have her. I'll take the girl."

This disruption to his plans clearly disgusted Curtis, but he accepted Toby's decision. "Suit yourself."

With a lecherous look at Yvette, Toby said, "Oh, I plan to."

Yvette wrapped her arms tightly around herself and stared at her feet.

Cannon still hadn't moved, hadn't spoken.

Other than an occasional flinching in his jaw, he remained perfectly still.

When Curtis barked, "Goddamn it, Saul, don't make me tell you again!" Yvette jumped and cried out.

Putting his arm around her, Toby held her tight to his bulky body. "Easy now, little girl. Things are just getting started." He rubbed his goatee against her face, bit a little roughly at her ear. "No screaming before I give you a good reason."

Margo held out her arms while Saul — oh, so cautiously — snatched away her purse. He grabbed the gun off the table and literally bolted, high-stepping around the kerosene to place everything on the dining room table behind them.

"You share the videos," Margo said.

"With each other, of course."

"No." She shook her head. "With other swine."

She could tell her insults were starting to grate on him. The muscles in his neck and shoulders flexed and twitched. "Yes, on occasion, I share. It pays to appease people in high places just in case my plans go awry and I need assistance."

High places? Like . . . in the police department? Her stomach knotted and her lungs compressed.

"Now," Curtis said to Cannon, unconcerned with her distress. "Who exactly are you?"

"He's no one," Yvette rushed to say. "He's just a neighbor. He —"

Toby grabbed her face in his big hand, squeezing so that she had to look up at him. He stared into her eyes . . . and laughed. "Damn, but I think she's smitten."

Curtis smiled over that. "A boyfriend? Interesting."

"He's not!"

Ignoring her, Curtis pondered things. "I can imagine all kinds of interesting scenarios between the two of them."

"Fuck that," Toby said. "I'm not sharing."

At the same time, getting so excited he damned near drooled on himself, Saul asked, "Like what?"

"I'll tell you after we set up the camera. Now, young man." He waved his finger in a circle. "Hands up while you turn around so we can see that you're not hiding a weapon."

Cannon raised his hands and slowly did a turn. Margo saw the bunching of his muscles under his shirt and in his thighs. He was coiled so tightly she wondered that the trippy trio didn't worry more about it.

"Good, good. Saul, go and secure his hands." And then to Cannon, "Make one wrong move, and Toby will break her neck. Do we understand each other?"

With no discernible emotion at all, Cannon stared at him. "Perfectly."

*Wow,* Margo thought. Cannon was so contained. Both he and Dash were handling things as well as could be expected. No posturing, no drawing undue attention or escalating the tension with ineffectual cursing and struggles.

Cannon stood docile while Saul wrenched his hands back and looped the nylon cuffs around him, zipping them tightly. Cannon's gaze met hers, and they both understood.

Saul didn't realize that the restraints needed to be against the skin, not over a long-sleeved T-shirt and jacket.

Cannon turned his back to the wall and stood still. With any luck, Yvette had secured Dash the same way — meaning Dash might be able to get his hands free.

*Oh, God, please let us have an advantage.*

"She's up to something," Toby said.

Margo gave a caustic laugh. "Easy, Toby. Keep that up and everyone is going to think you're afraid of me!"

"No." Still holding the knife, Toby rubbed his hand over Yvette's stomach. "I just don't want you."

"Because I make you nervous," Margo

taunted. "I do understand."

Curtis moved Tipton forward and pushed him roughly into his lounge chair. Tipton bit back an agonizing groan. "Sit in the chair, old man, and don't move." Then he grinned at Toby. "You know, I'm starting to think she might be right. Does the little lady scare you?"

"No."

"She's . . . what? Five-four? Maybe weighs a buck-ten?"

Margo shrugged. "Height is right, but you're off by seven pounds." Sneering, she added, "Maybe it's those extra seven pounds that concern old Toby."

Taking the bait, Toby stopped his unwelcome caress on Yvette and glared at her.

"What?" Margo said, and she prayed Dash would understand. "You want me to play the victim, Toby? Is that it? You want the helpless little woman to cower and cry over the big, bad man?"

Dash's head jerked up and he breathed harder.

"Yes." Pushing Yvette aside so roughly she almost fell, Toby took a step forward. "That's exactly what I want."

"Toby," Curtis said in soft warning. "I have plans for her. Do not even think about stealing my fun."

Filled with evil intent, Toby put his gun and knife behind him on the dining room table, right next to Margo's purse and weapon. "I won't kill her," he said. "I'll just get her warmed up for you."

"Don't be stupid." Curtis handed over the heavy can. "Douse the men in kerosene first."

Yvette was nearly hysterical, but Toby grabbed her hair and licked her cheek. "No more on you, honey," he said against her skin. "I'm going to play with you and I don't want that shit on me. But if you don't stand there quietly and be a good girl I'll fucking drown you in it, then just give you a bath before I have my fun."

Wanting their attention on her, not anyone else, Margo got snide again. "Chickenshit bastard."

Forgetting his order, Toby started for her, his intent plain.

Dash struggled to free his arms.

Margo ignored him — and his lack of trust. "Afraid of a real woman, aren't you, Toby? It's easy to dominate a girl, to play caveman and conqueror against someone so young and —"

Reaching her in three long strides, Toby backhanded her.

Margo staggered but didn't fall. Her cheek

throbbed, her jaw ached, but luckily he hadn't broken anything. She didn't show any pain, didn't rub her face or tear up.

"Toby," Curtis chastised, but he sounded entertained.

"You're going to watch," Toby said, "as I rape her."

Margo made herself stare into his black eyes, her own gaze unflinching. "That makes you more comfortable, doesn't it? Attacking a child instead of a woman? Bullying someone who's so young and afraid. Maybe," she continued, "because you can't get it up otherwise."

"Jesus," Cannon mumbled under his breath.

Dash just stared at her. Did he remember their game of victim, how she showed him her ruse? *Please don't let him interfere,* she thought. If he pushed them and got shot, or . . . She almost shuddered at the awful thought. No, they wouldn't burn anyone. Not yet.

"I bet none of you prickless wonders would know what to do with a real woman."

Toby reached for her — but Curtis said, "No."

Breathing hard, Toby stopped, even stepped back from her.

Maybe because she'd included him in her

insults, Curtis went coldly furious. "You're going to regret that smart mouth, bitch."

"A smart mouth is better than a dumb ass any day."

Toby stared at her like *she* was the insane one, then he laughed with derision. "Seriously, Curtis, just shoot her already."

"No." Curtis curled and uncurled his fists. "I've decided that I'll take her myself. You two can work over the child after I finish with this one."

That took Toby by surprise. He ran a hand over his goatee. "You sure, Curtis? I mean, you never risk being seen on camera."

The corners of his mouth lifted with determined meanness. "Usually," he said to Margo, "I prefer only to watch. Touching the girls . . ." He slowly shook his head. "Not really my interest. But for you I'll make an exception."

Her heart started racing but she kept her tone unconcerned. "Wow, I feel so special." The more enraged she got them the more likely they would be to make a mistake. All she needed was one opportunity, and she would react.

Saul actually clapped his hands. "Can I videotape?"

"No, you may not." Curtis's attention never wavered from her. "Toby is right. I don't want to be on film. This will be for my own private memory, not for anyone else."

Cursing, Dash drew their attention. That slowed things as Toby went over and soaked his legs with the kerosene all the way to his upper thighs. "Just settle down now," Toby said. "That kerosene is going to itch and burn pretty soon, but at least you'll have a front-row seat to the show." He laughed at his own twisted humor and moved to do the same with Cannon.

Bypassing Margo, Toby said, "We'll leave you clean and dry for now," but added, "There'll be plenty of time to fuel you up later."

She half expected Cannon to react, to kick or fight. Instead he stood still, looking almost bored.

While the men all watched that, Dash wrestled with his bindings.

Margo knew that Dash was trying to send a message. The three stooges might not have noticed, but in her peripheral vision she'd watched him cautiously tug and twist.

She was counting on him getting free, because she wasn't sure she could do this without him.

Now with the men effectively contained, Curtis took a step closer to her, his attention on her breasts — and her cell phone rang.

Silent as death, Logan, Reese and Rowdy crept up behind thick shrubbery to survey the house. Thanks to the high sun they were able to stay out of view in tall shadows.

"I had hoped Cannon was wrong." Rowdy glanced around the area, taking in every shrub, every source of concealment.

"He wasn't," Logan said. They each sensed the gloom in the air, the tension that good cops learned to pick up on. Good cops — and men like Rowdy, men who had lived most of their lives on the edge.

Things were off, and they could all feel it.

"Maybe this is why Toby wasn't at his place when I got there," Reese said.

"Probably." Earlier that day, the custom-car dealership had come through for them with an address. Reese had gone there to "talk" but found the wooded cabin empty.

The twisted lunatic was here, instead.

"That's Margo's rental," Reese added, nodding toward the car parked out front of the house.

"Yeah, it's a regular fucking party inside." Logan stared at the darkened front windows, trying to decide how to proceed. "How did they get in?" He turned to Reese.

"No way did Yvette or her grandpa invite them. But if they forced their way in, why didn't the patrolmen notice?"

"They're supposed to come by every fifteen minutes, but I haven't seen anyone and we've been here —" Reese checked his watch "— almost twenty-three minutes." Logan didn't like the significance of that oversight. "Who the hell would have called them off?"

"Oh, yeah." Rowdy sat on his haunches, his gaze studying the house from front to back. "My snitch says it was a tall silver-haired man who hired the hit on her house."

"The hell you say." Reese stared at him. "You just now think to mention it?"

"Yeah." He shrugged. "After Cannon called, that bit of news went secondary."

Reese turned to Logan. "So maybe the commander also called off the extra surveillance." And under his breath, "I never did like cheaters."

Logan didn't want to get distracted, not now, not with his brother inside. But he had to share. "The address Cannon gave me? I just found out an hour ago that it's the house Dan inherited from his folks."

Reese shifted, listening while also surveying the surroundings. "I'd say that seals the deal." And then he asked, "You asked him about it?"

"Right before Rowdy called us." They'd each been off following their own leads, but now everything was coming to a head at the same time. "Dan said he hadn't used that house for months, so whoever gave me the address must've gotten it wrong."

"Of course he'll be able to come up with an alibi if he needs to."

"Yeah." Logan hoped like hell Margo's father hadn't aligned himself with Dan. All of it was twisted enough, but the idea of a dad setting you up as kindling for a bonfire would fuck up anyone's life. "I think Dan has a lot to answer for."

"Soon as we get this settled."

"Right." Logan pulled out his phone and punched in Margo's number.

It went unanswered.

Grim, he said, "I'll try Yvette." Again, nothing. "Straight to voice mail."

"Maybe she turned it off."

Maybe murderous scum turned it off for her. Logan turned to speak to Rowdy, but found him gone. "Damn it."

Reese looked, too. "He is so fucking competent." Sounding impressed, he asked, "Where do you think he went?"

"Knowing Rowdy, he's probably finding a way to play the hero." Logan punched in another number, this time Dash.

He finally got an answer.

"Get his phone," Curtis told Yvette. "And hurry it up."

Breathing in short, gasping breaths, she skirted over to Dash and then waffled helplessly, undecided.

"Front pocket," Dash told her gently. "Right side." He helped by lifting his hips a little . . . and used that movement to further loosen his hands from the nylon cords.

Awkwardly, her face hot, Yvette dug in his pocket and finally got the phone out.

"Put it on speakerphone," Curtis ordered her, and then to Dash said, "One wrong word and the lady cop is the first one dead." To shore that up, Saul pointed his gun at her.

With trembling hands, Yvette opened the phone and held it out.

Knowing who it would be, and knowing his brother was too slick to give anything away, Dash said, "Hey."

"What the hell, Dash," Logan said. "You stood me up."

"Yeah, sorry." He and his brother had talked often enough about cases that he knew how to convey a message without actually saying it. "I forgot to call."

Already the kerosene on his legs grew uncomfortable. He saw Cannon shift a few times, too. He could only imagine how miserable poor Yvette had to be. He thanked God that they hadn't put that shit on Margo.

There was a single second of thought, and then Logan asked, "You hanging out with Margo, or Cannon?"

"Both." He glanced over at Margo, so afraid for her but determined to keep his facade of calm. Somehow they had to get out of this — nothing else was acceptable.

And then he had to tell her how much he loved her.

"Well, don't sweat it," Logan said. "Reese and I got called in to work anyway."

Meaning they knew what was going on.

"I'll see you soon, though, okay?"

So they were already right outside. If necessary, they could bust in — all he'd need to do was clue them in.

"Sure, but it won't be anytime real soon." If they tried to enter now, Margo might be shot. "I'll give you a call when I have some free time."

"Sounds like a plan. Hang in there."

"Sure, thanks, Logan."

"Bring me the phone," Curtis demanded as soon as the call ended. He tossed it onto the table and glared at Dash.

"We were supposed to meet for lunch," Dash lied.

Toby laughed. "You are so full of shit."

Dash continued to look at Curtis. Toby was harder to convince, but luckily Curtis was — for whatever reason — in charge. "You wanted me to throw him off but I didn't have to. He's a cop, like you said. Stuff came up."

Still Curtis frowned. "What stuff?"

"You heard what I heard. But you know he tried calling Margo first because she's his lieutenant, so whatever he's working on must be routine police business."

After some thought, Curtis nodded. "I believe him. If he'd given his brother any cause for alarm, they'd already be at the door."

Agitated, Toby paced, his suspicion cast on everyone. "I don't like it."

*"I didn't ask you."* Curtis took a deep breath, visibly calming himself. "Saul, give her the shot."

Shot? What the fuck? Dash worked his wrists. He almost had his right hand free. No way in hell would he let them inject anything into Margo. If it became necessary, he could attack with the damn chair still strapped to him.

Curtis took in his expression, but had no idea that he was close to being free. "Now, now. Don't worry. It's nothing lethal. Just something to help her be more compliant." He smiled. "I agree with Toby. She will not be easy to control."

Dash knew the woman in the video had been drugged. *He would not let that happen to Margo.* He'd die before he let her be used like that.

Saul snickered as he stepped into the kitchen and returned with a half-full hypodermic needle. "I'll dope her up real good. She won't give you any trouble."

*Jesus,* Dash thought, as panic sliced into his composure. Should he yell for Logan now? Had they just run out of time? Curtis still flicked that damned lighter — but he'd have to hand it off to someone else if he planned to . . . *No.*

The psychopath would not touch Margo.

"That's right," Margo said, still in her abrasive manner — nowhere near a victim — which made it difficult for Dash to understand her strategy. Not that he doubted she had one. "Fill the syringe full, you little worm. Make sure or you'll be sorry."

Not a victim, although she'd clearly sent him a message when she'd mentioned being a victim earlier.

As Saul paused, uncertain, she laughed, goading him. That got Toby bunching up, too, and had Curtis twitching with rage.

And then it hit him.

Margo wanted them all rattled. She wanted them to lose sight of their absurd game so that they'd make missteps — and she could take advantage.

As the truth settled in, Dash felt an eerie calm envelop him.

Hands down, the most dangerous person in the room was Margo.

He drew a slow breath while still working to free his hands. As he'd told her many times, she was an excellent cop, able to quickly evaluate any situation. She had a plan, and he'd have to do his part to help her.

His right hand finally slipped free, but he kept it behind him. Whatever happened, he would be ready. She would be fine.

Nothing else was acceptable.

# CHAPTER TWENTY-FOUR

Sticking close to the bricks, flattened to the outside wall, Rowdy went around the back of the house. He had to assume that the girl and her grandpa hadn't willingly let in the very people who had abused them. That meant the sick fucks had gotten in another way.

At the back of the house he found a narrow window. Someone had pried open the ancient lock, leaving it unsecured. It'd be a tight fit, but a man could get through there if he wedged in flat. Constantly surveying the area, Rowdy opened the window and peeked in.

It led to a dank, dark basement filled with cobwebs. He saw a few boxes, and to the side, several cans of kerosene. Ropes hung from the cans, leaving him to believe they'd been lowered in.

Were they planning to burn the house to the ground? It appeared so.

Probably with Margo and Dash inside.

He pulled out his phone and sent Logan a succinct text: Going in through the basement. With the sound already turned off, he slipped the phone back into his pocket, turned around and lowered himself inside.

Few basements had high ceilings so the drop was short. He landed on the balls of his feet without making a sound. The door at the top of the wooden stairs was closed, but he went up anyway, pushing aside floating cobwebs that had already been disturbed.

At the top step he listened, and heard it all. Everything. Too much.

If the door squeaked, he would be caught.

But if he didn't go now, much worse things could happen.

He turned the doorknob and, with sharp satisfaction, slipped silently into the room.

Margo prepared herself as best she could — but then Toby stopped Saul from going toward her.

Holding out a hand, his expression thoughtful, Toby said, "Wait."

Anxious to play his games, Saul jiggled in place. "What? Why?" He twisted the needle in his hand. "I want to stick her."

Turning to Curtis, Toby said, "Have her

take her shirt off first."

Dash cursed, making her silently plead for him to be quiet. To keep their attention, she said, "No. I won't."

"Ah." Pleased, Curtis rubbed his upper lip. "So you balk at the idea of showing us some skin? Well, I'm afraid I'll have to insist."

She lifted one shoulder. "Insist all you want, you miserable little puke. I said no."

Curtis grabbed Yvette and dragged her into his side. "You'll do it, or I'll strip her shirt off, and then light her up and let you watch her burn."

Doing her best to block Yvette's terror-stricken face, Margo weighed the seriousness of the awful threat. They all looked deranged enough to do it. "I thought Toby wanted to rape her?" She shifted her gaze to Toby. "I thought he needed an intimidated girl that he could easily control. If you toast her, then what will he do? Excuse himself to the bathroom to play with himself?"

Toby locked his jaw.

Nervously, Saul snickered.

She knew they waited to see what Curtis wanted. She prayed he wouldn't make her strip. She was afraid if he did, it'd force Dash to react too quickly.

Releasing Yvette, Curtis walked to the dining table and picked up Toby's knife. "He's fucked bleeding women before."

Cannon took a step forward.

Quickly she did the same, causing him to halt. Calmly, meaning it with every fiber of her being, she said, "Then for that, he'll die." And she pulled off her shirt. Without fanfare, without even really caring. She wanted Saul to get close so she could end this. She would enjoy killing the sick fool.

Dash was breathing hard. Cannon looked away.

Tipton kept his worried gaze on his granddaughter.

But Toby . . . Toby breathed deeper, put a hand to his crotch and rubbed. "The bra, too."

Uncaring, Margo opened the front catch to her bra and let it drop. She didn't slump, didn't let her shoulders droop or her chin lower. Stuffy air washed over her naked breasts and shoulders, her waist and belly above her slacks.

Toby thought she'd be less cocky if he got her half-naked. Well, he could bite the big one. She wouldn't cower — no matter how mortified she felt.

"Now?" Saul asked, staring at her chest while shifting from foot to foot. "Can I stick her now?"

"Yes," Curtis said softly, his gaze locked to hers, hoping to see some wayward emotion. "I think it's time."

Dash was deathly still, Toby distracted by her boobs, Curtis expectant. Only when Saul got close did Margo shift her attention to him.

Yvette softly sobbed, and poor Tipton suffered in silence.

Cannon kept his gaze averted, but Margo would bet on him being very aware, and very prepared.

With a low, guttural giggle, Saul looked at her chest and wiggled the needle, maybe thinking of where he'd like to stick it. In his other hand he held the gun . . . loosely. Jaw slack, eyes vacuous, he inched closer — and finally put himself within her reach.

As fluid as possible, Margo lunged. She knocked aside Saul's gun hand while grabbing his wrist and forcing his hand up and into his own chest . . . where she depressed the plunger.

At the same time Dash sprang from the chair. He only had his right hand loose, but that didn't stop him from hefting the dining chair and swinging it straight into Toby's head, where it shattered off a leg and a slat from the back.

Cannon reacted, too, kicking out and sending Curtis backward into the table.

Screaming, Curtis squeezed the lighter, but from out of the kitchen, Rowdy grabbed his wrist — and broke it with little effort. The lighter fell from his grasp and Rowdy kicked it away.

Yvette had dropped down to the floor, curled in on herself, hands over her head, sobbing.

Logan and Reese burst in, guns drawn.

Saul quietly went numb, slumping down, spittle dripping from the corner of his mouth.

Ignoring her own near-nakedness, Margo quickly relieved him of his gun.

In the middle of the floor, Toby and Dash fought in a tangle of arms and legs. Toby was meatier, but Dash was far more pissed. He pounded on him, and in the process took a few blows himself that barely registered. Parts of the chair still hung from his left wrist, handicapping him only a little.

He half sat up and with undeniable force, punched Toby right between his legs.

The bastard gave a throat-stripping groan and curled in on himself. Still heaving, Dash stood and turned to her.

Toby, too dumb to know when to quit, picked up one of the broken chair pieces and drew it back.

Margo shot him. Once, twice. Right in the chest.

Yvette screamed.

Chaos reigned.

Toby went blank, his eyes losing their evil glint. Sinking back, he hit the floor, sprawled out and just . . . died.

Shirtless, her recovering arm now hurting like a son of a bitch, Margo crossed her arms over herself. "Dash?"

He was there in the next second, pulling her up and into his arms, holding her so tightly she couldn't breathe. Her breasts were now hidden against his chest, but that left her naked back still exposed. She was vaguely aware of Logan giving orders, or other cops now crowding in.

Reese took Curtis from Rowdy, roughly cuffing him, uncaring of his broken arm.

"Cut me loose," Cannon demanded, and it was Rowdy who produced a big folding knife and took care of that.

Immediately Cannon went to Yvette. He lifted her in his arms and went down the hall and into the bathroom. Margo heard water turn on.

Dash ran his hand through her hair, keeping her tucked close. "He's washing off the kerosene," Dash explained. "It burns."

Burns? "Call an ambulance," Margo said to the room at large, knowing Logan or Reese would handle it. And then to Dash she asked, "Are you okay?"

"Yeah." Dash opened his big hands on her back, pressing her ever closer. "I am now."

"I need my shirt," she whispered, feeling a little slow. "And we should call the fire department about the fumes, and —"

"Ambulance is on the way." Logan, gaze averted, handed over the shirt. "Fire department will be here soon." He nodded at Dash's legs. "If that's kerosene, you need to get it washed off."

"Right." He kissed Margo's temple, her cheek. "Come on." Holding her close, still shielding her with his body, he walked with her into the kitchen.

Once they were alone, he set her back from him, his hands on her head, smoothing, touching her everywhere as he looked her over. "You're okay?"

She nodded. "Take off your jeans."

At the same time he said, "Put on your shirt." With a shaky smile, he shook his head. "God, things are fucked up."

He helped her first, lifting the shirt and smoothing it over her head. He swallowed hard, then drew her in for a warmer, longer kiss to her mouth.

Hands cupped to her face, he put his forehead to hers. "Is your arm okay?"

No. Nothing was okay. She felt tears well up, but no way in hell would she cry right now. Nodding, she choked out, "Yes."

Dash studied her face, and sucked in a slow breath. "I love you."

*Oh. Dear. God.*

Talk about timing. She tried to get air into her lungs, but none of her important organs seemed to be working. She felt her lips move, but not a single sound came out.

Dash's smile went crooked, reassuring her that he wasn't insulted by her lack of a response.

Yet.

But God almighty, she had to get it together. "I —"

Logan stuck his head in, saw Dash with his jeans still on and scowled. "Get them off, already. You could end up with blisters. Wash off in the sink." Then he said to Margo, "Paramedics are here. Do you need —"

Still reeling, she shook her head and said, "No." She hadn't been hurt. Not physically. "Have them tend to Yvette."

Normally, that would have been enough for Logan.

No longer.

He stepped into the kitchen and moved close, watching her like he might any other vic who could possibly be traumatized. He even touched her chin, turning her face to the side to inspect the growing bruise from where Toby had slapped her.

"Logan . . ." she began, unsure what to say. *Your brother loves me.* No, that wasn't something she wanted to start blabbing about here and now, especially when it could just be emotion talking. Dash wasn't used to life-or-death scenarios. He wasn't a cop.

He was just . . . awesome. Incredible. Cool under pressure. Burning-hot in the sack. Sweet but controlling. And how he controlled . . .

Oh, God, oh, God.

Ignoring her, Logan again turned to Dash. "Damn, do I need to strip them off you myself? Because I will if you don't immediately —"

"All right, yeah. Got it." Dash hurriedly kicked off his soggy shoes and peeled off his socks. Opening his jeans, he pushed them down and off. All while Logan continued to hold Margo's face — and for some stupid reason she let him.

"Did you get any on your boxers?"

"No, they're dry."

Logan said nothing as he waited until Dash went to the sink and ran water over a dishcloth.

Satisfied, he turned back to Margo. Finally he released her face and . . . handed over her bra. He didn't look discomfited by it. Apparently he'd gotten over the idea of her being a woman.

Glad that her underwear wasn't still out in the middle of the floor where any number of cops might've stepped over it, she nodded. "Thanks." Putting on a bra was the least of her concerns at the moment, so she just let the lacy garment hang from her hand.

"I checked on Yvette and Cannon." Logan glanced at Dash. "He got them both stripped of their pants and in the shower. She's pretty shook up, but he already talked her into letting the EMTs check her legs. The skin looks raw, broken in a few spots. But I think she'll be okay."

Margo knew better. It was going to be a very long time before Yvette recovered. "That poor girl." Twice now she'd gone through this mess.

"Hey, thanks to you she's alive and we have the bastards." Logan ran his big hand over the side of her head, smoothing her hair in a way similar to how Dash often

572

touched her, only without the hot look. "That is, we have two of them. Toby is dead."

"Good," Dash said from the sink.

Margo didn't say anything. She'd promised the pervert that she'd end him, and she had.

Her only regret was that the other two hadn't given her cause to shoot them, as well.

Logan searched her face. "Before things get too crazy, we need to talk."

In his black boxers, Dash rejoined them, his legs now dripping water all over the floor. His skin looked sunburned, making her frown.

Logan folded his arms over his chest. "Rowdy's snitch said it was a silver-haired man who ordered our perp to your house." He waited one heartbeat. "The patrols were pulled back. That's how the creeps got in here in the first place."

Her heart dropped into her stomach. "Dan?"

"He fits the description. Plus that address you gave me?"

"No way. Dan? Seriously?"

"Afraid so. He claims the address is wrong, but . . ." Logan shrugged. "Has he ever had a chance to unlock your window?"

She blinked twice while thinking. But of course she already knew. "It's possible. He's been to my house several times." She said to Dash, "Remember that's why I didn't want to answer when he called? I didn't want him to know I'd be gone and I didn't want him to invite himself over."

Dash put his arm around her waist. "I remember."

Pulling it together wasn't easy. But she needed to get this sorted out. "For a while there he made a real pest of himself, always trying to talk his way in."

"Hitting on her," Dash said.

"Obviously not, if he wanted me dead!"

"I'll take care of it," Logan assured her, and she heard the steel in his voice.

"Not without me you won't." It struck her, really sunk in, the enormity of it. "That slimy bastard! I knew he was up to something, I just never realized . . ."

Dash gave her a hug, tucking her in close, his chin on top of her head. "Take it easy."

She knew she was talking too loud, but so many possibilities jumbled together. She desperately wanted her father to be un-involved. The idea that he might not care at all, that he might actually despise her enough to want her dead, made her ill inside. She hadn't wanted to admit it to herself, much less anyone else. "Would he go that far to defend my dad?"

"We'll find out." Then Logan cleared his throat. "Only because I think it might matter to you, I'm going to tell you that it's obvious you're not wearing a bra. And assuming you want to come take control of this mess —"

Jerking around, her face hot, she gave him her back. "I'll be right there."

She actually heard the smile in his voice when he said, "All right, Lieutenant. Don't take too long, though."

Dash's arms came around her. "If you want to put on your bra, I'll keep watch." He kissed her temple. "About what I said . . ."

Her heart started bouncing around in her chest and her knees went shaky. *He loved her.* "Yes?"

"I know you've got to do your thing. We can talk later, okay?"

*A reprieve.* The knotted stress loosened from her shoulders and finally she was able to take a deep enough breath. "Okay, thank you." She turned and smiled up at him — but said nothing else. What could she say? *I hope you mean It but you just might be hysterical? Overwrought? Emotional?*

He wouldn't appreciate any of those

considerations. So she said nothing.

Flexing his bruised knuckles, Dash searched her face, touched the corner of her mouth and with shadowy acceptance turned to ensure no one walked in on her.

Cannon kept Yvette on his lap, his arms folded over her middle, hiding her upper thighs and her now transparent panties. They were both soaked from the waist down, but knowing how his own legs burned, he'd thought only of getting the kerosene off her. The shower seemed the quickest option.

She hadn't protested when he'd carried her into the bathroom, stripped the jeans off and set her into the shower — with him. The cold water stung at first, but it felt better than kerosene.

Yvette kept her face tucked into his neck as the EMT put ointment on her burns. Cannon couldn't help but notice the length of those shapely legs, how slender she was, how pale.

He glanced at the EMT but that guy looked only intent on aiding her.

When he felt Yvette tighten, he shushed her with sympathy. The ointment shouldn't hurt, but she was so devastated, so wounded and afraid.

His legs from the knees down were hot and itchy, but nothing like hers. Because she'd already had the kerosene on her once before, her skin was far more tender.

Hell, she was tender all over.

That thought bothered him enough that he put his jaw to her cheek and hugged her again.

Once the EMT finished, he stood.

"My grandpa?" Yvette asked from the safety of Cannon's embrace.

"He's okay," the EMT said. "Because he already had broken ribs we're going to take him for some X-rays, but you have a few minutes yet."

"Thank you."

The EMT nodded to Cannon and stepped out, closing the door behind him.

For a few minutes Cannon just held her . . . until he heard her sniff. That tore at his heart, made him feel helpless rage and so much more.

"Hey." He touched her chin and lifted her face. Her eyes and cheeks were blotchy but he didn't see any more tears. "You're safe now. They're going away for a very long time, maybe even life."

She looked embarrassed. "I'm pretty useless in a crisis, huh?"

Cannon shook his head. She was young,

and scared. But she hadn't really gone hysterical until the end, until those earsplitting gunshots. People watched movies and thought they understood how it would be, but until you found yourself in the middle of a shit-storm, you just didn't know.

He eased back her dark hair, brushing it behind her shoulders. "You did great."

She looked down, touched his chest with restless fingers and then snuggled in close again. "I don't know how I'm ever going to face your friend and that lieutenant."

"You don't have to worry about that. They understand, believe me."

"Everyone else was so brave."

"And you think you weren't?" He held out a hand and showed her how badly he trembled. "I was so damned scared it was all I could do to keep it together."

She put her hand in his and drew it to her cheek. "When they put that kerosene on you —"

"No." He shook his head, not wanting her to understand. "I was afraid for you." *Shut up, Cannon.* But of course he didn't.

Yvette stared up at him, her eyes so big and wounded, her expression so soft and sweet.

And her mouth . . .

"When that bastard touched you —" *For*

*the love of God, don't go there.* "I wanted to kill him." He still did. He'd taken great satisfaction in kicking Curtis, but it was Toby he'd wanted.

She gave a rough laugh. "That makes two of us." Then she shuddered.

Recalling how Toby had manhandled her, the threats he'd enjoyed making, Cannon ran his hands up and down her arms. "Did he hurt you?"

Shaking her head, she said, "Before you got there, he . . . he kissed me." She squeezed her eyes shut, her breathing going shallow. "They hurt Grandpa and . . . and mauled me and made me call the lieutenant. . . ."

Cramping, Cannon wondered if Toby had died. Sure looked that way to him. And good riddance. "He'll never touch you again."

"I know." She drew a broken breath. "But I'll always remember."

"No."

She looked at him again, her gaze pleading. She touched his mouth. "I don't want to remember him."

Oh, God. Cannon knew what she was asking, but how could he give in to temptation? Yvette wasn't herself right now. She was desperate and frightened and she'd always had a heavy-duty infatuation with him.

Plus, he'd be leaving. He didn't yet know for how long or how far away he'd go. But no way in hell would he be turning down the SBC. It was his long-term dream.

What he felt for Yvette . . . Well, it was just here and now. It was immediate and hot, but he wouldn't — couldn't — let it knock him off course.

"We should join the others."

"No." Her breathing accelerated. "I can't. Not yet."

"Shhh. It's okay. They've already taken the bastards out of there. I heard them leave."

*"No."* She hugged her arms around herself and started to leave his lap.

Just to escape. Just to flee . . . but to where?

"Yvette . . ."

"I can't go out there! I can't face all of them. I can't . . . can't stay in this house. *I can't.*"

Knowing it was wrong, knowing he should get up and join the others, knowing lust was the very last thing she needed, especially from him, Cannon drew her in close again. "Yes, you can."

She shook her head.

Holding her close, he stood with her. "Yes." He was so very aware of her bare legs, of those silky little panties she wore.

Of the way she clung to him.

"Cannon?"

Looking at her was his undoing. Slowly, he leaned down.

To his surprise, she met him halfway.

And when his mouth touched hers, he forgot everything else, all the reasons why it was wrong, the people milling in the other room, the burns on her legs.

He turned his head, gently moving his lips over hers, tasting her uncertainty and her need.

Almost of its own volition, his hand slid down her back.

She wiggled closer, urging him on.

Cupping a hand over her bottom, he felt the insubstantial damp cotton of her panties and the silky, warm flesh beneath.

She made a small sound of surprise and something more. Something out of place for the circumstances. "Cannon . . ." Knotting a hand in his shirt, she dragged him closer.

It was the knock on the door that brought Cannon back to his senses. *What the hell are you doing?* He cleared his throat and managed to say, in a mostly normal voice,

"Yeah?"

Lieutenant Peterson spoke softly. "Tipton found a dry pair of jeans for Yvette, and a pair of his jogging pants for you. I'm going to leave them right outside the door."

"Thanks."

With only the slightest hesitation, the lieutenant added gently, "You both need to come out now. We'll be waiting." He heard her retreating footsteps.

Damn, but she was one impressive female. Almost to the point of being intimidating, although she sure didn't affect Dash that way.

The interruption had helped Cannon to get his head on straight.

Putting some space between their bodies, he looked down at Yvette. Confusion, need and uncertainty all smoldered in her gaze. He smoothed his thumb over her damp bottom lip, and God, more than anything, he wanted to take her mouth again.

But he wasn't an animal. He was a grown man and up until a few minutes ago, he'd always been honorable.

He opened the door and retrieved the clothes while Yvette stood there in silence. He pulled on the jogging pants, which were a little too loose. Then he knelt and held the jeans for Yvette to step into.

A nice gesture, but dumb as shit since he was now eye-level with parts of her anatomy that he was trying very hard not to think about. "Step in."

She braced a hand on his shoulder and did just that. He tried not to let the material scrape her raw skin as he eased the jeans up and over her trim hips, then was even fool enough to zip and snap them for her, his knuckles brushing the soft skin of her belly.

When he finished, he smoothed down her shirt, tipped up her chin and said with convincing assurance, "You can."

To his relief, she nodded, and together they left the room.

Later, Cannon thought, he'd tell her about his news. But not tonight. She already had enough to deal with.

# CHAPTER TWENTY-FIVE

Her father's car was in Dan's driveway when they reached the house. Margo stared at it, her heart swelling like a melon to lodge in her throat.

But by God, she would do her job. "My father is here."

"Shit." Since he was driving, Logan made the decision to pass the house and park around the corner.

Were they conspiring together? The thought hurt. Down deep inside where no one could see, she ached so badly. . . .

In the seat behind her, Reese took in her expression and put a hand on her shoulder. "I still think —"

"Stow it, detective."

Logan sided with Reese. "You know you should —"

"No." She would not sit this one out. It didn't matter what Logan and Reese thought. It didn't even matter what Dash thought.

*Dash.*

Even thinking of him weighed her down with guilt.

He hadn't liked staying on the sidelines, but he wasn't a cop and he had no place in this. Beyond being tangled in her dysfunctional life, which included work and family, he had his own obligations. His own friends, family, house, business . . . And so she'd convinced him to go home.

But it had been a concession under duress.

*He loved her.*

It was going to take time to wrap her mind around that, if in fact he still felt the same way after all the dust settled. That could be days, even weeks.

She was going to be very, very busy for a while.

Not really sneaking, but definitely being unobtrusive, they went together up the street to Dan's house. Clouds crawled over the sun, making the late afternoon feel more like early evening. A slight breeze stirred the air, ramping up her anxiety.

Wearing a mask of inscrutable nonchalance, she hid the discomfort in her arm, ignored the pain in her jaw from Toby's slap, and the worse pain in her soul from her father's deceit.

Reese led the way up the walk to the front door — but then he held up a hand. When Reese drew his weapon, both she and Logan did the same.

Normally, she wouldn't be armed now, not after shooting Toby. It was protocol for an officer to hand over his firearm under those circumstances. If she'd waited any time at all, she knew she'd be put on leave with all the restrictions applied to an officer shooting.

That's why she'd insisted on dealing with this right now.

From inside Dan's house, they could all hear her father's booming, enraged voice.

Reese sent her a look of inquiry, and she nodded. He tried the doorknob and to their surprise it turned.

As they stepped in, they also heard West speaking. If anything, his quieter voice only sounded more furious than her father's. Knowing he was there as well sent acid down her throat and into her stomach.

Dan shouted, "It was necessary, God damn you! What would you have me do? Go down for fucking a hooker?"

"Ex-hooker," West insisted, "and Margo didn't know anything about your involvement!"

"She was still snooping. She was going to
—"

The sound of flesh hitting flesh, followed by a moan, led them to the kitchen. A chair fell. A cup broke.

They stepped into the doorway to see West trying to pull the senior Peterson off Dan Ford.

"I'll fucking kill you myself!"

West said, "Dad, damn it, stand down."

Instead, West got shoved back and her father landed another meaty blow on Dan's chin. "You crossed a fucking line when you went after her."

"You didn't rein her in!"

"I warned you to back off." Jaw clenched, her father wrenched Dan up close. "You should have listened."

Margo stood there, waiting to see if the pieces would come together. No one noticed them. They were too involved with their melee.

"I tried getting close to her!" Dan defended. "I thought if we were sleeping together —"

Holding Dan by the front of his now bloody shirt, her father slammed his head into the tile floor, silencing him. "She's smarter than that." Going nose to nose with the commander, he snarled, "She is my

587

*daughter.*"

Beside her, Reese shifted, Logan frowned. Their impatience was palpable, but she was too fascinated to interrupt.

"You don't even like her," Dan accused.

He hauled up Dan. "She. Is. My. *Daughter!*" He rattled Dan like a rag doll. "We have our differences, but you actually think I wanted her *dead*?"

More uncertain now, Dan ran a forearm over his bloody face. "I figured she'd be scared, not dead. It wasn't personal. It was just a . . . a solution."

"I have another solution," West said, putting a hand on their father's shoulder in an attempt to calm him. "You can rot in jail."

"You aren't even involved in this," Dan accused.

"Asshole, she's my sister," West said with rank humor. "That makes me involved enough to want a piece of you myself, so don't push me!"

"All right," Dan conceded. "I deserved your anger. But you need to calm down now. No one is going to jail."

Whether it was relief, disbelief, or morbid amusement, Margo couldn't quite say, but she laughed.

Three faces jerked around. One badly battered. One enraged. Only West seemed to understand how the proverbial shit had just hit the fan.

And damn it, that made her laugh even more.

Frowning, Reese muttered to Logan, "She's getting hysterical."

Logan nudged her. "Get a grip, Lieutenant."

"Right." Still chuckling, she wiped her eyes. "A grip."

West narrowed his gaze on her . . . and saw her bruised cheek. "Jesus, what now?" He started toward her.

Until Logan stopped him with his raised gun. "That's far enough."

"What the hell?"

Reese stood next to Logan — both of them defending her.

Doing what, until now, her family hadn't done.

Grinning, Margo stepped between them. "Looks like you're complicit, West." She tsked. "When exactly did you plan to report him?"

Not in the least intimidated, West crossed his arms. "Soon as Dad finished handing his ass to him, actually."

"Oh, really?"

"What? You thought a few punches would cover it?" He chided her with a shake of his head, saying softly, "No. He's going down. I'll see to it."

"Now that everyone is calmer . . ." Logan holstered his weapon and stepped forward. "Sorry, Mr. Peterson, but you'll have to turn him loose."

"I'll call it in," Reese said.

Her father still looked . . . flummoxed. On his knees, a mitt-sized hand twisted in Dan's shirt, he held the commander suspended above the floor and stared at her. "You're here."

"Alive and well."

Having trouble taking it in, he visually searched her over, stopping on her bruised cheek. "Another skirmish?"

Refusing to be drawn in by false concern, she smirked. "Call the mayor," she told Reese. "I have a feeling he'll want to know about this first thing."

Dan protested — until her father dropped him hard to the floor.

Like a turbulent thundercloud, her father jabbed a meaty finger toward Dan. "He opened your bathroom window! The fucker even hired that little shit to come to your house and . . ." He gulped. Hard. And his voice lost some of the rage, the anger replaced by something else, something that choked him. "He was to burn your house down."

"I didn't think she'd be there," Dan protested.

Eyes narrowing, her father turned and kicked him in the chest, knocking him flat again, his rage again taking over. "That is not a fucking excuse!"

Reese stepped up and, wrapping both arms around the thicker, older man, pinned his elbows down and immobilized him. Her father jerked, trying to shrug him off, but it had no discernible effect on Reese, who said calmly, "Bring it down a notch, Mr. Peterson."

Wow, that impressed Margo. True, Reese was a behemoth, but still. Her father was a bear of a man.

With him contained, she came forward. "That bothers you, Dad? That I might have been cinders?"

He stopped fighting Reese to face her. "What the hell do you think? That I'd want my own daughter hurt? Dead?"

"I have to admit," West said, "there were a few times I wondered."

All the fight went out of him. He looked away, his jaw working.

Cautiously, Reese let him go.

He stood there while Logan cuffed Dan.

When he finished he said, "You, too, sir."

Still staring at her, her father paid little attention while Logan caught first one wrist, then the other, to fasten the handcuffs. "Margo?"

She felt remarkably like a little girl again, sitting in the kitchen chair with the obscene sound of the clippers buzzing over her head.

That damned squeezing sensation returned to her throat. "You have disliked me a great deal, Dad."

"No." He seemed to realize what Logan had just done and while it disgusted him, he didn't fight. "I was furious over things you did, but . . ." His brows came down so heavily he looked ready to attack again. "You actually think I'd want you hurt?"

"I assumed you wouldn't care." She'd been hurt — and he'd only criticized her.

He breathed harder. "You think I'd let someone like Dan get away with that?"

"What difference does it make if it's Dan?"

For the first time that she could ever recall, her father looked defeated. Not enraged, not bullying, not self-righteous or in control. "I would never —"

"Dad, please." She refused to be drawn in. Before Dash . . . maybe. But Dash had given her new perspectives and, though she only just now really realized it, new self-worth. "I was ambushed and almost killed in that car wreck, and you acted like it was my fault."

"I want you to always be careful so shit like that doesn't happen! I raised you to be alert so you would survive, not so some asshole like Dan could . . ." He took one heavy step toward her. "Damn it, Margo, what was I supposed to say? Should I have cried over you? Babied you?"

*Yes,* she wanted to reply, *you could have shown an emotion other than disdain.* But instead she just shook her head. What could she say? That it would have been nice if he'd cared just a little? No, she wouldn't.

Her daddy hadn't raised that kind of woman.

She put up her chin. "What made you think it was Dan?"

At the mention of the other man, his eyes went flinty again. "The prick was forever insulting you, worrying that you'd come back and start investigating again. That you'd find out he was involved."

That sent her left eyebrow high. "Is that why his wife left him?"

"Yeah. That and he's a hound for porn. She found out, but he bought her off, gave her whatever she wanted in the divorce to keep her trap shut."

So respectful of the scorned wife, Margo thought.

West nodded. "It's true. Dad came to me and said he suspected Dan. I rode along with him to keep everything right and tight, but . . ." He rubbed the back of his neck. "Yeah, shit went south when Dan was so cavalier about it."

"He expected me to understand," her dad said with another evil glare for Dan. "He wanted me to cover his ass if anyone questioned him."

"Doesn't matter now," Logan said. "It's all out in the open."

Reese looked at West. "Unless you have any confessions you'd like to make?"

"Not me, no." West let his arms drop. "Not about that, anyway. Other stuff but . . ." He shook his head. "But Margo and I already cleared the air on that. At least, I hope we did." He watched her, waiting for confirmation.

Margo wouldn't let him off the hook that easily. "There will be another investigation, and your name will come up."

Dead serious, he told her, "It's not a problem."

Meaning he truly wasn't involved? God, she hoped that was true.

West waited. "Now, about us?"

She believed him, and relief flooded her system, making her so damned tired. "We'll work on it."

That seemed to be the permission he needed and he strode forward, lifting her chin and examining her face. "Are you all right?"

Suspect as it might be, his concern still felt nice. "I'm fine." Sirens sounded out front.

West put his arm around her. "You ready for this, sis? It's going to be far uglier than the first investigation."

"Regrets already?"

"No." He gave her a one-arm hug. "I just want you to know that this time you won't be alone. I'm here and I'll support you any way I can."

His show of affection got interrupted with a ringing phone. Logan pulled out his cell and, with Dan and her father both cuffed, leaned against the counter to answer. Margo watched him, saw the way he tightened, and blew out an impatient breath.

What now?

As soon as he ended the call Logan strode over to her, took her arm and moved her away from West. "That was Karen Ford."

"Dan's ex-wife?"

He nodded. "When Dan denied using his

parents' house, I asked Karen about it. I know they're divorced, but they still share a social circle. Karen was more than happy to turn him out. She said he's had multiple parties there, almost every weekend since he got the place. Their friends have talked about it, a few with praise, others saying he's off the deep end."

Smiling, Margo looked over at Dan. He sat on the floor, his face bloodied, his shirt torn. A defeated man.

Reese joined them, but only to hand over his phone. "The mayor's on the line." He leaned closer. "I told him all of it, and he wants to talk to you now, before you talk to anyone else."

Please, she thought, not another attempt at a cover-up.

But as she walked into the other room to speak privately, she discovered that the mayor's idea of damage control wasn't to hide anything. Nope, he wanted it all handled by the book, resolved once and for all, and for that he wanted her counsel. She almost wanted to crawl through the phone and kiss him for his honor.

Given her personal involvement, Margo knew she couldn't be in charge of the investigation. Logan was out, too. Thanks to her relationship with Dash, who had also been threatened, Logan would be too close. It was an easy decision to hand the duty off to Reese. But she didn't delude herself; she and Logan would both be in the thick of it. At least this way they had some checks and balances in place.

To complicate her life more, the mayor assigned her as temporary commander until further notice.

Since reconnecting with Dash, her life had been upside down, sideways and confusing as hell. And things had just gotten worse. Whether or not Dash actually loved her, she supposed she'd find out later. It was going to take her at least a few days to get things settled.

For now, she'd have to put him — and her entire personal life — on the back burner.

Duty called.

A long bath hadn't relaxed her, not enough. Dressed in jeans and one of Dash's T-shirts that he'd left behind, she took her Coke and settled on the couch with Oliver.

So many decisions to make.

As she was thinking it, first her cell phone rang, and then her landline. Margo huddled deeper into her couch, her face hidden in a throw pillow. Seven days had gone by — an entire week — and she still hadn't seen Dash. With each day that passed, any relationship with him seemed more improbable.

They'd talked that first day, and he'd again said he loved her. But she'd just found out that maybe, just maybe, her father, in his own way, loved her, too.

Knowing it left her . . . strangely empty. Maybe because, after everything, she couldn't trust in his caring.

Now West . . . for the first time he was totally backing her, even going so far as to give information from the first investigation. He'd even joined Dan's ex in verifying Dan had, in fact, been to his parents' house multiple times. West swore he never saw any drugs or pornos, but his visits had been during the day, not for parties.

They'd talked to other visitors who verified that. Most who admitted to seeing the porn swore they thought it was just that: cheap entertainment, not abduction and rape.

She was so relieved that West wasn't mired in any of the mess. But could they actually repair their relationship? She didn't really trust in that possibility, either.

For certain her mother was thoroughly disgusted with all of it. No reason to even wonder about that. But then, her mother had been cold and unfeeling for years. Margo suspected that had more to do with an unhappy marriage than any real animus toward her children.

Margo dropped the pillow and groaned. Oliver, being sympathetic, pressed against her and purred. She stroked him while trying to order her thoughts. Sooner or later she had to see Dash. She had to learn whether or not he really did love her, or if he'd just been caught up in the moment. She wanted to believe him. God, how she wanted to.

But what did she know of love?

*Nada. Zip.*

She was so confused. And maybe even a little needy. And that was uncomfortable enough to completely throw her off her game.

Disgusted, she put her head back and squeezed her eyes shut.

For most of her life her parents hadn't understood her, her brother had been annoyed by her, her officers resented her.

Her commander wanted her dead.

Dan Ford — the man who had initiated the corruption at the station, the official who had first drawn in the ex-hookers, forcing them to play or face possible trumped-up prosecution.

A man who had actually enjoyed watching women be victimized by a trio of psychos.

She was a strong person, she knew that.

But she was now officially overwhelmed.

If she met with Dash, what then? Even if he still wanted her, even if he wanted to continue their relationship, she couldn't help thinking . . . what if he *didn't* love her?

Lacking any real time off to help it heal, her elbow ached, especially when she tried to sleep. But it was nothing compared to the dark of night turmoil that plagued her head, or the hollowness that invaded her heart when she should have been resting.

With Toby dead and Curtis separated from Saul, Saul fell apart like a frightened child. He gave them everything they needed to fully prosecute Curtis: addresses, names, location of evidence. Saul's testimony wouldn't save him, but it could spare him a possible death sentence. For a cowardly little worm like Saul, a life sentence would be worse than death anyway.

Earlier that day she'd met with Tipton and Yvette again. Because of the memories, the resurgent fears, Yvette wasn't sleeping well. Margo had wanted to talk with her about the upcoming trials, to help her understand what would be happening. But the girl seemed doubly shamed when around her, so she'd reluctantly handed off that duty to Logan.

She wanted Dash. She *needed* him. And that was such an untenable sensation that she automatically balked, fighting it, and in the process made herself more despondent — which was also a terrible feeling.

"What am I going to do?" she asked Oliver.

When the knock sounded on her door, she nearly jumped a foot. It was well after work hours, already dark outside.

Could it be Dash?

Her heart launched into her throat, then dropped to her feet. If Dash demanded that she let him in, he could take the decision for a confrontation away from her. She bit her lip.

Did she want that?

Rowdy's voice came through the closed door. "Open up, Margo. I know you're in there."

Extreme disappointment had her squeezing her eyes shut. It took several deep breaths before she got herself together, then she called, "Coming."

Working up to her everything-is-fine face, Margo sat the cat aside, straightened her clothes, smoothed her hair and went to the door. She opened with an absurd show of welcome. "Hey, Rowdy. Shouldn't you be working?"

"Cannon is covering for me." With a smile of sympathy, Rowdy pushed his way in, checking her out from head to toes. He tweaked a curl. "Lookin' a little worse for wear, aren't you?"

She should have known she couldn't fool him. Turning away, she dropped back into her seat on the couch. "I'm exhausted."

"Yeah, so?" Standing right in front of her, he folded his muscular arms over his chest. "You've been exhausted before."

Physically, sure. But never so emotionally beat. "What do you want?"

For the longest time he continued to stand there, dissecting her, until finally he dropped down beside her — so close that their thighs touched. "I want to talk about you being single."

Her stomach sort of bottomed out. Before Rowdy had married Avery, she'd have been flattered. Before Dash, she might have even been tempted. But now . . .

Summoning up her most stern and direct stare, she looked into his eyes and said, "This isn't happening."

"Yeah." He put his arm around her shoulders and gave her a hug. "It is." And then with a grin he said, "But get your mind out of the gutter because it's not what you're thinking."

"No?" Her eyebrow went up. "Then what is it?"

"A long overdue lecture."

*Oh, hell no.* "Thanks, but no th—" She got her ass two inches off the couch before he pulled her right back, almost into his lap!

"A lecture that's coming from me for several reasons." Anchoring her to his side, his muscled arm keeping her immobile, glued to his scrumptious body, he said, "First, Avery insisted I come over. She literally shoved me out the door."

Margo snorted.

"The woman thinks I walk on water. I don't understand it, but —"

"Rowdy."

He smiled. "Secondly, I had a shit childhood. You maybe know that. Maybe not. I'm not going into detail, but understand that it was pretty bad."

She rolled in her lips and dared a look at him. So close that she could count the eyelashes on his beautiful eyes, she whispered, "I'm sorry."

"Yeah, me, too. Thing is, I think you know something about that. For you it wasn't the same. You had a house and clothes and . . . parents. But it wasn't fun for you, either. It wasn't the way it should have been."

She definitely couldn't compare herself to Rowdy's background. "I don't see how —"

"When I couldn't smother away the bad memories, I tried to fuck them away."

Well . . . there was a confession. More attentive, she listened.

"For the most part, I was successful. Screwing was the best way I knew to block a bad memory. I could so easily lose myself in a woman."

Just as she lost herself in Dash. "Rowdy . . ."

He pressed a finger to her lips and continued. "A nice lady or a bitch. A beauty or just some gal who was willing. Didn't matter if I liked her or not because all I wanted was a lay."

She removed his hand. "A quick lay?"

His smile went cocky. "Can't really block heavy-duty nightmares with a quickie, now can I? But the point is that I used women."

She wasn't exactly surprised. Rowdy's sexuality was a blatant part of him, pretty much up front and in your face. "I doubt the ladies complained over that."

Grin widening, he shrugged. "Mostly they just complained when it ended. But my point — because I do have one — is that you and I are kindred spirits."

Fearing he might be right, she tried to joke her way around his understanding. "Actually, I'm not into women."

"No, I have a feeling you're into something altogether different. Not entirely about sex, but maybe more about losing the responsibility for a while."

Her blood surged and her eyes narrowed. "Did Dash talk to you?"

Pitying her, Rowdy shook his head. "You know better — and it'd piss Dash off to know you even suggested such a thing."

Blowing out a breath, Margo dropped her head back onto his thick biceps. It felt kind of nice — comforting, warm, safe — to be held by Rowdy Yates. She could see why his sister, Reese's wife and Rowdy's wife had all so easily fallen under his protective umbrella.

But she was different. For her entire life she hadn't needed anyone. No way was she ready to give up that persona. Not yet.

Not with Rowdy.

She turned her head. "So what are you saying?"

"My life changed so much for the better when I met Avery. I would never do anything to hurt her. I love her. More than life. More than I even knew was possible."

"You still have nightmares?"

"Sometimes. The shit I remember . . . it's a part of me, so I doubt it'll ever go away. But to deal with it, all I need is Avery, not some string of nameless women."

Knowing where he was going with this, she shook her head. "And you think all I need is Dash?"

His expression gentled and he tightened his hold. "I think for a badass cop who wallows in taking control with an iron fist, at heart you're a coward."

That awful accusation hit her like a slap. Stunned, and then infuriated, she said, "I'm not —"

"And," Rowdy emphasized, cutting her off, "if you're not a coward, if I'm somehow wrong — or if I'm right and you want to correct things — then you'll go and talk to Dash."

She prepared to lambaste him. God knew he had it coming. She even had her mouth open to do just that.

But Rowdy watched her, his brows pinched with the seriousness of his claim, waiting to see if she'd own up, or deny it . . . like a coward.

"Damn."

The stern expression eased. He even smiled. She saw it in his eyes, how he expected her to man up and accept it. And she did.

"There you go," he said gently. "There's that backbone of steel."

Stupid, lame, crybaby tears blurred her vision.

Rowdy pulled her closer against his hard chest, his hand on the back of her head, his fingers in her hair, massaging her scalp. He didn't tell her not to cry. He didn't tell her everything would be okay.

Rowdy was more honest than that.

"Much as you're suffering, I can promise you that it's worse for Dash. He's fought every instinct known to man to be there for you in whatever way you needed, and still you cut him out."

Unable to squeeze a single word out for fear it'd be a squeaky, choking sob, she shook her head.

"No?"

She shook her head again. She hadn't cut him out. Never that. She didn't even think such a thing was possible. Not talking to him pained her. Not seeing him was worse.

Even during her job, while dealing with the seriousness of a major investigation, he'd been on her mind.

But she had given in to the fear. She'd hidden away.

A coward. A miserable, lowly coward.

It took several deep breaths before she felt confident she could talk without disgracing herself. "What if he doesn't love me?"

"Know what you should do?" He kissed her forehead. "Go to him. Right now. Ask him outright."

"Put myself out of my misery?"

His gravelly laugh was a sound more of compassion than humor. "Yeah, something like that." Then he tipped up her chin.

Margo knew what he saw. She was a terrible crier. Nothing pretty about it.

His smile went crooked. "Aw, hon." Using his thumb, he brushed away the tears. "I know how you feel, not wanting to put too much stock in love. But I can vouch for the awesomeness of it. All you have to do is trust Dash."

"I wouldn't know what to say."

"You're a female. You don't have to say anything. Just go to him, strip off your clothes and lead him to bed. Men are not as complicated as women. Trust me, he'll get the message."

She laughed around her uncertainty. "You are so sexist."

He shrugged. "After you've both let off steam and your brains are temporarily blank of the external problems, then you can talk."

Yes. Yes, that's what she wanted to do. She

put her arms around Rowdy and hugged him tight. "Thank you."

Unfortunately, that's precisely when Dash opened her door and stepped in.

# CHAPTER TWENTY-SIX

What the fuck.

Dash looked from Rowdy's smirking face to Margo's wide-eyed shock, and he lifted both brows.

He'd figured Margo was lying low, that she was probably second-guessing him and even herself. She wouldn't answer her phone, but that didn't mean she wasn't home, or even that she was busy. He'd checked with Logan first and found out that she'd finished her day an hour ago. They were overloaded, yes. Logan confirmed it. But she wasn't working literally around the clock. She could have called him if she'd wanted to.

With everything she'd gone through, she had good reason for wanting to take a time-out. But it had been a week and his patience was gone. And so he'd come to find her.

But he had not expected to find her . . . Well, like *that.* Wrapped around another man, all cozy and intimate.

For a suspended moment in time, Margo looked stricken. Then suddenly she was disengaging from Rowdy so quickly that she elbowed him in the throat before getting to her feet.

Rowdy, always unpredictable, just laughed.

So maybe Rowdy had been . . . what? Comforting her?

Yeah, her eyes looked red. Dash stepped closer. Shit, she'd been crying. And she'd gone to Rowdy instead of him.

Knowing that made him want to act like a caveman, breaking shit and beating on people until he made her feel better.

Of course, he wouldn't do that. The people he wanted to beat on weren't available. And even if they were, he probably couldn't demolish them.

Despite everything, she loved her father. That's why it hurt her so much. And Dan was locked up, well out of his reach. West . . . Logan said her brother was trying. He couldn't ask for more than that.

Rowdy, other than seeming to have an affinity for comforting every woman within his realm, didn't really deserve his anger.

Margo said, her voice husky, "Dash?"

At the same time Oliver left the couch and

walked over to wind around his legs. "Hey, puppy-cat." Dash scooped him up. At least the cat was purring in happiness, glad to see him.

In less of a hurry, Rowdy pushed to his feet. "Do I need to tell you that it isn't what it looks like?"

Dash shook his head and said, without much venom, "Get out."

"Right." As he went past, Rowdy leaned in and said, "You can thank me later." Dash heard the front door close. Still holding Oliver, he studied Margo. She wore his T-shirt . . . without a bra. The big shirt swam on her, making her skinny jeans look even slimmer — and sexy as hell.

But first things first.

He sat the cat back on the couch and went to lock the front door. Once he got things started with Margo, he didn't want any interruptions.

When he turned back again, she had the shirt off and was working on her skinny jeans. With every anxious movement, her full breasts moved enticingly.

Whoa. He had a lot to say to her, but if she got naked, all bets were off. "Hold up, honey."

"No." She pushed the jeans down, favoring her arm a little, until they caught on her ankles. Without much finesse she tried to kick out of them, lost her balance and fell back on the couch.

In a peach-colored thong. God help him.

Oliver hissed, jumped down and went to his bed to groom himself. He watched the cat a moment while he tried to recover from the sight of her with her jeans down.

He worked up the willpower to face her just in time to watch her toss the jeans aside. She reached for that skimpy thong, but he came down over her, catching her hands and pressing her into the couch.

"Sorry," he said. "But I need a minute."

Breathing hard, she stared up at him. "One minute."

She was so beautiful, even with blotchy cheeks and puffy red eyes. "You were crying."

Her chin lifted. "So? I'm a woman."

Rubbing himself against her, Dash said, "Yeah. Noticed." But what did she mean? "You've never cried before."

"There are a lot of things I'd never done before . . . before *you.* Let me get naked and we can talk about it later."

Apparently he had some catching up to do. "So I made you cry?"

"No."

He waited, but she said nothing more.

"Why are you throwing off your clothes?"

"Because I want you."

Totally lost, he nodded. "So much so, you wouldn't even answer your phone, much less call me back."

Her breath caught and she looked away, but only for a second. "I'm not pregnant."

"No?" Damn, but he felt like he'd walked into a scripted play without knowing his lines. He hoped he hid his disappointment, especially since he knew it wasn't what she wanted.

"I just finished my period yesterday."

Dash shifted, moving both her wrists into one of his hands so he could touch her. He started by gliding his thumb over her temple. "So maybe that's why you're so emotional."

Eyes narrowing, she whispered, "Are you accusing me of PMS?"

She looked so mean, he couldn't help but grin. Slowly he drew her arms up and over her head. "It's a fact of life, honey, not an accusation. You just said you're a woman, so you aren't immune."

She struggled against him, trying to free her hands.

Dash held on. "Does your arm —"

"No!"

He studied her face. "You can be such a

614

little fibber." He kissed her lips, keeping it light and quick despite her effort to the contrary. "I think it does pain you, but I like holding you like this, all stretched out under me." He looked down the side of her body. She had one slender leg sprawled over the side of the couch, her foot on the floor. He turned and looked at her other side. That leg was half-squashed into the couch. "Let's reposition you a little."

"Let's just go to bed so we can both be comfortable."

"I'm comfortable right here." He wouldn't explain that a bed would test him too much. He'd been in agony trying to give her the time she needed, trying to be respectful to the demands of her job. Suffering extreme withdrawal from her sweet little body.

"Dash —"

"Shhh. Quiet down, honey, and let me decide how I want to arrange you."

It didn't surprise him at all when she did as asked.

"Let's try this." He caught her inside leg and raised it up high so that it rested on the back of the couch, opening her legs wider so that he could settle more closely against her.

She had her bottom lip caught in her teeth, her breath rushing. Damn, but the things she made him feel . . .

Levering up on an elbow, he looked her over. "I've missed these," he said about her breasts and bent to gently draw her nipple into his mouth.

Gasping, she shifted, lifting up to him.

He sucked and licked, leaving her nipple wet and tight. "Hold still, Margo." He waited, and when she didn't move, it excited him unbearably. "Now, how does your arm really feel?"

"It's sometimes achy."

Her honesty pleased him. "But not now?"

"Only a little."

"Not enough that I need to —"

"No." She tugged gently, then admitted, "I like this, but then you already know that."

As long as she was being honest . . . "You've missed me?"

Her eyes clouded, grew damp again. "So much."

Relieved, he filed away her emotional reply. "You were . . ." He couldn't say afraid, so he amended, "Worried?"

After an audible swallow and a sniff, she nodded.

"Do you believe that I love you?"

"I don't know." She quickly added, "I hope you do."

Cupping her breast, his thumb teasing her

616

nipple, he asked, "Do you love me?"

"Yes."

She said that so fast, her eyes dark, her lips trembling. Relief slammed into him and he put his head down by hers, and whispered, "Say it."

"I love you so much."

Heart hammering, he took her mouth, kissed her hard and slanted his head so that he could deepen the kiss even more.

She pressed up into him, undulating her hips, wrapping her legs around him.

But not yet, he told himself. Not just yet. "You're moving."

"You're not." She hugged her legs high around his waist. "But you should be. After you get naked."

He smiled, and cupped her breast. "Do you have any idea what the past week has been like for me?"

"From what Rowdy said, it was maybe, but not quite, as bad as my week."

He knew she'd been inundated with the job and personal family stuff. More than anything he'd wanted to be there with her, to help however he could. "A lot going on at the station?"

She shook her head. "A lot going on with missing you."

Ah. So she'd suffered the same? Lightly,

he tugged at her nipple and watched her eyes go heavy-lidded. "Rowdy was here to sing my praises?"

"I think —" her breath caught "— it was more about saving me from myself. Or something like that. Hard to tell with him." Squirming, she licked her lips. "He told me to get naked with you and everything else would work out."

Dash had to grin over that. Yes, he would thank Rowdy when next he saw him. "He gave that advice . . . why?"

Her eyes closed. She even turned her face away. "Because I'm a coward."

Ending the sensual torment, Dash instead brought her face back around and then just waited.

"I love you, but . . ." She licked her lips again. "So many things have gone wrong. In my life, I mean. Even with my family I haven't had a solid relationship. I've never really known . . ." Her voice trailed off and she stared at him helplessly.

Dash smoothed her hair. "Love?"

She nodded.

God, he adored her hair — more so now that he knew how she'd first come by the sexy style. "You will always have it from me."

"My job, my family . . ." Worry etched a frown in her brows. "They can be difficult."

Dash cupped her face. "It doesn't matter if you're being the badass lieutenant, the independent daughter, or the submissive woman, I love you so much you're going to drown in it."

Tears glazed her eyes again. "Let my arms go."

He did — and she wrapped them around him, holding tight, hiding her face against his throat. He felt the dampness on his throat, but he knew everything would be okay now, so he just held her, kissing her cheekbone, her shoulder.

"Dash?"

"Hmm?" The thong left the satiny skin of her cheeks exposed. He turned, putting her atop him so he could stroke her sexy ass.

"Please don't think I'm awful."

"Never."

Mustering up her backbone, she said, "When I realized I wasn't pregnant, I was . . . disappointed."

His heart expanded — because he was disappointed, too. "A baby would mean permanence."

"I know."

Did she? Did she realize everything he wanted from her? "It would mean marriage, a lifetime together. The whole thing."

Her tentative fingers moved over his chest.

"Yes." Suddenly she came up to her elbows. And what a great pose that was. He had both hands on her backside, keeping her pressed closed to his erection. Her naked breasts were right there, tempting him to nuzzle. And her mouth . . . whether she was ordering, teasing, kissing or cursing, she had one of the sexiest mouths he'd ever seen.

"I want that."

Thrown off a little, Dash looked up at her face. "You want what?"

"You." As if she might lose her nerve, she came down to kiss him hard and fast. "Love. Marriage. Kids. The whole thing."

The grin crept up on him. "You want to marry me?"

"If you laugh, I swear —"

"What?" He held on to her behind. "What would you do?"

She let out a sigh. "Love you." Her forehead to his, she said, "I swear, Dash, I do love your laugh."

"Hold on." Locking an arm around her bottom, he stood, lifting her with him.

"Dash!"

He pulled her legs around his waist and, with one devouring kiss, headed for the bedroom. "Just so you know, I was halfway hoping you'd be knocked up, too."

"You're so romantic."

He laughed. "I have a mostly naked woman making me insane. How romantic did you expect me to be?"

"You mean it? You want a baby?"

"Or two or three." He paused in the hallway, pinning her to the wall, touching between her legs until she panted. "With you, Margo. Only with you."

*"Yes."*

In her room he lowered her down to the bed and sank in against her.

"To your proposal, yes. Whenever you want. Whatever you want."

He took her mouth and then didn't want to stop kissing her. But this was important. Breathing heavier now, he said, "As for kids, I know your job is important to you, and it can get complicated. So just let me know when you're ready."

Wide-eyed over all that, Margo laughed. "You are far too accommodating."

Again he stretched her out, using his knee to nudge her legs farther apart. With new heat roughening his voice, he said, "I expect you to be accommodating, as well." As he sat up, he trailed his fingertips down her arms to her breasts. "Don't move."

She shivered. "Dash?"

Her husky voice pleased him. "What, baby?"

"I love the way you love me."

He bent to kiss her stomach.

"Soon," she whispered.

"What's that?" He hooked his fingers in the waistband of the provocative thong and drew it down her thighs.

"I want to marry you soon."

"Sounds like a plan." Leaving the skimpy material at her knees, he bent to kiss her inner thigh.

"A baby right after that."

Growling, he stood and stripped off his clothes, rolled on a condom and returned to her. "You're making me hot."

She laughed — but she didn't move.

And neither of them did any more talking.

At the front of the rec center, freshly showered and dressed after a grueling workout, Cannon leaned on the reception desk and finished his phone call. In three days he'd be heading to Harmony, Kentucky. It was only a three-hour trip, but it was far enough to be a complete game changer.

He was signing with the SBC. He still couldn't believe it, but he'd just talked with Havoc and had it confirmed that he'd be meeting Drew Black in person. Havoc and Simon Evans ran a gym in Harmony, which meant a lot of prime competition hung out there. He'd get additional training with some great exposure.

Damn, he'd worked hard for this.

At the same time, he'd miss working at Rowdy's bar full-time. Not that he'd be moving away for good. He'd handed off some of the responsibilities for the rec center to Armie Jacobson, another fighter who was good with the kids. Cannon would retain a supervisory position. Between fights, and training for fights, he'd be back.

So then why did vague discontent gnaw on the outer edges of his satisfaction, blunting some of the pleasure?

"Cannon?"

That faint, whispery voice drew him around. As if he'd somehow summoned her with his churning thoughts, Yvette stood in the doorway, her body outlined by the floodlights out front.

As usual she wore jeans, but these were a boyfriend cut, not like the tight denim she'd always preferred. Since the night was cool she'd pulled on a hooded sweatshirt a few sizes too big. Her long dark hair trailed over her chest, around her breasts.

At his continued scrutiny, she shifted.

Realizing he was staring, Cannon unglued his feet. "Hey." He looked beyond her but didn't see her grandpa. "What are you doing here?"

"I'm sorry to bother you." She, too, looked around. "You're closed?"

"Just locking up, yeah." Since he wasn't working at the bar tonight, he'd planned to find a little female recreation before calling it a night. But despite the ill-advised kiss he'd given into in her bathroom, Yvette wasn't an option. For a dozen different reasons, she was off-limits.

"I thought you'd be at the bar, but . . . you weren't."

She'd gone to Getting Rowdy looking for him? "You're not twenty-one." *Number two reason why he could never again forget himself.* "You can't go in there."

A smile teased the corners of her mouth. "So Rowdy told me, very quickly." She continued to stand in the doorway instead of coming in. "He's the one who told me you'd be here."

Had Rowdy frightened her? He was big and imposing . . . and she'd been through so much. *Number one reason he had to keep his attention off her curvy little body in the slouchy clothes.* "You're okay?"

Nodding, she said, "I wanted to talk to you. I mean, if you have a minute. I don't want to interrupt anything."

"Come on in." He held the door wide and then secured it behind her. "How'd you get here?"

"I drove." Trailing a hand along a rack of weights, she explored the rec center. "I'm almost twenty you know, not twelve. I got my license a long time ago."

No, he didn't know that. And he'd be better off thinking of her as twelve. "I thought you just graduated."

When she looked away, he wanted to kick his own ass. Way to bring up a failure.

Gliding over to a speed bag, she gave it a shove, watched it a minute, then said, so softly he barely heard, "I live with Grandpa because my parents are both gone. They died with I was thirteen. I . . . lost a few months of the school year and had to redo it. Only I was moving around a lot, from my aunts to my cousins and then finally here." She shrugged. "I hadn't attended enough school in any one place to count the year."

That had to be really rough. "I'm sorry." He came up behind her, but not too close. No reason to tempt himself. "Things didn't work out with the other relatives?"

She pushed back the hood of her sweatshirt and gave the speed bag another tap. "I guess not." Flashing him a smile, she asked,

"How's this work?"

Drawn to her despite his better sense, Cannon stepped up to the bag. "It's hung a little high for you." He moved his feet into position and held his arms at the right angles. "Like this, okay?"

She nodded.

"After you're in the proper stance . . ." He struck the belly of the bag and immediately circled his fist back. "You count the rebounds to know when to strike again." After showing her what he meant, he did a thirty-second round, repeatedly and fluidly hitting the bag.

Smiling, she said, "You make it look so easy."

He stilled the bag, wondering why she was here, what she wanted. *What he wanted.*

Turning away and heading for the heavy bag, she laughed. "Actually, you make . . . everything seem easier."

Cannon watched her. "If I could, I'd make it easier for you."

She kept her back to him. "You already have." She ran her hand over the bag. "I'm leaving tonight."

His heart skipped two beats. "What does that mean? Leaving where?"

Pasting on a bright and completely false smile, she faced him. "I'm going back to

California. Remember the aunt I mentioned? Well, she's ill and could use some help with her store. I'll stay with her and in my free time I can get my associates degree and . . ." She stopped. Cleared her throat. "Grandpa is going to retire. He'll sell the pawnshop and just take it easy. He said he can visit often, or I can visit him. And of course, I'll have to come for the trial. But . . . I can't stay here."

Cannon took a step toward her but she held up a hand.

"No, please. Don't tell me I can. Don't tell me it'll all be okay." She closed her arms around herself. "I can't sleep, I keep jumping over every little sound, and I smell kerosene even when there's none around and . . ." She held out her hands. "I can't stay." Now she came to him, rushing over. "You've been such a huge help. To me and to Grandpa." Her hand touched his chest, but not for long. She was already walking away when she said, "I can't thank you enough, and I won't ever forget what you did for us."

By the time she reached the door, she was practically running. She fumbled with the lock a moment and finally got it open. A bell chimed as she darted out into the night.

Cannon hadn't yet moved. He had his

hand over his chest, on the spot she'd touched so very lightly.

He'd worried about her making more of that kiss than he'd meant for there to be. He'd thought she might consider it a commitment of some sort. That she'd consider him obligated to explain.

Instead he was the one left standing behind, wondering how she could walk away without even acknowledging it.

Striding to the big front window, he watched Yvette rush across the street to a small car parked beneath a big security light. She didn't look his way, and she didn't look back.

She just drove off into the night.

In three days he'd be gone anyway. But in his subconscious . . . he'd always figured on her being around when he came home.

"Shit." Locking up, he decided against female company and instead went to Rowdy's bar. He didn't drink often, but tonight was a special occasion — one he might regret for a very long time.

# EPILOGUE

It was just past the dinner hour at Rowdy's bar, and Dash sat back on the bar stool, watching as Margo came through the door. Wearing skinny jeans that hugged her ass and showed off her small waist, a soft white tank top and heeled strappy sandals, she looked sexy as sin.

Every guy in the place swiveled his head to look at her, but Dash didn't mind. Four months ago they'd married and he still couldn't stop smiling.

Next to him, Logan laughed. "You're more pathetic than I ever was."

Pathetic. Deliriously happy. Either worked.

Reese leaned around Logan to see Dash. "She's really taken to the whole letting-loose thing, hasn't she?"

"Yeah."

Rowdy laughed at how he said that, at the note of lust in his voice. He shoved drinks to the bar and leaned forward on his forearms. "She looks as happy as you, Dash, so you must be doing something right."

Margo had paused to talk with Cannon. He was in town for a visit, hanging with some of his friends. Pretty soon he'd fight for the SBC. That made him a local celebrity — although most already considered him that.

Next she paused to speak with the ladies. Logan's wife, Pepper, Reese's wife, Alice, and Rowdy's wife, Avery, all shared a table. Normally Avery tended bar, but not tonight. Tonight was special.

Tonight they were celebrating Dash's impending fatherhood.

"She doesn't look pregnant," Logan noted, and the rest agreed.

Dash didn't say that he'd found subtle differences in her breasts, in her sexual appetite — which had already been pretty damned healthy, thank you — or in her desire to nest. She'd literally taken over the entire house, rearranging and remodeling and doing all those things women often liked to do, but that he'd never envisioned Margo doing.

She still kicked ass when necessary.

And she was still the most honorable, brave, amazing woman he'd ever met.

Pepper pushed out a chair, inviting Margo to join them. She agreed, but held up a finger indicating that she needed just a minute first. Then she joined Dash at the bar.

As soon as she reached him, Dash said, "Hey," and pulled her in for a soft kiss.

Logan coughed.

Reese muttered, "Get a room."

Margo just sighed against Dash, then slanted a look at her detectives.

They each laughed, which made her roll her eyes.

"Today," she said, "I am officially back to being just a lieutenant."

Logan choked. "Just?"

"No 'just' to it," Reese added.

Dash pulled her up to his lap, cradling her close. "You're happy about that?" During the investigation she'd worked entirely too hard. But she came home to him each night, and that was what mattered.

"Very." At her ease perched on his thighs, she leaned in to whisper, "I'd rather put all my free time into being with my husband."

Blatantly eavesdropping, Logan said, "I'm glad you're back to your old position, because we need you."

Slowly Dash turned his head. "For?"

Reese again leaned around Logan.

"There've been three armed robberies in the past week, and we think they're all by the same group."

Margo slid off his lap. "Anyone hurt?"

"That's the weird part. The robbers are polite about it."

"How so?"

As they started talking shop, Dash grinned and turned to complain to Rowdy. But damn it, even as he filled drinks, Rowdy listened in.

It might have worried Dash more, how often her work came home with her, the peril she put herself in. He knew she could take care of herself, and with Logan, Reese and Rowdy helping, too, she was in good hands.

With a kiss to her temple, Dash excused himself so Margo could have his stool. When the police talk finished, she'd be going home with him.

He loved her, everything about her, all her various personas.

But he loved her best as *his*.

Smiling, content, Dash went to join the wives at their table.

# ABOUT THE AUTHOR

**Lori L. Foster** is a best-selling American writer of over 70 romance novels as Lori Foster. She also writes Urban Fantasy novels using using her first and middle initials, L.L. Foster. She and her husband have three sons, and a grandson. They live in rural Ohio.